MY BELOVED FRIEND, JUDAS

Vincent L. Di Paolo

authorHOUSE

1663 LIBERTY DRIVE, SUITE 200
BLOOMINGTON, INDIANA 47403
(800) 839-8640
www.authorhouse.com

First published by AuthorHouse 08/25/04

ISBN: 1-4140-0767-1 (e-book)
ISBN: 1-4140-0766-3 (Paperback)
ISBN: 1-4184-9011-3 (Dust Jacket)

This book is printed on acid free paper.

Front cover photo by Theo Uva (Montreal, Canada)

Dedication

This book is dedicated to my father, Lorenzo, who possesses so much knowledge and the most wonderful and vivid memory I have ever seen.

Table of Contents

Chapter 1

MEMORIES

The pain was so excruciating that Judas could only think of suicide, an easy and quick way out. He knew he did not have long to live, a month at the very most. He had seen so many of his people die from the same horrible painful cancer and he had long known that not too far in the future his life would also end in that painful way. Several of his people had chosen euthanasia because their pain had become unbearable. He had reached that unbearable stage and was considering a quick way out. He thought of euthanasia on that gray September morning as he sat by his window, looking out at the devastated countryside. He recalled, from the canyons of his memory, the green and fertile valley surrounded by mountains decorated with every shade of green imaginable to the human brain. How lush and pristine it had been! He opened his eyes, slowly looking out, hoping for a thousandth time that it was all a bad dream. He scanned the view as his dream of what it had once been came to a halt. He saw nothing but misery, devastation, and the darkest gray shrouding the countryside and sky. The thousands, millions of trees were bare and inanimate, their lives stripped by the venomous ever present dark gray mist that enshrouded the entire country, and possibly the entire world.

Tomorrow, Friday, September 8, 2023, would be his birthday. He would be forty years old. Two years ago, he would have still been considered young at forty. Today, forty was old. He had managed to subsist in the past twenty-four months only through sheer willpower and whatever canned food he and his people could scrounge around small mountain villages, which had escaped direct hit. A year ago, he had led a group of slightly over four thousand people, who followed him like a modern messiah, to this valley. Today, his people barely numbered six hundred and forty. More than five sixths of his people had died a painful death. And by tomorrow there would be one less, himself. He was going to die without ever finding out if He had been the true One. Maybe he would find out at his death. Killing oneself went against everything he believed in, against everything his father had taught him; but the pain was too unbearable. His inside was literally being eaten away by that foul sickness. He was doomed. They were all doomed. They were all going to die, day by day. Everyday someone had died. At times, two, three or more had died the same agonizing death. Still, they had hoped. He had hoped that someone would come up with a cure to this most horrible cancer, nuclear cancer.

It had all started back on Friday, August 27th, 2021, about ten days before his thirty-eighth birthday. Judas had just spent a week with his son, a young man, sixteen years old, second-degree black belt in tae-kwon-do, and twice U.S. champion. He had spent that entire week watching him practice and spar every day for six to eight hours. His son was part of the U.S. Tae-kwon-do team, which was training for the Tae-kwon-do World Championship, to be held in Honolulu the following week, on Thursday, September 2nd, 2021. His coach, a former world champion had told him that David was one of the top three contenders for the middleweight gold. He had lightning kicks and powerful punches and was not afraid of any opponent, including the North Korean and the German, who were the other top contenders in the middleweight category. Tae-kwon-do had been reintroduced into the Olympic Games in 2016, which had been held in Pyongyang, North Korea. The Olympic Committee had granted the 2016 games to North Korea as a sign of peace and friendship. Since then it had been kept as an Olympic event and his son, David, was preparing for the 2024 games, whose bid had been won by Naples, Italy. He could not wait for those games, a great chance to visit Italy again and watch his son possibly take a gold medal. It was an exciting time! He had been so proud of him. Not only had he been a great martial artist but also he had been a handsome young man. Handsome enough that girls would literally search for him. He had wanted to be a movie star, just like Bruce Lee!

They had enjoyed that week together, relishing a couple of movies and a great dinner at Paolo's with the whole family and friends. David's coach had been a former world champion and he had kept up with any possible information on world contenders. He had told him that with his son's lightning speed and superior power there were only two other martial artists that might give him a good fight, a North Korean and a German. However, the coach had felt that David would take the middleweight gold. He had been very impressive during practice.

Two days later, his wife, David, and a few other parents, together with the U.S. Tae-kwon-do team had left for Hawaii. David was the most promising U.S. competitor. Judas would join his wife and son the day before the championship, together with his daughter, who had been very busy working on her last chapter of her second novel. He was the proud father of an author. Her second novel would be a best seller, her publisher had told her. She was only seventeen years old, but she was a gifted writer. Her first novel, "Fish Crack", was the story of a young female rock climber and her adventurous climb of Fish Crack, a very steep and difficult route in Yosemite. It did well among rock climbing aficionados. Her second novel was a science fiction about astronaut climbers on Olympus Mons on Mars. The following day, he and his daughter had received an invitation to climb Seneca Rocks in West Virginia. Being avid climbers, they could not refuse.

He and his daughter, Catherine, had driven to West Virginia, which was only three hours away by car, and had met with their friends. It would be a day's climb and after a good supper in Petersburg, they would spend the night at a cozy inn. The following morning they would drive back to Washington, D.C. to prepare for their flight to Hawaii, on Monday, August 30, 2021.

Judas recalled the Day of Infamy, September 11, 2001. He felt that it had been that horrible day which had catapulted the Western World into a long, costly, and strenuous war against worldwide terrorism. He also recalled the attack on Iraq and the destruction of Saddam's evil regime. The war against terrorism never stopped, costing the United States over a trillion dollars.

Judas remembered when Russia, with the financial backing from the United States had become a true democratic country and America's strongest ally. Together, the U.S. and Russia, with some financial investment from Germany and Japan, had successfully completed a manned Martian exploratory mission. During the winter and spring of 2009, two American astronauts, two Russian cosmonauts, a German scientist and a Japanese micro-physicist had spent four months on board the spaceship Mars I. The new spaceship had been a larger and much faster vehicle developed from the Columbia-Atlantis series. It traveled up to ninety thousand miles per hour and was more than double the size of spaceship Atlantis. The outside shell had been made of a new alloy, which supposedly had been replicated from a piece of U.F.O. The sensational news of the new alloy had been leaked through the media, which had had fun with it in creating several good stories and news documentaries. There had been two possibilities in creating this new alloy named *galactis*: one was that *galactis* had been a true terrene invention; or that American, Russian, German, and Japanese scientists had really managed to separate the elements forming the U.F.O. alloy and had also managed to recreate it. The result had been a whitish silvery alloy, which was virtually indestructible and yet extremely light in weight. The scientific research team, which had been working together with N.A.S.A., had named the new alloy *galactis* because of its color and also in honor of our galaxy. The cost of Mars I had been astronomical but it had become realistic once Japan and Germany had decided to become two of its major financiers. The cost of manufacturing *galactis* was almost unthinkable because it included also the use of platinum; however, the result was a light and indestructible alloy.

The four-month mission had been very successful with only a few minor problems. It had taken slightly over a month to reach Mars, using a side-by-side approach with the Red Planet. During the beginning of that mission the distance between the two planets had been only 56 million kilometers away, the closest that the two planets reach every two years. The six astronauts had combed the northern Amazonia Planitia, Olympus Mons, and the Alba and Tantalus Fossae during Mars' northern spring. Searching for signs of forerunners of amino acids, and signs of water, the six astronauts had spent a month on Mars without ever encountering signs of organic molecules with carbon or microbes. They only found more fossilized globules of calcium carbonate; and the insects that they had brought for experiments had died. It took almost double the time to return to earth because the two planets were by then farther apart. Scientifically, it had been a disappointment. Exploratively, it had been the most successful space voyage ever executed by humans.

The production of *galactis* had been one of the greatest scientific achievements, permitting the manufacturing of almost indestructible jets, warships, and spaceships. Since the year 2009 there had been no more voyages to Mars or any other planets. It was too expensive and without justification. During the following nine years N.A.S.A., together with Russian, German, and Japanese scientists and astronauts successfully installed a lunar base, Luna I. By 2018, the Mars I spaceship had been used dozens of time as a lunar shuttle, proving to be the most reliable spaceship ever built on planet Earth. By 2020, hundreds of wealthy earthlings had spent a week vacation on the moon. The prohibitive cost of such a vacation funded longitudinal research on Luna I. Also, by the end of 2020, the joint space program had been renamed Galactic International Space Alliance (GISA). Italy, France, England, and Canada had been welcomed into the program, bringing more money into GISA, permitting the manufacturing of two more *galactis* spaceships, Luna I and Via Galactica. While those eight peaceful but powerful countries had spent twenty years and trillions of dollars in building a true and dynamic space program, North Korea, China, and Persia had been spending their time and money in nuclear armament. Persia had become a powerful and ruthless opponent from the unification of Iraq, Iran, and Syria in 2009. Twelve years later, on January 11th, 2021, China, North Korea, and Persia formed a triumvirate, an evil union with the sole intention to use their nuclear forces to monopolize world power.

Judas' father had been born in Italy in 1949, four years after World War II. He had moved to New York City with his family in the summer of 1960. He had been an excellent student and an exceptional artist with a bright future. By 1970, his father, Nicholas Cariota was already teaching art in a New York college. He had great memories of his father. He had been a true Christian. He had been raised as a Catholic, but had later rebelled against some of the Church's teachings and followed his own beliefs of Christ's true teachings. Even though he did not go to church anymore, with the exceptions of weddings, funerals, and baptisms, Nicholas had been a true Christian. He had practiced respect and love towards all human beings and he had been respected and loved by so many people from every walk of life. However, there had been one specific difference in his father's Christian beliefs which differed from any other Christian teaching: that Judas Iscariot had not been a traitor but that he had been Christ's right hand man and the pivotal character of Christ's life on Earth. Also, his family name, Cariota, his dad would explain to him, was a variation of Iscariota, the Italian version of Ish-Kerioth, Hebrew for "man from Kerioth". Kerioth or El-Qereiyat had been a village in the Plain of Moab during Christ's time.

Nicholas Cariota had not been a tall man. Actually, he had been on the short side, approximately five feet four and a half inches tall. He had always included that half-inch when he told people about his size; no one was going to take that half-inch away from him. Although a short man, he had been ruggedly handsome. He had resembled that classic western actor of the 60's and 70's, excluding his height. What was his name? Flint or Clint something wood. Flint Lockwood. Clint Westwood. Flint Eastwood. Clint Eastwood. That's right! He looked like Clint Eastwood minus seven or height inches. Nicholas Cariota had met his mother in the Brooklyn Jewish ghetto, in a Jewish delicatessen, while eating a super size old-fashioned pastrami sandwich. The deli had been a small but crowded Jewish eatery on 13th Avenue. He would frequently meet some Jewish friends and colleagues and together they would enjoy great old-fashioned pastrami and discuss religions. He enjoyed talking about religion.

"What are Christians?" he would always say. "Nothing, but reformed Jews. What did Christ do? He reformed the Hebrew teachings, that's what he did!"

His friends liked him and enjoyed his company. He and his friends had also been movie buffs and they would spend at least three evenings a week watching movies on the biggest screens of Greater New York.

"Going to review a new movie, honey. Wanna come?" Judas remembered his dad asking his mom.

"Review! You mean, you're going to watch a new movie, dear," she would always answer with a laugh.

"Watch a new movie! You must be kidding. People watch new movies. I review them. I study them," he would retort, as he would exit their house.

It had been a windy cold Saturday, on January 2, 1971, and Nicholas and his friends had been digging their teeth into their respective super-sized, old-fashioned pastrami sandwich and greasy French fries, when she walked into the deli for protection from the bitter, cold, January, New York wind. She undid her shawl and unbuttoned her coat, revealing her voluptuous body as she took a seat at a nearby table. Her long dirty, blond hair cascaded over her cheeks and coat, framing that gorgeous face. She looked like Rita Hayworth. Nicholas stopped eating and began focusing on the newly arrived beauty. She noticed him and smiled. Her lips were succulent. He had no desire to finish his second half of the pastrami sandwich. The only things on his mind were those lips, that face, and that body. His friends had noticed what was happening and asked him if he was going to finish his other half of the pastrami sandwich. He had said no. They quickly divided it into three sections and shared it. Mordecai Silverstein, one of his Jewish friends, suddenly noticed the Rita Hayworth facsimile and also became interested. He looked like the Big Bad Wolf as he dug his teeth into the last bit of the pastrami sandwich, his eyes engulfing the view of the beautiful stranger.

"She's mine!" declared Nicholas.

"Yours? You don't even know her. She doesn't know you. Besides, she's Jewish," replied Mordecai defiantly, as bits of the old fashioned pastrami and rye bread flew from his mouth, splattering all over the table forcing the other two friends to give up their last bite.

"So what if she's Jewish!"

"So what if she's Jewish! So what if she's Jewish!" repeated Mordecai. "You're a Christian. Her parents would never accept you!"

"She's not orthodox. Look at how she's dressed. An orthodox girl would never dress that way. It's too sexy! And look at that hair."

"I still don't see..." Mordecai did not have a chance to finish what he was going to say as Nicholas got up and walked towards Rita Hayworth's younger sister's table.

His friends were flabbergasted at Nicholas' uncontrolled behavior. However, Nicholas was not going to give Mordecai the chance to even dream about her. He wanted her for himself. She was the woman of his dreams, and he wasn't going to let her go. He approached the opposite chair and gently grabbed its back with his fingers.

"Hi, my name is Nicholas Cariota. May I sit down?"

"Sure, Nicholas!" she whispered.

Nicholas sat as his flabbergasted friends gawked at his presumptuous boldness.

"I feel kind of foolish," began Nicholas, "But if I don't talk to you now I probably will never get a second chance."

"You might as well talk, then," she whispered again.

"Do you always whisper when you talk?"

"Only when I want to keep a conversation private."

"I'm sorry," whispered Nicholas.

"Eve."

"I'm sorry, Eve, but I couldn't help but talk to you. I find you irresistible. I'm...I'm in love with you!"

"But, you don't even know me."

"I know what I see and I love what I see. I want to spend the rest of my life with you. I adore you. Marry me."

For the following three months Nicholas would not relinquish his hold on Eve and by then she had fallen in love with him. He wined and dined with her every other day, spending most of his money on expensive restaurants. Finally, they planned to get married; however, neither rabbis nor priests would marry them unless one of them planned to change to the other's religion. Nicholas' parents had wanted a nice Italian girl; but he had warned his parents that it would be a girl that he loved no matter what color, religion, or looks.

They were married on Friday, March 26th, 1971, at city hall. He was twenty-one and she was barely eighteen. They studied, worked, and traveled together for the following eleven years, finally settling down in Northern Virginia.

Nicholas had wanted a son.

"A son!" Eve would say. "What happens if it's a girl?"

"I'll love her just the same;" he would reply, "But we'll try again for a boy, okay?"

"I'll do anything to make you happy."

"You make me happy!" he would say as he hugged her.

On Thursday morning, September 8, 1983, a healthy baby boy was born to Nicholas and Eve Cariota. Nicholas named him Judas, after his favorite apostle.

Judas' smile suddenly disappeared as he opened his eyes; the wonderful images created by his memories had disappeared, replaced by the view of the devastated countryside for one last time.

Chapter 2

MEMORIES OF YOUTH

Friday, August 27, 2021

Judas picked up the receiver after the second ring. It was a friend, John Leblanc, a geologist and a great rock climber. He was inviting Judas and his daughter, Catherine, to climb Seneca Rocks in West Virginia.

"I've got a tight schedule, John. As you already know, Catherine and I are leaving for Hawaii on Monday morning. That's barely three days away. And I've got to call the university about next week."

"Relax, Jude. It's only a day's climb. You make your call, pack your ropes and rack; and, we'll pick you up by two, this afternoon. Okay?"

"You don't have to pick us up, John. I'll drive my jeep. Catherine and I need to be back by Sunday morning. You and the gang could relax for a couple of days. Is that alright with you?"

"Sounds great. Be at my house by two; we would like to have supper at the Inn in Petersburg and check in for the night. I've already made reservations."

"You son-of-a-gun!"

"Hey, what are friends for? See you at two."

By five o'clock, Judas, Catherine and his friends had all reached Petersburg, West Virginia.

Coming from a mixed marriage, Judas had learned about both religions from his father. His father had truly believed that there were very little differences between Christianity and Judaism. Both believed and followed the laws of the Old Testament and that Jesus Christ had simply reformed some of the Mosaic Laws and the Hebrew religion. His dad would always tell him that. His mother was a very beautiful and extremely intelligent woman, but she was not religious and would only observe some of the Jewish holidays. Her parents were good people, and even they were not religious. They would go to the synagogue only on holidays. However, Mrs. Bettie Yanowitz was kosher and kept a kosher kitchen, which was not an easy thing to do. Mr. Yanowitz, Eve and her brothers enjoyed bacon and eggs, French fries, pepperoni pizza, seafood, and all kinds of non-kosher food; but Mrs. Yanowitz remained kosher throughout her life.

Judas celebrated Christmas, Easter, Chanukah, Passover, New Year's, and Rosh Hashanah. As a child, he thoroughly studied the Old Testament and loved all the colorful stories of the ancient biblical era. Noah, Moses, Samson, and King David were some of his favorite heroes. Judas also learned about Jesus and the New Testament in a private Catholic school. His father would review stories of the New Testament with him; but Nicholas would change a few passages that he strongly believed should have been changed long ago.

Judas' friends called him Jude, after the Beatles' song "Hey, Jude", or Judd. His teachers called him Judd. Children who did not like him or chose to taunt him called him Judas, Judas Priest, or Traitor. The teachers and administrators would always reprimand those children because Judas was always a well-mannered and exceptionally bright student. Like his father, he was a gifted young artist. Before the age of ten, Judas had already won three international art awards and was already selling some of his works. Most of his sketches and paintings were of beautiful facades of cathedrals, churches, and old buildings. By eleven years old he had already been commissioned to do a painting of the Roman Forum. As a child he had often traveled with his family and had visited ancient ruins and cities. The Meso-American and South American Civilizations and their enchanting ruins had always fascinated his father. Judas had enjoyed them; however, the ancient ruins in the Middle East had bewitched him. He wanted to be a biblical archaeologist most of all. His parents, especially his dad, liked that idea very much.

By the end of grade four, Judas had been given a battery of tests ordered by his principal and approved by his parents. Once the tests were scored they had held a conference concerning Judas' immediate future. The principal had suggested that if Judas and his parents did not mind he would be placed in sixth grade instead of fifth. Not only was he the top student of the school but he had also scored extremely high in all the tests that had been administered to him. Of course, it was understood that if he would not do well in sixth grade he would be placed back to fifth. His parents were thrilled and agreed to Judas skipping fifth grade. By the end of his sixth grade, Judas had covered all the advanced algebra, geometry, social studies, and advanced sciences and had still managed to come out as top student of the year. Mrs. Browne, the principal of the middle school had suggested that Judas be given a higher battery of tests. Once again, Judas took several tests, which covered mathematics, sciences, language, and social studies. He also took I.Q. tests and a psychological test. Once again, Judas and his parents had held a conference at Mrs. Browne's office. The school psychologist and guidance counselor were also present. Mrs. Browne had told his parents that Judas' scores were extremely high and that she was recommending either a private school or placing Judas in ninth grade at Thomas Jefferson High School, the top academic high school in Virginia and one of the top in the country. It was June of 1993 and Judas was not yet eleven. Nicholas stood up and circled around Mrs. Browne's office, as everyone stared at him with puzzled expressions on their faces. Nicholas Cariota seemed worried about something. He had asked Mrs. Browne if Judas could leave the room for a few minutes. She had agreed; but Judas had been greatly disappointed by his father's request for he never did find out the results of those tests and what his I.Q. was.

On Tuesday, September 7, 1993 Judas began his ninth grade at Thomas Jefferson H.S. and on his second day of school he turned eleven. His parents had a big birthday party for him that following weekend. All four of his grandparents and all of his best friends were present. His mom had even invited his two former principals. It was a big pool party and there was a mountain of food and tropical juices and fruits. They had had fun in the pool and had played water polo and other aquatic games. His eleventh birthday party had been a smash and he had received lots of gifts.

At Thomas Jefferson, Judas kept an **A** average; however, socially, he felt like an outcast. He was the youngest and probably the smallest student in that school. He had a few friends. Some of them were girls and they were only interested in studying with him and being friends. He wanted a girlfriend! But, he was just too young for them. So, he had contended himself with their friendship and their closeness while doing homework and projects. By age thirteen, he looked older and more mature. He had a slight moustache and lots of pubic hair and he could have passed for fifteen, maybe sixteen years old. His dad would tell him that it was the Italian side of him that made him look more mature. However, he was not tall. Both of his parents were only five feet four. Of course, his father would always include that extra half-inch, which got him nowhere when his mother would wear high heels and would look a few inches taller than he. They still looked great together, no matter what. And they loved each other after almost twenty-five years of marriage. That was really something at that time when divorce had become the norm. Most marriages did not last long. People were not willing to compromise. His dad would often tell him that love was an equal give and take. Love was to make sacrifices and sometimes giving up something for the person you loved.

Judas was barely five feet tall and that was small compared to some juniors and seniors in the basketball team who were six feet tall and a few were much taller. There was an African-American student who was six feet seven inches and at seventeen he was still growing. Most students at Jefferson High liked Judas and recognized his genius. Finally, he met Hanh-Phuong Nguyen, a beautiful Vietnamese girl, and fell madly in love with her. They began to date. She was sixteen and a junior. He was thirteen and a senior. What was great was that she was smaller than he by a couple of inches. She was gorgeous and extremely intelligent. They became inseparable for most of that first semester until her brother, who was extremely jealous, had found out about them and beat Judas up by using some type of martial art on him. That day he went back home with bruises, a cracked rib, and a bleeding nose, which took hours to stop.

Nicholas was furious. His mother, worried, catered to him for the next four days as he lay in bed. Judas' father had visited Mr. Nguyen and had told him that he was going to press charges of assault and battery against his son, who happened to be six years older than Judas. Mr. Nguyen was ashamed of his son. He had taken away his son's driving privilege and had given him an early curfew for the next six months. Nicholas was not satisfied. Mr. Nguyen did not want to lose his son. He begged Nicholas Cariota to forgive his son's stupidity. Khanh was not a bad boy. He had been jealous that Judas had become very close to his sister. Nicholas stormed furiously out of the Nguyen home promising to bring a lawsuit against the Nguyens.

That evening Hanh-Phuong spoke to Judas on the telephone. She was worried about him and about her brother. She begged for his forgiveness and Mr. Cariota's forgiveness. That same evening Judas had telephoned Khanh and had forgiven him. He then proceeded by begging his father to also forgive Khanh. Nicholas was still obstinate about it; however, he changed his mind when Judas told him that Jesus would have forgiven him and that it was the only Christian thing to do. That cold winter night, his dad telephoned Mr. Nguyen and told him that he and his son forgave Khanh. Mr. Nguyen was grateful and thanked both of them several times.

That weekend, Mr. Nguyen and Khan had come to visit Judas, bringing him a large brown envelope. Mr. Nguyen told him that it was a special gift from Khanh and that he had paid it with his own savings. Judas nervously opened the envelope, not knowing what to expect. Inside was a six-month contract of tae-kwon-do classes in Judas' name. Judas had been excited and had thanked Khanh. They all shook hands and the incident had been closed.

Khanh was a first-degree black belt in the Korean martial art of tae-kwon-do and he personally assisted Judas' initiation into it. Judas became a faithful student in the art and also continued to see Hanh-Phuong for the rest of that school year. By then, he had passed the green belt exam in tae-kwon-do.

By June of 1996, Judas had managed to cover four school years at Thomas Jefferson H.S. in three years. He always took an extra advanced subject or two and still managed an "A" average. He had also received top honors and recognition from the administration during his graduation and a scholarship at Harvard University. He continued his tae-kwon-do classes during that summer. He was barely fourteen when he began his first year at Harvard University, in the Anthropology and Archaeology Department. His professors and administrators quickly recognized his genius and his thirst for more knowledge. Because of his many trips to ancient cities with his parents and all the information he had acquired from his father, an archaeology buff, his knowledge of ancient architecture and cities was exceptional, especially in the history, geography, geology, and archaeology of the entire Middle East. His professors would, at times, ask Judas for his approval on certain details because his memory and knowledge were impeccable.

By June of 1999, only three years later, he graduated from Harvard, receiving a Bachelor's degree in Archaeology with *summa cum laude*. He had also become a first-degree black belt in tae-kwon-do. He had kept up with his martial art at a local tae-kwon-do school in Boston. His parents were beaming with pride during the graduation ceremony and then visited his tae-kwon-do school, where they met his instructors and some of his friends. Judas gave them the tour of downtown Boston and they enjoyed an excellent seafood lunch. That evening, while having supper at a classy Italian restaurant, Nicholas and Eve surprised their son with a family summer vacation. They would be spending a month in Israel and its neighboring countries. Also, they would be flying the Concorde to Paris first. Judas was delirious. He would get a chance to explore the Dead Sea area and prepare a special presentation for his first year in the Master's Program at Harvard.

Flying the Concorde was a thrill. Judas and his parents landed at Orly Airport two hours after taking off from John F. Kennedy Airport. After a two-day stay in Paris they flew to Israel. They first stayed in Jerusalem; exploring Old Jerusalem from the Temple to the Via Dolorosa to the Church of the Holy Sepulcher, and from Antonia to the Kidron Valley. Judas would inspect every rock of the old fortified city that fascinated him. His parents, patiently and lovingly, looked on as they admired his determination and interest for biblical history. They visited Megiddo, Haifa, Tiberias and Nazareth. In Tiberias, on the shore of the Sea of Galilee, Judas daydreamed of

15

Jesus and His apostles in a fishing boat during a bad storm. He also admired the hard work that the people living in kibbutzim had put in fertilizing that valley. He wandered if it had been fertile by the Sea of Galilee during His time. They drove back south along Highway 90, along the Jordan River, visiting the most important ruins they encountered, oblivious to possible attacks by terrorists. They stopped at the town of Yeriho, ancient Jericho, where they found a place to stay for the following four days. Every morning, after a hearty breakfast, they would drive to Khirbat Qumran, bringing along a good supply of bottled water and freshly picked oranges. As Nicholas and Eve had promised their son to spend sometime on the northern shores of the Dead Sea, they had faithfully kept their promise for it meant so much to him.

During their flights to Paris and then to Israel Judas had not stopped talking about Khirbat Qumran, Khirbat Mazin, Khirbat Mird, and Mar Saba. He had come equipped with detailed maps of that area and he seemed to know where important ruins and caves were located. They explored the Essene ruins at Khirbat Qumran: its tower, the well, the courtyards, the pillar bases, the southern esplanade, and the Herodian Door at Ain Feshkha. He had thoroughly inspected any signs of ancient stone carvings with his magnifying lens and spent a good half hour studying the Herodian Door. Judas had led his parents through the chasms that scarred the Wilderness of Judea. It was as if he had been there before as he pointed to some big holes near the top of the western rocky walls and explained to them that those holes were Cave 4 and the remains of Caves 7 and 8. Judas proceeded to tell his parents that some Biblical archaeologists and historians believed that Jesus had been buried in Cave 8. Nicholas told Judas that that theory had been falsified, but he seemed to have already known about it. They explored the platform at Khirbat Mird and the Kidron Valley. On the morning of the fourth day they drove through a rocky dirt road to reach Mar Saba, a fifth century monastery. Eve became very upset when she was not permitted inside the monastery. She had to contend herself by exploring the spectacular walls of the canyons of the Kidron Valley. Those four days had been extremely hot; and, although the heat had reached the low 100 degrees Fahrenheit Judas seemed totally undisturbed by it.

He had been totally mesmerized by the rugged land around Qumran and the Kidron Valley.

The third week had been spent visiting the famous oasis at En Gedi, Fountain of the Kid, and the caves of Nahal Hever. They stayed in the town of En Gedi where they swam and floated in the Dead Sea. The following morning Judas woke up his parents at 4:00 so that they could drive to Hervot Mezada, Massada, and climb the steep Snake Path, which leads to the top. In total darkness, it took Judas and his parents a little over an hour to reach the top of the cliff a few minutes before sunrise. Judas had not been interested in taking the cable car; he wanted to experience the climb along Snake Path. On top of the fortress, the spectacular sunrise they witnessed over the Mountains of Moab justified getting up at four o'clock in the morning, driving to Hervot Mezada, and climbing the steep trail that led to it. The rest of that morning, they explored the entire ruins of Massada: Herod's hanging palace, the store houses, the bath house, the middle terrace located about 65 feet below, the lower terrace of the palace, up to the administration building, the Synagogue, the casemate rooms, the Byzantine Chapel, the Western Palace, the swimming pool and the Herodian Villas, the Columbarium, the lookout tower, the cisterns, the mikve (pools), and the rest of the casemate wall and rooms. Beguiled by the Spartan beauty of the fortress, Judas, Nicholas, and Eve spent the entire six hours of that morning examining every detail, while munching on dried fruits and nuts. They rode the cable car to get down and that was also a spectacular experience. They had lunch at a small restaurant in Arad, where they spent the evening and night.

The following morning, after breakfast, they continued on Road 31 to Newe Zohar, where they thought best to fill up their rental's gas tank. After a one-hour stop at Sedom (Sodom), where they viewed the famous "Lot's Wife" and the Dead Sea Salt Pans, they continued south to Elat. It took five hours to reach Elat, having stopped at Ammude Shelomo (Solomon's Pillars) to visit the famous red columns and Egyptian temple, which had been built before the Exodus. At Elat, they enjoyed the beautiful waters of the Gulf of Aqaba, great hospitality and seafood, and the swimming and snorkeling in the warm water of the coral beach. Three days later, feeling tanned and rested, they drove back to Yerushalayim

(Jerusalem) by the way of Be'er-Sheva. It was a longer route but they explored the ruins at Mamshit (Kurnub), Hevron (Hebron), and Lakhish. Before reaching Jerusalem they visited Jesus' birthplace at Bayt-Lahm (Bethlehem).

Back in Jerusalem, they visited the Archaeology Department of the Hebrew University. There, Judas felt at home talking to some biblical archaeology and history professors. They were impressed by his knowledge, his age, his school and invited him to do his doctorate at their university. Judas was intoxicated by the offer and he promised to fill an application. They spent the rest of their vacation in Jerusalem and in Tel Aviv-Jaffa. The entire trip had been an unforgettable experience for Judas, which would be cherished for the rest of his life.

Chapter 3

VCDs

Twenty-four years ago was a long time but those wonderful memories of his youth with his parents would always be kept alive in his memory. How he missed them! He thought, as tears ran, like two rivulets, down his cheeks. He missed Judith. He missed David. The only consolation was that their deaths had been immediate. He missed his daughter. Where was Catherine? Tears continued through their marked paths. She had gone on a searching party, looking for canned goods and bottled water. Catherine had left for the town of Buckhannon with two other young people on a small '20 Toyota Scrooge pick-up truck. John Taylor and his son, James maintained all of their vehicles. They were the best mechanics of the *Seneca Climbers*, the name chosen by Judas' group because of the many mountain climbers who belonged to it. John and his son maintained their best vehicles with the lowest gas consumption; no gas-guzzlers could be afforded. Whatever gas was left in all the existing stations, which had been missed by direct hit, was up for grabs by any surviving group. There was no other pick-up or van that could better the 2020 Toyota Scrooge pick-up in miles per gallon. Toyota had named it Scrooge because it averaged 110 miles to the gallon. It was an extremely light and small pick-up, with a three-cylinder engine and enough room for three adults.

The Scrooge's fine fuel injectors sipped the gas permitting Catherine and her friends to scout the town of Buckhannon within a three miles radius, which included a couple of small villages, and return to the Seneca Rocks Compound using less than two gallons of gas. Since gas was scarce, every vehicle was equipped with several sturdy gas containers and was used only in searching for food, drinks, and other needed supplies.

Catherine was sick but her cancer was not as advanced as Judas'. It seemed that all the younger people had a little more strength than middle-aged or older members of the Seneca Climbers. She and her friends had left the day before and they should soon be back. Two days was the maximum time allowed when searching within a one hundred mile distance, he thought. He missed her! He would wait for her before he would terminate his painful existence. Tomorrow would be his birthday. He was going to be forty years old. At least he would complete forty years and would see the beautiful face of Catherine.

He looked out through the big panoramic windows as he reclined on his leather lazy-boy. The sky was covered with the same ugly and poisonous clouds that enshrouded the entire planet. He hadn't seen the sun in the past twenty-four months, since that foredoomed day. It was the end of summer, but it was a cool fifty-two Fahrenheit. By the end of the month it would begin snowing again. He truly believed that the earth had begun a new ice age. He felt his lazy-boy with his fingers and smiled. He smiled because he had bartered two VCDs for it. VCDs had become the most powerful commodities. If his memory was correct the VCDs had been *Terminator II* and *The Fugitive*, two classic video compact disks. VCDs had been introduced into the market towards the end of 1996. Judas was a young teen-ager then and he remembered receiving a VCD player and his first VCD, Jurassic Park, for Christmas. He remembered the heavy Christmas promotion Sony undertook to launch their new VCD player and about a dozen films on compact disks. The beauty of watching a VCD was its color. It was perfect. By the end of that decade VCDs sold like wildfire; however, most people still kept their VHS players and videotapes. By 2005, VHS videotapes were no longer produced. Every new movie had been marketed as VCDs because their prices had dropped and everyone owned a VCD player. Videotapes had become obsolete but many people kept them because of their large personal libraries.

About four months after the apocalypse Judas, Catherine, Major Coolidge and Major Nichols, two astronauts, and Dr. Jeffery Weinstein, a top-secret federal government scientist, had come upon a huge video rental store in Charleston with thousands of different VCDs. The store was for sale. They had managed to laugh at the sign as they entered the locale. They had gone to Charleston to buy some supplies only to find that all the canned food and bottled drinks had been completely sold out. The grocery stores were all closed, empty, and barricaded. Thousands of people had died from contaminated meat, fish, fruit, and vegetables. Only canned food and bottled drinks seemed to be safe. At least, canned goods did not have an immediate effect on people and animals. They entered the VCD rental store; it was empty with the exception of the owner, who sat morosely by his counter. Judas had asked for the price of all the VCDs. The little old man had announced that one can of food or a bottle of any drink would be a fair trade per VCD. They all laughed, including the morose man. I'm ruined! He had exclaimed. No one was renting because no one could get his or her TVs to work again. Judas presented himself and then introduced his daughter, Major Coolidge, Major Nichols, and Dr. Weinstein. The morose man's name was Lloyd Kearney, who had moved to Charleston, West Virginia, in 2116. He was from Pittsburgh, Pennsylvania. Judas had told him that he was lucky to be alive in Charleston, West Virginia, than being burned to a fine crisp in Pittsburgh, Pennsylvania.

He began to cry like a baby. All five consoled him and he finally calmed down to a hiccupping sob. Judas had offered the lonely Mr. Kearney a therapeutic proposition. His store was worthless and so were his VCDs. Judas offered him a safe haven with his rapidly growing group at Seneca Rocks for all his VCD players and VCDs. The Visitor Center at Seneca Rocks had become their home and he was welcome to join them. He would always be provided with two meals a day, with protection from wild gangs, and enough time to view all the VCDs he cared to. How? He had exclaimed. Judas had explained to Lloyd Kearney that Dr. Weinstein was a famous scientist who had managed to restore a VCD player and TV; and, although they couldn't receive any channels, they could watch any movie on VCD they could get their hands on. Mr. Kearney had suggested going into business together to service the entire population of Charleston. They could get rich. That was not a good idea, Judas had replied. Charleston had been ransacked for food, drinks, gas, and ammunition. People in Charleston were dying like flies; disease and death were prominent. In the country, TV service and VCDs were used to barter for food and drinks, gas and ammo. Although sick, people still enjoyed watching a good movie. It was food for the mind and soul. Judas told Lloyd that he would provide all his stock and that they would provide TV service and barter. They would be set for the rest of their miserable lives. Money was worthless except to light fires with. Judas would make VCDs the new money. Lloyd Kearney thought about it for a moment and finally bought the idea; and, on that very cold winter day, he helped his new partners and friends box all the VCDs, VCD players, TVs and accessories. They loaded his van and their army truck with all the boxes and drove east towards Seneca Rocks.

The two vehicles traveled east on the **60**, a state highway, which crossed routes **219/55**, taking them home. About thirty odd miles east of Charleston, they stopped at Glenn Ferris and Gauley Bridge, two villages connected by several houses outside of their centers. There, they actually found a grocery store with canned food and bottled drinks. An old man came out, holding a five-cartridge Remington shot gun, and threatened them to move on. Judas had sweet-talked him into an exchange of goods. The old man had not seen a movie in four months and would part with a few boxes of goods in exchange with some good VCDs and TV service. The old man had a concrete building in the back that looked like some type of warehouse, secretly stocked with boxes of canned goods and bottled drinks. With a southern accent, he told them that he, kind of, expected that what happened was going to happen. The few weeks before Armageddon, he had watched nightly news on TV and all the signs of what was going to happen were there. He spoke to them with a whining accent. So he had decided to stock up, spending most of his savings on canned food and bottled drinks. But since it had happened he couldn't watch TV anymore and all his damned videotapes and VCDs were a sorry waste. A real shame! Thousands of good American dollars had all gone down the drain. He had tried to fiddle with 'hem several times but got nowhere. He even called Joey Smallwood, the village TV and VCR repairman, but he couldn't fix 'hem. He didn't see how they were going to fix 'hem if Joey Smallwood couldn't.

Dr. Weinstein began rewiring his two VCRs and a VCD player on his two TVs and a giant screen projection. The old man promised one hundred assorted cans of food and five cases of Coors if the doc could fix everything. No deal, said Judas. For fifty boxes of food, twenty cases of beer, and thirty cases of soft drinks they would fix everything and give him ten new VCDs of his choice. The old man got upset and ordered them to get out at gunpoint. Twenty new VCDs! Judas had offered once again. OUT! The old man shouted, pointing his gun. Thirty! Judas had shouted as they ran out of the store. They were getting in their vehicles when the old man opened the store door and called them back in. For fifty new VCDs of his choice and for fixing his three TVs and machines they could have fifty boxes of food, twenty cases of beer and thirty cases of soft drinks. Judas had looked at Lloyd for approval, which he eagerly gave with a twinkle in his eyes that clearly showed everyone his excitement and a sense of mischief. It had been his first big sale since last August. He then realized the trading power of VCDs. He was impressed by Judas' leadership and friendship and he was glad that he belonged to the Seneca Climbers.

It took about two hours for Jeffery to rewire the three machines and reconnect them back to their respective televisions. One VCR was connected to an old 2009 39" RCA, the second VCR was connected to a 42" multi-cellular, high-resolution Sony, which was only a couple of years old, and the VCD player was connected to a nine-foot Panasonic screen, which had the optional and very expensive 3-D image maker. Wow! The old man loved his TVs. There had been a glint in the old man's eyes as Dr. Jeffery Weinstein played an old Clint Eastwood spaghetti film on the 39" RCA, *Platoon* on the high-resolution TV, and an *Unforgiven* VCD on the 3-D giant screen. The old man had a grin on his face as wide as his facial muscles permitted. He had told Dr. Weinstein that he had never seen his TVs as sharp as they were on that day. Then the old man had wanted to choose his VCDs first. He spent a good hour choosing his new fifty VCDs from westerns and war movies. He was an old Vietnam War veteran.

Luckily, they had boxed the VCDs by topics. In exchange, they had chosen ten boxes of 24 vacuum-packed packages of crackers, ten boxes of 24 jars of peanut butter, ten boxes of 48 cans of chunky light tuna in oil, ten boxes of microwave turkey dinners, and ten boxes of 50 cans of corned beef imported from Argentina. Judas had felt that the peanut butter and crackers would make nutritious morning meals for everyone. The tuna, the turkey dinners, and the Argentinean canned corned beef were luxuries they could not refuse. They also chose ten cases of Coors, ten cases of Michelob, ten cases of Mountain Dew, ten cases of Perrier, and ten cases of Coca-Cola. All of that supply, together with whatever they had already collected, would last a while among the 236 members of the Seneca Climbers. Little had Judas known then that the membership would increase to four thousand within the next ten months.

They bid farewell to the old man, who had finally told them his name, Don Norton. He was a native of Charleston. Judas had asked him if he would be interested in another trade a couple of months down the line. The old man agreed as long as the VCDs were westerns and war movies. Within the following six months, they managed to trade over one thousand VCDs and fix over one hundred TVs and VCD players for nearly two thousand boxes of food and drinks.

Catherine had left with Sue Parrish and Jay Morrison, taking fifty mixed VCDs and tools with them. Their goal was to trade all of the VCDs and fix as many TVs and VCD players for as much food and drinks as possible. Jay was a great climber and had become Dr. Weinstein's apprentice. He loved to overhaul VCRs, TVs, and VCD players. Jeffery had taught him how to reconnect VCD players or VCRs with TVs and make them work. Buckhannon was approximately sixty miles away; and, they would soon be back.

Chapter 4

BIBLICAL ARCHAEOLOGY

On September of 1999, Judas had begun his master's degree in archaeology, specializing in Biblical Studies, at Harvard University. That year had been a troubled one for many Christian religions and religious sects for they believed that the world would end by midnight on New Year's Eve. The year 2000 entered without any major interruptions and with the usual festivities for most people. Business went on as usual. Several religious sects kept postponing their doomsday; but by the end of that year most of them had eased on their predictions. However, there were two or three sects who dragged their doomsday all the way to the end of 2001. The infamous terrorist attacks of September 11, 2001, on New York City and on Washington, D.C. were a glimpse of what would follow, culminating into a nuclear Armageddon on Saturday, August 28th, 2021.

By June of 2001, Judas had graduated with a Master of Archaeology in Biblical Studies with Summa Cum Laude. He had also been accepted to do his doctoral studies at the Hebrew University in Jerusalem. He had been so happy and his parents had been so proud of him.

From September of 2001, till June of 2003, Judas studied Biblical Archaeology in Hebrew, which he learned to speak, read, and write. He also studied ancient Aramaic, the precursor of Hebrew, Arabic, Armenian, Pahlavi, Uighor, and Brahmi. During those two troublesome years in Israel, filled with numerous terrorist attacks,

Judas learned an immense wealth of information during archaeology field trips and digs. He had the Biblical backyard at a daily reach. His professors quickly realized that Judas was an exceptional and gifted young archaeologist. He became an assistant to one of his professors on his final year of his doctoral studies. Judas lived, slept, and devoured archaeology.

By June of 2003, Judas was a Doctor in Biblical Archaeology; and, he had been offered a teaching position at the university. His parents had flown over to celebrate his prodigious accomplishment at the incredible young age of nineteen. They were intoxicated by the presentation that the Hebrew University of Jerusalem had done for Judas, declaring that he was going to be the youngest professor at campus and a most invaluable staff acquisition.

On Monday, September 8, 2003, Judas had completed his twentieth birthday as he began his post as associate professor in Biblical Archaeology. That evening he and his older colleagues celebrated his birthday at Fink's, a famous restaurant in Jerusalem. Judas was a handsome young man, who looked a little older than what he really was. He could have easily passed for a young man of twenty-four. He had the body of a slender Hercules with powerful, sinewy muscles. However, he had also inherited his parents' height. At twenty, he was barely five feet six inches tall. Although short, his muscular body and his knowledge of tae-kwon-do reassured his puissance within himself and to anyone who might gaze at him. That Monday, he had noticed a very beautiful young lady in one of his classes. Her name was Judith Levy.

That first week of teaching had not been easy for Judas with Judith's presence in his classes. His presentation of biblical information was interesting and dynamic, full of energy and personal conviction. Miss Levy had been mesmerized by young Dr. Cariota's presentation and energy. Judas, of course, had tried his hardest to impress the beautiful young lady. Daily, she stayed after classes to ask Judas questions in biblical archaeology. That Friday, Judas had told her that he was going to meet a friend at Fink's and asked her if she would join them. There, they would have ample time to discuss biblical archaeology. She had been ecstatic by the invitation; and she had gladly joined him. At Fink's, Judas' friend never showed up, of course. They spent the evening talking about themselves and their parents. They had fallen in love with each other. From that evening on, Judas and Judith spent as much time as possible together. On weekends, they would scout the arid hills of the West Bank by the Dead Sea, from Khirbat Qumran to Masada, for new clues to possible ancient ruins, tombs, or caves, totally oblivious to the ever-present danger of terrorism. They became inseparable and their close friendship worried Judas' older colleagues. However, Judas clearly saw their disappointment with him and he countered by announcing his engagement to Judith on the day before Chanukah.

Judas' parents flew over from America to celebrate their son's engagement to Judith. A big party had been planned at Fink's and many of Judas' colleagues and Judith's family and friends had been invited. His parents loved Judith and her family. Everyone had a great time and everyone was happy for Judas and Judith. They looked great together, even though Judith was two inches taller than Judas. Height did not matter to them for they were truly in love. Judith was a modern ballet dancer and her slender and sinewy body accentuated every move she made. She was a sensuous and beautiful young lady. They had planned a Christmas wedding after finding out that Judith had missed her menstrual period. Chanukah and Christmas came and they were married. They honeymooned at Elat, enjoying the sun and waters of the Red Sea.

On July 25, 2004, a healthy baby girl was born to Judith and Judas. They named her Catherine Eve. The following year, on July 11, 2005, Judith gave birth to a baby boy. They named him David Nicholas. Judas and his young family lived in Israel until the end of May of 2011. Judas had lived ten years in Israel and eight of those years he had taught at the university. During his last two years at the Hebrew University he had been promoted to full professorship. He had scouted Israel with a fine toothcomb, looking for tombs of famous biblical personages. He had found a few, but never the one that had intrigued him for the past thirteen years. He had searched for something that, maybe, did not exist. He probably would have remained in Israel if he hadn't been offered the prestigious position of curator at one of the Smithsonian museums.

By spring of 2010 Judith had received her doctoral degree in Biblical Archaeology. She had managed to take care of the children and finish her program at the Hebrew University of Jerusalem. She began as an assistant professor during their last year. Of course, Judas had been a great help with the children and with her studies. Their colleagues were going to miss them both and the administration promised to keep the university doors open for them if they ever decided to come back to Israel. Leaving Israel was not easy for them. They had made many friends and everyone who knew them loved and respected them.

During the summer of 2011, Judas, Judith, Catherine, and David moved to Annandale, in Northern Virginia. Annandale was a suburb of Washington, D.C., on the Virginia side, inside the infamous beltway. From there, it was only a twenty-minute drive to downtown Washington. Judas' new job as curator of Ancient Middle-Eastern Civilizations at the Smithsonian was prestigious and rewarding. Judith began her teaching career of Biblical Studies at the Catholic University. Catherine was in second grade and David in first grade on that September. Life for Judas and his young family was exciting and full of weekend adventures. There was so much to explore in Washington, D.C. and in Virginia: all the museums and the neo-classical buildings, all the battlefields, the Blue Ridge Mountains, the Shenandoah Valley with all its caverns, the beaches, and West Virginia. It was in West Virginia that both Judas and Judith began some serious mountain climbing. By autumn of 2011 they had both spent over fifty hours in rock-climbing lessons. The following year they had acquired all their own equipment and had made many friends; some of them were rock-climbing addicts.

During the summer of 2014, both Catherine and David began tae-kwon-do and rock-climbing. Although Catherine and David were ten and nine years old, they enjoyed both sports and the many challenges they offered.

Chapter 5

ARMAGEDDON

Thursday, September 7, 2023

As Judas slowly moved from his bed to his desk the excruciating pain in his abdomen was so powerful that he felt as if his inside was being eaten away by a monstrous amoeba with a voracious appetite. His legs weak, he clutched his stomach as he forced himself to reach his desk. Finally, he sat on his chair, only to realize that his right knee was barely holding on. He reached for an Ace knee brace, which had a customized inner pocket with a round magnum-ferrite in it, and put it around his knee. That gave him enough support to walk without fearing the loss of his right leg. The magnum-ferrite extracted most of the pain on his right knee. He still had a few of them left; his father had given them to him as part of a first-aid kit he had bought for him for camping. After twenty-six years three of the magnets still looked new. Since that fateful day in late August of 2021, Judas had had trouble with his right knee. Had it been the 27th, 28th, or 29th of August? He couldn't remember which date it had been; but he would never forget how he had banged his right knee. No, he would never forget that fall.

Judas and Catherine had gotten out of the jeep and had walked towards the Inn at Petersburg, West Virginia. It was five o'clock in the afternoon. He remembered that it had been a Friday. John Leblanc and his wife, Carole, were already seated at a table with Brian Nesbitt and his new girlfriend. He couldn't remember her name. Brian had gone through a divorce and several girlfriends. Judas had thought he was an immature, selfish, and very shallow man; however, he was an excellent rock climber. They had had a great supper that evening and had enjoyed a drink while discussing which side of Seneca Rocks they would climb and who would lead the climb. They had all agreed on climbing the south peak and east face of Seneca Rocks and it would be Judas' turn to lead. They knew all of the east face's walls, cracks, and their cruces. It would be a day's climb. Always a challenging one, of course!

Having had a lean but effective breakfast at six-thirty, the following morning, Judas, Catherine, and their friends drove to the parking lot of Seneca Rocks' Visiting Center. They began by rearranging their racks on the parking lot's pavement. They were already dressed for climbing with the latest bodysuits and rock shoes. Their new Italian rock shoes, made by Alpinista, were far superior to any other type. They were flexible and their soles were extremely malleable to every shape of rock. Literally, the soles of the Alpinista rock shoes would mold to the shape of any rock and regain its original shape when released. Every top rock climber was probably wearing Alpinista rock shoes.

The sky was clear and not a cloud could be seen anywhere. By eight o'clock they were all marching towards the rocks, carrying their racks, ropes, and knapsacks filled with dried fruits, nuts and drinks. It took about an hour to climb the foothill and boulders leading to the walls of the south peak-east face of Seneca Rocks. Judas was eager and ready to begin the climb that was to be his seventh lead on that wall. John anchored himself to a tree and got ready to belay Judas on Frosted Flake, a 5.9 two-pitch climb. Having checked his rack, making sure that his seven camalots were in the right order and having chalked his fingers Judas began to climb the crack. Using a layback technique, he climbed about ten feet before placing his first cam. He held himself with his left hand as his left foot pushed on the corner of the crack, his weight pulling towards the left as his right foot extended to the right. His right hand reached for the first cam and placed it into the crack and quickly secured his rope into the cam's carabiner. He could have rested but Judas wanted to climb the first pitch without taking a rest. His right hand reached higher, permitting his left foot to step higher on the crack as his right foot followed. Left, right, his hands jammed on the crack as his body lay back to the left. He placed the second cam and secured his rope into its carabiner. Judas made the climb look easy as his powerful body performed rock ballet with every move he made. Within a few minutes he had placed four of his camalots, reaching the flake, which curved to the right. The protection was excellent! He had saved the last three cams for the crack underneath the flake. His hands were beginning to hurt but he wasn't going to hangdog. Hangdogging was against his principles as a climber. The flake became thicker to its right forming a small overhang and the only way Judas could climb it was by under-grabbing the crack and pulling his body out as his weight forced his feet to wedge against the wall. Quickly, he placed his fifth, sixth, and seventh cams reaching the end of the flake where it formed a small overhang. He held himself with his left hand as he chalked his right, and then switched hold to chalk his left hand. With his last energy he brought his right hand and foot over the overhang, pushing and pulling himself over the bulge. The Alpinista shoes were wonderful, giving him the best possible footholds. He began traversing to his left as he climbed towards the cold shuts where he would secure himself and set up a belay station to belay Catherine and his friends up. It was at that moment that it happened! Before reaching the cold shuts, Judas instinctively turned around as did every single person and animal to witness the explosion and glow which had illumined the entire eastern sky. He knew, as did everyone else, that something awful and unspeakable had just happened. The entire eastern sky had blanched to a pale white, and it was then that Judas lost control and fell backwards. His instinct was to grip the edge of the bulge but his tired fingers slipped as he fell, his body swinging to the right and over the overhang where the last two cams held his rope. He fell approximately thirty feet, about sixteen feet below his last two cams, banging his right knee against the wall. He felt an instant stab inside his knee followed by an immediate swelling as he hung on. Judas had been lucky because the cams had been properly placed and easily held his magnified weight from that sudden fall.

31

Below, John had been pulled up several inches by Judas' fall as he had also turned to witness the annihilation of Greater Washington, D.C. It was one hundred and twenty-five miles, as the crow flies, from Seneca Rocks to downtown Washington, D.C.; nevertheless, the explosion had illumined the morning sky. It was twenty past nine! John looked up at Judas, realizing his predicament, feeling bad about what had just happened to him.

"Do you need help, Jude?" he yelled.

"No!" yelled back Judas as he clenched his teeth to withstand the stabbing pain, "I can manage. Just bring me down!"

Although hurt, Judas managed to descend quickly, using only his left foot against the wall. Immediately, he searched inside his knapsack for an emergency Ace bandage, which he always kept in one of the inner pockets. He bandaged his knee as he studied his daughter and friends' pensive and fearful faces.

"I banged my right knee badly," he volunteered, "I fell when I heard the explosion."

They all looked up at the sky as mushroom-shaped clouds could be seen in the distant skies, towards the east, southeast, west, and north. Washington D.C., Norfolk, Pittsburgh, and Columbus had just been hit by nuclear missiles, as every other major city in North and South America, Europe, Africa, Australia, Japan, and Israel had experienced the same fate. United States, Russia, and Europe had immediately responded with hundreds of nuclear missiles bringing total destruction to Persia, North Korea, and most of China. Most of the population on planet Earth had been destroyed, leaving the survivors to die a slow and painful death.

The ominous nuclear clouds mushroomed enormously, quickly enlarging, as they enveloped the distant skies. Judas and his friends rushed down along the steep path leading to the parking lot, carrying all of their equipment. Judas tried to keep up with the quick pace by hopping and walking along with a stick. When they reached the parking lot, there were about two to three hundred frightened people, who had quickly returned from their hikes or climbs. There were climbers still trying to rappel down. Some had been parking their cars when the explosions occurred. A few had already left. People were panicking and there was much confusion and screaming when Judas had decided to shout "SILENCE!" by cupping his hands around his mouth. Everyone stood frozen as Judas spoke, succeeding in calming them down. He told them to thank God that they were all alive and that together they would try to learn what had happened. He suggested to everyone to remain calm and he forbid anyone to leave the valley. He told them that most probably they were in a safer zone and that he would find out any possible information by phone or radio at the Information Center. People began to console each other as some sat on the pavement, talking in small groups. Parents held their children. Others sat in their vehicles, waiting for Judas to return. Catherine was holding a young girl, who seemed to have misplaced her parents. John followed Judas as he hopped towards the Information Center.

Inside the Seneca Rocks Information Center, which was part of the Monongahela National Forest, were six forest rangers, four men and two women, and eleven visitors: five women, three men, two teen-age boys and a young girl of four to five years old. The visitors were frightened and the rangers were trying to calm them down as Judas and John entered the main exhibit hall. One of the male rangers, Patrickson, turned around and told them that the center was closed for the day. Judas asked to use the telephone because his cellular was not working. Ranger Patrickson told Judas and John to get out of the center because it was about to be closed. Judas insisted that he use the telephone to find out what was happening. Ranger Briggs, a petite blonde woman, informed Judas that the telephone and electricity were not working and that they were going to close the center and go home to their families. Both Judas and John exited the center, disappointed and troubled by the implications of lack of electricity and telephones. Many of the people in the parking lot were driving away, indifferent to Catherine's begging to stay. Judas and John ran towards the cars, unable to stop some of them. Judas begged everyone to sit down on the asphalt pavement and listen to what he had to offer. That became the first meeting and the incorporation of the Seneca Climbers.

Judas then remembered. It had been Saturday, August 28, 2021. How could he ever forget that day!

Chapter 6

DR. WEINSTEIN'S MACHINE

Thursday, September 7, 2023
(6:00 p.m.)

Judas rearranged the Ace knee brace so that the magnum-ferrite disk was on the right side of his knee. The pain on his knee would shift from left to right and, at times, to the back of it. That felt better! He looked out the window to see if Catherine was back but the Toyota Scrooge wasn't there. He really wanted to see her again before he would actually put himself to sleep forever and finally meet his Maker. Then he would find out if Jesus truly were the Son of God. Would he be punished for doubting? He had been a good man, a good husband, a good father, and a good son! He had been a good person throughout his lifetime. He hadn't hurt anyone with his doubts. Thomas had also doubted and he had not been condemned by Him. He had been merciful with Thomas. Would He be merciful with him?

He had thought about using a gun but decided that it would have been too messy. A lethal injection of cyanide would be a smooth and quick way to cross the street of life. Death is the other side of life. It could not be bad. Nothing could be worse than the present world, he thought. Life had become hell itself; and, if that were hell death would be heaven. As he tried to imagine what it would be like to cross from life to death within sixty seconds there was a knock on the door. Seconds passed and then there was another knock. Judas was unable to hear it for he was far away, exploring the long tunnel that led to the afterlife. The third knock was loud and frenetic accompanied by cries of JUDAS.

Finally, he awoke from his deep meditation and answered back, "Coming. I'm coming! Just a minute, please!" and faltered to the door.

He unlocked the door and opened it. It was Catherine, together with Dr. Weinstein, Major Coolidge, and Major Nichols. Catherine quickly embraced him as he held her for what seemed to be a very long time. The three men entered Judas' bedroom-study and sat down as he lovingly held his daughter cheek to cheek. He kissed her cheeks, her forehead and the tip of her nose.

He turned around, still holding Catherine, and whispered to his friends, "I'm dying."

"No, daddy! Please, don't say that daddy!" cried out Catherine.

"My sweet child, it's so good to see you. I'm so happy to see you...and you, my dear friends."

"I have some great news!" interjected Dr. Weinstein, "I have finished my top-secret project."

"You have?" replied Judas, doubting that remote possibility.

"Yes! And, tomorrow it will be your birthday."

"You remembered, Jeff!"

"I didn't forget it, neither, dad. I might as well give you these now," exclaimed Catherine, taking two CDs from her pocket, "I've been searching for these two for months. Happy birthday, daddy."

She hugged and kissed him.

"River of Dreams! Billy Joel, and, and...I can't believe it! Where did you find this, my sweet angel?"

"In a little store in Buckhannon."

"ABBA!" he exclaimed, "ABBA GOLD! Thank you, honey. Wow, Billy Joel and ABBA."

"And my birthday gift to you is the ride of your life in my machine!" exclaimed Dr. Weinstein. "Come on, Jude, you must see it now!"

"I'm too tired and hurting, Jeff...Maybe tomorrow."

"Please, daddy, come now. I'll help you," Catherine said, placing her arm around his shoulders to support him.

"You've got to see this. It's magnificent!" uttered Major Coolidge, who was almost a replica of a young Gary Cooper.

"And, since there is no government left in the U.S., you will be the official person to try it out. You're our leader; and Doctor Weinstein's experiment with his wonderful machine doesn't really count. It only lasted ten minutes," continued Major Nichols, who was a little shorter than Major Coolidge.

"What! You've already tried it!" Judas exclaimed at Dr. Weinstein.

"I had to find out if it would really work. Well, it works! It was scary, Jude; I almost got killed."

"And you want me to try it as a birthday present. Great!"

"No, Jude. The machine is faultless. A red coat in the Revolutionary War almost killed me. I went back to seventeen seventy-seven, hoping to find George Washington."

"You went back to the American Revolution. You actually went back in time and were able to return. That's impossible, Jeffery!"

"No, my friend! I've spent the last nine years and more than five billion dollars of our tax money and I did it. I actually did it, Jude!"

There was a glint in Judas' eyes and he suddenly seemed to come alive with an energy that he must have saved for such a moment. He finally cried out "You were physically in the American Revolution. That's mind-boggling, Jeff. And, frankly, I never thought that this would be possible. I thought you were wasting your time, money, and energy on this project...How long were you there? In...during the American Revolution."

"It seemed like an entire day; however I had set the time for ten minutes only."

"I still find it difficult to believe in the whole idea. It seems impossible. How can it be possible to travel back in time or, maybe, to see the future? Once it's gone, you cannot bring it back; and, if it hasn't happened, you can't possibly be there!"

"Time does not really exist. We, humans, have invented time to measure our daily life and to suit our needs here on earth; but in the

36

universe time is meaningless. I have used the most precious stones money can buy, together with *galactis*, to create a vehicle that traverses time. I have used precious stones for they hold, locked within them, the secret to time; and, I have used *galactis* for it seems to be an alloy with the characteristics of disintegration and reintegration when traveling at the speed of light. It seems that true time and light are interrelated. Together they form a synergic pure energy."

"If what you say is true, can you bring me back in time?"

"That is exactly what I intend to do, Jude. Tomorrow is your birthday and that is my birthday gift to you!"

"You are a true friend, Jeff; however, that is going to be very difficult. You know where I really wish to go back to."

"We all know where you would like to go back to and to make that possible, Majors Coolidge and Nichols will take us all there tomorrow. That's their birthday gift to you."

"I don't know what to say, guys. I'm overwhelmed!"

"Say, yes!" exclaimed Major Nichols.

"Yes, yes, YES! Of course, I'll accept if it's not a major problem. Can the Stealth G-1 carry such a vehicle?"

"Yes, it can! The Judas-1 can fit in the storage room underneath," answered Major Coolidge.

"The Judas-1?"

"I had to name it, and since it's your birthday...you know!"

"Jeff, guys, I love you. I love you Catherine."

He kissed her on her forehead.

"Alright, help me get out of here; I want to see this wonderful device."

Jeff and Catherine helped him out of the door and out of the building. They all got into Jeff's U.S. Army All Terrain Vehicle and he drove them to his building, which was four miles northwest of Seneca Rocks Visitor Center, at the foot of Spruce Knob Unit. The former U.S. Government had built a research facility into the mountain. A large remote-control electronic door permitted them to enter. The huge door was shaped like a rock, which followed the outline of the rocky cliff. It was impossible to get in unless you had a remote-control device, which had been especially made for the Spruce Knob Research Unit. They arrived there within five minutes. Jeff used his special remote-control device and he drove into the man-made cavernous research facility of Spruce Knob Unit. Judas had been there several times; but this time it was for a very special reason.

They walked into Dr. Weinstein's laboratory. Computers, T.V. monitors, and other electronic gadgets that he used covered an entire wall. The opposite wall was blanketed by books, videos, CDs, and VCDs. The third wall had a working counter which ran the entire length and was loaded with papers, books, small tools, and dozens of beakers and glass containers of all sizes and shapes, and all filled with chemicals. The upper part of the third wall held a two-way mirror. From inside the lab you were able to see outside; and, from outside the lab, it was a long mirror. The fourth wall held larger tools, a smelter, and two doors, one at each end of it. A large white sheet covered something in the middle of the lab. The hidden object was not too big; it was about six feet high and four feet wide by four feet deep. They all walked around it and stood silently, waiting for Jeff to unveil his new invention, his masterpiece of time.

"Well," began Jeff, "go ahead. Unveil it!"

"You want me to unveil it!" answered Judas, puzzled.

"The honor would have gone to the president of the United States of America. Unfortunately, he's not present. You're our leader and a very good one; and it is an honor having you officially unveil it and baptize it!" Jeff grabbed a bottle of Mumm's Cordon Rouge Champagne and proudly held it with both hands.

"You don't expect me to break that bottle? Do you?" asked Judas.

"Yes, we do!" exclaimed Jeff.

"Can't we first have some and then break it."

"No, that would not really count."

"Where did you get that bottle? Do you realize how difficult it is to find a bottle of good champagne?"

"I've been saving this bottle for years...for this moment. Now, please, unveil it."

"Okay!" Judas agreed, giving up the idea of tasting the champagne.

He grabbed the white sheet and slowly pulled it down, revealing a most beautiful throne made of *galactis*. The throne seemed to be made of one solid piece of the white metal, highly polished, with smooth round corners. A one piece of thick round glass covered the front up to the top and hugged the sides of the throne, allowing clear visibility.

"That is beautiful, Jeff. It's a masterpiece; but, where is the control board or computer? It seems to be empty."

"It's all hidden inside. You must touch certain parts to activate its command board and precious stones time traveler."

Catherine, Major Coolidge, and Major Nichols quietly looked on, admiring the simplicity and beauty of Dr. Weinstein's invention. Both majors had been present during Jeff's trial test of Judas-1, witnessing the atomic decomposition and reintegration of the machine.

"Look!" Jeff continued by pressing the center of the *galactis* frame of the glass bubble. The molded glass door automatically opened, revealing a leather seat inside the throne. At the bottom of the door a control board, also made of *galactis*, slowly positioned itself upward. It was studded with the most beautiful precious stones he had ever seen. At the center of the board stood a huge diamond. It must have been easily over one hundred carats.

"The diamond is one hundred and thirteen carats. It is almost double the size of the Hope Diamond."

"Where did you get it? Where did you get all of these beautiful stones?"

"Government money!"

"You mean taxpayers' money!"

"Yeah, taxpayers' money. Mine, yours, and the rest of America's."

"How much did this cost, Jeff?" Judas pointed to the throne.

"It's not important. It's the result that counts."

"My Lord, do you know how many people could have been fed with all that money?"

"I know, Jude. Please, don't do this. I've succeeded and that's what's important. Please!" Jeff begged handing Judas the champagne bottle as he gently shut the glass door.

"Ah, what's another few bucks!" exclaimed Judas. "I baptize you Judas-One." He smashed the champagne bottle on the *galactis* corner of the throne. The bottle broke as the champagne splashed everyone. They all clapped and congratulated Dr. Jeff Weinstein.

Tom Johnson, one of Jeff's assistants, came into the lab through the left door holding six champagne glasses and another bottle of Cordon Rouge, which had been chilled to perfection.

"You son-of-a-gun! How many bottles did you save?"

"Oh, a few cases!"

Everyone laughed and drank to Jeff's honor and to Judas' birthday.

Later, that evening, a general meeting was called and the six hundred and forty members of the Seneca Climbers were all present, all of them sick, some more than others. Judas told them of Dr. Weinstein's invention; and, that thanks to Majors Nichols and Coolidge his dream would soon materialize. There was excitement and hope in the crowd. Hope that Judas would succeed in finding the Christ, their Lord. They also prayed and hoped for a future on earth.

Friday, September 8, 2023
(6:00 a.m.)

Judas woke up to the music of ABBA, feeling a bit more energetic and hopeful than the day before. The beautiful machine, the champagne, his people, and his parents' favorite CDs had lifted his spirit up; and, after all, it was his birthday. He was forty years old and alive.

By seven o'clock Judas and Catherine were outside by the parking lot. On the field beside the center loomed the black **Stealth G-1**, like a bird of prey about to spring and attack its victims. Major Nichols and Major Coolidge were busy packing boxes inside the storage bin in the belly of the big bird. People were coming from their homes and makeshift habitations to see their leader leave for the most important mission of their lives.

A light mist shrouded the whole countryside and the whole scene did not seem quite real, like a painting by Dali. The sky was covered with a blanket of dark gray clouds and the western wind was sharp enough to chill your bones. Snow was soon coming. Another long terrible bleak gray winter. Judas held Catherine in a warm embrace. Was this to be their last day together? A tear slowly bubbled out from his right eye and streamed down his cheek. How he loved this sweet child. How he missed his beautiful wife and his wonderful son. How he missed his mother and father. Would he ever see them again? Maybe soon, in the next life! Anything was possible!

"Happy birthday, daddy," Catherine whispered in his ear for the umpteenth time. She softly kissed his cheek. How she loved this gentle man. Her daddy! How she missed her beautiful mother and her younger brother. How she missed her grandparents. Was today to be the last day with her dad? She silently prayed that he would be successful in his mission. She knew how much this adventure into the past would mean to him. She knew that he had searched for and struggled within his soul to find Christ in his life. How she knew! She had gone through the same struggle within herself. She prayed that he would really find Him and spent a few days with Him. Her dad would know if Jesus was truly the Son of God or just a wonderful human being. She felt excitement at this thought. She hugged and kissed him again and told him how much she loved him. Everyone looked on. Some looked sad while some looked hopeful. Some looked happy.

"You are an angel, my sweet child. You are proof that angels really exist, my sweet Catherine!" he replied.

They turned around upon hearing Jeff's army A.T.V. humming towards them. Having parked his army All Terrain Vehicle, he jogged towards them carrying a U.S. Air Force duffel bag.

"Good morning, Jude, Catherine, everyone. Happy birthday, dear friend!"

"Thank you, Jeff. Thank you for this wonderful gift."

The three friends walked towards the Stealth G-1, which was only a few hundred yards away, as people joined them, wishing them a safe journey. When they reached the formidable jet the two majors greeted them and wished Judas a happy birthday. A thousand eyes watched them silently.

"Do you have your coordinates with you, Judas?" asked Major Coolidge.

"As a matter of fact, yes!" answered Judas as he searched the inner pocket of his leather jacket. Having found the paper, he proceeded to read it before giving it to Major Coolidge, "It's thirty-one degrees and forty-four north and by thirty-five degrees and twenty-seven east. That's where Khirbat Qumran, or Mesad Hasidim once stood."

"That is great, Judas. We are ready and the Stealth has been fueled with enough liquid hydrogen and quartz to go twice around the earth without refueling; however, we will use only about one fourth of that for this round trip. We also have enough canned food and bottled water for all of us to last us ten days. Is that enough food Doctor Weinstein?" volunteered Major Coolidge.

"More than enough. The entire mission should last eight days maximum. We should be back by next Friday, September fifteenth."

Major Nichols checked the storage room in the belly of the Stealth to make sure that Judas-1 was secured. And, it was!

The Stealth G-1 had been used only three times during the past two years. Those three flights, within the United States, were to reconnoiter other small surviving groups. Most of those groups lived in the mountains and forests of sparsely populated states.

During the third flight, the two majors had witnessed the western part of California, from San Francisco to Baja California, submerged into the Pacific Ocean. Debris of skyscrapers stood out of the waters like man-made coral reefs; and, the Pacific Ocean stretched out to the foothills of Sierra Nevada. Life was never going to be the same. Planet Earth was doomed had thought Major Nichols. Their only hope was survival. They felt lucky that two years before they had landed on the field at Seneca Rocks and had met Judas and Dr. Weinstein. They had become their new hope. And today they were to begin a mission more important than any space flight they had ever experienced. Today they would puncture a hole through the veil of time to discover Truth itself. With Judas and Dr. Weinstein there was hope for any survivor on earth.

The Stealth G-1 was a revamped F-117 Stealth. Its high-tech hardware was the most advanced ever. It operated on liquid hydrogen and quartz. The two compensated each other, giving it almost a fifty thousand mile flight range. It was the fastest jet ever built and could fly through the thermosphere, where it was capable of reaching up to seventeen thousand miles per hour. Dr. Weinstein, Major Nichols, and Major Coolidge had modified the back seating space from two to three seats. They boarded the two billion dollar black bird and Major Coolidge shut and secured the hatch. This mission would be their first trans-Atlantic flight since the nuclear attack; and, they would finally get a chance to scout Europe and the Middle East.

Having worked all the preliminary computerized check-points, the two majors were ready to fly. They would first fly over the ruins of Washington, D.C. and New York and then break through the thermosphere to gain maximum speed. There was no need to wear oxygen masks inside the Stealth. Its insulation, aerodynamics, and air-tightness equaled Spaceship Mars'.

People waved good-bye as they stepped back, far away from the Stealth, forming an enormous circle as they held hands and in chorus they chanted *Happy Birthday* and *For He's a Jolly Good Fellow*.

Inside the Stealth the five friends had fastened their seat harnesses and were eager and ready to fly this most precious mission. Major Nichols was on the pilot seat and turned on the powerful turbo engines of the G-1 as Major Coolidge assisted him. Surprisingly, the noise was muffled by the ultra-insulation and only a humming of the powerful engines could be heard. The chanting of their friends was also muffled by the outside noise of the engines and by the ultra-insulation.

"Ready, everyone?" Major Nichols broke the concentrated silence of the enclosed cockpit.

"Ready!" exclaimed everyone with rather enthusiastic voices.

Major Nichols pushed a green button and suddenly the Stealth G-1 lifted itself up and continued its way up until it reached two thousand feet. The Seneca Rocks looked like giant teeth. Their habitations seemed like tiny boxes below, and their people were waving good-bye as they encircled the huge field.

The black Stealth turned ninety-five degrees and came to a stop, its nose pointing straightly eastward. Major Nichols pushed a second green light and the G-1 shot eastward like a bullet, climbing to six thousand feet within a minute. Its speed was unbelievable; and, although it was flying only at two thousand miles per hour it had flown over the Appalachian Mountains within two minutes. In less than five minutes they had reached the Washington, D.C. area, where Major Nichols came to an immediate slow down, descending to one thousand feet. The Stealth G-1 suddenly behaved more like a giant helicopter, hovering over the former capital of the former United

States of America. Devastation reigned everywhere. Not a single soul could be seen. No animals. No life. It looked like a giant plastic model of a great city that had been burned and melted by an unforgiving force. It was the first time that Judas, Catherine, and Dr. Weinstein had witnessed the devastated capital as tears flowed easily from their eyes for the Greater Washington Area had been their home.

Sadly but decisively, Major Nichols pointed the big black bird towards northeast and once again, pushing the second green button, the Stealth shot forward like a giant bullet. The four screens on the cockpit scanned the trajectory of the flight. The first one was a digital map of the entire Northeast coast. The second screen showed a digital relief map of the trajectory, which included tall buildings. The third showed detailed maps of the ever-moving four square miles of the trajectory. The fourth screen was an infrared view of the trajectory. The speed climbed digitally. There were so many buttons on the cockpit that Judas was flabbergasted with the speed and efficiency of Majors Nichols and Coolidge. They were constantly pushing buttons with great ease and calmness, as the Stealth G-1 piloted itself towards New York.

The entire Washington, D.C.-New York corridor had been pulverized, and only the burned remains of millions of vehicles dotted its mangled highways. But, the most impressionable and horrifying sight was the witnessing of the remains of what once was New York City. Not a living soul had been seen on the infrared screen. Millions of people burnt to a crisp and millions of people dead through a horrifying and painful cancer. Desolation and devastation were forever present.

Major Nichols broke the silence, "Everyone must wear these oxygen masks for the trans-Atlantic flight.

"I thought we didn't need to wear them in this space jet?" asked Judas.

"We don't, but we are being extremely careful. After all we will be flying within the thermosphere and at mach-twenty speed. That's a little over thirteen thousand miles per hour and about seventy-five miles above the earth," answered Major Nichols.

"The fastest I have flown until today was the Concorde," said Judas.

"The Concorde was a turtle compared to this. This babe can reach up to twenty-seven thousand miles per hour in space, just as quickly as Spaceship Atlantis. But for this trip we will go half its potential speed. So, everyone, wear these oxygen masks. We are not taking any chances at all, especially with this mission!" commanded Major Nichols.

Everyone wore his or her mask as the two astronauts shot the Stealth G-1 upward into the thermosphere. For the first time in two years they saw the sun in all its splendor, rising from the east. A giant layer of gray clouds covered planet earth, masking its blue beauty. Would it ever be like it was? Thought Judas. Catherine was looking out the window as the sun shone on her beautiful face. Dr. Weinstein was glued to the right window, preoccupied with the speed and height. Judas patted both their backs, reassuring them with a smile. He leaned to his left and kissed Catherine's cheek, and, then returned to his deep thoughts about the future of the earth and about finding Jesus of Nazareth.

Major Nichols woke them up from their concentration, "We are about to descend. We are sixty seconds away from France."

"But it's only eight o'clock!" exclaimed Dr. Weinstein, removing his mask.

"I'm afraid it's later than that. It's the fourteenth hour or two p.m. There is a six-hour time change; and, please, keep your mask on. We are descending," ordered Major Coolidge.

Suddenly they were into the gray clouds and finally they could see the ocean. Everything was gray and dark once again. There was no sun anywhere on earth. They flew over Paris, which had been entirely devastated. They reconnoitered over most of Europe only to find out that no one had survived. There had been a concentration of hits and all major cities had been at a closer range than American ones, ensuring a total decimation of its population. Stricken with grief at the sights of total devastation the five flew towards their destination, Khirbat Qumran.

Chapter 7

RIVER OF DREAMS

Friday, September 8, 2023
(3:00 p.m.)

The black Stealth G-1 slowly descended on latitude 31, 44'
and longitude 35,27' as it had been computerized by Major Nichols.
For the past few minutes Judas had witnessed the total destruction of
the Middle East and of the holy city of Jerusalem. Not a soul was
alive. Major Nichols instructed them to keep their oxygen mask on
because of the heavy concentration of post-nuclear dust. The
powerful engines blew that dust in a circle forming a cloud around the
Stealth. Major Coolidge suggested that they waited ten minutes until
the dust settled before they would open the hatch.

Finally, when the dust had settled, they could see that the ruins
of Khirbat Qumran were still standing; and, they could see the Dead
Sea in the east. Major Coolidge opened the hatch and, one by one,
they climbed down from the jet. The air felt thick and it was rather
cool for mid-afternoon. Judas looked around recognizing the ruins of
the round well, which stood west of what remained of the tower.

"This place gives me the creeps!" exclaimed Dr. Weinstein.

"It was once an enchanting site," suggested Judas.

"I don't doubt you, my friend; but now, it smells of death."

"That smell is everywhere!" exclaimed Judas resignedly.

"We must find a place for Judas-One. Where would you like it, Judas?" asked Major Nichols.

Judas looked around, searching for a safe place. He thought of the ruins of the monastery, southeast of the tower. It contained a small courtyard. He thought that to be a safe place for Judas-1. He showed the spot to Dr. Weinstein, the majors and his daughter. They all agreed that there was plenty of space for Judas-1. Major Nichols suggested placing it with the Stealth. It would take only a few minutes. He instructed everyone to move back, behind a major wall. He reentered the huge black bird and he gently maneuvered it up to twenty feet over the ruins of the monastery. He gently lowered Judas-1 into it. Once it had touched the ground he released the cables that had held it in place. Judas-1 stood in the middle of the monastery's courtyard. Major Nichols hovered the Stealth back to the original landing as gently as a butterfly, without stirring much dust.

Dr. Weinstein explained the control board of Judas-1, which was a modified computer studded with precious stones. He had set the time back one thousand nine hundred ninety-four years, at 29 A.D. He instructed Judas that by simply pushing the yellow topaz would activate Judas-1. To return, he had to push the large diamond. Jeff had programmed everything. He showed the compartment underneath the seat. It had a GISA knapsack loaded with canned food and seven bottles of water. Its pockets held a folding knife with two surgical steel blades, a tiny but powerful quartz flashlight, a miniature 35mm spy camera, a small first-aid kit with two Adrenalin kits, and an anti-poison injection. Inside was also a 6mm 100-foot climbing rope. A white kaftan was neatly folded on the top of the knapsack.

"A camera?" questioned Judas.

"You must take pictures of Jesus, the apostles, His mother, the Baptist and any other important person. This camera holds a roll of seventy-two photos and there's an extra double roll. The film is one thousand ASA; you can shoot in dark rooms and you don't need a flash. Use them both and, please, bring them back," answered Dr. Weinstein.

"I will do my best if I come back."

"You will, my friend, you will; however, I must tell you something very important about going back in time and returning. When Judas-1 reaches the speed of light it will turn into pure light, including you and everything else in it. As it slows down you, Judas-1, and everything else will reintegrate into what you are. I know that this will probably be a frightening experience; it was for me. But I'm back, alive, and exactly the way I was before I left."

"Death doesn't frighten me, Jeff. I am ready now."

"Don't talk about death; we will see you in exactly seven days, my friend." said Dr. Weinstein as he embraced Judas.

Judas embraced Catherine, kissing her on the forehead and cheeks and whispering how much he loved her. He embraced Major Coolidge and Major Nichols. Judas was now ready, dressed in GISA white pants and shirt with the GISA insignias on the left pockets. The two majors had also given him a matching belt with a GISA buckle and white leather Mars boots. It had been a birthday gift. He still carried the portable miniature CD-player and the two CDs Catherine had given him as a present. He carefully held them as if they were precious artifacts from another era. In a way, they were. Although, he had lost a lot of weight, Judas still looked good and seemed to be happy.

Dr. Weinstein embraced Judas again wishing him a successful trip. Major Nichols told him that his trip would be the most important voyage ever taken by a human and that he considered him a great man and a great explorer. Major Coolidge wished him a safe voyage and that they would be waiting for him. Finally, Catherine embraced her father for the last time. Tears ran down her cheeks as she kissed him. Once again, he told her how much he loved her as he kissed her for the last time. Judas reassured her that it would be only seven days. Only a week!

Judas sat on the throne of Judas-1 and Dr. Weinstein helped him in buckling up and in closing the glass door. The four watched him from the outside as Judas placed the ABBA CD in his miniature CD-player. He fixed his earphones and set the CD to *I Have a Dream*. He waived good-bye and pressed the yellow topaz. The sound of a guitar or sitar began to clang in his ears as Judas-1 began to spin slowly. Judas thought that something was wrong for the machine was spinning extremely slowly. Dr. Weinstein, Catherine, Major Coolidge, and Major Nichols stepped back behind the wall of the ancient monastery.

The song began with the angelic voices of Agnetha and Anni, the two lead singers of ABBA. By this time the machine had completed a revolution. As the song continued on the spinning had picked up a bit more speed. Judas saw his loved ones through the glass bubble and waved again. The four waved back. A tear rolled down Judas' cheek as he saw a vision of his parents holding him up and dancing to the words and music of that very same song. By then the machine was spinning at a speed faster than any Lamborghini. As the song reached its midpoint the machine and Judas were now blurred into a white funnel.

The four friends were looking at a small white tornado spinning at thousands, maybe a million miles per hour. The small white tornado broke up into pieces, into particles, into trillions of microscopic micro-particles disappearing from their vision.

The song was reaching its end as the trillions of atomic particles began to reassemble into the figures of Judas-1 and Judas, rotating in a micro-universe of their own. Judas opened his eyes, looking for his daughter, Dr. Weinstein, Major Coolidge, or Major Nichols. They were nowhere to be seen. He blinked his eyes. Impossible! He was in a pretty courtyard with orange and fig trees. He opened the hatch of Judas-1 and stepped out of it, admiring the courtyard. He looked at himself and at Judas-1. Both were intact and untouched. He could not believe that it had actually worked. His eyes were everywhere, as he put on the kaftan, admiring the walls of the Qumran Complex, Mesad Hasidim. Light flickered through the branches of the fig and orange trees. He followed the light into the open sky. He saw a blue sky with the sun shining above his head. It was so beautiful and so hot! It was at least ninety degrees Fahrenheit and almost noon. Suddenly, he heard a distant voice coming from outside. He took the knapsack and shut the hatch of Judas-1. He looked around, spotting a corridor leading out of the courtyard. He turned right and entered a room. Seeing an exit straight ahead he took it and entered another room. He turned right in another entrance, which led him into another room and then another, and another. He entered a tiny room that had no exit. He was lost in a labyrinth of the complex. He retraced his steps with the aid of his flashlight finally reaching the courtyard and Judas-1.

Suddenly, a voice whispered *Angel* in Aramaic. A man, dressed in black, with long black hair and beard, fell to the ground with his limbs outstretched, showing total submission. Judas grabbed his arm and, in broken Aramaic, told him to stand up. The Essene monk covered his eyes; his entire body trembled as if entering a state of convulsion. Judas turned off his flashlight, realizing that it was causing the Essene's fear. He asked the man to lead him to the voice. The monk did not quite understand his question. Judas mentioned Yehohanan the Baptist and the monk nodded and led him out of Mesad Hasidim. The middle-aged monk pointed southwest towards the Wadi Qumran. In broken Aramaic, he recommended the man to be the keeper of Judas-1. In exchange of his care he promised his flashlight on his return. The monk faithfully promised to guard the sacred object with his life as he bowed in reverence of Judas.

Judas began walking south towards the Wadi Qumran. As Judas got closer to a sloping cliff the voice became clearer and immediate. The Wadi Qumran was on the other side of the cliff. As Judas circled the promontory he came face to face with the Baptist, who stood on a large rock on the other side of the wadi. A crowd of approximately sixty to seventy men, women and a few children listened attentively to the Baptist.

"Repent, for the Kingdom of Heaven is at hand!" His shouts came to an end as his eyes locked with Judas. His auburn hair and beard were those of a wild man. His camel skin garment was fastened with a wide leather belt. Suddenly, the Baptist pointing to Judas, shouted with a newly acquired fervor in his commanding voice, "Turn around, and witness the mashìah himself!"

Everyone turned and stared at Judas. Some fell to the ground and some into the shallow waters of the wadi, prostrating down and asking for forgiveness.

"I am not the mashìah. I am only His messenger from the future. I am looking for Ishia of Nazerat. Do you know where he might be?" asked Judas in broken Aramaic.

"You must come from far away; it is the first time that I hear such an accent. You search for Ishia the Nazarene, oh, Angel from the Future. What can you tell me about my future or Ishia's future?"

"I know that you are the voice crying in the Desert of Yehuda, making ready the way of the Lord. You are the one preparing His path. And, of Ishia the Nazarene, once I meet him I will know if he truly is the Son of God or simply another holy man. Now, please, my time is short and I must find Ishia of Nazerat. If you know where he is, holy Baptist, please, tell me so that I may see if he is truly the Anointed One!"

"He is praying in the Wilderness of Yehuda for forty days and forty nights. You can find him on a hilltop at Jebel Har Montar. It is far and you will not be able to reach it today. It is now the sixth hour and it will be getting dark by the great hour. You will reach it tomorrow by mid-morning. You must follow this wadi until it splits into two. At the split, take the northern wadi until you come to its source. There you must climb the northern cliff of the wadi. That will be Jebel Har Montar. He is at the top, praying. The distance is about fifty-four stadia and it will take you ten to eleven hours of walking. At night sleep in one of the caves along the Wadi Qumran. Continue your walk in the morning. May the Lord be with you, oh, Angel from the Future."

"When I return, holy Baptist, if Ishia the Nazarene is with me, then He is truly the Son of the Most High. If he is not, then I will resume my search for the True One. May the Lord be with you, Yehohanan!"

"Angel from the Future, if you come back with Ishia the Nazarene you will not find me here. I will be at Bet-ha-Arava by the Ha-Yarden. There you will find me."

"I know Bet-ha-Arava. I will be there with the True Messiah!" And with that promise, Judas began his long walk along the northern bank of the Wadi Qumran.

Within minutes the powerful voice of the Baptist had become faint; and, as Judas continued on, it had totally faded away. He was alone once again. Only the sound of the Wadi Qumran was heard, at times broken by the quick movements of lizards and snakes. Judas searched in his knapsack for his CD Walkman and Billy Joel's CD, *River of Dreams*. He listened to the songs as he continued his walk. He checked his wristwatch only to find out that it was not working. It probably needed a new battery. It must have been discharged during the time travel. He looked at the sun, which was slightly to the west of the sky's midpoint: it was about one o'clock in the afternoon. He then remembered the Baptist's sixth hour and great hour. The sixth hour was noon, the sixth hour of daylight; and, the great hour was six o'clock, time for prayer. He had to move at a quicker pace; he wanted to reach the place before dusk. As he moved with an energetic pace, he listened to the wonderful songs, remembering his father. He had been almost eleven years old when *River of Dreams* had been released. It had become his father's favorite CD and within that year it had also become his favorite. There was so much to Billy Joel's words: they were meaningful words pertaining to life.

As Judas marched, listening to Billy Joel's songs, he had to concentrate at every step he took; rocks and bushes were everywhere and little crawling creatures lived under them. He kept on without stopping. Fifty-four stadia were approximately eleven kilometers or seven miles, seven miles of hilly desert. He was determined to reach Jebel Har Montar before sundown. He moved on at a brisk pace, determined to arrive there on time. When the CD was over he pushed on the play button, starting it from the beginning again. He arrived at the fork where the waters of the Wadi Qumran joined, from the northern and southern branches. He remembered the directions of the Baptist, "At the split, take the northern wadi." Judas kept to the right and followed the northern Wadi Qumran for several minutes and then came to a stop. He took a liter of spring water and a three-ounce bag of salted peanuts from his knapsack; and, he proceeded to wet his lips and to swallow a mouthful of the bottled water. He continued his march along the wadi as he chewed on a few peanuts, listening to *River of Dreams* for a third time. He could never get tired of it: it had definitely been Billy Joel's best production, a classic album with so many wonderful memories of his loving parents. He loved and enjoyed all of the songs as he kept on along the winding wadi whose angled banks had by then become the walls of a canyon. The sun was so powerful that Judas had to cover his head with the hood of his kaftan. He was sweating and he began to feel pain inside his knee. Going back in time seemed to have produced in him enough epinephrine to make him forget his terminal sickness and deteriorating knee. But the pains in his knee and in his stomach did not stop him from walking on. The vision of the Nazarene kept his languished body in a constant motion along the Wadi Qumran, totally oblivious to the sweltering heat. He was lost into Billy Joel's *River of Dreams* and his steps seemed almost synchronized with the music.

Judas had forgotten the number of times he had listened to Billy Joel's songs—their lyrics were a powerful drug, full of meaning and vigor, as they reverberated in the microcosm of his brain. Suddenly, he fell, tripping on a rock, as his eyes had closed for a moment. His bad knee throbbed with a new and sharper pain. He lay flat on the arid soil, not wanting to get up in that moment of anguish and desperation. Where did he think he was going? How was he going to find Ishia the Nazarene? Or was he going to die a lonely death in such a forsaken place before finding him? Yes, he would die if he would not get up and continue his search. He slowly and painfully sat up and rested his back against a large rock by the wadi. He reached for some water from the wadi to wash his face—it was surprisingly refreshing. He drank a little water from the plastic bottle and munched on a few nuts. Slowly, he resumed his march along the wadi; but he seemed to have lost the strength he had possessed when he had begun from Khirbat Qumran. However, he knew he must go on to find Ishia of Nazerat.

As he continued walking he felt the pain in his knee; and, as he forced his way along the wadi he also felt the sharp pains of the cancer eating his inside. From time to time he munched on some nuts for energy and washed them down with some bottled water. He was extremely tired and his body was burning from the sun. He stopped to feel his forehead—it was burning hot. He felt the water—it was cool and refreshing. He had a fever! He removed his kaftan and the rest of his clothes, laying them on top of the knapsack. In his underwear he stepped into the refreshing waters of the wadi and sat against a rock. The wadi was not very deep but its waters were cooling. He decided to lie down, the water streaming through his burning body, refreshing it, bringing the temperature down. After fifteen minutes Judas felt better, his temperature near normal. He got dressed and continued his march along the wadi and stopped only to check the location of the sun. It was anywhere between three and four o'clock. He must move quicker! He began to set a quicker pace but after half an hour his energy was depleted and his pace slowed down to a trudge. His stomach hurt and his legs had no strength left. He stopped and sat on a rock to munch on the rest of the nuts. The ten-minute rest and the nuts and water gave him some extra energy to go on. He had to find Ishia of Nazerat before he would die; he realized that he had little time left to live. He felt death catching up to him. His worn-out body would be ready to cross the street after he would meet the Nazarene. His legs and the rest of his body moved only by sheer will power. He looked like a rag doll or puppet, or like a drunken hobo without a destination.

Time passed as his weary body trudged on towards Jebel Har Montar. He looked up at the western sky, squinting his eyes to better focus on the afternoon sun. The sun was near the western horizon—a maximum of two hours of dimmer sunlight were left before nightfall would move in. He continued along the wadi, still listening to the ever-repeating Billy Joel, his body wobbling along like a puppet controlled by a novice puppeteer. Suddenly, his knee gave out and Judas fell face down on the sandy, rocky bank of the Wadi Qumran. He was at his end—he had no energy left within his languid, sick body. His lips pressed against the sandy soil, tasting the saltiness of the Judean Desert. How could he possibly go on? How could he get up and continue with his search? How could he possibly find Ishia of Nazerat? Jesus—Ishia! That was why he had traveled back in time, almost two millennia back! Unbelievable, but it was true. The thought of Ishia gave him his last hope. He had to muster his last gleam of hope and vigor and reach Jebel Har Montar. He lifted his head to look for a view of the canyon walls only to notice that the wadi was coming down from the northern hill. It was Jebel Har Montar! He had reached it and now he had to climb it. He looked westwards and only the last rays could be seen over the hills. He did not have too long before nightfall. He quickly searched into his knapsack and upon finding the Adrenalin kit he immediately injected himself with the epinephrine hormone. He had to move quickly—he had to reach the top of the mesa.

Having drunk some water, Judas washed his face at the source, which came from rainwater seeping through the cracked hilltops and mesas that shaped the Judean Wilderness. The water was refreshing and surprisingly sweet. He looked up at the top of the mesa—he could not see anyone. Ishia must be at the center of the plateau! He removed his kaftan and neatly placed it into his knapsack. With the newly acquired adrenaline within his body he began the climb. The first few hundred feet were easy and Judas had no major difficulties in climbing. Judas estimated the rest of the climb to be four to five hundred feet. As he continued ascending the bottom half of the wall the grade of the climb shifted from the high 4s to 5.0 and 5.1. Suddenly, more energy was required and Judas struggled on. The landscape and rocks reminded him of Arizona and Utah. He continued the ascent inching his way through the crux of the climb, which had become between 5.4 and 5.6. Judas followed the cracks of the face, using hand and fist jams and at times finger jams to protect himself from falling. His right hand pushed into the open crack and then twisted into a fist, jamming it into the crack, holding his weight until his left hand would reach higher into the crack searching for a hold. He continued on with his right and left, right and left, jamming his hands, twisting them into fists when there was enough space, or cupping his knuckles and fore-knuckles between the sides of the cracks. He climbed on using his hand and fist jamming to protect himself from falling. The jamming was painful at times as Judas' hands got scraped and cut as he struggled towards the top of the mesa. He came to a sudden stop on a small ledge, realizing he could no longer see—the last rays of the sun had extinguished and darkness had set in. He estimated that approximately one hundred feet were left to climb. Jamming his right foot into the crack and carefully standing on the thin ledge, Judas succeeded in finding his flashlight. Having strapped his flashlight on his right wrist Judas attempted to resume his climb, but his wasted body wanted to abandon that last attempt. Judas searched and found the second Adrenalin kit. He tied a tourniquet on his left forearm and with the help of the flashlight he injected the adrenaline into one of his larger arteries. He waited until the adrenaline reached his brain, creating a new energy within him. With the help of his flashlight he was able to grasp some of the holds, relying more on his arms than his legs. Inch by inch, foot by foot, Judas edged and smeared the wall with his feet, sensing for footholds. With his last willpower and adrenaline he gradually climbed on, finally reaching the top. His past hour had been an excruciating and difficult climb in almost total darkness. He then breathed a sigh of relief as he dragged his emaciated body towards the safety of the plateau. His hands were all cut and bloodied. His eyes, closing with fatigue, wanted to sleep; however, Judas chose his last moment of energy to scan the top of the plateau with his flashlight. After several searches he spotted the body of a man, sleeping on his side, covered by a white mantle. He had found him but he was too exhausted to even think of waking him up. He lay on the stony top, covering himself with his kaftan, as his mind slowly drifted away into the silence of the night.

Chapter 8

ISHIA THE NAZARENE

Tuesday, March 1st, 29 A.D.

The bright sunlight of the early morning sun reached Judas' eyes, forcing him to open them. He saw the man in white sitting in a lotus position, meditating. His immediate desire was to go to him to ask him if he was Ishia of Nazerat. He tried to move but his aching muscles did not respond. He could barely move his arms to reach for some water and mixed nuts. He was able to sip a little water but he had no energy to chew the nuts. He contended himself with a little more water, pushed in ABBA's CD for repeated playing and went back to sleep, listening to one of his favorite collections of songs as images of his parents became more vivid within the memories of his mind.

Judas woke up again, the hot sun beating on his face. He was so tired that he could barely open his eyelids. With great effort he managed to roll over on his side. The man in white was still meditating. He looked up. The sun was directly over him—it was noon. ABBA's songs kept on playing for the latest crystal cells could last for months on repeated playing. He managed to sip a little more water and went back to sleep, lost in the deep musical memories of his childhood.

It was night again and Judas experienced a fantastic dream. In his dream he saw the man in white meditating in the night. Up in the starry firmament a bright star crossed the sky, becoming larger as it reached the center of the sky above his head. The bright star became larger and larger until it reached about one hundred feet above the plateau. It was so big and bright that the entire plateau and its surroundings became illumined, brighter than the sunniest day Judas had ever experienced. A hatch opened from the star and three men in bright white descended as if riding on an invisible escalator. They walked towards the meditating man and helped him to get up and escorted him inside the star. As they passed through the large entrance, the four men had become light, four human shapes of bright light. Moments later the three men in bright white came back towards Judas and carried him inside the star. He could see their faces—they had no facial hair and they were extremely handsome. The dream ended. Judas was sleeping very heavily, still exhausted from the long walk and strenuous climb.

The sun was still shining brightly over him—the heat of the sun felt great. He was breathing in the wonderful energy it radiated. He was enjoying that hot, beautiful, warm sun that he had missed for the past two years. He kept soaking it in, even though he realized that he was dying. Any day, now! Any day! He shifted his eyes to the left; he saw the man praying, sitting in a lotus position. He managed to crawl his fingers to the bottle of water, which lay about a foot away, and was barely able to hold the neck of the plastic bottle. He experienced a lot of difficulty in turning its cap but succeeded after several feeble attempts and managed to bring the bottle to his lips. He sipped the little water that was left; but he was still thirsty. He remembered that there were six more water bottles in his GISA knapsack, which was beside him. He could not recall removing his knapsack from his back after the climb. He had been exhausted after such an arduous day. He slowly managed to open the Velcro flap, feeling his way in with his fingers, and count the bottles. There were still six bottles left. With deep concentration he pulled one out and with whatever little energy he possessed he succeeded in opening its cap. To his surprise, the bottle was not full—about one quarter was missing. He smiled as he stared at the meditating stranger. I hope you liked the water, he thought. He took a few more sips and closed the mouth of the bottle with its cap. He placed it beside him, next to the knapsack; and, slowly he abandoned his dying body to that deep sleep he had exited.

Judas dreamed that the man in white had come to him and had placed his index and middle fingers, together with his thumb, on his temple. He proceeded to press on his temple as he continued his meditation with his eyes totally shut. He kept on pressing on his temple for a long time—it seemed like an eternity. Visions of his birth were vividly reviewed from his deep subconscious mind. Judas had given his mother a lot of trouble during birth. Visions of every meaningful experience during his childhood flashed within the deep canyons of his memories. Flashes of his school days and his vacations were reviewed in his brain. Every little meaningful event projected like microscopic holograms within his memories. His teaching in Israel and his ongoing search for Christ's tomb were once again real within his mind. Falling in love with Judith and the birth of his children and all the wonderful experiences in his life were reviewed like a fast film. Flashes of all he had learned and studied, and of all he had written, were quickly reviewed in his brain. His children growing up and his happy marriage with Judith were all reviewed. David and Catherine's accomplishments, as young adults, were relived in a flash of scenes. His rock climbing and all his friends were seen once again. The terrible nuclear destruction of the earth and the way he and his new family and friends had lived in a dying planet had all come back in vivid pictures. Judas moaned and cried, his eyeballs almost coming out of their sockets, as he witnessed the man in white probing the most remote secrets of his life. He thought that those vivid images were the last moments before death—it was his entire life, from birth till his last experience on Jebel Har Montar, flashing within his memory before he would meet his Maker.

The flashes had continued up to his experience of time travel, meeting the Baptist, and his search for Ishia of Nazerat. His climb, Billy Joel, ABBA, and the man in white were his last visions. Finally, the man in white released his mesmerizing touch and returned to his meditation. Judas, exhausted, fell back into a deep slumber. Was it a dream? Or did the man in white really review his life? He continued to sleep, thinking that he was about to meet his Creator. Judas slowly managed to open his eyes—it was still daylight. He remembered the strange dream as he looked at the man in white. The man in white was still meditating and he, Judas, was still alive. Had it all been a bad dream or had the strange man really delved into his memory? He was thirsty! This time he couldn't move his arms or his legs. His last energy had been spent in opening his eyelids. He tried to cry out but his lips wouldn't move. He tried to call ISHIA but no sound came out. He tried again and again without success. He was dying—he felt it. He closed his eyes because it was too painful to keep them open. In desperation, he abandoned himself to death.

His mind drifted away as his reclining body floated into a long white corridor, as the sweetest rendition of ABBA's *I Have a Dream* resounded from everywhere. He had never heard such complex and sweet version of that beautiful song. But it now played for him as his body floated along the brightest corridor he had ever seen. His body floated into an immense but extremely bright circular room. It was so bright that he could not distinguish details and his eyes hurt. That was silly! How could his eyes hurt in a dream? His body gently lowered itself on some type of long white table, very much like a hospital's operating table, and he fell into a deep sleep as he continued to hear that wonderful rendition of *I Have a Dream*.

Judas woke up. His eyes opened slightly, squinting to keep the powerful light of the sun from blinding him. He tried to reach for the bottled water and, to his surprise, had no trouble moving his arms. He grabbed the bottle and twisted its cap off and drank from it. The warm water felt good in his mouth—he was still alive and he felt slightly better. He turned around to see if the man in white was still there; and, there he was in his meditating position. Didn't he ever get tired of meditating? Was he ever going to get up? Should he call him? Or, even better, should he go there and wake him up? His better judgment told him to wait a little more and not to disturb the meditating man. He decided to listen to Billy Joel's *River of Dreams* once again. As he listened to those meaningful songs, Judas slowly closed his eyes again and went back to sleep. He dreamt of the star once again coming towards them until it reached about one hundred feet above them, blanching the plateau and its surroundings with the brightest light he had ever seen. It was brighter than the brightest noon at a white sandy beach or in the desert. Once again, three handsome men came down from the open hatch and helped the meditating man into the bright star. The dream was so vivid that it seemed almost real. More like surreal! The three men escorted the meditating man down the invisible escalator; and, then they went up and vanished into the bright star, which took off at a speed faster than anything he had ever seen, disappearing into the starry night.

Judas woke up with a slight headache, as the sun came up from the eastern horizon, its rays illuminating the early hours of the day. The night had seemed so long with so many weird dreams. He looked to his right—the meditating man in white was getting up, having finished with his meditation. The man in white put on his sandals and then proceeded towards him.

"Good morning, Judas! How are you feeling today?" he began.

"Weak!...Are you Ishia the Nazarene?"

"Yes, I am Ishia of Nazerat, the Jesus you have been searching all your life!"

"How do you know that?...How is it possible that you speak English? The English language will not be invented for another thirteen centuries!" exclaimed Judas.

"Everything I know about you and about the English language I learned from you."

"That dream I had last night...that was no dream, was it?"

"If you mean the night I reviewed your memory, that was not last night. That happened three nights ago."

"THREE NIGHTS! How long have I been lying here?"

"Five nights and four days. Why is time so important to you?"

Judas touched his face, feeling his six-day-old beard, and said, "I have only two days left; I must go back to my world by tomorrow."

"You are too weak to travel and I desperately need you to be with me for the next three years."

"How can that be possible when I'm dying? I have only days to live. I would like to go back so that I can see my daughter before I die."

"You came to this world to find me, to see if I really did exist, and to see if I am truly the Son of Yahweh. In order to experience the Truth you must follow me for only you seem to know all the prophecies about my future in this world."

"But I don't have much time left. I'm dying!"

"If your cancer is cured, would you stay with me until my last day on earth."

"If you can cure this abominable sickness I will be with you until the end."

"Only you can cure it, Judas."

"How is that possible? I have very little energy left."

"Do you believe in the power of the mind, my friend?"

"I know that the human brain will be able to do wonders in the future, if there is a future left."

"You cannot be cured until you believe. You must believe that your mind can cure it. I will simply stimulate it to begin the production of the necessary endorphins to fight the nuclear cancer; but you must firmly believe. You must have faith."

"I believe, Ishia of Nazareth!"

Ishia placed all his ten fingers on Judas' temples and said, "You are still doubting, my friend. There must be no doubt in your mind. Your faith must be whole, leaving no place for doubt. Concentrate, Judas! Concentrate, my friend!"

As Ishia sensed Judas' belief, he began pressing on his temples. Judas squirmed from the pain, his eyeballs bulging out. Relentlessly, Ishia kept the pressure on his temples and continued praying until Judas lost consciousness after his last spasmodic wriggle. Finally, Ishia released his hold on Judas and stood up, looking at his emaciated body, waiting patiently for him to regain consciousness. As Judas slept, drained from his last ordeal, Ishia proceeded to listen to ABBA's and Billy Joel's CDs.

The sun was shining brightly over them when Judas opened his eyes, witnessing Ishia the Nazarene gently moving to the beat of ABBA's music. Suddenly, he turned around, simultaneously removing the earphones; and he said, "Ah, welcome back, my friend. How do you feel?"

"Tired," he whispered.

"Of course. The energy I passed on to you is being used by your brain."

"Energy. Brain. What do you mean?"

"Your energy was very low. It was necessary to give you some of my energy so that your brain could begin to synthesize the endorphins needed to fight the nuclear cancer within you."

"Am I cured?"

"Your brain has begun the production of the anti-nuclear endorphins which will fight the cancer within your body system. Of course, you must understand that it will take some time for your body to regain its vitality. Some good food and a little wine will surely help you to speed up the process."

"Where can we get good food and wine?"

"Commander Ghabriel will not mind a guest for this special occasion. I think he will enjoy your company, my friend."

"Commander Ghabriel? Is he the captain of the temple guards or is he a Roman general?"

"No, Judas. Commander Ghabriel was sent by My Father to ensure that His promise to His Chosen People would be followed through to His last Word. Please, get up," explained Ishia as he extended his arms to help Judas up.

Judas extended his right arm and was grabbed by Ishia's hands and stood up easily with his help.

"Is Commander Ghabriel an angel?" asked Judas as he stood face to face with Ishia. He was at least six feet tall and had a handsome yet rugged face. He had deep blue eyes and a fine nose. He wore his dark blonde hair long, resting on his shoulders. His dark blond beard was full but not extremely long. There was something wonderful about his face and the way he spoke.

"Yes, he is in so many ways," He replied, giving the CD player and earphones back to Judas. "Nice music and good lyrics. Those ABBA girls have angelic voices and Billy Joel is very prophetic in his songs."

"You liked them! They're my favorites. They were..."

"Your parents' favorite songs."

"Yes, My Lord, they were."

"You miss them, don't you?"

"Yes, Lord, I do...Lord?"

"Yes, Judas?"

"Who were those three bright men with you last night?"

"Commander Ghabriel and two physicians."

"Archangel Ghabriel...two physicians? What about the star?"

"You mean the space shuttle. Commander Ghabriel was assigned by My Father to carry on this promissory mission."

"Space shuttle! The star is a spaceship! From which planet?"

"The name of My Father's world is Paradise, which is halfway towards the center of this galaxy, which you call Milky Way, or Via Galactica by the Romans. Once my mission is finished here I will join Commander Ghabriel and his brave astro-travelers on a voyage to Paradise, where I will rest with My Father, Yahweh the Almighty. Come now, let us get ready; the space shuttle will soon be here. Commander Ghabriel knows that I have ended my fasting. Come, my friend, Judas."

Judas followed Ishia to the center of the plateau. Ishia began to stare up at the southern blue sky. Judas did the same but could not see anything.

"Where are they coming from, Lord?" he asked.

"From the moon."

"Is that their base?"

"Yes, it is. Commander Ghabriel feels it is a very private place to land the mother ship. He does not want to scare anyone on earth."

"If what I saw was the space shuttle, how big is the mother ship?"

"It is bigger than Yerushalayim."

"That's immense!"

"Yes, it is, Judas. Look!" Ishia pointed up at the beautiful blue sky.

Judas looked up but did not see anything. "I don't see anything, Lord!" he exclaimed.

"Keep looking towards the direction that my finger points to."

Judas stared at the sky, concentrating on Ishia's direction. Suddenly a shiny dot appeared and it became larger by the second. Within ten seconds Judas clearly recognized a round metallic spacecraft flying towards them. In a few seconds it cut through the Judean sky and halted its course over their heads, hovering about one hundred feet over Jebel Har Montar. It was magnificent! It seemed to be one solid piece of metal with no hatches or windows. It was difficult to guess its dimensions; nevertheless, Judas thought that its diameter was at least the length of the old space shuttle Atlantis. Suddenly, a large hatch opened at the center of the shuttle's belly. Two human figures appeared and seemed to descend on an invisible escalator. They were dressed in impeccably white uniforms and molded white boots, which showed the shapes of their ankles and feet. They were young, clean-shaven or with no facial hair, and with beautiful shiny light hair. When they reached the top of the plateau they began to walk towards them. The two men from Paradise stopped three feet in front of Ishia and reverently bowed to Him. No words were spoken but Judas knew they were mentally communicating with Ishia. Both men were extremely handsome and tall. One of them seemed to be a little older and taller than the other. Judas thought that he was at least six foot four and the other man was as tall as Ishia. Both had big blue eyes, very fine noses, fine mouths with fine lips, smaller ears than humans, and handsomely elongated faces. Their heads were larger, probably containing extremely advanced brains.

Chapter 9

COMMANDER GHABRIEL

"Commander Ghabriel, this is Judas Cariota, from the future," Ishia introduced.

"The pleasure is mine, Judas," spoke the tall Commander Ghabriel in perfect American English, extending his right hand to Judas.

"Commander Ghabriel…is this a dream?" uttered Judas as he shook Ghabriel's firm and powerful hand, "You…you speak English!"

"I learned it from you. It is quite complicated, containing many unspeakable words. This is Sha-el, the chief physician of this mission and one of Paradise's best," replied Ghabriel.

"It is a pleasure to meet you, Judas! You look better already," said Sha-el.

"It is my pleasure to meet you, Doctor Sha-el."

They all smiled.

"Come my friend, Lord Ishia has been surviving on paradisiacal water. He and you are greatly in need of some nutritious food. Please, Lord Ishia."

Ghabriel bowed and Judas also bowed, following Sha-el and Ghabriel's example. Ishia began to walk towards the center of the plateau as Commander Ghabriel and Sha-el helped Judas to walk. Suddenly, they stopped and an invisible staircase began to transport them up into the shuttle. A bright light illumined the opening and

Ishia disappeared into the light as they followed. Once inside the shuttle Judas was escorted to a throne-like seat. As he sat, some type of seat belt automatically fastened him. Everything was ultra white and the entire spaceship was brightly illumined. Judas looked around and after focusing he noticed several men, all dressed in the same uniform, who were busy preparing for flight. Ishia sat next to Commander Ghabriel at the center of the circular spacecraft, which had three thrones and a control center shaped in a semi-circular fashion. On the other side of Ishia sat another man, who was probably next in command. The hatch automatically closed as windows appeared all around the circular walls of the shuttle, unfolding the terrestrial landscape of the Judean Desert. A circular window appeared at the center of the shuttle's ceiling, which Judas guessed to be about twenty feet in height and approximately double than its circular wall. All of this took place within seconds. Everyone on board seemed to be seated and fastened by automatic belts. The spacecraft gently turned, showing a panoramic view of the landscape and then took off like a bullet into the blue sky, which became bluer by the second, and then darker, reaching total darkness within twenty seconds.

They were in space! Judas clearly saw the beautiful blue planet Earth adorned by streams of white and patches of browns and greens. Judas was flabbergasted! He never expected to be traveling into space and with some of the most wonderful people in the entire universe.

"It is a beautiful planet, isn't it?" Ishia broke the silence.

"Yes, My Lord, it is," replied Judas, as tears ran down his face.

"Why do you cry, Judas?" asked Ishia.

"I cry because it is so beautiful and two millennia from now it will be raped, robbed, and then destroyed by selfish and evil people. I cry because I won't live to see it so beautiful again."

"In death, through death, and by death a new life is born," spoke Ishia in a most gentle yet sad voice.

"We are about to arrive, Lord Ishia," suggested Ghabriel.

"My good Lord, that is the moon! Isn't it?" exclaimed Judas.

"Yes, it is," answered Ghabriel. "We will be landing in a moment."

The shuttle circled around the dark side of the moon where, to Judas' surprise, an illumined area shone brightly in the cold darkness of the cosmos.

"That, Judas, is our mother ship, the Paradise One," said Commander Ghabriel.

Within seconds they were hovering over it, a beautiful illumined town on the moon.

"It is magnificent!" exclaimed Judas.

"Yes, it is. It is home away from home," spoke Ghabriel as the shuttle hovered through an opening, which had automatically appeared on one of its side.

The shuttle gently landed inside and the opening automatically sealed. A whistling noise inside the huge hangar changed the air as everyone prepared to disembark. Judas' seatbelt had automatically disengaged. Judas got up, taking his GISA knapsack. He followed Ishia through the hangar into a hall. As everyone had entered the hall, its entrance was quickly sealed. They were inside Paradise I. Judas observed that there were no joints anywhere. Everything seemed to be molded from one gigantic piece of alloy. And, yet there were doors and windows that automatically appeared when needed. He followed Ishia, Commander Ghabriel, and his men down the large hall. Out of the right wall an entrance appeared and they all went inside a wonderful large room, with several large round tables and throne-like chairs around them. The tables and chairs all seemed to be made of the same molded alloy. Commander Ghabriel waited for Ishia to sit and everyone followed by taking a seat. The entire crew of the shuttle, including Judas sat around one table. Suddenly a door unfolded from a wall and a beautiful young woman, dressed in the same uniform, walked in and approached their table. She bowed first to Ishia and then to Commander Ghabriel. The beautiful woman stood in front of Commander Ghabriel without speaking; but Judas knew, by now, that they were communicating.

"Judas, Ariel, my assistant in the arts would like to borrow your ABBA CD. She and her artists would like to play some of the songs for the mother ship," said Ghabriel.

"Please, help yourself to anything in my knapsack!" volunteered Judas, giving the knapsack to the beautiful Ariel.

Ariel removed the ABBA CD and the miniature CD player from the GISA knapsack, bowed to Ishia, to Ghabriel, and then made a small bow to everyone and left the room.

"Ariel thanked you for your kindness, Judas," spoke Ghabriel.

"It is a pleasure to do anything for you all," replied Judas.

Suddenly, two other beautiful women and a young man entered the hall carrying large platters of fruits, nuts and vegetable dips. The fruit platter contained various grapes, figs, and persimmons. There were mixed nuts and the biggest dates Judas had ever seen. There were four different vegetable mixes and dips decorated with evenly cut pieces of pita bread. Everyone was given a smaller dish for the food and lemon scented towels for wiping. The three young people returned with beautifully decorated cups and jars. They filled the cups and served everyone.

Commander Ghabriel stood up, holding his cup high, and said, "I thank the Almighty Lord Yahweh for all these wonderful foods and this wine, His best. I thank Lord Yahweh for choosing me for this most precious mission to this beautiful planet. I dedicate this simple, yet delicious meal to Lord Ishia, the Only Begotten Son of Lord Yahweh, for having ended His long fasting and meditation, and to His good fortune to have found such a true friend, Judas. To Lord Ishia, Son of the Most High!"

Everyone, including Judas, stood up and cheered, "To Lord Ishia, Son of the Most High!"

Ishia and everyone present drank the red wine.

Judas had never tasted wine as delicious as Lord Yahweh's wine. He wanted to ask someone about the wine, the delicious fruit and nuts, the garlic vegetables dips. Were they all vegetarians? Did Lord Yahweh Himself make that wine? He had so many questions as he ate figs, a persimmon, grapes, nuts, whole grain pita dipped in the most delicious mixes he had ever tasted. He felt so good. It was the first time since the nuclear Armageddon that he had actually felt good. The food and the wine, there was something wonderful about them. He felt good because he was in the presence of the most important person on planet earth, Lord Ishia. But, they were having dinner on the moon. Was it all a dream?

As they had begun to eat, the sweetest and most powerful rendition of ABBA's I *Have a Dream* began to play. It was the most wonderful music with the most melodious voices he had ever heard. It sounded like ten groups of ABBA were all playing and singing simultaneously. Judas enjoyed the music, the food, and the wine. Everyone seemed to be enjoying the food, the wine, and the sweet renditions of ABBA's best. The musicians played also *Chiquitita* and *Fernando*; however, the songs seemed to last so long.

When they were all satiated, Commander Ghabriel asked Judas if he would like a tour of the mother ship, Paradise I. Judas was thrilled. He followed Lord Ishia, Commander Ghabriel, Sha-el, and a few others through the mother ship. Doors would open from solid walls; Judas could not understand how it was possible. He followed them through their private rooms, their art room, their music room, their storage rooms, workout room, bathrooms, control room, their library, their meditation hall, many other rooms, and finally to their arboricultural hall. Judas was astonished by its size; it was as big as a football field with every imaginable fruit plant, nut plants, flowers, vegetables and other experimental hybrids they were working on.

As Lord Ishia wandered into the wondrous garden, smelling the flowers and looking at the birds and butterflies, Commander Ghabriel whispered to Judas, "My good friend, I would like to answer some of your questions that you wanted to ask during dinner time. Yes, we are mostly vegetarians, but we at times enjoy fish. All our fruits, nuts, and vegetables are of the highest quality and their most precious vitamins have been genetically enhanced with Lord Yahweh's everlasting properties. Many millennia ago Lord Yahweh, through his ongoing studies and experiments, found the genetic secret of everlasting properties. These properties were found in some fruits, vegetables and animals, like fish. He genetically enhanced those qualities, creating fruits, vegetables, nuts, and fish so rich in everlasting properties that when eaten, their vitamins keep all of our cells and organs young and extremely healthy. Our bodies can last for many millennia. Look at me, Judas! How old do you think I am?" Ghabriel smiled.

Judas looked at Ghabriel, studying his young face and youthful body. Finally, he said, "You look in your late twenties to early thirties, but I know I am off. After what you told me I wouldn't be surprised if you are thousands of years old."

"You are right in both guesses. I was only twenty-eight earthly years old when Lord Yahweh discovered the everlasting properties, but that was more than twenty millennia ago. Since then I have been faithful to My Lord and He has given me the power to command many missions. But this mission is the most important of my long career: to come back on Planet Earth, for the fourth time, to implant His Most Precious Seed into the womb of the gentlest and purest maiden to be found from the bloodline of King David and to fulfill every promise He had made to His Chosen People. I will see this mission through its final days and then bring both Lord Ishia and His Most Holy Mother, Miryam, back to Paradise…Oh, yes; the wine we drank is Lord Yahweh's best production. You are also wandering about my musicians' renditions of ABBA's songs. Most of us from Paradise, if not all of us, are gifted in the arts and in science. They go hand-in-hand; science and art do. Lord Yahweh is the greatest scientist and artist of this galaxy and of all galaxies in this universe. That is why all the other great leaders of their respective galaxies chose Him as the Supreme Leader…Judas, I must ask an enormous favor. Lord Ishia considers you His friend and I know that you are a good man; therefore, I ask you, as His good friend, to be always with Him. Your knowledge of Lord Ishia is pivotal to His mission and your presence will ensure that every action taken by Him will be true to Lord Yahweh's Holy Words and to the words of the prophets."

Judas stared at Commander Ghabriel, his mouth open, looking like a total idiot, flabbergasted by the implications of what he had heard. He was unable to speak.

It was Lord Ishia who awakened him with a more mundane reality, "Come, my friend, I have work to do back on earth. We must leave as soon as possible; I have to meet the Baptist the day after tomorrow at Bet-ha' Arava."

"Yes, My Lord," he mumbled.

Judas had wanted to stay longer in the mother ship. He had wanted to explore the arboricultural hall, the music room and every little part of that wonderful spaceship. Commander Ghabriel did not have enough time to explain and to answer all his questions. And, they were stationed on the moon—he wanted a chance to go out and mark his footprint on its sandy soil. He had always dreamed of a moon vacation but could never afford it.

"Judas, I will answer all your questions on the way to Bet-ha'Arava and when my mission is over I will make sure you get your turn to walk on the moon."

Judas did not respond but Lord Ishia felt his excitement about the promise He had made to him. He smiled at him and began His way back towards the hangar. Doors magically appeared from nowhere within the molded walls of the mother ship. Judas followed Him like a lost puppy. Commander Ghabriel and his assistants followed Lord Ishia's brisk pace. They all stopped in the dining hall, where they had eaten that delicious meal and waited a few minutes. No one was talking but Judas knew better. These superior beings were able to communicate by thinking. He wished he could do that. He wished he could have some more of those fruits, nuts, vegetables, and wine. Oh, that wine was delectable. But he couldn't ask. He did not want to be presumptuous with Lord Ishia and His angels. After all, they were the angels of the Old and New Testaments. Suddenly, the beautiful young lady called Ariel returned with Judas' CD player and the ABBA CD. She also carried two golden colored aluminum-like bags. One was tiny; the size of a pocket book; and, the larger one was about a cubic foot in volume.

"Ariel does not yet speak English, but she would like to thank you with her gift. She hopes you do not mind that she recorded most of the ABBA CD," volunteered Commander Ghabriel.

Judas smiled but was unable to say anything; however, he managed to whisper "Thank you!" in the presence of such a beauty.

Ariel placed the bags on the table and went up to Judas and hugged him. Judas felt wonderful by her touch; he felt young again. She went up to Lord Ishia and gave Him the small bag and then hugged and kissed Him on the cheeks. Lord Ishia smiled at her as He touched her face with His long fingers. Then, He turned around and preceded towards the hangar, everyone followed Him as magic doors opened before them. When, they reached the hangar, the entire crew of Paradise One was there to bid Him farewell. There were at least a dozen women and over thirty males, all of them young and beautiful, some of them were black, and some of them looked oriental. Everyone, including Commander Ghabriel hugged and kissed Lord Ishia and Judas, on their cheeks. Surely, it must have been a custom of Paradise.

Commander Ghabriel whispered to Judas, "Be always by His side. He will need you. We will not interfere unless it becomes imperative."

Judas nodded as he followed Lord Ishia and four men into a shuttle. The hatch of the shuttle sealed itself as all the other angels of Paradise One left the hangar. Within minutes, the shuttle was flying out of the mother ship towards planet earth. Judas saw the moon getting smaller as the spaceship approached earth's atmosphere. The reentry was quick and smooth and in less than two minutes the shuttle was hovering over Jebel Har Montar. The safety belts having unbuckled themselves, Judas followed Lord Ishia towards the invisible hatch, which magically opened before them. Judas followed Him down the invisible escalator and found himself on top of the same plateau. The shuttle shot away like a missile, disappearing in the afternoon sky.

Judas broke the silence exclaiming, "We're back on the plateau, My Lord. Why couldn't they let us off near Bet-ha'Arava?"

"Because I need to fulfill my mission as an earthly man, not as the Son of Yahweh. Besides, we need the walk; we haven't exercised our leg muscles in a long time. You are feeling better, aren't you, Judas?"

"Yes, Lord, I do feel stronger after that meal. Those were no ordinary fruits, were they?"

"You are very perceptive! No, those fruits, nuts, and vegetables have been bred for millennia. You already know, Commander Ghabriel explained it to you. You have been given some of that fruit by Ariel; they're in that bag that you hold."

"She must have read my mind. And, what about that wine? I have never tasted better wine in my whole life."

"Everyone sensed your strong desire to have more of the food. And, that wine is also my favorite. It is My Father's very best; and as you can see I have some of its concentrate." Ishia held up the small golden bag.

"It's concentrate! Do you mix it with water?"

"Yes, my friend, we mix it with water. This will be most invaluable for me," Ishia said as He put it back in a pouch, which was tied to his belt and hidden under his white robe. "Now, we must move on. We can walk the rest of the day and rest along the wadi tonight. We will speak then. Come now. Follow me. I know a safer path that leads down to the wadi."

Judas followed Ishia towards the northern side of the plateau, where a winding path zigzagged all the way to the bottom. He stopped for a moment to tie his GISA knapsack and then quickly moved on to catch up with Lord Ishia, who moved at a brisk pace for a man who had fasted for such a long time. It took about half an hour to get down to the bottom of the promontory by the wadi.

Chapter 10

THE BAPTISM OF LORD ISHIA

Judas followed Ishia along the Wadi Qumran, trying to keep up with His quick pace and thinking about Mary and Joseph. Did Joseph have sex with Mary during her pregnancy with Ishia or did they wait until after His birth. Judas kept on with his silent march with those thoughts ruminating in his brain.

Suddenly, Ishia came to a halt and broke the silence, "Joseph, my earthly father, had a difficult time understanding what my mother had told him about her pregnancy; but, being a good man, just like you, Judas, he tried to understand. Finally, Commander Ghabriel met with him and then did he fully understand the implications of my mother's pregnancy. No, he did not have sex with my mother during the period she was pregnant with me. He was patient and he felt blessed by being chosen to be my earthly father. And, yes, my mother was a virgin throughout her pregnancy with me. Now, please Judas, do not dwell with these thoughts. We must move; we have a lot of walking. We will talk tonight," Ishia had answered Judas' thoughts without losing His cool and had been extremely gentle with him.

Judas followed Him, feeling ashamed about his thoughts. He tried to recall the faces of his loved ones but had a difficult time picturing them. Faces appeared in his memory but they were not the faces he was searching for. He kept on following Lord Ishia as he labored through his memory to recall the faces of his loved ones.

The sun was offering its last rays of warmth when Lord Ishia stopped.

"We will sleep in a cave above those boulders, Judas. Let us look for any kindling to make a little fire to warm us during the night. It will be cool tonight," said Ishia.

"Yes, My Lord, that is a very good idea."

Both men looked around for any dry piece of wood. There wasn't much; Judas managed to find only small washed up branches but nothing substantial enough for a big fire. When his arms were full of kindling, he returned towards the boulders. He tried to look for Lord Ishia but it was already dark. Suddenly, He appeared standing on the top boulder, waving at him, "Come up around the right of these boulders, it's an easier climb."

Judas followed His instructions, finding the walk up quite easy, finally reaching the top of the boulders. On the side of the cliff was a cave, and a fire was already burning. And there was a pile of branches beside the wall of the cave. Judas looked at Ishia with a puzzled look on his face.

"Please, do not be afraid to talk to me, my friend," He said.

"How did You...how did You make the fire, Lord? Do You have matches or a lighter?"

"No, Judas, I willed it."

"You told the wood to begin a fire!" said Judas, dropping the kindling on top of Ishia's wood.

"I concentrated my wish until the wood made a flame."

"Will I ever be able to do the same?"

"Yes, but not yet. You have so much to learn still. Be patient and I know that one day you will be able to do anything."

Judas smiled at the thought and sat on one of the two stones that Lord Ishia had placed near the fire. Both men sat by the fire; Ishia fed it with more wood.

"The fire feels good, doesn't it?" asked Ishia.

"Yes, it does, My Lord...Lord, what does Your Father look like?" Judas asked, timidly.

"If I shave my beard, you would see the Image of My Father. Would you like to see the image of your father and of your loved ones, my good friend?"

"Very much, My Lord. I am unable to remember their faces."

"Begin by trying to remember your father and mother…there you are. Now try to focus on their faces. Concentrate Judas. Do not let your mind wander through your memory. Concentrate on those two faces, only on those two faces."

"I see them, Lord. Hi mom! Hi dad! I miss you very much…Oh, you miss me, too. You were right, dad; you were right! You have to go, now? Stay a bit longer, please! You must go…good-bye, I love you both, so much." Judas exclaimed, stretching his arms out exactly like he had done so many times with his parents.

"Now concentrate on your memory of your wife and son. Focus on them, my friend," suggested Ishia.

"Judith! It is you, my love. You look so beautiful," said Judas, excited at the vivid pictures of his memories of her. "You look alive. I can touch your beautiful face. I can hear you speak. Where is David? Our wonderful David…There you are, my son. You look great…I miss you, too…You are alive…You and mom will always be alive in me, always!" cried Judas as their faces grew less and less focused. He began to concentrate on his memory of Catherine, which quickly came alive in his mind. She would wait for him, together with Dr. Weinstein, Major Coolidge, and Major Nichols. Their faces spoke to him. They told him that they would wait for him. "Will I ever see them again, My Lord?" asked Judas.

"Yes, you will, my good friend; you will see them again."

Judas wanted to know if he would see them during his lifetime, but did not have the courage to ask Him; and, Ishia did not volunteer the answer. There was silence for a while. Finally, it was Ishia who spoke first, "Are you hungry, Judas?"

"A little, My Lord."

"Would you look in the bag to see what's in it?"

"Of course," replied Judas as he tried to open the sealed bag. "Lord, I can't seem to open it."

"Let me help you," recommended Ishia, gently drawing an imaginary line on the bag with his index finger. The bag opened as if Ishia had pulled an invisible zipper, exposing two persimmons, about a dozen figs, and over twenty dates lying on a bed of mixed nuts. "We should eat the persimmons, they are your favorite fruit and the most perishable."

"You are right, My Lord. Please, take one," offered Judas, passing the golden aluminum-like bag to Ishia. "How do they manage to grow persimmons at this time of the year?"

"They have programmed different trees to bear fruit throughout the year. They have persimmons, figs, grapes, and other fruits and vegetables all year round. A wonderful work of My Father."

"It is an absolutely magnificent enterprise!" exclaimed Judas, tasting the ripe persimmon. "I have never tasted a more delicious persimmon than this one."

"It is also one of my favorite fruits," volunteered Ishia, "It is delicious and extraordinarily nutritious."

They both proceeded to eat the persimmons, making them last as long as possible, savoring the luscious fruits. Judas finished his first, exclaiming, "Mine had a pit, My Lord. I will save it; I can plant it somewhere."

"You may have mine, too," said Ishia, giving him the pit. "Save them in your bag; you will plant them in the near future."

"Would you like a couple of figs or dates, Lord?"

"I will have one of each and that will be enough for me."

Ishia and Judas each enjoyed a black fig and a date. They relished the fruits and they talked about life, about the earth, about Paradise, and about the future. Judas asked Ishia, "Did Your Father really create Adam and Eve?"

"My Father, Lord Yahweh came to earth many millennia ago, when the earth was under a glacial period. During that mission He created the first man and woman by changing the genetic structure of the most advanced hominids. He also created many new animals and plants through genetic engineering. He is the Greatest Scientist, the Creator of everlasting life."

"How long did Lord Yahweh stay on this planet during His first mission?"

"He remained here on earth for thousands of years, guiding His new people, teaching them how to live. However, most of them had inherited their earthly nature, which is destructive, and they began to kill each other. They became more and more evil, driven by greed, by violence, and by disgusting sexual behaviors. My Father, realizing the impossibility of His mission, decided to destroy them all.

However, through His Wonderful Goodness, He searched for some people who might have been peaceful and good. And, He did find a few scattered all over this planet. Having given them instruction and assistance in building very large boats, He proceeded by flooding this planet and, simultaneously, ending the glacial period by melting ice fields in the northern hemisphere. You know the stories."

"So, Noah's ark was real?"

"Noah and his ark were real; but he was not alone to survive My Father's wrath. Several good men and their families, from different continents, were chosen to survive. Everyone received instruction and assistance from My Father on surviving. Different families of animals, depending on the region, were saved by those chosen few. After the flood, those chosen people began anew. They were good men and led good lives by abiding to My Father's Laws."

"What happened with Sodom and Gomorrah, Lord?"

"Because of man's evil nature, again people turned to evil with time. When My Father asked Abraham and Lot to travel to the land of Canaan, many people had resorted to evil ways; but none could be more evil than the inhabitants of Sodom and Gomorrah. Those people had no respect for one another, not even for their children. Stealing, lying, and killing had become habitual for them. They sexually abused each other: fathers and mothers with sons and daughters, brothers with sisters, men with men, men with animals. Nothing was sacred for them; they had no values, no morals. Lot was unlucky to have chosen such a wicked city to live in; but he was lucky to have had Abraham as his good friend. It was Abraham who begged My Father to spare Lot and his family. Sodom and Gomorrah were destroyed with nuclear bombs. My Father had no choice. If a branch of your favorite fruit tree becomes sick and dies, you must remove it lest the entire tree perish."

Judas sat silently, watching the fire and feeding it more of the kindling. He dared not ask any more—he was afraid to ask any more questions about Lord Yahweh.

"Why are you afraid to ask any more questions? This is the perfect time, Judas. Please, ask your questions."

"Did Lord Yahweh help Moses and his people? Why were the Jews the Chosen People?"

"The Jews were and are My Father's experimental group. Lord Yahweh implanted them with the scientific gene. And, yes, it was My Father who helped Moses and His Chosen People."

They talked until late, until Judas' eyes were closing from the fatigue of that very long and exciting day. Judas fell asleep by the fire, as Ishia fed it some more wood so that it would last a while longer. Finally, exhausted, He also fell asleep by the fire.

Ishia opened his eyes—it was still dark outside the cave. Still, he gently stood up, noticing that the fire had died at least two hours before. He felt the urgency to move on for he knew the distance they had to travel. Bet-ha'Arava was approximately sixty-two stadia away and He wanted to be there before nightfall. He decided to let Judas sleep a little longer; he needed it. He made His way down the rocks, reaching the wadi. He washed His face—the cool water felt wonderful and invigorating. He cleansed His teeth and mouth and then drank some of the cool water. He climbed back up and found Judas still sleeping in a fetal position. He gently touched his shoulder, calling his name.

Judas woke up, saying, "My Lord!"

"We must go soon, my friend. We have a lot of walking to do. I would like to be at Bet-ha'Arava before sundown. Are you feeling better, this morning?"

"I haven't felt this good since I was a young man. I am feeling great, My Lord," he replied, quickly getting up.

"It is almost sunrise. The sun will soon illumine the path to the wadi. You need to wash up, Judas."

"Yes, My Lord. I will go now; I can use my flashlight to see."

Judas began to search for his flashlight inside his knapsack. Having found it, he switched it on. The beam of light illuminated the ceiling of the cave. Ishia stared at it, admiring it. Judas offered it to Ishia, "It is called a flashlight, Lord. It is powered by a quartz battery. It can last for a couple of years more. Do you like it?"

"It is a wonderful invention and a very useful one."

"Would you like to have it, My Lord?"

"No, thank you, my friend, but you will need it. It will save your life. You should wash up, now."

"Yes, Lord. I will go." He began to step out of the cave. He turned around and said, "I will be quick, Lord."

Judas went down to the wadi, his steps guided by the flashlight. After a few minutes of prayer Ishia picked up His bag and the golden fruit bag and went down to the wadi, where Judas was rearranging his knapsack.

"We could eat while we walk, Judas. We have much distance to travel," said Ishia, handing the golden bag to Judas.

"Of course, My Lord," answered Judas, taking the bag and trying to open it without success. "Lord! I can't open this bag."

"It will open if you simply draw a line with your finger along the top. The body temperature of your touch will open it."

Judas drew the imaginary line with his finger and, to his amazement, the bag opened. Still mesmerized by his accomplishment, he took several figs and dates and offered them to Ishia. Smiling, Lord Ishia took one of each and gently bit into the black fig.

"Please, take some more, Lord," offered Judas.

"No, thank you my friend; we must conserve this food. After meeting with the Baptist we will have a long journey to Nazareth. You may eat more than this, Judas."

"Oh, no, My Lord. This fig and this date will be enough for breakfast. After all, these are no ordinary fruits, Lord!"

"No, my good friend, they are not."

Together they walked along the same path that Judas had taken to find Lord Ishia, savoring the heavenly fruits. Surprisingly, Judas felt as if he had eaten much more. He felt better and stronger and ready to follow the wonderful and mystical Lord Ishia anywhere on earth. Finally, the sun's rays showed their splendor, illuminating their path and bringing a touch of warmth to their bodies, which were cool from the chilly night. Judas kept up with Ishia's brisk pace, which seemed like a never-ending cycle of footsteps. The sun became warmer and inviting as the hours of marching flew by—by then it had reached the center of the cerulean sky. They had been walking for nearly six hours without rest.

"Would you like to take a rest, Judas?" offered Ishia, sensing his thoughts.

"If time allows, Lord."

"Yes, it does, my good friend. Can you walk for a few more minutes for we are near Mesad Hasidim, where you left your machine? We could take an hour of rest and a little something to eat; and, you could examine your machine before we leave for Bet-ha'Arava."

"We are near Mesad Hasidim. My machine! Lord, thank you! Thank you, My Lord," Judas exclaimed excitedly.

"However, there is a problem concerning me at Mesad Hasidim. Therefore, I must ask your cooperation on this very sensitive issue. Do not refer to me as the Son of Yahweh for the monks and priests of Mesad Hasidim feel I am a blasphemer and a liar when I refer to who I am. I will be simply Ishia of Nazerat, a lowly sojourner, taking a rest from our long trip."

"I will do exactly that, Lord," answered Judas, sincerely and troubled by what Ishia had told him.

"Do not trouble over this, my good friend; you know that many will never believe who I am. Even if I resurrect the dead, they will never believe. Come now; time is precious."

They resumed their walk; and, as they reached the end of the chasm they could clearly see the walls of the monastery and its tower. Quickly they reached the gate. Ishia knocked at the wooden door and a monk, all dressed in black, came to open it. He welcomed them in for a rest and to sit down with them to share some food. They followed them into the courtyard, where the time machine stood. The same monk to whom Judas had asked to safeguard the machine sat in prayer facing it. As they got closer to the machine, the monk turned around and upon recognizing Judas, prostrated himself on the stony floor exclaiming *Angel* in Aramaic. His shout was heard from every corner of the monastery and, within seconds, all of the monks came running and also prostrated their bodies down in adoration of Judas.

Judas felt disgusted at them for not recognizing Lord Ishia and was about to speak when Ishia whispered to him in English, "Do not be troubled by this, my friend. Please, do not mention who I am. And, after all, you are a messenger from the future and that is something wonderful."

"My Lord..."

"Do not trouble yourself over this. Simply, they are afraid of you. Let me talk to them." Ishia spoke to the monks in Aramaic, telling them that Judas was an angel from the future. This seemed to puzzle them. He then told them about guarding the machine, which they revered as a holy object.

The monks finally stood up and they led Ishia and Judas into a large room with tables and long benches. Some sat down with Ishia and Judas and some quickly left the room. They returned with plates of bread and two other large bowls. One bowl contained a red wine; the other contained a creamy dip. They offered the food to Judas first. He took the plate of bread and offered it to Ishia. Ishia took the loaves and begin to break them, passing each piece around. When everyone had a piece of bread, Ishia dipped it into the creamy dip and tasted it. The monks waited for Judas to dip his piece. Then, one by one, in hierarchical order, the monks also dipped their pieces of bread. Everyone ate the bread, staring at Judas and Ishia, trying to understand what was happening. The dip tasted like *hommus*, a chickpea blend with olive oil and spices. It was good; but Judas did not like the wine dip because it had turned into strong vinegar, which everyone, including Ishia, seemed to enjoy.

Ishia thanked them for their hospitality and got up. Judas and the monks followed Him to the courtyard where the machine stood. It was Ishia who broke the silence, "You may go back, now, my beloved friend. It is the seventh day. You have seen me and been with me these last six days. Here is your door to the future—go back to your daughter and your loved ones and bring back my message of peace and love to them," He spoke in English. Then He proceeded to open the hatch of the time machine telepathically.

The monks fell to the ground as Ishia shone like a light. Judas could see Him and yet he could also see through Him. Judas, too, fell to the ground.

"I can't go, My Lord. I want to be with You. I want to die beside You," cried Judas.

"I leave you in charge of this time machine. No one, except angels should touch it. Can I have this commitment from all of you?" asked Ishia to the mesmerized monks, who were still lying on the floor of the courtyard. The monks promised. Ishia telepathically sealed the hatch as the monks silently witnessed it.

Having thanked them for their hospitality and care, Ishia and Judas left the monastery and walked towards the shore of Yam Ha-Melah, the Dead Sea. Feeling rested, Judas kept by Ishia's side, asking Him questions, and listening to His wonderful answers. Judas was happy and had hardly any regrets for the decision he had made: to follow Him, and even die beside Him. They moved quickly along the shore of Yam Ha-Melah, often wetting their feet to cool them down. It was more pleasant to walk along the shore of the Dead Sea than along the Wadi Qumran. After three hours of constant walking, they reached the mouth of Ha-Yarden, the Jordan River. Ishia came to a halt by the west bank of the river, as Judas continued until he was knee-deep into the river. Judas looked back at Ishia—He was smiling.

It was late afternoon when they reached a hillock near Bet-ha'Arava. They would spend the night on the hillock. That evening Ishia and Judas enjoyed a can of boneless mackerel, nuts, dates, and some bottled Naya water. Ishia had enjoyed the mackerel and the bottled water. Later, they talked and gazed at the stars, as Ishia would point at all the different stars and planets. He told Judas that Saturn, Mars, Venus, Mercury, Jupiter, and Neptune would be nearly aligned in the southern cosmos—the following day would be very meaningful for both of them.

Tuesday, March 8, 29 A.D.
(5:00 a.m.)

Ishia awoke and stood up, stretching His arms outward towards the moon and the stars. He concentrated His thoughts in the direction of the moon; and, then He turned to the sleeping Judas and gently touched his shoulder. Judas opened his eyes and quickly got up, understanding Lord Ishia's urgency. Without a word, Judas took his knapsack and followed Ishia down the hillock, heading towards the Jordan, which was nearly two stadia away. It was still night and Judas noticed how clear the moon and the stars were—there wasn't a cloud in the sky. It didn't take long to reach the river where, to Judas' surprise, hundreds of people were flocked by its banks. At Bet-ha'Arava, a smaller river emptied into the Jordan from its east bank—it was at this spot that the crowd waited. Several different dialects were being spoken as the crowd impatiently waited for Yehohanan the Baptist. Ishia did not want to be recognized for He hid His face with His white robe, which covered His head and shoulders. Judas did not ask any question; he followed Him silently, absorbing His mystery and the crowd's confusion. People were everywhere: in the cool water, standing on rocks, on the opposite bank, and on the banks of the tributary.

Suddenly, people quieted down as several of them told everyone else to hush. As a figure appeared on the top of the west bank everyone, except Ishia, turned around. Judas saw the Baptist once again, clothed in camel skin held by a thick leather belt. A leather water container hung by his belt; and, he held a staff with his right hand. Still holding the staff, he stretched his arms up to the sky, which had acquired hues of red, pink, and orange, and cried out in a powerful voice, "People of Yisrael, listen to me for I am the voice who cries in the desert to straighten all of your crooked paths so that you may be ready to see the Lord."

"Are you Elijah?" asked a voice from the opposite bank.

"Are you the mashìah?" cried another.

"Silence, you brood of vipers! I will show you how to flee from the wrath to come. I will show you the straight path to the Lord," retorted the Baptist. "As I am here, the axe is laid by the roots of the trees; and, every tree that is barren of fruits shall be cut down and used for firewood."

"What are we to do?" yelled several people.

"If you have two tunics, give one to someone who has none. If you have plenty of food, share it with others. Do not be selfish, but learn to share everything that is yours," replied the Baptist.

He jumped down and walked towards the river, continuing with his sermon, "I will baptize you with the waters of the Ha-Yarden; but, One mightier than I is coming, the straps of whose sandals I am not worthy to loosen. He will baptize you with the power of the Holy Spirit or with fire. Beware, you sinners, change your ways before it is too late for no one knows when He will arrive."

"How will you know when He is here if you do not know who He is?" asked a young man from the other side of the river.

"The angel from the future will point Him to me."

People looked puzzled and began to talk among themselves. It was then that Ishia touched Judas' shoulder. Judas knew exactly what to do. He quickly moved towards the Baptist, making his way through the crowd. He reached the Baptist and spoke to him in his poor Aramaic, "Do you remember me, Yehohanan. I am the angel from the future. I have found Him, the Only Son of Yahweh. He is here."

"Silence, everyone! You are the luckiest people of Yisrael for this very morning you will witness the most wonderful happening in your lives. See the Angel from the Future; look at him and make way so that he may reveal the presence of the Holy One, the Only Son of whose Name I cannot dare to utter," shouted the Baptist, pointing to Judas.

Everyone stared at Judas as he made his way towards Ishia. People moved out of his way until he reached the Lord. He bowed his head and cried out, "Behold, oh people of Yisrael, Ishia, the only Son of Yahweh."

It was then that people began to protest, accusing Judas of blasphemy for uttering the Name of God. And it was then that Ishia dropped the white robe from His head, revealing Himself as the sun unfolded its first rays from the mountains of Ammon. He did not say anything but pointed to the moon, where a nearby star began to move. It grew bigger as it traveled towards the earth; and, the people fell to the ground, afraid of judgment and death. Within seconds, the star was a few hundred feet above them, its lights illuminating the entire area. Everyone except Ishia, Judas, and the Baptist hid their faces to the ground, afraid for their lives.

"I am blessed for You have come to baptize me, My Lord!" said the Baptist.

"No, my beloved friend, I have come here to be baptized by you, the holiest and purest of all men. Now, baptize me, Yehohanan!" spoke Ishia; and, then proceeded to remove his robes and sandals until only His loincloth remained.

The Baptist followed Him into the waters as everyone watched. When the water reached their waistline they stopped. It was at that moment that a white dove was released from the star-shuttle. The dove must have been well trained for it flew in small circles over Ishia's head and a majestic voice came from the star-shuttle, speaking in perfect Aramaic, "THIS IS ISHIA, MY BELOVED SON, IN WHOM I AM WELL PLEASED." Everyone, except Judas, fell to the ground in awe of Yahweh's powerful voice.

Some trembled in fear and others cried for witnessing such a glorious sight as the Baptist immersed Ishia into the waters of the Ha-Yarden.

Early that March morning the water of the Ha-Yarden River was rather cool but Ishia did not seem to mind it at all. As Ishia came out of the water the white dove flew three more circles above His head and then flew upwards, disappearing into the star-shuttle. The shuttle took off like a speeding bullet, rapidly shrinking until it became a bright dot by the moon. It then disappeared around the moon as the crowd fearfully gazed at it, mesmerized by that most sacred event. Ishia waded back to the riverbank, followed by the sacrosanct Baptist. Yehohanan seemed to be in an ethereal state of enlightenment. Judas assisted Ishia by handing His robes to Him, as He got dressed under hundreds of watchful and eager eyes. Once dressed, the crowd mobbed Ishia as everyone desired to touch His robes or kiss His hands. They asked for forgiveness of their sins. They asked Lord Ishia to bless them. They asked to be baptized by Him.

Finally Ishia spoke to them, "My brothers and sisters, for that is what you are. You are all children of My Father; therefore, you are all brothers and sisters no matter where you come from or the color of your skin. I must leave now for I must travel back to Nazerat; but I leave you with the holy Baptist, Yehohanan. There is no better Baptist in this world than he; he will baptize you with these waters and with the Holy Spirit, whose presence you all experienced on this wonderful morning. I leave you with my message of peace: love one another like good brothers and sisters; love everyone that you come in contact with, especially your enemies, for if you become loving you will have no enemies. Share your wealth, food, and love with everyone and you will become richer in spirit. Accept strangers from all corners of the earth into your beliefs for Yahweh, My Father, is the Father of every human being that will be born on this earth. I did not come here to fight the Romans, for they too are My Father's children. I was not born on this earth to fight anyone. I am here to show you the way to love and understand your fellow men for if you learn to love, to care, to share, and to be understanding with everyone, no matter who they are, you will enter the kingdom of My Father. Before I leave I must ask the holy Baptist to baptize my beloved friend, Judas, who wishes to be baptized by him."

Judas, once again amazed that no thought could escape Ishia, stepped forward near the river and undressed himself. Everyone stared at him, studying his underwear and knee support bandage. They had never seen such material before. They also studied his GISA boots, which were made of fine white leather and had the GISA insignia, a space shuttle flying into the cosmos. Under the watchful eyes of everyone present, including Ishia's, Judas was immersed into the cool waters by Yehohanan the Baptist. As he waded back to the bank everyone knew that he too had become enlightened.

Ishia spoke again, as Judas got dressed, "My brothers and sisters, I must leave you now. I recommend you to be baptized by this holy Baptist and I leave you my love so that you all may learn to love everyone."

As mysteriously as He had come into the crowd likewise did He leave it. Judas tried to follow Him as he struggled through the excited crowd. Finally, he saw Him heading towards the same hillock and quickly moved towards that direction. When both were on top of the hillock they witnessed the crowd queuing to be baptized as Yehohanan baptized them one by one. He would be busy for hours with such a crowd.

"Come, Judas, we will go to Yeriho. It will be our first stop on the road to Nazerat."

Judas rearranged his knapsack and quickly began his way down the north side of the hillock, following Lord Ishia of Nazerat.

Chapter 11

THE YOUNG LADY OF YERIHO

The sun had not reached its midpoint by the time that Ishia and Judas stood in front of the gate of the ancient city of Yeriho. It was the oldest of all cities in the old world and its first foundations had been laid well over ten thousand years before. Judas studied the thick walls of the fortified city and concluded that they had been rebuilt and repaired several times. He touched the mortar between the stones and noticed its various grades of hues due to different time periods when the repairs had been made. Its massive walls had been rebuilt to withstand the enemy's attack.

"Studying ancient buildings and cities was your job, Judas; wasn't it?" asked Ishia.

"Yes, it was, Lord."

"A noble task to study antiquities and to learn from past mistakes!"

"I think so, too, Lord. I loved my job and I am enjoying looking at these most ancient walls. Although this city is probably one of the three most ancient cities on earth, it is still post-diluvial, isn't it, My Lord?"

"You are partially right, Judas. Any wall or edifice you see is postdiluvial. However, the inner walls of Yeriho are the original walls. I'm afraid that the deluge erased any sign of civilization that existed before. Even the Tower of Babel is postdiluvial."

"Lord, I'm a little hungry. Would you like to share some of the nuts as we look around?"

"I will taste a few. We can enter Yeriho and go to its synagogue. I need some time to meditate, Judas; you may search for a room to sleep for the night while I pray."

"Yes, My Lord, I will," replied Judas as he offered Ishia some of the nuts from the golden bag. He took only three small dried nuts and began to chew on one. "Please, take some more, Lord. You must be hungry. You have not eaten since last night."

"I usually do not eat until supper, Judas. Therefore, these three nuts are plenty for me. And, I have the feeling we will have a wonderful supper tonight, my good friend."

They both entered the main archway, which led into the city. The narrow streets were made of stone and the old houses and buildings seemed so close together that they formed a labyrinth throughout the city. People stared at them as they made their way towards the center of the city. Judas felt that people were really staring at him and the way he was dressed. Finally, they reached the city square where stood a synagogue, several larger homes, and a market. A crowd of buyers and vendors were noisily bargaining as people busily moved on.

Ishia stopped in front of the synagogue; and, said to Judas, "Do not mention who I am to no one, for my hour has not yet come. Go and look for a place to dine and stay for the night. I will be in the synagogue."

Ishia walked up the seven stairs leading to the door of the synagogue and Judas moved towards the market. In his broken Aramaic he asked several people for a place to dine and sleep. Some of them did not bother to answer and some pointed to a two-story house, which had an Aramaic inscription on its stone doorjamb. It simply translated to inn. He reached the open door and was about to enter the inn but the powerful stench of wine immobilized his next step. There were several rowdy men drinking and constantly trying to grab a young woman who seemed busy carrying jars and cups of wine. Judas decided that this was not the place for Lord Ishia to dine. He retraced his two steps and stepped out as laughter erupted from the malodorous inn. He walked away from the city square entering another street. He walked along a wall, which seemed to surround a large property with trees protruding over, when he heard several voices crying in desperation. He reached a studded wooden door, which was locked from the inside. He decided to knock. He waited but there was no reply. He vigorously knocked again and impatiently waited until he heard footsteps clacking on stone. A young woman's voice came from the other side.

"Who is it?" asked a gentle voice.

"Do you need a doctor?" asked Judas in broken Aramaic.

The heavy wooden door opened, revealing a beautiful young woman. She couldn't have been more than sixteen. She was still a child, but fully developed into a gorgeous young woman. She was younger than his daughter, thought Judas. Nevertheless, her beauty and maturity were extraordinarily attractive.

"My mother is dying!" she cried.

"I will be back very soon with the greatest doctor on earth. Wait for me," uttered Judas as he made hand gestures, which she understood better than his poor Aramaic.

Judas ran quickly, reaching the synagogue within seconds. He covered his head and entered the pillared hall. There were several people praying and talking. Lord Ishia sat by a corner, whose view was partly blocked by a column, praying. Judas moved towards Him under suspicious looks from a few, who had turned to look as he had entered the synagogue. He reached Ishia and whispered the message in His ear. He slowly got up and followed Judas and did not seem to be worried as He sauntered across the synagogue while Judas impatiently waited for Him outside.

"Quickly, My Lord, she's dying!"

"She is already dead. She died when you told me about her."

Judas' face saddened as he listened to Ishia. Both walked towards the young lady's house. When they reached the door it was shut. Painful wails of desperation and loss echoed from the stone fortress. Ishia pushed the heavy door open. Judas followed Him inside a wonderful walled garden, laden with flowers, spices, and fruit trees. A large stone path led to the house, dividing into a smaller path that circumambulated the fragrant garden. Ishia allowed Judas to knock at the door of the villa. Heavy footsteps resounded as a person approached the door. The door opened and a richly clad young man, whose face clearly showed his sorrow, stupefyingly stared at them.

He was Judas' height and his face looked more Roman than Hebrew. His face was clean-shaven and his curly locks were neatly trimmed.

"It's too late," he whispered.

"May I see your mother?" asked Ishia, His voice simultaneously suggested compassion and authority.

"Please, come in," offered the young man politely.

They entered an atrium, where the sun's rays reflected on the water of its pool. The shallow pool was surrounded by a Roman colonnade, which firmly supported the open roof. It was a Roman villa, equal to any vacation home in Pompeii. It was an impressive house. They followed the young man to the first room on the right side of the atrium. The cries of mourning had dissipated into sobs. As they entered the vast bedroom, Judas greeted the young lady with his eyes. She knelt by the side of the large bed, holding her mother's hand. The dead lady had been a beautiful woman and she looked more like the young lady's older sister than her mother.

Ishia offered His hand to the young lady, which she took as if she had been mesmerized by His presence.

"Do not cry, my child; it is not too late," said Ishia, leading her out of the room. "I must be alone with her."

The young man quickly began to protest when Ishia interjected before he had time to speak, "You must do as I say if you want your mother back; there is no time to waste!"

Judas gently helped the young man out of the room as Ishia quietly shut the door. Judas tried to comfort the two young people as they sat on a stone bench outside the bedroom. Not a sound was heard from the bedroom. Minutes passed, which seemed to last forever. The young man paced around the atrium, too nervous to sit down and too preoccupied by the total ignorance of the miraculous event that was taking place inside his mother's bedroom. Suddenly, a faint voice was barely audible through the thick bedroom wall. The young man stopped pacing and the young lady stood up, both staring at the bedroom door. As if telepathically being called by Lord Ishia, Judas knew that it was time for them to go inside the bedroom. But before they had a chance to walk towards the door, it opened and Ishia helped the lady of the house walk out of her bedroom. The two youths rushed to embrace their mother, holding her and kissing her, manifesting a strong love for her. The three now cried from joy and happiness, as they turned around to Ishia, thanking Him for their mother's life, kissing His hands in adoration, realizing that He was no ordinary man.

"Go and call Eva, Lydia. Tell her to prepare a feast for we must celebrate this wonderful miracle," cried the young man. Turning to Ishia, he continued, "My Lord, would You, please, dine with us. We must celebrate for our mother is alive and You have graced this house with Your presence. Our father will be here any day for I have sent our servants to Kfar-Nahum to tell him that our mother was dying. Stay with us until he comes. Our house is yours, My Lord."

Ishia and Judas followed the young man, as he held his mother's side. They entered an open dining room, which was connected to the kitchen. The kitchen had four fire pits and a brick oven. Young Lydia was helping a middle-aged woman in preparing food, and baking fresh bread. A large table, surrounded by large wooden benches, occupied the center of the large dining room. The walls were gaily painted with scenes of their garden, fruits, and flowers. It was a cheerful room. Ishia and Judas sat on one bench as the young man gently helped his mother to sit down.

"You must be starved, mother. You have been sick for nearly two weeks, and you haven't eaten in several days."

"I am hungry, my son. When did you sent for your father?" she whispered.

"Five days ago, mother. He should be here by tomorrow, at the latest. Simon and Yehuda are good horsemen and they must have reached Kfar-Nahum by the third day. Father should be here by tomorrow."

"Your father is a Roman officer, a centurion?" asked Ishia.

"Yes, he is, but how...?" mumbled the young man.

"And you, my lady, are a Jewess?" continued Ishia.

"Yes, My Lord. I met my husband twenty-three years ago in Tiberias, by Yam Kinneret. I was a young lady, then; and, he was a young Roman soldier. He was kind and generous. It didn't matter to him that I was not Roman. We were married three months later and we love each other more than ever. He is a kind and loving man. We have a loving family, My Lord. You will like him when You meet him," replied the lady.

"I am sure that he is a good man, Miryam. Goodness seems to be everywhere in this house. Let me introduce my beloved friend, Judas Cariota, and I am Ishia of Nazerat," spoke Ishia.

"My name is Linus Horatius, son of Augustus Horatius, and my sister is Lydia. Our wonderful servant is Eva, wife of Shimon of Yeriho, mother of Yehuda," said Linus, as Lydia and Eva came to the table, carrying a bowl of cured olives, dates, various seasonal fruits and wine. Eva poured the wine into six silver goblets and offered them to everyone.

"To my mother's health and to Lord Ishia of Nazerat, who brought her back to this world," cheered Linus.

Everyone, including Eva, toasted to Lady Miryam and Lord Ishia. The wine was good, imported from Sicily; and a wonderful aroma, coming from the brick oven, stimulated everyone's appetite. The olives, which had been marinated in olive oil, wine, and various spices, were delicious; and, the dates and fruits were sweet. They enjoyed the food and Sicilian wine, while the various breads were baking in the brick oven.

Linus explained that his family had been living in Yeriho for the past six years, since his father had been assigned to the Yeriho post. He was now in Kfar-Nahum looking for a house for he had been recently reassigned to that post. His father and his family were very happy because they loved living around Yam Kinneret, the Sea of Galilee. Both Linus and Lydia had been born in Tiberias and Kfar-Nahum was close enough to it, on the northern shore of the Sea of Galilee. Miryam, his mother, had become very sick two weeks prior to that day, only three days after his father had left. Linus thanked Lord Ishia again for his mother's life and thanked Judas for his concern.

As Eva opened the iron door of the brick oven, the aroma intensified throughout the house. Both Lydia and Eva brought three large wooden spatulas, which had been specially made to scoop bread from the oven, which held three different shaped breads. Eva explained that the large flat bread was dressed with olive oil, sliced olives, garlic, and many spices from the garden. The second bread, which was round, had been stuffed with spices, dried fish, and olive oil. The third bread had been stuffed with sliced dates, and local dried fruits—it was a sweet bread. She proceeded to slice all three breads, serving Lord Ishia first, followed by Judas, Lady Miryam, Linus, Lydia, and finally herself. Lydia had refilled the goblets with more Sicilian wine. The breads were delicious, still hot from the oven. Everyone, including Ishia, praised Eva's cooking. She had learned it from Augustus Horatius' mother when they had first visited Italica and she had, since then, created many variations of stuffed bread, depending on the seasons of fruits, vegetables, meats, and spices.

Lord Ishia and Judas had been given their respective bedrooms, and a hot bath had been made ready for them, heated by the heat of the brick oven. After bathing, Ishia walked along the garden path with young Lydia. Lydia had been mesmerized by Lord Ishia's ethereal power over sickness and death. She followed Him and every move He made with her beautiful eyes, listening attentively to every word He spoke. Lydia had immediately recognized who Ishia was, the Mashìah, the Son of the Almighty One. She wanted to be with Him. Do anything for Him. She realized that she loved Him and wanted to spend the rest of her life with Him. Ishia knew her thoughts and desires and He was extremely gentle with her. He did not want to hurt such an angel for she was pure of mind and heart.

Having bathed and dressed, Judas had seen Lord Ishia and Lydia from the window of his bedroom. Both were seated on the stone bench under a pomegranate tree. Ishia was speaking to Lydia as she focused on every spoken word and gesture He would make. For Lydia, every syllable that He uttered, every movement that He made, every smallest detail that came from Ishia was sacred. Judas, upon realizing Lydia's love for Ishia, had decided not to disturb them with his presence. After all, Lydia had every right to love Lord Ishia. He loved Him and would die for Him. He had cured him from an incurable cancer. The least he could do was to love Him and follow Him; and, he was ready to die for Him or with Him. He understood Lydia's feelings perfectly. He decided to spend some time with Lady Miryam, Linus, and Eva. They talked until late, munching on the rest of the breads, olives, fruits and dates and enjoying more of the Sicilian wine. No one mentioned Ishia and Lydia for each one of them understood the delicacy of the situation that He was experiencing with her.

That night, as everyone slept, drained from the emotional pain and joy of that day, Judas got up from his bed and went to the window to breathe in some fresh air. As he focused his vision from the starry sky to the wonderful garden he noticed Lord Ishia praying under the same pomegranate tree. He thought about joining Him but decided that Lord Ishia needed that privacy to consider His next move. Judas knew that his Savior did not have time to waste; but he also knew how badly Lord Ishia needed sleep. Every hour, he would get up and go to the window, hoping that He had gone to sleep, only to observe Him praying. Finally, exhausted, Judas had fallen asleep.

As the first rays of dawn shone through the window, Judas woke up and went by the window. Rubbing the sleep from his eyes, he noticed the Lord, sleeping under the tree. He rushed to the garden, tip-toeing on his bare feet not to wake anyone up. As he reached the stony path, another figure appeared in front of him. It was Lydia. She was carrying a beautiful blanket, which she used to cover Lord Ishia. She, then, sat by the bench, guarding her Lord. Judas retraced his step and went back to his room.

Later that morning, Eva and Lydia had prepared breakfast for everyone. The sweet rolls, dates, and fruits were delicious and refreshing, and freshly hand-squeezed citrus juice was a real surprise. Lord Ishia ate very little, tasting a bit of everything. Both He and Lydia were very quiet. Lady Miryam, Linus, Eva, and even Judas made small talk about the food and the sunny day. Having eaten, Lord Ishia told everyone that He and Judas must leave. Linus and Miryam begged Him to rest for a few more days. Linus begged Him to wait and meet his father. However, Lord Ishia told them that he must reach Nazerat as soon as possible. Linus offered his last two horses but Ishia declined the offer, telling him that they would need them when moving to Kfar-Nahum. It seemed strange to Judas that Lydia did not seem perturbed at all by Ishia's sudden decision to leave.

Lord Ishia promised them that they would soon meet again for a very joyous occasion and that would be a more appropriate time to meet Lydia's and Linus' father. Obviously, having previously known of this sudden decision, Lydia had prepared some food and wine for Ishia and Judas' journey. Ishia and Judas hugged and kissed Lady Miryam, Linus, Eva, and finally Lydia. Ishia gave Lydia a very special hug and, to everyone's surprise, kissed her gently on her lips. They took their bags and the GISA knapsack and walked out of the house and out of the garden under Lydia's devoted eyes as she watched them disappear past the crowd towards Yeriho's gate.

Chapter 12

ON THE WAY TO SHOMERON

Judas was having difficulty keeping up with Ishia's pace. For nearly three hours he had speed-walked to keep up with His longer pace. Finally, Judas decided to say something about it, "Why are you walking so quickly, My Lord. My knee hurts me. Can't we stop for a few minutes?"

"We are nearly there, Judas. We must reach the Wadi Mallaha; it is only two stadia away. If we move quickly enough, we could reach it by midday."

"But for what reason, My Lord?"

"Judas, do you believe in me?"

"Yes, of course!"

"Then, we must move. We must reach the wadi to stop an ambush."

Judas did not want to pursue it further and did not want to disappoint Lord Ishia with trivial questions. He had come to a realization that being with Him would be the greatest adventure of his life for extraordinary events took place wherever He went. So he continued his fast walk as he tried to imagine what was about to happen at the Wadi Mallaha.

When they reached the southern promontory of the wadi Ishia came to a halt. Looking down at the wadi, Ishia pointed at the bottom of the northern promontory where several deep recesses formed. Inside the two recesses, which flanked the bottom of the winding path that led to Shomeron, were two parties of armed men ready for attack. Far on the northern promontory, on the road from Beth-shean, arose a dusty cloud from a traveling party. Judging by how quickly the cloud moved the horsemen were galloping at full speed. How did Ishia know about this event that would soon unfold in front of their very eyes? What were they to do?

"Quickly, Judas, give me the golden bag."

Judas took it out of the top of the knapsack and gave the glittering bag to Ishia who immediately used it to reflect the sun onto the galloping party. As Ishia placed it on an inclined position, reaching the exact angle, a beam of golden light reflected from the golden bag. The golden beam instantly blinded the horses' visions and the galloping party came to a stop as some of the riders were thrown off from their saddles. Judas was amazed at Ishia's ingenuity and stared at Him in awe.

"Come, Judas, we have enough time to stop the ambush."

"My Lord, there are too many of them!"

"Judas, Judas! Believe, my friend! Believe!" He exclaimed as He began to run down the winding path that led to the wadi.

Judas had no choice but to follow. He ran down as best as he could, bad knee and all. Ishia had already reached the wadi and had begun to cross it; however, the wadi was chest deep at its midpoint. Ishia moved on, undaunted by the strong current. Judas held his knapsack high as he crossed the waters at a slower pace. He struggled through the midpoint of the wadi but succeeded in crossing it. By the time he reached the northern bank, Ishia was already facing the two parties, which had joined forces. Judas counted fourteen plus their leader who stood facing Ishia at about twenty paces away. His sword hung by his side as he held a lance in a throwing position.

"You will die for this!" screamed the angry brigand. "You have spoiled our attack!" The leader rapidly shot the spear at Ishia's chest.

Ishia instantly stepped sideways with His right foot, catching the shaft of the lance with both hands. Immediately, He broke it on His right thigh as He brought His knee upwards, and threw the two pieces on the sand. The five horsemen who had, by then, reached the top of the northern promontory witnessed Ishia's advanced style of self-defense.

"They are Romans, our enemies. They deserve to be killed!" shouted the frustrated leader.

"If you kill with lances and swords, you shall die by lances and swords," fervently replied Ishia.

"Who are you?" shouted the leader.

"I am Ishia of Nazerat."

"And I am Bar-Abbas. And you, Ishia of Nazerat will not stop me!" screamed Bar-Abbas as he took another lance from one of his men and hurled it at Ishia.

Once again, with an easy and simple move, Ishia moved sideways and caught the second lance using only His right hand. Throwing it to the ground, He commanded Bar-Abbas and his men to leave immediately and promised that no harm would come to them.

Frustrated and angry, Bar-Abbas withdrew his frightened men and began to run along the bank of the wadi, which led to the Ha-Yarden Valley. While running, Bar-Abbas turned around and shouted, "We'll meet again, Ishia of Nazerat. We'll meet again."

By then, the five horsemen had managed to reach Ishia. Three of the horsemen were Roman soldiers, one of them a centurion. The other two were Jews.

"Thank you, my good friend. We owe you our lives," spoke the centurion. "And where did you learn to catch lances. I have never seen anything like it. You would make the greatest fighter. In Rome…"

"I do not believe in fighting, Augustus Horatius. I was not born in this world to fight. My mission is a mission of peace."

"Who are you? How do you know my name?"

"I am Ishia of Nazerat. This is my good friend, Judas. We come from your house in Yeriho."

"How is my wife, Miryam? Is she in good health?" asked the alarmed centurion.

"Do not despair, my friend. She is in good health. Go in peace, Augustus Horatius. Give our love to your family. We shall soon meet again," said Ishia.

"How can I thank you, Ishia of Nazerat. How can I repay you for saving our lives?"

"By granting permission to your daughter's will, my good friend. Lydia will speak to you this very day. Be gentle and try to understand her wish for only goodness will come out of her desire. We must now part for we need to reach Nazerat before the end of this month."

"Please, take two of our horses; my men can ride double for we do not have long to go before we reach Yeriho."

"Thank you, my good friend, but you will need your steeds for the move to Kfar-Nahum. Go on now; your family is waiting for you. We will meet again, my good friend, for it is all part of my plan. Go in peace for I bless you and your men with my spirit."

Mesmerized by His words and His voice, the centurion and his men bowed to Ishia. "Farewell, Ishia of Nazerat. Until we meet again!" saluted the centurion as he and his men began to cross the wadi, heading for Yeriho.

Ishia and Judas stood watching as the horsemen went up the winding path, finally reaching the top of the southern promontory. The five men stopped their horses and turned them towards their Savior. All five waved farewell and then began to gallop until they disappeared from view. It was Ishia who spoke first, "Do not hide your thoughts from me. Ask me what you need to know. Let us walk along this wadi; it will bring us towards the road to Shomeron. It is a safer road to travel on. We can talk as we move on."

"Lord, how could You possibly have known about the ambush?"

"I know this area very well; I have walked and slept around lower Shomeron for months. I have come upon many wounded people who had been attacked by the same brigands and by other robbers. Several of those people had been attacked at this very same spot. It is a perfect spot for an ambush. The attackers are well hidden and by the time their victims reach the bottom of this winding path they are attacked from the back. Also, I knew that Lydia's father would have taken this road because it is the most direct one and less mountainous than other roads," explained Ishia, pausing for a moment. "Early this morning, before I fell asleep, I had a premonition of what was going to happen today."

"Is that why we left in such a hurry?"

"Yes, my friend. I had no choice but to move as quickly as we did. If we would have taken a little longer at breakfast, Augustus and his men would have been killed."

"Had You told Lydia about your premonition?"

"No, Judas, I could not; she would have worried for her father and for us."

"Then, why didn't You accept the horses, My Lord? We would have reached this place earlier."

"The brigands would have heard the galloping from a distance. This way, we quietly surprised them. Please, my friend, do not be shy to ask your next question. You must consider that we will be together for the next three years and you should know as much as you need to know about me."

"Who taught You self-defense and where did You learn how to catch lances directed at You at such speed?"

"I returned to this land only last year. For the past twelve years I have visited the most remote regions of this earth. Commander Ghabriel took me to those remote places in every continent of the earth. He knows all of the holy men on this planet and he made sure that I spent some time with each one of them. All of those holy men and their people worship My Father under different names. The last place I visited is the most cherished to me, next to Hagalil. That place is on the highest mountains of this planet; it is called Thi-bet. I lived three years in a monastery, high up on the Himalaya Mountains. I studied all of their arts, including fighting-without-fighting, which consisted of blocking or evading someone's attacks and of evading and catching arrows and lances aimed at my body. My teacher was the leader of the Buddhist monks and his name was No-Name, which he had chosen to symbolize how insignificant men are when compared to the universe. Yet, he also taught everyone how important men are and how each man must fully use his talents to reach self-realization."

Judas followed the Lord for the rest of that day, traveling along the sandy banks of Wadi Mallaha, until the sun had settled down on the western sky, creating a wonderful multi-colored sunset. He asked many questions which Lord Ishia gladly answered, but he kept one question to himself. It was too private of a question and he did not dare ask. They had reached a large recess on the wall of the northern plateau, which was almost a cave, protected by large boulders on both sides. They would spend the night there.

Together, they gathered dead branches for a fire, which the Lord allowed Judas to start with one of his waterproof matches. Ishia smiled as He inspected the matches, while Judas fed the small fire with more branches as he broke them on his left knee. The flames grew as they sat on two rocks, which they had placed by the fire. They ate half of the stuffed bread, which Lydia had given them along with some fruit, and they sipped Sicilian wine from a leather flask. As they ate, Judas could not escape his nagging question, which he had chosen not to ask.

"It is really irritating your mind, isn't it, Judas!"

"What, My Lord?"

"When I said to you that you may ask me any question, I really meant it, including the one that is biting the innermost part of your spirit."

"But, Lord, it is too personal!"

"Nothing is too personal between you and I...I know everything you have ever learned, even things you have forgotten. Why should you not know some of my personal thoughts?"

"You really don't mind?"

"Please, my good friend, gather some courage and ask."

"Is Lydia in love with You?"

"Yes, she is. And I'll save you from asking the next question. Yes, I am in love with her. I have never met a woman, in all my life and travels, that has aroused within me feelings and love I have never felt before."

"But, Lord, You are the Son of Yahweh, the Lord of this Universe."

"Yes, I am the only Son of Yahweh, and that side of me is asking all the questions. But, I am also the son of Miryam, and that manly side of me is captured by her love for me and by my love for her. Am I to negate my manly feelings because I am the Son of Yahweh? Am I to abstain from the most wonderful qualities of mankind: to love and to be loved by a most wonderful woman? Am I to neglect the most wonderful feelings that man was born to experience? Do you understand this, my friend?"

"Yes, My Lord, I do understand. But are you to..."

"Marry her. Yes, of course. Not to would be negating my human nature. I would always wonder what it would have been like and I would be depriving myself of my human rights."

"I was never sure if You would marry or not, My Lord."

"Judas, as a man I will never be fully a man until I marry; and even then, I would never be fully a man until I become a father."

"What about men that don't marry or do not become fathers?"

"Woman was created for man. The two will not be fully realized as persons until they marry and have children. Only then, may they be considered fully man and woman. My Father consecrated the unity of man and woman and anyone breaking that union is sinning against the holiest covenant in mankind…All the problems of the future of this planet will arise from the breaking of that holy covenant between men and women. You are a perfect example of what I tell you, my friend. You have kept faithful to your wife, even though you sense that she died."

"My Lord, I could not think of another woman."

"Not even Lydia?"

"My Lord, it was only for a moment. She is so beautiful! But afterwards I thought of her like my own daughter."

"You are a good man, Judas; and because you are so faithful to the woman you loved, you should understand what I am going through."

"I do, My Lord, and I couldn't be happier for You, My Lord, for truly she is the purest and sweetest of them all."

"What you tell me means a lot to me for I know that it comes from your heart."

"When will You marry her, My Lord?"

"She is asking her parents this very moment. They will give her their blessing for they both realize who I am. They will arrange for a wedding within a few months, after their move to Kfar-Nahum. It will take place in Kfar-Nahum or at the house of my mother's friends, who live in a small town north of Sepphoris. And for this very reason I must reach Nazerat to tell my mother about this wonderful happening in my life."

Judas took all of that news in, slowly digesting it within the innermost recesses of his brain. What was about to happen was so meaningful and wonderful that Judas broke into a smile. Ishia knew what the smile was all about and He was happy to have Judas as His beloved friend.

Chapter 13

NAZERAT

Friday, April 1, 29 A.D.

Ishia and Judas had spent the past two weeks walking across Yehuda and Shomeron by first following the Wadi Mallaha until they reached its source. They had continued along the plateau until they reached the Tirza River, which they had followed faithfully until its source. After a week of travel, they were about fifty stadia north of Har Gerizim. Ishia had tried to stay away from people, wanting more time to contemplate on His mission. For the following two weeks they had traveled through the Shomeroni hills and valleys, staying away from Salim, Aenon, and Beth-shean. The days were divided into three parts: traveling from very early morning till noon; meditating from early afternoon till evening; and ending the day with supper, a long conversation, and sleep.

Their breakfasts and lunches had consisted of either a fruit or a small handful of nuts and dried fruits, accompanied by a little water. Their suppers had been the sharing of one can of salmon, or some of the stuffed bread and fruits. They had skimped during meals, stretching whatever food they had and making it last for nearly three weeks. The empty plastic bottles and the leather wine container had been replenished with water from the wadis or rivers. By the time they would reach Nazerat they would have no more food and only one full bottle of water.

They had traveled safely, meeting only a few people, one of which had been beaten and left for dead. Ishia and Judas had found a middle-aged man by the Shomeroni foothills, northwest of Aenon. The man, whose name was Eleazar, had been robbed of his horse, money, and clothes; and, he had been left half naked and bleeding from wounds, which had been inflicted by a knife or sword. Judas had helped Ishia wash the man's wounds and then witnessed the miraculous cure of Eleazar, the Shomeroni. Once the wounds had been cleaned Ishia had taken a handful of sandy earth, spitting into it several times until it became moist. He then used the mix to cover the stab wounds. There had been no reaction from the wounded man for he had been barely breathing. They had waited a while until the mix had dried up together with some of his blood. Finally, Ishia began to wash away the crusty brown mix with some water, exposing the healed wound. All of Eleazar's wounds had healed within the hour— how was that possible? How could the process of cell division be accelerated at such an unbelievable speed? Judas could only wonder in awe at the wonderful Ishia, Son of the Almighty Yahweh.

Once all the wounds had been cleaned, Ishia spread His right hand over the man's forehead, allowing His thumb and little finger to reach both temples. Murmuring a prayer or a command, Ishia kept a strong pressure on Eleazar's temples. Judas watched in amazement, witnessing the greatest doctor at work. Minutes passed without any physical response from the stranger; but the Lord intensified His concentration. After nearly a quarter of an hour of deep concentration, Lord Ishia called the man by his name, Eleazar. As if woken up from a long coma, the man opened his eyes and smiled. The Lord helped him up and Judas offered him some water, which he drank. He bowed to Lord Ishia, thanking Him for saving his life. He, then, proceeded in recounting his misfortunate story.

Eleazar was from the city of Shomeron and had gone to Aenon to sell his work, gold jewelry. He was a gifted goldsmith, whose beautiful gold necklaces, bracelets, and rings had been purchased by Romans, Greeks, and rich Jews. On his way back to Shomeron, he had been followed by two men he had seen at the market square in Aenon. He was ambushed around the foothills. The two men took all his money, his beautiful clothes, the jewelry he wore, and the horse. One of the men did not wish to let Eleazar go free, for fear of being recognized, and attacked him with a dagger, stabbing him eight times. He remembered his vicious look as he continuously kept on stabbing him while his accomplice cruelly laughed at Eleazar begging for mercy. He would never forget their cruel faces as long as he lived.

Ishia took His best robe and offered it to Eleazar, which he took. He thanked the Lord for His kindness and generosity and for saving his life, as he continuously checked his wounds, not understanding how Lord Ishia had managed to rejoin his deep cuts in such a wonderful way. It was at that moment that Eleazar realized who Lord Ishia was, as he fell on his knees before Him. He praised Him as his savior and as the Savior of Yisrael, the mashìah.

Having shared some of their food, Ishia and Judas parted with Eleazar for he suddenly felt invigorated with newly found strength. Before they parted, Eleazar promised Lord Ishia a gift that he would handcraft for Him as a token of gratitude for what He had done for him. Lord Ishia had told him not to bother himself with jewelry for He wore none and that His life here on earth would be very short. He told him that he should share his wealth with the poor people living in Shomeron. Eleazar had promised Lord Ishia that he would share his wealth with the poor but that he still wanted to handcraft a gift for Him, and that it would not be jewelry. Ishia hugged Eleazar and wished him a safe journey home. Eleazar hugged Judas and then departed, turning around and waving good-bye at every few paces until he disappeared around the base of a rocky hill.

Finally, after fifteen days of traveling from the Wadi Mallaha, the place where Ishia had saved the centurion and his men, Ishia and Judas arrived at Nazerat. Ishia's hometown was a village on the rocky hills of Lower Galilee (Hagalil), a three-day walk to Tiberias or Magdala, and only four days to Kfar-Nahum, pronounced Capernaum by the Romans. As they entered the outskirts of the village they were welcomed by several children, who took Ishia and Judas by their hands and led them to the village center. Judas took whatever nuts and dried fruits they had left and distributed them among the children, who laughingly thanked them and ran away to continue their games. Judas followed Ishia along the rocky alley leading to His home, where they were greeted by His younger brother Yakov. He had taken over his father's work as carpenter since his death twelve years before. Yakov, which is James in English, resembled Ishia in so many ways but he was no taller than Judas. His face resembled some of Ishia's features that they had inherited from Miryam. However, his hair and beard were deep black, while Ishia's were a dark blond. Ishia introduced Judas, as the angel from the future, to His brother. As they embraced, the wooden door of the stone house opened wide and a middle-aged woman stepped out—it was Miryam, the mother of Ishia and Yakov. Ishia walked to her and hugged her, kissing her soft and gentle face. Miryam's face radiated love and awe for her son, Ishia, for she very well knew who He was. She was shorter than Judas and he thought that she was approximately five feet two inches. Her body was well proportioned; and she was not fat and had a healthy look. Her face was oval and smooth framed by healthy long black hair, covered by a blue material, which had been embroidered with flowers. She had big dark eyes and a fine nose and the most beautiful full lips any woman would desire. She looked in her early forties but Judas knew that she was at least ten years older; and, he could not help himself from staring at her. Judas felt blessed at that moment for he was in the presence of the two most adored people in the history of mankind, Ishia and His mother.

Finally, Ishia introduced Judas to His mother. He held her hand, bowed and kissed it. Miryam invited them in and prepared a fine meal for them: hommus with olive oil, freshly baked bread to dip into the hommus, green olives spiced with aromatic spices, a baked fish which had been stuffed with spices, and Galilean wine. They enjoyed the meal as Ishia recounted some of His travels in the past twelve years, never boasting of His wonderful miracles, telling them of the far away places He had been. It was Judas, with an improved Aramaic, that told them of Ishia's miracles, especially of his own cure. Ishia helped Judas with some words, allowing him to express himself more smoothly. There was only one matter that Miryam and Yakov had great difficulty understanding, the thought that Judas was from the distant future. Ishia tried to explain it in so many ways but they could only accept His words but could not understand the concept. Judas took his knapsack, opened it, and removed the 100-foot, 8mm climbing rope, the knife with the surgical blades, the miniature CD-player and the ABBA CD, and the 35mm miniature spy-camera. Judas placed the CD in the portable player and arranged the earphones on Miryam's head. She smiled at the beautiful music;

and although she did not understand its words she clearly appreciated its sound. He gave the beautiful knife to Yakov, who marveled at its sharpness and purity of metal. He then asked Ishia if he could take a picture of His family. Ishia smiled at the idea and asked His mother and brother to pose for Judas. He took two photographs of them and then Ishia instructed Yakov to take a picture of Judas together with Ishia and their mother.

Later, Yakov gave Judas a tour of their modest house and his workshop, where he was working on a long table for a wealthy family in Sepphoris. They spent the rest of that day talking to several Nazarenes who had come to welcome Ishia back to His hometown. Once everyone left, later that night, Ishia and Judas shared Yakov's workshop as their bedroom.

Chapter 14

REJECTED

Saturday, April 2, 29 A.D.

Early that Shabbat morning, every Nazarene in Nazerat anxiously waited for Ishia to come out of His house. They quietly crowded the immediate streets and allies next to His home, waiting for any window shutter or door to be opened.

Inside, Miryam was about to wake up Ishia when He sat up and spoke to His mother, "Good morning, mother. They are waiting for me; aren't they?"

"How do you know that, my son? You have been sleeping and the crowd has been quiet throughout this early morning."

"I can feel their presence and their eagerness to hear me. Nevertheless, today will be a bitter and disappointing day for all of us, dear mother."

"Why do you say that, my son?"

"Nazerat is eagerly waiting for me to speak and cure the sick; and, all of Nazerat will be amazed when I speak and when I heal its loved ones. But, when I will tell them who I am they will become enraged and irrational. They will throw me out of our synagogue and they will want to stone me over the cliffs of Nazerat. You and Yakov will be in danger, here in Nazerat."

"What are you saying, my brother?" asked Yakov, as he entered the workshop.

"Do you know who I am, Yakov?"

"Yes, you are my brother through our mother; but, you are also the Only Begotten Son of the One I dare not mention His Name."

"You may say My Father's Name, Yakov, for you are not saying it in vain."

"You are Ishia, the Son of Yahweh," cried out Yakov.

"Today, because of me, you and our mother will be forced to abandon your work, your house, your personal possessions and flee Nazerat."

"Why is that, my brother and My Lord?"

Ishia's face became suddenly sad, as a tear appeared from His right eye, followed by another from His left. Judas sat up and shared His sadness for he knew what was about to take place on that very Sabbath morning.

"Today, at our synagogue, I will be rejected, condemned, and attacked by all the Nazarenes present. They will not be able to accept who I am; and, because of who I say I am they will want to stone me and throw me over the cliffs of Nazerat. I say to you, pack whatever you need, some food and water, for you will never come back to your hometown again."

"Where will we go, my son?"

"To Kfar-Nahum, to the house of my bride-to-be."

"I thought you would never marry, Ishia!" exclaimed Yakov.

"While I am on this world, I must experience the full meaning of what it is to be a man: to marry, to conceive a child with Lydia, to be a father for a little while. That will be the most wonderful experience of being a man. One is not fully a man until he marries and becomes a father. That is the realization of being a man. Surely, you understand, Yakov?"

"Yes, I understand; and, I want to follow You and die with You, My Lord!"

"You will not die with me, Yakov. You will live a long life and you will bring my message of peace and love to many places far away. Also, you will take care of my son and Lydia when I am gone. They will need you when I leave this world."

"Where will you be going, Ishia?"

"I will go into the heavens, to my world."

"How is it possible for You to know that your bride-to-be will bear a son?"

"I know this from Judas; he is a messenger from the future."

"How can he be from the future when the future has not yet come. How is that possible, my brother and My Lord?"

"I know that it sounds impossible, and I know how difficult it is for you to understand this; but, Judas does come from the future. I can verily say this as I say I am the Son of Yahweh."

"I believe You; but, it is very confusing to me…Ishia, when You leave I will also take care of our mother."

"Yakov, our mother will be coming with me to Paradise, my world. It is My Father's Wish."

"I understand," said Yakov sadly at the thought of losing his mother and brother.

"What is the name of the young lady, Ishia?" asked Miryam.

"Her name is Lydia, the daughter of a Hebrew woman and a Roman centurion. She is pure in body and in spirit," replied Ishia.

"And she is the most beautiful young lady I have ever met," added Judas. Miryam smiled at Judas, realizing that he also liked Lydia who would soon become her daughter-in-law. "I know for sure that you, My Lady, will love Lydia for she is full of love and, in so many ways, she is like you."

"Yes, she is, my mother!" exclaimed Ishia, happy at the thought of Lydia, "Like Judas said, she is full of love for everyone; and, we love each other very much."

"She sounds wonderful. I cannot wait to see her, my son!"

"Thank you, my mother, for being so full of love and understanding about what I am about to do."

"I was born on this earth to be Your mother and Yakov's; and, that is the most wonderful reason in the world for me to be alive. I will gladly give up this house to be with You and Lydia. I will be there to help her in every possible way."

"Thank you, my mother; but now, we must get ready to go out. Prepare what is necessary while I pray."

Judas helped Miryam and Yakov pack some bread, dates, olives, a small leather container of wine and a large one of water. They packed two thicker bed covers for the cold Galilean nights and a few other personal objects. They were ready to leave their home, where Ishia, Yakov, and three other brothers had been raised, where her dear husband, Yoseph, had made so many wonderful tables, chairs, beds, wooden toys and other wonderful objects. Miryam became emotional and Yakov hugged her. Judas, understanding their situation, hugged both of them as they accepted his comfort.

"It is time," whispered Ishia, entering the main room.

The three turned around, looking at Ishia as His countenance clearly manifested the deep sorrow of what was about to unfold.

"We must go now. They are waiting for me. Yakov, after the crowd you will accompany me into the synagogue. Judas, you will stay with my mother; she will guide you to the cliff. Set up your rope; I will need it to descend the cliff. Yakov, you will leave the synagogue when the crowd becomes mad and you will quickly join mother and Judas. You will use the path; it will be easier for mother. I will join you at the bottom."

"My Lord, it is too dangerous. At least, let me show You how to rappel. It will be safer," volunteered Judas.

"I know how to rappel, Judas; I have seen it done many times."

"Where, My Lord?"

"Thousands of times within your mind."

"Forgive me, My Lord!"

"There is nothing to forgive, Judas. You are concerned about my safety. I appreciate that very much. Now we must leave. Yakov, please open the door and try to separate a path through the crowd."

Yakov nodded while taking the wooden bar off the door, opening it. The crowd began to chant, "ISHIA, ISHIA OF NAZERAT!"

Slowly, Judas and Mary followed Yakov to help him separate the crowd. Finally, Ishia stepped out, tall and lonely. He looked lonely at that moment. The crowd went berserk, chanting and pushing. Ishia immediately held up His right hand and the crowd became as tame as lambs.

"My beloved Nazarenes, I want to thank you for this warm welcome you have given me. I am here for you, all of you, for anyone of you who needs help. Come to me, my brothers and sisters, if you are in need," gently spoke Ishia.

"My wife, cure my wife!" screamed a voice from the crowd. "She is dying. I have been waiting for you, Ishia, son of Yoseph."

"Where are you, my brother?" asked Ishia as the crowd made way until He reached the man who had called Him. He held his wife in his arms. She was very light, skin and bones, her beauty had been lost long ago. He looked at the man and saw his strength in the way he held her. There was suffering written in his face, but his strength was prominent.

"Is she able to talk?"

"No, my Lord. She's been like this for months. I have kept her alive because I love her. She is my wife; she is the mother of my children. She has been a wonderful companion and mother; and, now, look at her. She's nothing but bones; help me, please!" begged the man as he sobbed from the emotion and suffering.

"Do you believe in me, Shimon?"

"You remember me, Ishia!"

"How could I forget you, my friend? We were best friends as children, and we still are," said Ishia, gently stroking the sick woman's forehead. "Do you believe that she can be cured?"

"I have heard great things about you; they say you can bring back the dead. Is that true, Ishia?"

"That's not important, Shimon. Do you believe that your wife can be cured?"

"I believe in you, Ishia. I believe you can cure my wife."

"Then, she is cured. You may put her down."

Shimon gently put his wife on her feet, still holding her arms.

"Eva will be fine, Shimon. She now needs nutritious food. Take care of her, my friend. She is a wonderful lady."

Shimon fell on his knees, kissing Ishia's feet, as Eva moved to embrace Him, "It is You, Ishia; it is really You. I feel so strong, now. I feel so good. Thank You, My Lord."

"I love you both. I will never forget all the beautiful things we did together as children," whispered Ishia, kissing Eva's forehead.

Shimon and Eva held each other as Ishia moved along, reaching a middle-aged woman who had not stopped calling His name. As Ishia slowly advanced, the Nazarenes were contended in touching His robe, His hair, or being close to Him. Everyone marveled at His power as they had witnessed Eva's miraculous recovery.

"My Lord, help my son. He is blind!"

"Has he been blind since birth?"

"No, My Lord. He began to lose his sight four years ago. He has been blind for the past two years. Can you help him, please?"

"Do you believe that your son will see again?"

"I believe you can cure him, My Lord."

Ishia placed His index fingers on the boy's eyelids, as both of His thumbs rested on his nose and the other fingers around his temples, and began to pray. The three minutes seemed to last a lifetime as the crowd held their silence, witnessing wondrous miracles by Ishia the Nazarene. At that moment, they were proud to be Nazarenes because of Ishia.

"Open your eyes, my son," whispered Ishia as he released His hold on the boy's brain, "For this will be the only moment that your eyes will witness your redeemer."

The twelve-year old Zebulun opened his eyelids and quickly protected them with his right arm for the morning sun was too bright. Slowly, he allowed more light in by lowering his forearm, as the crowd watched every movement He made so that they might witness another miracle by Ishia of Nazerat.

Ishia scanned the crowd, noticing so many sick and crippled people of all ages. Poverty and misery shrouded the Nazarenes; and, He felt their misery, their hunger, their pain, and He took it all for it would be the last time that He would see His fellow Nazarenes. As Ishia took all that anguish, incorporating it within Himself, young Zebulun screamed a joyous cry, which broke His deep concentration. Everyone stared at young Zebulun, mesmerized by what had happened.

"I can see; I can see. Oh, so many beautiful colors. Oh, I can see; I can see!" he chanted on as the crowd stared in disbelief.

"How is that possible?" exclaimed a woman.

"Isn't that Ishia the carpenter, the son of Yoseph?" asked an old man.

"How can this be? A Nazarene with such mighty power!" asked a young man.

"People say that Ishia is the mashìah," answered an older woman.

"I believe He is. He can cure anything. They say that He has revived the dead," said another man.

"Only the true mashìah can do such wonderful things," continued the older woman.

"Blessed be Ishia, son of Yoseph and Miryam!" exclaimed Zebulun's mother.

The crowd continued to wonder at Ishia as He continued to work miracles on His way to the small synagogue. The crowd chanted blessing His name, calling Him the mashìah. Finally, He reached the synagogue and turned around before entering. He looked at His fellow Nazarenes and then stared at His mother, and at Yakov and Judas. At that moment Ishia's countenance was filled with sadness for He knew what was about to happen. As He turned around, entering the synagogue, all the men in the crowd began to flock into the small house of prayer. The women and young children remained outside contended to hear His voice as Miryam, Yakov, and Judas made their way towards the cliffs of Nazerat.

The rabbi welcomed Ishia as everyone present anxiously waited for Him to speak. The rabbi handed Him the scroll of the prophet Ysha-Yahu; and, He proceeded to unroll it until He found the passage He wanted to read. He began to read in a strong yet gentle voice, "The spirit of the Lord has been given to me, for He has anointed me. He has sent me to bring good news to the poor, to proclaim freedom to the captives and to restore sight to the blind; to set free the oppressed and to proclaim the favorable year of the Lord and the day of recompense."

Pausing, He rolled up the scroll and gave it back to the rabbi's assistant. Everyone stared at Him as He began to speak, "These very words are being fulfilled today even as you listen and as you look at me."

The crowd was astonished at the way He spoke the gracious words, approving and welcoming Ishia as the mashìah. An old man exclaimed, "Is not this Yoseph's son, Ishia?" Others began to whisper, asking each other how could a Nazarene be the mashìah.

Suddenly, Ishia stood up and replied with a powerful voice, "Some of you will surely quote me the passage, `Physician, heal yourself', and you will tell me, 'We have heard all the wonderful things you have done in Judea—why not do the same in your own town.'" He looked at the crowd and continued, "Amen, I say to you, no prophet is ever accepted in his own town and country. There were many widows in Yisrael during Eli-jah's time, I can assure you of that, when it did not rain for three and a half years and a great famine raged throughout the land; however, Eli-jah was not sent to any of those. He was sent to a widow at Sarephat, a town near Shidon. And during the prophet Eli-shiah's time there were many lepers in Yisrael, but none of those were cured. The only leper that was cured was a Syrian called Naaman."

Enraged by what Ishia had just told them, the rabbi and the elders stood up shouting accusations at Ishia for they hated the Syrians and Shidonians. Within seconds, the crowd which had been exalting Him and which had been mesmerized by Him was ready to kill Him. Ishia, knowing exactly what was about to happen, slipped through the maddened Nazarenes and walked quickly towards the cliffs, which Nazerat had been built on. Some of the Nazarenes had seen Him and ran after Him as they picked up rocks to stone Him. When He reached the cliffs, He noticed Judas' climbing rope around an olive tree with both ends reaching the first ledge below. He quickly grabbed both ends of the rope and rappelled down the cliff, controlling it with His right hand up and His left down. Within seconds Ishia reached the ledge as Judas quickly took the rope down. When the crowd reached the top of the cliff Ishia had vanished from sight and they could not see them below. Ishia, Miryam, Yakov and Judas waited as the infuriated crowd began to throw their stones down, hoping to hit Ishia. Together they waited until the crowd dispersed and followed the ledge to a walk-down, which led them to the bottom of the cliffs. They began their long walk to Magdala, which would take the rest of the day.

Finally, they reached the town of Magdala at dusk and found a room for the night at a small inn by the Sea of Galilee. Sarah, the wife of Yoshiyah, a fisherman, ran the small inn. She prepared the catch of the day and fresh baked bread for them. They enjoyed the food with some wine from Arbelah. That night, Ishia barely slept, thinking of the betrayal and rejection of His fellow Nazarenes. They stayed in Magdala for three more nights, enjoying the gracious hospitality of Sarah and Yoshiyah.

Chapter 15

THE CHOSEN

Having rested at Magdala, Ishia, Miryam, Yakov and Judas made their way along the coast of the lake towards the direction of Genne-Sareth, enjoying the gentle northern breeze sweeping across the waters. There were several fishing boats on the lake, hoping for a good catch. It was still morning when they reached Genne-Sareth. They continued along the shore, walking towards Kfar-Nahum, where they caught a boat to Beth-Saida. It was late afternoon when they reached that fishing town. A few fishing boats had already returned from a day excursion. A fisherman with a very loud voice and a quick temper was washing his nets. As they approached the boats, the stocky fisherman uttered something nasty to his younger partner, blaming him for the poor catch.

"Do not blame your brother, Shimon, for it is not his fault for the poor catch!" exclaimed Ishia.

Yakov and Yehohanan, sons of Zebedeus, who were fishing partners with Shimon and Andros Bar-Jonah, silently looked on. All the fishermen and people, that had been watching the boats coming back to shore, were suddenly intrigued by Ishia's meddling with Shimon. No one, who knew Shimon Bar-Jonah, would meddle with him because they all knew about his temper and strength. They had never seen him lose a fight, even with opponents who were much bigger than he. He was about five feet six inches in height with a powerful upper body. His height was considered tall for that epoch, when most men were a few inches shorter than Shimon. His strong torso and powerful arms were probably acquired by the daily sailing and pulling of the fishing nets. He had a round face with a prominent Hebrew nose, long curly black hair and a beard to match it. He was intimidating, at the very least. His younger brother, Andros, was almost the same height, but slimmer with sinewy muscles. His face was slightly slimmer with a sparse beard, giving him a gentler yet smarter look. Shimon turned around and was about to let the stranger have a few nasty words when Andros touched his shoulder, whispering something in his ear. Shimon dropped the net he was cleaning and, bowing his head, murmured something unintelligible. His brother, Andros, stared at him, upset that he could not speak clearly to the mashìah.

"Your thoughts are forgiven, Shimon! May we come into your boat?" asked Ishia, as He helped His mother step up into the vessel.

"My boat is your boat, Master," replied Shimon, confused and still upset.

The fishing boat was approximately thirty feet long but wider than a sailboat. It had one mast and sail but no cabin; but it had a large wooden container for the catch. Ishia helped His mother sit on a wooden bench and sat beside her. Yakov and Judas sat facing them. The boat smelled of dead fish, but no one seemed to mind.

It was Ishia who broke the silence as everyone stared at them, "Shimon, would you cast your nets once more?"

"I am tired, Master. We have worked all day and caught nothing," mumbled Shimon, until his brother gently elbowed his ribs, "But because You have told me to, I will lower the nets once again."

The boat began to move as Andros set the sail and as Shimon steered. The wind pushed the boat towards Magdala.

"You will need your partners' boat, Shimon," said Ishia.

"Master, I will be happy to fill this boat for I have never experienced that."

"Truthfully, I say to you, Shimon Bar-Jonah, that even two boats will not be sufficient to hold the fish of your next cast."

"I will call them, Master. YAKOV...YEHOHANAN... FOLLOW MY BOAT...WE WILL NEED YOUR HELP," yelled Shimon, motioning them to follow his boat.

Yakov and Yehohanan, the sons of Zebedeus, pushed their boat and followed Shimon's boat. It was clear that Yakov was doing most of the pushing for he was the older and stronger brother. Yehohanan was slimmer and only a teen-ager. Yakov had a full black beard and long coarse black hair. He was about the same height as Shimon but had gentler features. Yehohanan was a handsome young man with a sinewy upper body. His long black hair had been tied in a long ponytail and the few whiskers that grew from his face had been lightly bleached by the water and sun. Both brothers had their robes down to their waist so that they could work easier. The wind pushed the boats westwards, in the direction of Magdala. When the two boats reached the deep waters of Yam Kinneret, Ishia broke the silence that had reigned on Shimon's fishing boat since they had left the shores of Beth-Saida.

"Anchor your boats here and lower your nets. Tell your partners to do the same," suggested Ishia.

"Yes, Master," replied Shimon with a touch of sarcasm and then proceeded to instruct his partners, "YAKOV, YEHOHANAN... ANCHOR YOUR BOAT AND CAST YOUR NETS."

All four fishermen immediately began to lower their nets after they had anchored their boats. Ishia stood up and faced the waters and began to concentrate or pray. It was difficult to know what He was really doing. He concentrated for a good half hour thought Judas. Then He stopped His intense concentration and sat down.

"What do we do know, Master?" asked Shimon, still using a touch of sarcasm and it was clear to everyone that he was annoyed by Ishia's pretense of knowing everything. He was not a fisherman!

"We patiently wait until the fish I summoned enter the nets. I will let you know when the nets are full."

"No man can summon..." began Shimon but was stopped by his brother, Andros.

Shimon was silent but everyone clearly saw the rage building up within him and would surely explode if the catch would be poor. As he constantly examined the ropes, which held the nets, he saw that the ropes were being pulled down, inch by inch. Within only minutes that he had been silenced by his younger brother the ropes had stretched to their maximum length.

Yakov and Yehohanan screamed out to Shimon that their nets were being pulled and that they feared they would break. Shimon turned to Ishia and the look of rage had been replaced by fear.

"It is time to bring the catch in," whispered Ishia.

"BRING IT IN; BRING THE CATCH IN!" yelled Shimon to his partners, as the four fisherman began to pull the nets in, "We need help, the nets are too heavy."

Both Yakov and Judas stood up to help Shimon and Andros to bring in the first net, which was bursting with fish. Quickly, Shimon moved towards the second net as the first net was secured onto the boat. They brought in the second net and then the third, which was by the stern of the boat. Hundreds of fish, maybe thousands, covered every space available. There was no place to stand as the nets expanded from the squirming fish. The water was only inches away from entering the boat and the situation had become dangerous.

"Master, we are sinking!" exclaimed Shimon.

"Throw some of the fish back into the lake and set sail towards Beth-Saida," suggested Ishia.

Everyone frantically threw some of the fish back into the waters of Yam Kinneret. Yakov and Yehohanan screamed for help; there were too many fish in their boat. The boat was sinking. Shimon screamed at them to throw some fish back into the lake and to turn back towards Beth-Saida. He then turned around, faced Ishia and fell on his knees among the fish, which were squirming and jumping up all over the boat.

"Forgive me, My Lord, I am not worthy of Your presence for I am a sinful man," said Shimon.

"Do not be afraid, Shimon! Follow me and from now on you will become a fisher of man," replied Ishia.

The two fishing boats struggled back to the shore of Beth-Saida, where a multitude had gathered, anxiously waiting, curious to see if Ishia had realized the impossible.

"What shall we do with all the fish, My Lord?" asked Shimon.

"Everyone in that crowd would appreciate a few fish to take home to their families. Most of them have that look of hunger."

"Shall we keep a few for our families, Lord?" asked Andros.

"Of course you should. You are also hungry, are you not?"

"Yes, My Lord, we all are. Will You and Your family join us for some delicious fish?" smiled Andros.

"Yes, we will be happy to join you and your family."

Shimon spoke to the crowd but they were too excited and growing more restless to listen to him. It was then that Ishia made His way to the front of the boat and raised His arms. The multitude calmed down and only the beating of the water against the boat and the movement of the squirming fish could be heard.

"Make two lines on each side of the boats and each one shall receive three fish. You are to take these fish home to your families and share them with your parents, brothers, sisters, husbands, wives, and children. Do this for me," spoke Ishia.

As if hypnotized, the crowd began to split into four lines, one on each side of the boats. Judas and Yakov jumped off Shimon's boat and went onto the other boat to help Yakov and Yehohanan with the sharing of the fish. Each person, male or female, child or adult, received three fish. The entire village of Beth-Saida must have been there for it was late at night when the last eight were served. There were enough fish left in each boat that the four fishermen would have been proud to call it a catch.

Ishia, His brother Yakov, Judas and Miryam helped the four fishermen with their boats and to take home the rest of the catch. As they walked towards Shimon's house some of the people approached them to thank them for the fish. As they entered Shimon's house, his wife came to welcome them with tears in her eyes. She was a young lady, still in her late teens. She was pretty, with a full bosom and hips.

"Why are you crying, woman?" asked Shimon.

"My mother is sick in her bed. She is dying," cried his wife.

"Take me to her bed," said Ishia in a gentle and soothing voice. Having put the basket of fish down, He followed her to a small alcove, which housed her mother's bed, covered by a woolen drape. She opened the drape, exposing an elderly woman sweating and burning from a high fever.

Everyone looked on as Ishia wiped His hands and then gently touched her forehead. Ishia asked for a fish, which Shimon readily handed to Him. He placed the fish on her forehead and began to meditate or pray. Everyone looked on, puzzled by the use of the fish.

Ishia kept the fish on her forehead for several minutes, which seemed an eternity for Shimon and his wife. The sick woman spoke gibberish, delirious from the high fever. No one spoke, waiting for Ishia to finish His prayer. Finally, He removed the fish from the woman's head and gave it to Shimon, ordering him to bury it for it had absorbed his mother-in-law's high fever. The older woman now rested as everyone witnessed every detail of Ishia's movements and gestures. When Shimon came back, Ishia asked the name of his mother-in-law. It was Sarah.

"Wake up, Sarah, and get up for you are cured," ordered Ishia, offering His hand.

Sarah opened her eyes and looked at everyone. She took Ishia's hand and quickly got up saying, "Why didn't anyone tell me that we had guests. Quickly, Esther, we must cook for everyone."

All four fishermen and Esther, Shimon's wife, fell on their knees. Ishia asked them to get up and take care of the fish. As the four fishermen salted most of the fish, Miryam and Esther helped Sarah to cook some of the catch and bake fresh bread. Sarah was an excellent cook and they all enjoyed a delicious supper. That evening many people came to Shimon's house to see the mashìah.

Early the next morning, Ishia gently got up without waking anyone up and went outside to relieve Himself. Judas had also woken up and followed Him outside. It was still dark and only the gentle ripples of the lake could be heard as they brushed the shore.

"Is everything fine, My Lord?" whispered Judas as he had run to catch up with Ishia.

"I need some privacy to relieve myself, Judas. Unfortunately for us, these poor people have no idea of what a bathroom looks like. Unlike the Romans, in that respect, the poor are not concerned in living with comfort; their main concerns are My Father and finding enough food to survive the day."

"I am sure that Herod Antipas has bathrooms in all of his palaces."

"It would have been easier for me to have been born in the royal family; but, I was born in a stable and I do not own anything for my staying on this earth is short. Therefore, I must relieve myself like the rest of the poor people. Now, Judas, I do need a moment of privacy."

"Please, My Lord! I'm sorry for having troubled You."

"No trouble, Judas. I know that you are concerned for me."

The first rays of the morning sun were ending the darkness as Ishia entered Shimon's humble home. He gently woke them up and asked Shimon and Andros to follow him to Kfar-Nahum.

"What about my wife and my boat, master? And what about my mother-in-law?"

"Your wife and her mother are welcome and we can go by boat to Kfar-Nahum."

"What about the house, my father's house?"

"Give it away to a homeless family."

"Give it away! You are asking too much, Master. I will sell it."

"That will take too long. My time left on earth is quite short. I am asking you to follow me and to do so you must give everything away. Can you do that Shimon and Andros Bar-Jonah?"

"I am ready to follow You, My Lord!" exclaimed Andros.

"I will follow You anywhere, My Lord. I will help to cook and wash Your clothes," continued Sarah.

"You will need my help, mother," added Esther.

"Have you all gone crazy? You want to throw away everything that my father and I worked for. Are you all insane? I can't give up my boat, my house, and everything that's in it. I just can't."

"Do you know who I am, Shimon?"

"People say you are the mashìah. Some say you are Yehohanan the Baptist; and, some say you are a prophet. Who are you?"

"I am neither the Baptist nor a prophet. I am the One whom My Father promised to the Chosen People, Cephas."

"You are the Mashìah, the Son of the Most Holy!"exclaimed Shimon, stunned by the sudden realization. "But why do You call me Cephas, Lord?"

"For two reasons I call you Cephas: first, because you have a head as hard as a rock; and the second reason is that I need someone as strong as you to build my Church and lead it through its toughest time when I am gone. I am choosing you, Cephas, to follow me and I will make you a fisherman of men."

Shimon-Cephas fell on his knees begging for forgiveness. Ishia extended His right hand, which he took to get up.

"We must leave soon. Take whatever you need to survive with me. Andros and Yakov, find a homeless family and bring them here. We will go by boat to Kfar-Nahum; you can still keep your boat for a while, Cephas," instructed Ishia.

"Won't You call me Shimon, Lord? I bear the name of my grandfather," asked Shimon.

"From now on, your name shall be Cephas, the rock," replied Ishia. "And now, quickly prepare what you need to take along. Remember, we will travel far; therefore, take only what you can carry."

While Cephas went looking for his necessities, Miryam helped Sarah and Esther prepare a quick breakfast, bread and an olive dip. They also placed four loaves of bread, salted fish, and cured olives in a bag; and, readied a skin of wine and a large skin of water for the voyage to Kfar-Nahum. Finally, Andros and Yakov, together with Yakov and Yehohanan, the sons of Zebedeus, had returned with two women and five young children, two of which were babies. Their husbands had gone looking for work in exchange for some food to feed their families. Andros had found them by a rocky alcove where they had made it their home.

Ishia wanted Cephas to be the one to give his home away to the two homeless families. It was difficult for Cephas to do so; but, he mustered up all his courage and said, "I offer both your families my home. Use it and take good care of it; it is now your home. Any furniture or tool is also yours. The three containers of salted fish, the container of olives, and the sacks of flour are all yours. It should last you for the rest of this year."

The two women could not contain their happiness and good fortune and got down to kiss Cephas' feet; but he stepped back, exclaiming, "Do not thank me! You must thank Lord Ishia of Nazerat for He has instructed me to give up my home. Take care of it for it was built by my father."

The women wanted to kiss Ishia's feet; but He objected and began to play with their children. Finally, everyone was called for breakfast, which they shared by dipping pieces of bread into the delicious olive dip.

Chapter 16

KFAR-NAHUM

The two boats sailed towards Kfar-Nahum, riding the morning breeze. Cephas steered his boat and Andros took care of the sail. Ishia and the women were on Cephas' boat. Judas and Yakov were helping the sons of Zebedeus with their vessel. It was not a strong wind but it was steady, giving enough push for the heavy fishing boats to glide northeastward. It took a little over one hour to cover approximately seven miles of water. As the boats sailed closer to the bustling port of Kfar-Nahum, a crowd congregated on the shore. It was clear that they knew of Ishia's coming. As the boats reached shallow water, Judas recognized Lydia and Linus with their mother, Lady Miryam. The three anxiously awaited Ishia, as joy and happiness reigned over their countenances. It was not difficult for Judas to understand their excitement. Following Ishia had been a daily adventure full of excitement and unknown wonders.

The two boats came to a halt as their bottoms coasted on a sandy section of the pebbly shore. Ishia immediately stood up and raised His right hand. The clamor of the excited crowd diminished to whispers and then to total silence as He kept His right arm up. As He scanned the crowd, He noticed several Pharishaiya. He knew that they had been sent by Kaiaphas to make trouble and to try to turn the crowd against Him.

"Peace be with you. I am happy to be here in Kfar-Nahum, my new home," announced Ishia.

The crowd cheered Him, welcoming Him to their town.

Yakov and Judas jumped down from the boat to make way for Lord Ishia. The sons of Zebedeus, Yakov and Yehohanan, followed them to help. Cephas and Andros helped the women to get down from their boat. Ishia got down last, walked directly towards Lydia and hugged and kissed her. He then hugged and kissed Lady Miryam; and, then He hugged Linus. Judas hugged and kissed all three on their cheeks. Ishia introduced His mother and brother to Lady Miryam, Lydia, and Linus. He then introduced His first chosen four, and Sarah and Esther to His future in-laws.

"My husband and I have taken the liberty to purchase a house for You and Your family, My Lord," quietly spoke Lady Miryam.

"You will like it, sweet Ishia. I helped to find it. After all we will be living in it soon," whispered Lydia on His ear.

"You have gone through a lot of trouble and expenses for me, my dearly beloved," replied Ishia.

"There was no trouble but only love in searching for Your house, and no expenses but only sharing with the people we love," said Lady Miryam.

"You are so wonderful and generous with My Son. You are all as loving and as graceful as Ishia told me," spoke Miryam.

"It is our honor and good fortune, blessed mother!" exclaimed Lydia, as she proceeded to hug her with the greatest affection.

"You are full of love, my child," replied Miryam.

Ishia and His brother smiled at all the affection among His loved ones. Judas and the rest looked on, happy to see their Lord smile for He had a beautiful smile, which demonstrated His happiness at that moment. They all stared at Him, as did the crowd, for everyone clearly saw His wonder and splendor shining through.

A young boy at the left corner of the crowd caught Ishia's eye. He was no more than seven years old, yet he held the scars of a poor and miserable life. His right eye was purple and his nose was swollen, whose nostrils were encrusted with dried blood. His left leg bore the testimony of brutal beatings, full of badly healed cuts; and, he limped from a deformed right leg, which had four bumps protruding from its knee and a swollen ankle and a twisted foot. Ishia's smile suddenly changed to anguish as He felt the young boy's pain and misery. Tears swelled in His eyes as He incorporated the pain and torment of the emaciated boy. His misery and misfortune were the clothes he wore and people moved away from him as if he had leprosy. Ishia began to walk towards him, as His saddened heart could not stand the young boy's pain any longer. Ishia knelt down on His right knee to reach the young boy's eye level, as he looked down, embarrassed by his state of being.

"He is deaf and dumb!" exclaimed a rough voice from the crowd.

Ishia turned around and asked, "Who said that?"

No one answered.

"Who is the man who said that?" asked Ishia staring towards the direction that the voice had come from.

Once again there was total silence from the crowd. He sensed fear within some of the people near the man that had spoken. Ishia turned around to the young boy and offered His hand to him, which he took. As Ishia led the way, together they walked towards the center of the crowd. Ishia moved slowly, allowing the young boy to limp slowly beside Him. The boy stopped as Ishia had come to a halt, facing a wild-looking man who stood behind a few people trying to hide from Him. The man looked down for he could not return Ishia's powerful gaze.

"You are the boy's father!" exclaimed Ishia. "Come forth, I command you."

The wild man pushed the people out of his way and charged Ishia with a violent fury. His attack was stopped as Ishia's right palm connected with his face. The wild man was stunned and fell to his knees.

"You are the boy's father, are you not?"

"Yes, I am!" exclaimed the raucous voice emanating from the wild man. "And you are the Holy One of God!"

"He is possessed, Master," spoke an elderly man.

"How long as he been possessed, my good man?" asked Ishia.

"Since he was a young man, Master," replied the old man.

"You have been there too long; it is now time to come out," said Ishia as he faced the wild man once again. "In the Name of My Father, I command you to come out of this man!"

The wild man began to squirm around spasmodically, his body continually beating on the sand. Suddenly, his body succumbed to

Ishia's order and rested on the sand. The man had lost that wild look and seemed lost and confused.

"Stand up, Henoch, you are cured," gently spoke Ishia.

Many people in the crowd began to murmur, asking themselves questions concerning Ishia. He had commanded the evil demon in the Name of His Father. He had known the possessed man's name when no one had uttered it. That He was the Mashiah or the Son of God spread quickly through the crowd. The noise came to a stop as Ishia once again turned to the young crippled boy, who was silently crying.

"Do not cry, Manasheh, for your father will never hurt you again. Do you want to get better, my sweet child?" asked Ishia.

"He is deaf and dumb, My Lord," trembled Henoch.

"Being deaf and dumb was his only defense against the fury that possessed you, Henoch. Manasheh has never been deaf and dumb. Isn't it so my child?"

"Yes," whispered young Manasheh, crying.

"Do not cry, my son, for today you will be reborn. You want to be able to run and play with other children, my sweet child?"

"Yes, Lord," whispered the boy.

"Come into the water with me and let us wash away the dried blood and all the cruelty you have experienced, for today you will begin a new life with me," gently spoke Ishia as the crowd was mesmerized by His power and love for those two poor souls.

Manasheh clutched His hand once again and with some assurance he limped along with the Son of God until his crippled little feet touched the waters of Yam Kinneret.

"Take your robe off, my child," said Ishia.

The young boy hesitated at first, but for the first time in his life he had experienced courage and at that moment he removed his torn ragged robe, exposing his scabby and beaten back to the crowd. Cries of shock and anguish came from the crowd; but the most painful cry reverberated from Henoch. He had finally realized the pain and suffering he had inflicted on his own son in the past seven years since his birth.

Ishia stepped deeper into the water, inviting young Manasheh to join him, "Do not be afraid, my child; come into the water."

Still clutching His hand, Manasheh limped into the water until it reached his shoulders. At that moment, Ishia looked up into the sky and, raising His hands up high, He began to pray. He then took some water with His cupped hands and gently washed the young boy's face. He continued to wash his face until it was free of blood. He smiled at Manasheh and he smiled back, and it was a wonderful and beautiful smile. Ishia's heart had begun to be uplifted as He continued to wash Manasheh's back, totally oblivious to the crowd. He took Manasheh's crippled leg and began to wash it with intense concentration as the child held himself on Ishia's belt. Then, he repeated the same massage-wash on his left leg until He chose to end it. Judas had been hypnotized by the entire event and his belief and love for Ishia had immensely grown. He had never expected to witness such love and power. At that moment, Judas knew that the young boy had been entirely cured.

As they emerged from the water, everyone clearly saw the young boy's new body, completely free of any deformity or scar. His handsome face was free of scars, of bruises, and of encrusted blood. His legs were free of scars and his bones were not deformed any longer. He walked slowly for he would have to get used to walking normally. He would learn how to run! He smiled and hugged Ishia as He kissed his forehead. Lydia came to them, removing her new white shawl and wrapped it around little Manasheh like a robe. He hugged her like his own mother for his mother had died during his birth.

The three reached the crying Henoch, surrounded by a mystified crowd. Ishia spoke, "Manasheh, here is your father. Henoch, here is your son. I give you both my blessing and my love."

Both father and son embraced each other, crying.

"Henoch!" said Ishia, "Learn to love your son and everyone you meet. You shall never strike a person again. If your enemy strikes your cheek do not strike him back; instead, give him your other cheek. From now on, you and your beautiful child shall follow me wherever I shall go."

"Forgive me, My Lord. Forgive my wickedness," replied Henoch on his knees, as his son stood by him.

"Your wife died of complications at your son's birth; but he was not the cause of her death."

Henoch's face was in shock as he spoke, "How is it possible for you to have known this. You are truly the Son of God, Ishia of Nazerat. I will follow you until I die. I will never hurt anyone again, I make this promise in front of my son and all of these people shall be my witnesses."

"Get up, now; and, follow me," whispered Ishia. Then He turned around to his mother and Sarah and told them to feed Manasheh for he was desperately in need of nutrition.

The young boy ate some cold cooked fish and some bread as they followed Ishia and His friends to see His new home. Kfar-Nahum would be His new home; and, the crowd followed Him for they knew Who He was.

Centurion Augustus Horatius and Lady Miryam had not been skimpy with their money for they had purchased a beautiful home for Ishia and Lydia, and His immediate family. A retired Roman officer had gone back to Rome and had sold his furnished villa for a tidy sum. It had been a magnificent opportunity for Augustus Horatius to demonstrate his appreciation of Lord Ishia for having saved him and his beloved wife; and, it had also been good for the retired officer. He was going home with a fortune, which he could live off it for the rest of his life.

Augustus Horatius was from a noble Roman family, which dated back centuries when Rome was only a fortified city. One of his ancestors, Publius Horatius Cocles, had single-handedly defended the bridge leading to Rome against an attack by Etruscans. And three other Horatii brothers had fought the powerful Curiatii brothers at Alba Longa. The champions' city would rule the others'. The Horatii brothers had won and they had become the champions of Rome; and, they were given the status of nobility. Centurion Augustus Horatius was a direct descendant of that noble family, inheriting a fortune. Throughout his life the good centurion had learned to use some of that money very well, in rewarding many people who had been good to him. He had learned to be extremely generous with those people and he treated his servants as equal because he believed that all people were basically equal. He did not believe in slavery and had to close his eyes to Rome's slave trade; and, that was a major reason for living in Galilee. Life in Galilee was different than in Rome. Periodically, he and his family would visit Rome and his native house, where his parents still lived; but he would always look forward to return to his Galilean custom post. He had also paid for the building of a new synagogue in Kfar-Nahum, which had become his hometown. When he had been assigned to Yeriho he had taken the post with reluctance; but he had never stopped asking to be reassigned to Kfar-Nahum. The Jews of that city respected him and he respected them. Once again, Augustus Horatius and his family were back in their beloved city; and, they had done whatever possible to make it also Lord Ishia's new hometown.

The following day Ishia met two men who were looking for Him, named Philip and Nathanael. Philip introduced Lord Ishia to his friend, "He is the One that Moishe wrote about in the Law. He is the One who the great prophets wrote about. I like to introduce you to Lord Ishia, son of Yoseph, from Nazerat."

"From Nazerat?" questioned Nathanael. "Can anything good come from that Godforsaken place?"

"Now, there is an Yisraelite who deserves the name, *Incapable of deceit*," said Ishia to Philip.

"How did you know my name?" asked Nathanael.

"Before Philip came to call you," answered Ishia, "I saw you under a fig tree."

"How is that possible that you know that? Forgive me, Rabbi, you are truly the Son of God, the King of Yisrael," cried Nathanael.

"You believe because I saw you under a fig tree, far away from here; but, if you follow me, you will see greater things than that. Stay with me and both of you shall see the heavens lay open, above me, and My Father's angels ascending and descending from the sky."

Both men followed Him to His new home and became His disciples.

Ishia, Miryam, Yakov, Judas, and his first chosen followers had comfortably settled in the villa, which was protected by a stonewall and gate. However, Ishia could not accept such luxuries without sharing it. Within weeks of having moved in, the inside of the villa looked like a combination of a soup kitchen and an emergency room of a large hospital, thought Judas. The four fishermen were still fishing and their catch was used to feed the poor, which would line up daily for fish soup, bread and a piece of fish. This kept the fishermen and the women busy from early morning to late evenings. While they kept busy with their daily chores, Ishia was constantly taking care of the sick. He would cure them, whether they were physically or mentally sick. He cured the crippled, the possessed, the wounded, and people that were dying. At times, Lady Miryam and Lydia would not recognize the villa; but they would stay and help for it was evident how much Ishia loved the poor and the needy. It was wonderful for them and everyone to see their Lord curing the hopeless and the dying. It was wonderful to see how much love He had for His people. There was never a dull moment at Lord Ishia's villa.

One very busy morning, in the midst of hungry and sick people, several men and two women carrying a paralyzed man on a pallet were desperately trying to get him into the villa, where Ishia had been performing His wondrous works. When the crowd made it impossible for them to pass; they decided to take the paralyzed man through the opening of the atrium. Having climbed the tiled roof, four of the men lowered the pallet with ropes.

Ishia, knowing that a few Pharishaiya were present in the crowd, was waiting for the opportune moment to provoke them for He knew they had been sent to destroy His mission. As Ishia saw the pallet with the paralyzed man slowly descending from the atrium's opening He knew that it was an opportune moment to ridicule those vultures dressed in black.

"Man, your sins are forgiven," Ishia told the paralyzed man, waiting for a reaction from the two-faced Pharishaiya.

"Who are you to blaspheme in front of all these people? Only God can forgive sins," yelled the elder of the Pharishaiya present.

"Haven't you seen enough this very morning to realize Who I am? Why do you vultures argue in your hearts? Which is easier for me to say, 'Your sins are forgiven' or 'Get up and walk'. But, I will prove to you that My Father has given me the power to do both!" exclaimed Ishia. Then, turning to the paralytic, He said, "Not only are your sins forgiven but I order you to get up, pick up your stretcher and go back home."

The Pharishaiya were furious; but their hatred turned to confusion when they witnessed the paralytic slowly getting up from his pallet and slowly standing up. Without saying a word, the former paralytic untied the ropes, picked up his pallet and began to make his way home as the crowd made space for him to pass. The four men on the roof began to shout "Ishia of Nazerat, the Mashìah" and the crowd became hysterical with joy and began to mock the Pharishaiya, who quickly left the villa.

The boisterous morning had passed by quickly and the afternoon had begun with a series of questions from the crowd about the Mosaic Laws and about good and evil, which Ishia had gladly explained or answered. A middle-age man had asked Him, "Lord, why do the Pharishaiya and the followers of Yehohanan the Baptist fast often and always pray but your followers go on working, eating, and drinking?"

"Surely you cannot make the bridegroom's friends fast while the bridegroom is still with them?" replied Ishia. "But the time will come when the bridegroom will be taken away from them; and, that will be the time when they will fast."

At that moment Augustus Horatius made his way through the crowd, followed by his son, Linus, two Roman soldiers, and the Pharishaiya, which had been mocked. The crowd quickly made room, fearing the worst; but Ishia stood up and welcomed His future in-laws with an embrace and happiness.

"I haven't seen you in a while Augustus. You are very busy with your work, my good friend," Ishia greeted him.

"My Lord, I see that You are very busy yourself, helping anyone that comes to You," cried the centurion.

"What troubles you, my beloved friend?"

"My Lord, Shimon, my beloved servant, Eva's husband is dying. He is so sick, My Lord, that I don't think he will make it through the day. Please, Lord, cure him for I love him like my own brother."

"Quickly, let us go to him," suggested Ishia.

"Do not trouble Yourself, My Lord, for I am not worthy to have You under my roof. I know that You are the Son of God and that You only have to say the word and my servant will be cured."

Ishia closed His eyes for a moment and seemed to be in deep meditation. Once finished with His powerful meditation, He turned around to the crowd and said, "I tell all of you that nowhere in Yisrael Have I found faith as strong as this man's." Then, facing the centurion, He continued, "Go, my beloved friend. Your servant, Shimon, has been cured."

The centurion hugged Ishia and kissed His cheeks, thanking Him for the life of Shimon. He then bowed, as did Linus and the two soldiers, and left in a hurry. The Pharishaiya went along, as did most of the crowd.

It was the first afternoon in which the house was empty, with the exception of Judas and the women. His brother Yakov had gone fishing with Cephas, Andros, the other Yakov, and young Yehohanan. He asked Judas if he would join Him for a walk along the shore, which Judas gladly accepted for a change of scenery.

Some of the crowd went back to His home to announce the wonderful news that the centurion's servant had been healed. The crowd was excited for this had been no ordinary miracle and they were glad to spread the news. However, when they reached His home Lord Ishia was not there.

Chapter 17

HYPOCRITES DRESSED IN BLACK

Kaiaphas, the high priest in Yerushalayim, could not stand the idea of a *mashìah* when he had been chosen as the high priest of the Temple of Yerushalayim. And if Ishia of Nazareth was truly the Mashìah, why hadn't he come to see him. After all, he was the highest spiritual leader in Yisrael. Yehohanan the Baptist was nothing but a crazy wild man blurting out idiocies in the desert to a bunch of renegade religious fanatics. He was not worried about Yehohanan because one day he would rot in jail for saying something nasty about Herod Antipas and his brother's wife, Herodias. It was the Nazarene that bothered him. Together with the San-hedrin he felt justified to send some of his spies to see if Ishia was truly the Mashìah or another charlatan pretending to be the Holy One. And, he could not think of any better persons for that job than a group of law-abiding Pharishaiya who followed the Mosaic Law to the last letter.

The group of Pharishaiya and their scribes had tried everything and anything to be wherever Ishia was staying; but during the past several months they had had bad luck in locating the Nazarene. He and his strange traveling companion had traveled through the desert, along wadis and rivers, and cut through the steep rocks and mountains of Yisrael, knowingly or unknowingly eluding them like the plague. Even when the Pharishaiya reached Nazerat it had been too late; however, they had been thrilled in finding out that he, his friend, and the rest of his family had been thrown out of their

138

hometown accompanied by a shower of rocks. He might have even been wounded by one of those rocks for there were many in Nazerat claiming to have hit him. Once again, they had missed him in Magdala and Genne-Sareth; but one of their scribes had learned that his next town would be Kfar-Nahum and that he would remain there for years, making that port his new home. They had him now! They had immediately traveled to Kfar-Nahum and had been part of the welcoming crowd at the shore of Yam Kinneret.

The hot midday sun bleached the shore of Kfar-Nahum as the two boats touched its sand, coming back from an early morning fishing trip. Ishia, His brother Yakov, and Judas had joined the four fishermen for that morning's catch, which had been bountiful. As usual, a welcoming party of poor and sick people was waiting for Lord Ishia, the Mashìah. Among them were the Pharishaiya and their scribes carefully questioning several people in the crowd, concerning who Ishia was. They had to be careful with their questions for it was no secret that the people loved their Ishia. Of course, how could the poor and the lame not love him when he generously shared his rich villa, the catch of the day, and somehow heal their sicknesses and take away their miseries. Ishia of Nazerat was truly the long awaited Mashìah or he got his powers through the Devil himself. And, they were going to prove the latter; and, they would use any means to justify their end.

Many of the poor people who had been eating daily at His house had come to greet Him and to help carry the catch back to His kitchen. That day the fishermen had caught more than twenty basketfuls of fish and all of them with the exception of Ishia were each carrying a basketful. The other baskets of fish were being carried by some of the regulars who had been eating daily at Ishia's house. They would not allow their Mashìah to carry fish. Every time Ishia was ready to lift a basket of fish some poor follower would take it away from His grasp.

The Pharishaiya mingled with the crowd as they followed the long parade of basket carriers along the narrow streets of Kfar-Nahum. Suddenly, Ishia stopped at a small square and everyone came to a halt and rested. The Pharishaiya pushed their way to the front to see what *'the impostor'* was up to. Ishia had stopped by a customs house and had invited a tax collector, named Levi, to follow Him.

Levi left everything on his table and followed Ishia. No one would touch the money for two roman guards were present at the customs house.

"Will you follow me, Levi?" asked Ishia.

"My Lord, I know that You are the Mashìah, the Only Son of God. I will follow You, Lord; but, You must know beforehand that I am a sinner," responded the small rotund Levi.

"Admitting that you are a sinner, Levi, is the first step to healing your spirit. Your sins are forgiven!" exclaimed Ishia, knowing very well that Pharishaiya and their scribes surrounded him.

"There he goes again, blaspheming. Only God could forgive sins; and you are definitely not His Son," shouted one of the Pharishaiya.

"You hypocrites dressed in black! I can see your souls in broad daylight and they are as dark as the clothes you wear. Do not judge me or anyone else and you will not be judged. But you easily judge me and others you do not agree with; therefore, you shall be easily judged by me and by the poor people you attack with your accusations and false incriminations. Your self-righteousness has blinded your ability to judge what is right and what is wrong. Your hypocrisy and hatred of the poor and the sick has blackened your souls and withered your hearts. You cannot see who I am for you are blind. Look at Levi, a tax collector, and look at all these people. Who are they? Simple people, poor people, sick people, but they ask me for help, which I will not refuse. Their souls are only spotted and I can clean them. Their hearts are open and I fill them with my love. You vultures I cannot help for your souls are drowning in the sins of pride and self-righteousness and your hearts are closed to love. If you want to be saved you must open up your hearts and accept my love. I have permitted all of you, Pharishaiya and scribes, to enter my house, hoping that you might open up your hearts; but I see that you have no intention to do so. From this moment on, I forbid you to enter my house, unless you are willing to repent and are ready to accept my love. If you do not intend to repent stay away from me for I shall ridicule you and expose your dark souls for everyone to see," retorted Ishia.

All of the Pharishaiya and scribes made their way out of the square, heads bowed, shamed by the sharp Nazarene.

It was Levi who broke the silence that Ishia's fury of words had commanded, "Lord, this evening, would You and Your disciples dine with me and my friends at my house. The feast I will give will be in Your honor, My Lord, My Savior."

"How could I refuse such an honorable and sincere invitation? I and my disciples will gladly come," answered Ishia.

The crowd cheered and followed Ishia to His house, where He began to cure anyone who was sick, as His mother and the women, who had increased in number, were preparing a meal for the crowd.

The Pharishaiya had not given up that easily and later, that evening, they followed Ishia, Judas, Yakov and the other disciples, who had also increased in number, to the house of Levi.

Levi, the tax collector, had invited four colleagues, three other rich people in town, and three prostitutes to dine with Ishia and His disciples. Two long tables had been set in the open courtyard to accommodate everyone invited. A belly dancer and a musician were entertaining the group. Ishia and His followers had been seated, with Ishia on a special chair for the party was to honor Him. He was extremely polite with Levi and his friends; and, He had earlier instructed His disciples to behave in the same fashion. Everyone enjoyed the food, which was abundant; and, the wine from Arbelah was delicious. The belly dancer was entertaining as the music guided her every move. Levi was happy and kept toasting to Lord Ishia.

The Pharishaiya were once again part of the crowd that stood watching the party from the other side of the wall, which gave Levi's courtyard a little privacy. However, the wall was no more than five feet tall and most of the people in that crowd, including the Pharishaiya, were on their tiptoes to see what was going on.

One of the Pharishaiya spoke to the disciples, which sat at the end of one of the tables, only a few feet away from the wall, "Why does he eat with gentile tax collectors and sinners? Are you not ashamed to eat supper next to gentiles and whores?"

Ishia's keen hearing missed nothing that was said; and He promptly replied, "It is not the healthy who need the doctor, but the sick. I did not come to this earth to call the virtuous, but sinners." And turning once again to all invited, He said "Levi, are you ready to renounce your home, give away all your wealth and follow me?"

All of Levi's rich friends and colleagues, and the prostitutes were shocked by what Lord Ishia was asking of Levi; but the small rotund man had already made up his mind and seemed ready to answer.

"My Lord," he replied, "I am happy that You have chosen me and I am happy to give away all of my wealth. All my life, I have been taking away tax money from everyone. Now, it is my turn to give everyone some of that money back. I will sell this house at a fair price and distribute that money among the poor. And I will follow You, My Lord, until I die."

The other tax collectors and friends were shocked by Levi's answer. It was difficult for them to imagine Levi following Lord Ishia around Yisrael and living like the homeless, at times with no food and no money. The disciples were happy for Levi for having made the right choice. The crowd cheered Levi and the Pharishaiya were confused for they, too, enjoyed comfort and money.

Smiling, Ishia said, "You are a good man, Levi; and, now that you have accepted my calling your name shall be Matthias from this very moment on."

"Why not Levi, Lord?" asked Cephas.

"For the same reason that Levi will always be associated with a tax collector. Matthias, just like you, is starting a new way of life."

One of the other tax collectors had always liked Levi's house and he made him a reasonable offer, which Matthias accepted. He spent the following few days paying back any debts and distributed the rest of the money among the poor. He was then free to follow His Savior, Lord Ishia, Son of the Most High.

Chapter 18

THE IMPORTANCE OF PRAYER

From the very first time that he had seen Ishia, on top of Jebel Har Montar, until that very day, Judas had always witnessed Lord Ishia pray. The Lord would wait until everyone would be asleep and then He would pray. He had now been with the Lord for over a year and Judas had always tried to stay awake to be with His Savior, as each night He would kneel down and pray to His Father. No matter where they were, in the desert, on top of mountains, by the shore of a wadi or a river, or as a guest in someone's house, at night He would kneel by a large rock or under a tree or besides His bed and He would pray. Judas, quietly, without disturbing, would kneel nearby and join Him in prayer or deep meditation. At times, Judas would see rivulets of tears streaming down His cheeks for Ishia would incorporate within His powerful inner Self all the misery and suffering of His people. He would take in, within His Spirit, all the sins and horrors that He would encounter daily. He would see the starving and the sick and take all of that misery within Himself. And, all of that suffering and misery would haunt Him during His prayers. It was so much too take! Judas would cry along with Him, for he very well knew where all of that would lead to, His passion and crucifixion. Lord Ishia knew all that would happen to Him; and His human side found it difficult to accept. All of these sufferings would be so vivid in His mind that He would, at times, ask His Father if there was any other way to show His people how to love, for the ultimate proof of

143

His love was to sacrifice His human life to erase all sins and begin anew. But, He also knew that the original nature of mankind was evil. The basic Ten Commandments that His Father had instituted long ago had only touched a smaller percentage of mankind. Most people, throughout the earth, still stole, lied, coveted others' properties and wives, killed, enslaved their fellow men, believed in false gods, and showed no love for their neighbors, no understanding of their enemies. It would take at least two millennia for people to be aware of the most precious gift of love; and, still there would be evil people in power that would destroy entire nations and eventually annihilate most of the earth's population. Ishia knew this very well for He had living proof of what was to come with His beloved friend, Judas. But, if He would not go through His final Self-sacrifice, the people of this planet would not enjoy the beginning of the third millennium for they would obliterate mankind. He would come to that realization whenever He had doubts about His purpose and mission on earth; and, He would come to that realization whenever He would turn around and see Judas keeping Him company, trying to emulate Him in prayer. He would go through His ultimate sacrifice even if it were only for Judas. He knew that Judas would give up his life for Him; and, for that very reason it was clear that He would go through death itself.

One hot summer morning, a Shabbat, Lord Ishia wished to go to the mountains, northwest of Kfar-Nahum and midway on the road to Genne-Sareth, to instruct all of His followers on the importance of love and prayer. He had asked Cephas to take a dozen men with him and sail the two fishing boats along the shore. They would need thousands of fish to feed the thousands of followers that had traveled from the four directions of Yisrael to be with Him, to listen to His wonderful messages and to be healed by Him. During the two days before that hot summer Shabbat, He had instructed His mother to bake several hundred loaves of bread, to feed a large population. Dozens of women had been busy making dough and baking all of that bread. The two brick ovens had been working night and day. Cephas and his men would bring the catch to be cooked while He would be giving His sermon. All the bread and fish would then be loaded on two horse driven carts that Augustus Horatius had promised Him for that reason. Cephas and his men would bring the food to the foothills by early afternoon. That was the plan that Ishia had come up with to feed such a crowd.

As Ishia traveled along the road to Genne-Sareth, His disciples and thousands of followers created the longest procession of people that the Pharishaiya had ever seen. Some of them began to think about the Nazarene. Could he possibly be the true Mashìah? And if he was the Holy One, they were wasting their energy trying to falsify his claim and they were going against the prophecies. Would they be damned? Were their souls really as dark as their clothes? These questions probed through some of the Pharishaiya's brains on that hot Shabbat morning. As they traveled along the road, besides fields of golden grain, some of the followers had plucked some grain, and rubbing them with their hands, were eating them because they were hungry.

One of the Pharishaiya exclaimed, "Why are you plucking grain on this Shabbat morning?"

Another said, "If you are the Mashìah, why are you allowing them to break the law of Shabbat? It is forbidden to do anything on Shabbat!"

"Did you ever read what David and his followers did when they were starving?" retorted Ishia. "Didn't you read how King David and his men entered the Holy Temple, when Abiathar was the high priest, and ate all the loaves of offering. Only priests may have eaten those loaves; however, David and his men devoured them because they were in need of food. The Shabbat was made for man, not man for the Shabbat. I am the Son of Man and I am master even of the Shabbat. Now, would you likewise like to pluck your own and savor the fresh taste of mature grain?"

Outraged, the Pharishaiya moved to the back of the crowd, away from *the impostor*, still following him hoping to trap him in front of that multitude to expose his deceitfulness.

Ishia had reached the foothills northwest of Kfar-Nahum and had asked the people to sit down on the slope so that they might hear what He had to say. It took a while, with the help of His disciples to coach the large multitude that occupied the slope and all the boulders that surrounded it. Thousands of people had come from the surrounding villages and towns of Hagalil, from Yehuda, from Yerushalayim, from Idumaea, from Samaria, from Perea and

Decapolis, and from Tyre and Shidon. They had all come to see the Mashìah, the Savior of Yisrael. Most of them had a personal reason to see Him or even to touch Him; but, the sole purpose of the Pharishaiya was to expose him as a charlatan and the sole purpose of the zealots was to have him as their leader against the Romans. Ishia knew all of that and He was hoping that most of them would see the light to the words He was about to speak.

With the help of Judas, Ishia had managed to climb a large boulder, at least ten feet in height. It would be His podium for His sermon. As He stood on top of the boulder He looked taller and magnificent. Judas sat a few feet away from Him. As He raised His arms, stretched out wide, the tumult of the multitude began to decrease until only a slight wind could be heard.

"My beloved, I wish you love and peace on this sunny Shabbat morning. I recognize many of you who have been at my house; but, many of you are new, from faraway places and I am happy that you have come. How happy are the poor in spirit, for theirs is the kingdom of heaven. Happy are the gentle for they shall inherit the earth. Happy are those who mourn for they shall be comforted. Happy are those who hunger and thirst for justice for they shall be satisfied. Happy are the merciful for others shall be merciful to them. Happy are the pure in heart for they shall see God. Happy are the peacemakers for they shall be called children of God. Happy are those who are persecuted in their pursuit of justice for theirs is the kingdom of heaven. Happy are you if you shall be abused, persecuted, or falsely accused because of your belief in me: rejoice and be happy for your reward will be great in heaven. The great prophets of old were abused, persecuted, and falsely accused because of their belief in My Father."

"Blasphemer!" shouted a Pharish.

"Who accused me of blaspheming? I see that the accuser does not have the courage to admit his accusation. I do not blaspheme; I speak only the truth. If you seek the truth; then, you have found it, for I am the Truth. You are all like the salt of the earth. But if the salt becomes tasteless it is good for nothing, and it can only be thrown out to be trampled by everyone. You are the light of the world. A city built on a mountain is there for everyone to see. No one lights a lamp and hides its glow; it is placed on a stand so that it may illuminate the house. In the same way, your spirit must shine for everyone to see so that they may appreciate its splendor."

Absolute silence reigned over the multitude; and, the Pharishaiya were too afraid to shout any insults for the people next to them were showing anger and contempt towards them.

"Do not even think that I have come to destroy the Law or the Prophets. I have not come to this world to destroy the Law or prophecies; I have come to fulfill them. Truly, I tell you, until the end of heaven and earth, not one dot or stroke shall disappear from the Law till all of it shall be fulfilled. Therefore, anyone who breaks the least of My Father's Commandments and teaches others to do the same will be considered the least in the kingdom of heaven. But great will be anyone who lives according to the Commandments and teaches others to live according to the Law," spoke Ishia, and then pointing to the group of Pharishaiya and scribes He continued with a firmer voice, "And I say to all of you: if your morals are no better than the Pharishaiya's and scribes' you will never enter the kingdom of heaven. The Commandments say 'You must not kill', and if anyone kills he will be brought before a court. But I say to you this morning, if anyone is angry with another that person will also be brought before a court. If anyone falsely accuses or judges others he will answer for it in the fire of Gehenna, in the Valley of Hinnom, where criminals are executed and burnt. Therefore, if you are bringing your offering to My Father's altar, make sure you have already reconciled with your fellow men. If you are still angry with anyone, do not bother to present an offering at My Father's altar. You must be at peace with everyone before you enter My Father's Temple. Make up with your enemy or accuser before you enter the court or the judge will throw you into prison. And I truly say to you, you will not get out until you have paid the last penny."

Judas listened to everything that Ishia had said and sighed, incorporating it all within.

"The Commandments say 'You must not commit adultery'; but I say to you: if any man lusts after another woman, he has already committed adultery with her in his heart. If your right eye causes you to sin tear it out and throw it away, for it is better to have only one eye than to have your entire body thrown into hell. And if your right hand causes you to sin cut it off and throw it away, for it is better to have only one hand than to have your entire body thrown into hell. The Law also says that if any man divorces his wife he must give her a written notice of dismissal. But I say to you that anyone who divorces his wife, except for the case of fornication, makes her an adulteress; and, any man who marries a divorced woman commits adultery.

"The Law says that you must not break your oath and that you must fulfill your oaths to the Lord. But I say to you, do not swear at all: neither by Paradise for it is God's throne, nor by the earth for it is His footstool, nor by Yerushalayim for it is the sacred city of the great King. Neither should you swear by your head for you cannot change a single hair to white or black. Never swear again! You simply have to learn to say 'yes' if you mean yes and 'no' if you mean no. Swearing comes from the evil within man.

"The Law says 'An eye for an eye and a tooth for a tooth'. But I say to you: do not resist the attack of a wicked person. On the contrary, if anyone strikes you on the right cheek, offer him your left as well. If a man wants your robe, let him also have your cloak as well. And if anyone orders you to go one mile with him, go a second mile with him. Give anyone anything that he asks or wants to borrow; and, never turn anyone away."

A murmur traveled throughout the multitude.

"I never said that it was going to be easy! It is easy to break the Law and the Ten Commandments; it requires no effort. What is difficult is to obey the Law and to live by the Ten Commandments for it requires a daily struggle between good and evil within each one of you."

Everyone nodded, agreeing with what Ishia was saying.

"You have learned the old rule: love your neighbor and hate your enemy. From this day on, you must love your enemies and you must pray for those who persecute you. Praying is powerful and if you pray for your enemies and love everyone you will become the children of God in Paradise. The sun rises equally on bad and good men; and, the rain falls equally on honest and dishonest men. It is easy to love those who love you; that does not give you the right to claim credit. Even the tax collectors do as much, do they not? And if you greet only your loved ones, are you doing anything exceptional? You must learn to greet everyone equally; and, you must learn to love everyone equally. If you do this, you shall have no enemies but only friends. You might say: it is very difficult to do this. You are right! What I ask of you is extremely difficult; but unless you become full of love towards the whole mankind, you cannot reach perfection. Therefore, you must reach that perfection through love and then you will be part of that perfect Paradise, where My Father lives.

"Be careful not to parade your good deeds in front of everyone, like the hypocrites who do so in the synagogues and streets to win others' admiration. If you give alms, give them away secretly without letting anyone know who you are. God will reward you for He can see you. When you pray, do not imitate the hypocrites, who say their prayers standing up in the synagogues and street corners so that everyone can see them. Those prayers are lost and not heard by God. If you pray, do so in private, in your room or a in a secret place, for God shall be there to hear you and reward you. When you fast, do not be a hypocrite and let the whole world know. If you must fast, do it privately without letting it interfere with your daily duties. God will see you and He will reward you. Do not store treasures for yourselves on earth, for they can be stolen. Store the true treasures in your heart for no one will be able to take them away from you.

"The lamps of your body are your eyes: if your eyes are used soundly, your body will be filled with light; if your eyes are used wickedly, your body will be in total darkness. No one can have two masters: he will either hate the first and love the second, or treat the first with respect and the second with scorn. You cannot be the slave both of God and money. Give up money for it is the root of all that is evil.

"Do not worry about your future and about food. Do not spend all your time buying rich clothes for your body. Life means more than food, and the body more than clothing. Look at the birds in the sky!" He exclaimed, pointing to several birds that were flying above them, "They do not sow or reap or congregate in barns; yet, our heavenly Father feeds them. Are you not worth much more than they are? Can any one of you add one single second to his life by worrying? And why worry about clothes? Look at the flowers in the fields; they never have to work or spin. I tell you: not even King Solomon in his entire splendor was clothed better than any of those flowers. If God clothes the grass in the field which will be soon burned, won't He better care for you, you of little faith. So, do not worry; do not say, 'What are we to eat? What are we to drink? What are we to wear?' Pagans think and live that way! Your heavenly Father knows you need all of these things. Set your heart on His Kingdom and on being righteous and loving and all of those things shall be given to you. Do not worry about tomorrow for tomorrow will take care of itself. Each day has enough trouble of its own."

Ishia paused for a moment and then continued with His sermon, "Do not judge anyone and you will not be judged, for the judgments you give will be the judgments you get. Do not pray in front of others to show how pious you are for it will be in vain. Privately, ask God and it will be given to you. Search and you will find; knock, and the door will be opened to you. For the one who asks always receives; the one who searches always finds; and, the one who knocks will always have the door opened to him. Even if you are wicked, you do not give a stone to your son if he asks for food. Your Father in heaven will enrich your spirit to all of you that ask. Do not ask for money, for it can be stolen; do not ask for treasures for they can be lost; but, ask for love and good knowledge, for those riches will always be treasured in your hearts. Always treat others the way you want them to treat you. That is the meaning of God's Commandments. If you decide to follow me and you decide to spread my teaching, you better decide to first live the way I have told you and then you may preach it. You cannot spread my teaching if you cannot live by it. I will tell you to your face to be gone. You must become full of love and understanding to follow me; and then, you may spread my teaching.

"When you pray, do not pray out loud like pagans do. Pray in silence to be heard. And now, I want to teach you a prayer to Our Father. Silently, repeat after me, not with your mouths but with your hearts: Our Father in heaven, may Your name be held holy, Your kingdom come, Your will be done, on earth as in Paradise. Give us today our daily bread, and forgive us our debts, as we forgive those who are in debt to us, and do not put us to the test, but save us from our evil. Yes, if you forgive others, your heavenly Father will forgive you.

"And now, I will forgive anyone who wishes to be forgiven. Pray to Our Father with your hearts, with your minds, and with your spirits. Ask Him to forgive whatever you have done that was wrong. In the name of Our Father, I forgive your sins. Do your best not to sin anymore."

Ishia looked at the crowd, which was deeply in prayer; and, as He looked down the road, he saw Cephas, His mother, and the rest of the men and women walking along two Roman carts, each pulled by two horses. One of the carts was loaded with hundreds of bread, covered by a white cloth. The other was full of baskets, holding cooked fish, and it was covered with a light brown woolen spread. The small caravan was approximately two stadia away, only half an hour walk.

"My beloved, I want to thank you for your patience and your time that you have given me this morning. I want to let you know how much I appreciate all of you. And now, if there are any sick among you, please step forward and slowly make a line towards me. Be gentle and loving with your neighbors. Do not push anyone or try to steal someone's place. I will see everyone that comes up to me. When you have seen me, please return to your friends and family. When everyone will be taken care of, we will have bread and fish to eat. There is a spring of fresh water between those two boulders to my right. I know that some of you will be very hungry and thirsty by then."

As hundreds of people, male and female, and of all ages from old people to babies, from crippled to blind, some being helped and some being carried on stretchers, began to make a long winding line, Ishia and Judas down-climbed the big boulder, down to a small ledge. The first people were already there. Ishia closed His eyes for almost a minute Judas thought. He must have been preparing Himself for all those sick people. Ishia would be exhausted by the end of the day! Judas saw Ishia slowly open His eyes and one by one, He cured everyone either with a hug, or with a kiss, or with a loving touch. The long line moved quicker than Judas had expected. He had never seen such power in Ishia as He saw it on that day. It was clear that Ishia used peoples' energy to heal themselves. The touch, kiss, or hug was merely a trigger. What a glorious day that was by the foothills near Kfar-Nahum! He would never forget that day! And to top it all, everyone received two large slices of whole-wheat bread and a fish, even the Pharishaiya and scribes. They, too, were impressed by what Lord Ishia had done that day.

The cutting of the bread and the distribution of the fish kept all the disciples, male and female, busy for a couple of hours. Everyone looked healthy and happy. A nearby spring, which flowed through rocks, kept a steady supply of cold water for the large crowd. Everyone marveled at His words, at His miracles, and at all the food He had provided. Ishia of Nazerat was truly the Mashìah, the Son of the Most High.

Chapter 19

THE WEDDING

Monday, January 1, 31 A.D.

It was a cool and windy morning in Kfar-Nahum and Judas was assisting Lord Ishia with His new white tunic and red cloak. He was dressing for a very special occasion, His betrothal to the beautiful Lydia or their first wedding as it was called according to the customs of the Yisraelites. Their first marriage was going to take place in the columned synagogue that Augustus Horatius had financed to be built. Judas had learned that this betrothal or first wedding was a trial marriage, which permitted them to consummate it only for the purpose of having children. A second marriage ceremony would take place only if Lydia would be expecting, at the beginning of her third month of pregnancy. The woman would always be on her third month of pregnancy by the second and final wedding. If Lydia would not be pregnant, they would try again and hope for a pregnancy to finalize their marriage. That custom was observed by most religious Yisraelites. There were many who had adopted Hellenistic, Roman, and Egyptian customs, giving up most of the ancient and religious ones. Ishia and Lydia were observing that ancient marriage law.

On that cool January morning, the beautiful columned synagogue at Kfar-Nahum was filled with Ishia's family and followers and with Lydia's family and friends. Family members and honored guests were dressed in their best clothes. Augustus Horatius looked more like a Roman general than a centurion. Miryam, Ishia's mother was dressed in pure white and light blue; and, Lady Miryam wore a long white Roman tunic, made of silk, which had been made for her on their last visit to Rome. Young Linus wore a white tunic and a blue cloak, looking more Hebrew than Roman. Lydia wore her most precious white dress, also made of silk and embroidered with white flowers, and beautiful matching sandals. Her head was adorned with a crown of flowers, which also matched her dress and sandals. She was beautiful and as pure as the white lilies that grew in the Hagalil valleys. Most of Ishia's followers wore the same clothes, which had been washed for the occasion. Poor people did not have a second set of clothes.

The ceremony, which was presided by Jairosh, the rabbi of Kfar-Nahum, followed the ancient Mosaic Laws and it was rather lengthy. Augustus Horatius gave a lavish feast with imported Sicilian wine at his villa. Everyone, including Ishia's followers, had been invited. Although the tables, chairs, and benches could only accommodate the immediate families and friends, everyone was enjoying the good food and delicious wine provided by the good centurion. It was a wonderful reception and everyone enjoyed it, even the poor and destitute. Nothing went to waste. That night, after everyone had left, Ishia and Lydia retired to the villa's guest master bedroom to consummate their first marriage.

After three days with Lydia, Ishia was to leave her and continue His work; and, according to ancient customs, Lydia would still live with her parents until the second and final wedding. During that period, Ishia and Lydia were not allowed to see each other. That custom was very difficult for Ishia to accept; thus, He decided to dedicate that time traveling to the neighboring towns to help the sick, the poor, and the hungry. His disciples and followers accompanied Him, happy to be with Him. Miryam, His mother, and a few women remained in Kfar-Nahum, continuing to feed and help the poor that came daily. They also made frequent visits to Lydia and her loving family. Miryam felt that Ishia could not have found a more wonderful wife than Lydia. She was full of grace and full of love; and, she was extremely beautiful!

Ishia and His immediate disciples sailed to Genne-Sareth with the two fishing boats, while the crowd of followers traveled along the shore on foot. From Genne-Sareth they continued to Magdala, where they waited until His followers had reached them. While still waiting on the shore of Magdala, a hooded man walked up to them begging to see the Master. When several of the disciples realized that the man was covered with leprosy they stepped back, terrified by his appearance. Reaching Ishia, they told Him about the leper. Ishia and Judas began to walk towards the leper, cautiously followed by His disciples.

When they stood only five feet away, the leper fell down flat on the pebbly beach and implored Ishia, "Master, if you wish to, you can cure me."

Ishia bent down and touched the leper's shoulder and said, "Of course I wish to! Be cured!"

The man began to wriggle on the pebbles, his arms and legs squirming without control. Suddenly, he stopped; and, standing up, he removed his hood and worn-out robe. His face, his arms, and legs were free of leprosy. He removed his tunic, leaving only his loincloth on, and everyone present witnessed the miracle: the leper was cured. He fell down on his knees, praising Ishia, the Son of God.

"Tell no one of this," ordered Ishia, "But go to the synagogue and make your offering for you have been healed. Do this in respect of the Mosaic Laws."

Having secured the two fishing boats by the shore, Ishia and His disciples began to walk towards Arbelah. As soon as they had reached the outskirts of Magdala they heard two men shouting for help. Ishia and His disciples turned around and saw two men who were desperately trying to reach Him without much success. It was clear that they were blind. One led the other; but both were having a miserable time on the rocky terrain. Finally, Judas and Yehohanan ran to help them.

When the blind men reached Ishia, the older blind man said, "Take pity on us, Son of David!"

"Do you believe I can cure your blindness, my good man?" asked Ishia.

"My Lord, I know you can do anything!" exclaimed the blind man.

"You can raise the dead!" exclaimed the other.

"Your faith in me has saved you. Both of you deserve to be cured," replied Ishia, touching first the older man's eyes and then the younger's. The two began to see and as their sight became clearer they witnessed the Mashìah. They both fell on their knees, kissing His feet; but Ishia took them by their arms and asked them to stand up.

"You must do something for me in return!" commanded Ishia. "You must not tell anyone about this!"

The two men promised Him that they would not tell anyone and went back to Magdala, where they broke their promise and told everyone of the great miracle. By the time the crowd reached Magdala, Ishia and His immediate disciples were half ways to Arbelah, which was fifteen stadia away. Everyone in Magdala had heard the story of the two blind men who had been cured by Ishia. The Pharishaiya and scribes had also questioned the two men, trying to falsify their story, and accused them of pretending to be blind. Most citizens of Magdala knew the two men and supported their miracle story. Not only did the two men firmly maintained their original story but also became menacing towards the Pharishaiya, calling them blind for not recognizing the Mashìah of Yisrael.

The Pharishaiya narrowly escaped a stoning from the two men and their friends, running towards Arbelah to catch up with the Nazarene. Their hearts were full of hatred and jealousy, which had truly blinded them from recognizing Ishia as the Holy One, the Mashìah.

The following morning was a Shabbat and the synagogue in Arbelah was filled with pious Yehuda, including the Pharishaiya and scribes who were working for Kaiaphas and the San-hedrin. The old rabbi of Arbelah was eagerly waiting for a visit by the Mashìah, Ishia of Nazerat. He had heard of all His great miracles from the crowd that had followed Him, which had more than doubled the population of Arbelah. The rabbi had shushed the Pharishaiya as soon as they had begun their usual jeremiads; and, he had permitted them to stay as long as they would behave in front of the Mashìah. The old rabbi felt blessed by the presence of the Mashìah in his hometown.

Inside the synagogue was a man who had a withered right hand and arm. His right forearm was smaller, in length and thickness, than his left; and, its right hand was tiny, very much like an infant's hand. However, its tiny little fingers were not as developed as an infant's fingers; but they were more like five little buds. The man had been born with the deficient forearm and hand and could only use it to help his good hand. He had no real grasp with his tiny undeveloped fingers. Every citizen of Arbelah knew the man with the withered hand.

Suddenly, whispers traveled throughout the synagogue until everyone knew that Ishia, the Mashiah, was about to enter. The crowd began to make way so that Lord Ishia and His disciples could enter the already crowded synagogue. Ishia stood tall as He gently walked into the center of the temple, allowing anyone to touch His clothes, even His legs and arms. He embraced the old rabbi, who was ecstatic to have lived long enough to meet Israel's Mashiah. The old man clearly recognized Ishia as the true Mashiah as he looked into His eyes. No one had spoken a word about the man with the withered hand; but Ishia had received the message from the Pharishaiya's eyes, daring him to cure someone in a synagogue on a Shabbat morning. It was unthinkable!

Ishia turned to the man with the withered hand and said, "Stand up in the middle of this holy temple, my good man!" Then, He turned towards the Pharishaiya and spoke, "Is it against the law on any Shabbat day to do good or to do evil. Is it against the law to save a life or to kill on Shabbats?" He stared at the Pharishaiya and scribes for an answer but they were obstinate in their silence because they could not truly answer His question.

"Answer my question!" He exclaimed angrily. "...I see that you cannot truly answer it." He then turned to the man with the withered forearm and hand and said, "Stretch out your right hand, my good man."

As the man slowly stretched his withered right arm to Ishia the crowd began to whisper throughout the synagogue; but, that did not bother Him as He grabbed the man's withered hand, exposing the whole forearm. Ishia began to massage the man's withered forearm and recite some silent prayer. Ishia kept with the massage and prayer for two or three minutes until the man began to scream from an agonizing pain within his withered arm. The man continued to scream as his withered forearm, hand, and fingers began to stretch out in front of everyone's eyes. Disbelief and shock were on most people's faces because what was happening seemed to be humanly impossible. The screaming and disbelief stopped when the man's right hand and forearm had grown to the same size as his left. He stretched out both forearms and fingers, studying and comparing them. Everyone's eyes were on Ishia, including the Pharishaiya's.

"You are truly the Mashìah, the Son of the Most High!" exclaimed the old rabbi.

The crowd and His disciples praised Him and bowed their heads in adoration. The Pharishaiya and scribes, disgusted by this show of reverence, left the synagogue and began to plan a way to destroy him.

It was still dark the following morning when Ishia and His disciples left Arbelah, traveling westward on the road to Nazerat. Ishia had wanted to leave early to reach Har Tavor, an enchanting mountain east of Nazerat. They traveled at least forty stadia before they reached a smaller path, which forked southwards from the road to Nazerat. It was early afternoon when they reached the source of the Northern Wadi Tavor, whose waters originated from the drainage of the mountain. The group had been traveling for nearly nine hours and most of the disciples were exhausted. The valley west of the wadi was very fertile with wild oats and flowers, which covered it like an embroidered bedspread. Judas loved it and he was just like a little boy, rolling on a multicolored carpet. Some of the younger disciples imitated him, enjoying frolicking down the valley. The rest quickly fell asleep.

Having rested in the field of wild flowers for nearly two hours, Ishia's wish was to reach Har Tavor before sunset. Some of the disciples had to be woken up from their nap—the long march and the sweet fragrance of the wild flowers had contributed to their slumber. They resumed their walk along the northern wadi until they reached the slopes of Har Tavor. Ishia thought best to rest for He saw how tired His disciples were; and, after sharing some of the food and water they carried they fell asleep at the bottom of the slope. Ishia retreated behind a tree, where He knelt to begin a long night of prayer. While everyone slept, Judas watched His Lord struggle within Himself in accepting His ultimate sacrifice for the sake of mankind.

The morning after, Ishia, with the help of Judas, instructed His disciples on personal hygiene. Some of the men smelled like dead fish and others had not bathed or washed their clothes in weeks or months. After sharing some bread and water, they climbed Har Tavor. Once they reached the top, Ishia began to instruct them with His parables. He also promised them that He would come back to Har Tavor with His chosen twelve to witness a meeting between He and His angels. Judas already knew that Ishia's next rendezvous with Commander Ghabriel would be right on Har Tavor. The mountain had a flat top very much like a mesa—a perfect place for a spacecraft to land on!

Once again, like every other night, Ishia began His prayers on top of Har Tavor as soon as everyone, except Judas, had fallen asleep. Judas, as usual, remained awake to pray and to reflect on his unforgettable experiences with Ishia of Nazerat, nearly two thousand years back in time. He had given up the only chance to ever going back to his daughter, his friends, and his people; and, he had sacrificed that very love for them to be with Him, the Only Son of the Almighty Yahweh, Lord of the Milky Way. How he missed his daughter, his friends, and his people! He missed his wife and his son! He missed his parents!

The early morning sun shone on Judas' face. He opened his eyes but was very tired from little sleep. He had fallen asleep only after he had seen Ishia succumb from fatigue. And that had been only three hours before. He slowly got up not to awake anyone and silently went away from the group to relieve himself. When he got back Ishia was already up and He was gently waking up His disciples.

Ishia had decided to come down the western slope of Har Tavor through the valley where the Israelites had battled the Qanaanites thirteen hundred years before, in the War of Daberath. Ishia retold the story of the battle to His disciples as they hiked southwest towards Giv'at Moreh. They crossed the southern Wadi Tavor, which met with the northern tributary, flowing southeast and eventually emptying into the Ha-Yarden. After a quick-paced, three hour march the rocky slopes of Giv'at Moreh were within call. The stonewalls of the fortified town of Nain were visible as Ishia and His disciples clearly heard the cries and chanting of the lamentations of a funeral. As He and His disciples reached the gate of the fortified town the funeral cortege was making its way out of it, moving to the direction of the cemetery, which was situated outside the town walls.

The corpse they carried on the catafalque was that of a young man, sixteen or seventeen years old at the very most. The dolorous mother was a widow whose husband had passed away two years before. Her only son had fallen victim of a horrible disease, which had ended his youth within a month. A man who was part of the funeral cortege recounted this information to Cephas.

Ishia felt the mother's desperation deep within His heart and her pain was too great for Him. Would His mother go through such pain when He would be crucified? He knew He would resurrect on the third day after His death; but if He chose not to help the young man He knew that the widow's pain would only become greater. He walked up to the lady and hugged her, sharing her sorrow. The cortege stopped as the eight pallbearers rested the catafalque outside the stone gate. Many in the congregation wanted to know why they had stopped. Some of the disciples informed the rabbi and relatives that the man hugging the widow was Ishia of Nazerat. A silence came upon the group as they waited, ignorant of what was about to happen.

"Do not cry anymore; your pain is within my heart and it is too heavy to bear. Your love for your only son is great; and, his youth was suddenly ended by a most horrible and painful sickness. I know that he was a wonderful young man and he has been cheated by death. I want to help you," He whispered in the widow's ear.

He approached the corpse. The pallbearers stood still as total silence reigned by the gate of Nain. Only the chirping of the birds could be heard. Ishia uncovered the young man's face, removing part of the shroud. His face was whitish gray and had lost some of its flesh from the strange and fatal disease. He uncovered more of the shroud, exposing his wasted torso. He placed His right hand on the dead youth's chest where his heart was and His left hand touched his forehead. He concentrated or prayed for a moment and then said, "Young man, in the name of My Father I order you to get up."

Many uttered shocking cries as the young man's fingers began to move. Then, his heavy eyelids opened and his eyes began to search around.

"Mother," whispered the young man.

"Your mother is here, young man," said Ishia as the young man sat up.

Slowly the young man stood up. The widow ran to her son and embraced him as the crowd, including all of the disciples, fell on their knees in awe. They felt the presence of God as they praised Ishia of Nazerat. Finally, the funeral cortege turned into a joyous procession as it turned around and paraded into the fortified town. That day a celebration took place within the fortified walls of Nain that would never be forgotten. Everyone was happy and celebrating. Many brought their best dishes that they had cooked and the best wine they had. As the celebration went on, Ishia topped that wonderful day by curing anyone who was sick or lame. The feasting continued throughout the night celebrating a most wonderful visit from the Son of God.

After spending a few days in Nain, Ishia had decided to move on. He and His disciples had been showered with food, wine, and fruits to carry on to their journey. They walked along the valleys until they reached the Wadi Tavor and followed it to the Ha-Yarden. For two weeks Ishia and His disciples meandered along the sacred river and its valley, meeting many new people each day.

Judas noticed that the crowd had, once again, become enormous in number and he feared the worse for it was difficult to control thousands of people. He also remembered that it was along the Ha-Yarden Valley that Ishia had saved the centurion and his men from an imminent death.

Ishia had sensed his thoughts and He reassured Judas, "Do not worry for me, my good friend. Nothing is going to happen to me for there is still so much to do. My time has not yet come."

Each day, Ishia would cure anyone who would come for help, using the water of the Ha-Yarden as if it was a medicine for all sicknesses and diseases. As Ishia moved northward towards Yam Kinneret, the crowd moved along occupying both shores of the river. By the time they reached the fishing village of Sennabris the crowd numbered well over five thousands, instantaneously doubling its population. The wealthier people, following Ishia, gladly treating the poorer ones for a meal—they believed in Ishia's message of sharing and loving their fellow men. The people of Sennabris were happy to receive Ishia of Nazerat and happy with the booming business He had brought with that vast crowd of followers. For a few days, the village of Sennabris enjoyed a prosperity it had never experienced in its history—it had become a bustling fishing town. Unfortunately for the town of Sennabris, its booming business left with the crowd on the fourth morning as it followed Lord Ishia, the Mashìah.

Ishia led the immense crowd on a slow march towards Ammathus, another fishing town along the western shore of Yam Kinneret. He chose to walk slowly because there were older people and He did not wish any strain on their weary bodies. He also knew how much time He had left before the second and final marriage. Therefore, He had chosen that time to do some of His work. He took all day on a distance that Judas could have jogged in an hour. But, Ishia would stop every four or five stadia and recount a parable as the crowd listened to every little word uttered from His lips. Every syllable He spoke seemed to have a special meaning. Every word He said had become sacred to His disciples and to many followers in the crowd.

After several stops and parables, Ishia stopped again and moved towards the steep hills of the western shore. Having found a good-size boulder, Ishia climbed it with an ease that Judas had seen only with some of the best rock climbers before the Nuclear Holocaust. Everyone watched Him in awe for they had never seen anyone climb a steep boulder with such ease and grace. He turned towards the crowd, stretching out His arms, and said, "A farmer went out to sow his seeds. As he scattered the seeds, some of them fell on the side of the path, some were trampled by people, and some were eaten by birds. Some of the seeds fell on rocks and withered away, scorched by the heat of the sun. Some fell among brambles and as they grew they were choked by the thorns. However, some fell into fertile soil and they grew, producing an abundant crop. Listen to what I have to say, anyone of you who has ears to hear. Be like the fertile soil and let my words and my love grow within your minds and hearts."

The crowd and His disciples ruminated on the sacred words He had spoken as they continued along the rocky shore of the Sea of Hagalil, as the lake was sometimes called. At Ammathus the crowd became larger as more people listened to His eloquent and meaningful words and as they witnessed unexplainable miracles. *Ishia of Nazerat* and *the Mashìah* had become the most spoken words in Yisrael. Everyone claimed to have met Him or seen Him, even if they hadn't.

The town of Ammathus enjoyed three full days of prosperous business while Ishia and His disciples remained there. Early, on the fourth morning, Ishia and His disciples left for Bethmaus with the intention of bypassing Tiberias to get to Magdala. The crowd followed Him up the steep slopes to Bethmaus, where He cured a blind woman and a young paralytic. Finally, the day after the one night stay at Bethmaus Ishia and His followers reached the wonderful fishing town of Magdala. The two fishing boats had been taken care of by admirers of Ishia who had kept watch on them. Ishia remained in Magdala for two more days, spending most of His time curing the sick or speaking to the crowd.

On the first morning in Magdala Judas had gone fishing on the fishing boats with Ishia, His brother Yakov, Cephas and his brother Andros, and the sons of Zebedeus, Yakov and Yehohanan. They needed fish for the large crowd, which had been following Ishia. Once again, Lord Ishia repeated a miraculous catch and they brought back enough fish to feed thousands of people. The crowd had never seen such a catch: the two fishing boats barely made it back to shore as they were laden with thousands of fish. Only the Mashiah could work such wonderful miracles.

After the crowd was satiated with the freshly cooked fish, everyone rested by the shore as Ishia spoke from Cephas' boat. He told them that He and His disciples would sail for a few days along the shores of the lake and eventually sail back to Kfar-Nahum. Once again, He taught them the Lord's prayer. Having bid them farewell and having blessed them, Ishia and His disciples sailed away on the two fishing boats.

For days the two fishing boats sailed around the lake, stopping at the shores of many fishing villages. Ishia cured anyone who believed and fed many with more miraculous catches. By now, Judas had become His assistant. His beard and hair had grown long and his GISA boots were unrecognizable and had acquired an earthly and weathered look. After almost three weeks of sailing, fishing, and miracles, Ishia, Judas and the rest of the disciples finally reached the shore of Kfar-Nahum. Mary, His mother, Lydia and her family, and a large crowd had been anxiously waiting for them. Ishia, His brother Yakov, and Judas immediately hugged and kissed Mary, Lydia and the rest of her family, as it was customary. The families of the disciples hugged and kissed them. The shore of Kfar-Nahum was crowded with hundreds of people filled with emotion and love.

The following few days were spent in preparation of Ishia and Lydia's wedding. Lydia's pregnancy was healthy and the second wedding would finalize their holy marriage. According to ancient customs, Ishia and Lydia were not supposed to see each other until the wedding; but, Ishia felt strongly in changing some of those ancient customs. He wanted to be sure that their baby was healthy and that Lydia was following a rich and healthy diet for her sake and for their baby's growth. The wedding was going to be held in a villa of a friend of the family who lived in Qana, a Hagalil town approximately one hundred and fifty stadia east of Kfar-Nahum. At first, Augustus Horatius had tried to offer his villa for the wedding celebration; however, both Ishia and Judas had tried to explain to the good centurion the importance of celebrating it at Qana. Both had tried to tell him that changing the location of the wedding from Qana to Kfar-Nahum would most probably change the future of the world. It had been very difficult for the good centurion to even try to comprehend what Ishia and Judas were talking about; but he believed in what they were saying with a faith stronger than the base of a mountain. After all, he was listening to the living Son of God. He had seen what Ishia could do: revive his beloved wife, save him and his men from sure death, cure his beloved servant from a distant, and cure hundreds of suffering people. The centurion truly believed that Ishia was the Only Son of the Most Powerful Yahweh. His Roman gods were useless statues and his emperor, Tiberius Claudius Nero Caesar, was a weakling who had appointed the commander of his praetorian guards, Lucius Aelius Sejanus, to govern the Roman Empire while he rested at Capreae. To Augustus Horatius Ishia was the most powerful man he had ever met and his belief in Him was unconditional. However, as a Roman officer, he had to keep those feelings and faith private for he could be easily found guilty of treason by demented Roman rulers.

Qana was a town in Hagalil approximately one hundred and fifty stadia southeast of Kfar-Nahum; and, it would take one long day by horse-drawn Roman cart or at least three good days of marching. The wedding day had been set for Monday, April 1, the second day after the Shabbat, at the synagogue at Qana. The sacred meal following the religious ceremony would be held at their friend's villa and it would last until late evening. Both Ishia and Lydia needed to be there by Friday morning to pray and fast in preparation to their final wedding. Augustus had offered a second cart for Ishia and His immediate family; however, Ishia had wanted to walk there with His disciples and followers. His mother, Cephas' mother and wife, and a few other women would use the cart and leave together with Lydia and her family.

A week before the date of the wedding, Ishia and His disciples left for Qana. They first sailed to Genne-Sareth, leaving the two fishing boats on its shore. Having eaten at a local inn, Ishia and the men began their long march towards Qana. They kept along a creek, which flowed in the valley that led to Garaba. At the spot where the creek curved north, they marched southeast along the base of the northern cliffs which led to Qana, which was situated at the western foothills of Har 'Hazmon. It had taken three long days of marching and most of the men were tired and famished. They were welcomed at the villa by Cleophas and Miryam, friends of Ishia's mother, where a feast had been prepared for Ishia and His men. Cleophas and Miryam were very rich Hebrai and knew who Ishia was. It was an honor for them to have Him as their guest and to hold the wedding meal at their house. Ishia and the men rested and during the following two days helped prepare and set up all that was needed for the wedding celebration.

The two horse-drawn carts arrived by Friday afternoon, and once again, Cleophas and Miryam welcomed their guests with a wonderful supper. The following day, Shabbat, March 30, Ishia spent it in prayer on the top of the cliffs. Only Judas had been invited to be with Him. The rest of the disciples, including Ishia's brother, remained at the villa helping the women in setting up for the wedding celebration.

Judas and Ishia had soloed several cracks to reach the top of the cliff. They meditated all day long and slept there that night, too tired to come down. The following morning they finally descended the mountain by a winding path, which led back to Qana. Ishia spent some time at the synagogue praying; and, once the synagogue had been filled with devout men He was invited by the rabbi to speak to them. Ishia gave a sermon on the many faces of love.

Monday, April 1st, 31A.D.

As the rabbi ended the Song of Shelomo, everyone anxiously waited for the ceremony to continue. Both Ishia and Lydia looked resplendent in their beautiful wedding clothes. Ishia looked very much like a handsome king and Lydia like an angel from heaven. The good centurion, in his shiny regalia, stood proud and a gleam of joy shone from his eyes. He was the rare Roman welcomed in synagogues for all knew that he had funded the building of the beautiful temple at Kfar-Nahum and for his belief in Ishia the Mashìah. The women stood behind a wall, listening to the ceremony and peeping through the small spaces, which had been made between the stone blocks. The synagogue was crowded with Ishia's disciples and followers. Suddenly, the entire synagogue was silent as a tall hooded stranger came in. Judas recognized the face of Commander Ghabriel and, smilingly, nodded at him. He communicated with him by greeting him and then shifted to Ishia. Commander Ghabriel congratulated Him on His marriage to the beautiful Lydia and wished Him a most happy wedding. All of this took place without a word being said; but everyone felt the power present between the two. It was like a super charge of electricity. Everyone, except Ishia bowed down to the angel. When they had finished with their silent communication, Commander Ghabriel took his place behind Lord Ishia by His right side. The nuptial ceremony continued smoothly and joy and happiness reigned in the crowded temple as Ishia and Lydia finalized it with their marriage vows.

The nuptial cortege promenaded to Cleophas and Miryam's villa, where stewards had been busily preparing a luscious feast. Stuffed lambs had been slowly cooking over fire pits for hours. Various poultry had been roasted and basted with honey and spices. Fresh fish from the Mediterranean Sea had been stuffed with olives, breadcrumbs and aromatic spices and grilled over fire. Breads, stuffed with olives and spices accompanied the meat dishes. Many vegetable and fruit dishes adorned the huge serving table. Decanters of red and white wine imported from Sicily had been strategically placed in between plates. There were several smaller dishes filled with black and green olives prepared in various Mediterranean styles.

It was a feast, which would have pleased any king or emperor. The large atrium of Cleophas villa was crowded with nearly three hundred guests. There was plenty of food for everyone but the chief steward was worried about the wine. The purchasing of the wine had been estimated for an expected two hundred guests. But there were juices and excellent well water to compensate the wine. Ishia, Lydia, Commander Ghabriel and the two immediate families sat by the table of honor. Cleophas and Miryam sat with Judas and the chosen disciples next to the table of honor. The rest of the disciples, their families and invited friends were everywhere in the atrium, enjoying the delicious food and Sicilian wine. Musicians played the wonderful psalms written by King David and the latest songs, which told stories of brave men and of beautiful women. The merriment continued throughout the afternoon.

It was near dusk when the chief steward approached Cleophas and whispered something into his ear. Miryam, Ishia's mother followed the concerned chief steward with her eyes and stood up when she saw the look that governed Cleophas' countenance. She walked towards her beloved friend and while she held his hands she asked him what was troubling him. He whispered to her that the wine was almost totally consumed and that the evening was just beginning. What was he to do? While there was still plenty of food to last for the next few days, the wine was at its end. Mother Miryam offered to speak to her son. She approached Ishia and whispered the troubling message to Him.

"What do you expect from me, my Lady?" asked Ishia.

"Is there anything that you can do, my son?" she gently replied.

"Now is not yet the time. Do not worry, mother. I will take care of it."

Miryam kissed her son and went to speak to the chief steward. She told him to do whatever her son would tell him to do and she went back to her seat.

Almost an hour passed and the last glass of wine was drunk. The chief steward and Cleophas were frantic trying to offer juices and water to the puzzled guests. It was then that Ishia stood up and signaled Judas to follow Him. Judas knew and had been anxiously waiting for His call. He had already taken the pouch with the concentrated powder of paradisiacal wine. They went directly to the kitchen where six large stone water jars stood under the counter. The jars were half-filled with water. Ishia proceeded to pour an equal amount of concentrated powder into each jar. He then instructed two stewards to have them filled with water to the brim and to serve it to the guests.

"But, My Lord, we cannot serve them water. They will be enraged," whispered one of the stewards, perturbed by the idea.

"Do as I say and everything will be fine," replied Ishia.

"Yes, My Lord!" replied the steward.

The jars were filled with well water under the scrutinizing eyes of the stewards. As the water reached the jars' brims an aromatic scent emanated from the stone containers. Puzzled by the aromatic scent, the two stewards decided to sample the sweet smelling water. To their surprise, the water had turned into the most delectable white wine they had ever sampled. Ishia told them to bring a decanter of the wine to the chief steward. Excitedly, they followed His instruction.

As one of the steward poured the aromatic wine into a cup, the chief steward began to sniff the scent emanating from the cup. As he tasted it, he smacked his lips as he was taken by surprise by the most exquisite taste his palate had ever experienced. He drank the rest of the wine and ordered his steward to fill his cup, which he did excitedly. The chief steward drank more and then went directly to Cleophas and with gusto and decorum he announced, "Usually, people serve their best wine first, and, then when most of the guests are inebriated, they order us to bring out the cheap wine; but, you, my lord have kept the best wine I have ever tasted until now. Where does this wine come from, my lord?"

"You will have to ask Lord Ishia, my good man. That is His wine," answered Cleophas.

Ishia who was not too far away and had heard the chief steward's comment on the wine decided to answer his question, "That wine comes directly from Paradise, and now tell your men to serve it. Everyone is anxiously waiting to savor it."

When everyone present was served the paradisiacal wine, Cleophas made another toast to the bride and groom. To everyone's surprise, the wine was the most delicious anyone had ever tasted. The six stone jars contained enough wine for the whole evening and it became the main subject of conversation until the early hours of the next day. No one ever forgot the taste of that wine and no one ever tasted a wine as delicious as the one they had tasted at the wedding of Qana.

Chapter 20

FROM LEGION OF GADARA TO JAIROSH'S DAUGHTER

It was a hot overcast spring afternoon and the wind grew stronger as Ishia, Judas, and His most faithful disciples tried to push the two boats off the shore at Kfar-Nahum. Cephas was worried about his boat, as the wind rapidly grew stronger.

"My Lord!" he exclaimed, "I do not think that this is a good time to sail. A storm is brewing from the north."

"Cephas, Cephas! Are you afraid of a little storm?" replied Ishia.

"My Lord, the winds are gaining strength and dark clouds are moving in. I do not recommend setting the sail for it is too dangerous," pleaded Cephas.

"You do not trust my judgment, Cephas!" said Ishia.

"You are the Great One, My Lord, but You do not know much about sailing," answered Cephas.

"What are you saying, Cephas? Have you gone mad?" questioned Judas.

The others stopped pushing the boats and stared at Cephas, flabbergasted at his insensitive comment.

"Forgive me, Lord, for having opened my stupid mouth. I am not much of a speaker…I am a simple fisherman."

"You have already been forgiven, my friend. However, by the time you are ready to take my place on this earth you will not be a simple fisherman anymore for your catch will not be fish any longer. You shall be a fisher of men. Now, let us move these two boats before the wind reaches its culmination."

Cephas stared at Ishia, dumbfounded about His comment about taking His place and becoming a fisher of men. Finally, with all his strength, he began to push his boat out into the billowing waters, along with Ishia, Judas, his brother, and a few other disciples, still wondering at the meaning of His comment.

Other fishermen who owned boats were also pushing their boats, laden with people, into the stormy lake. People had paid fishermen to follow Lord Ishia into the lake. The rest of the crowd stood on the pebbly shore, some helping to push the boats, others disappointed that Lord Ishia was leaving. Finally, the two boats were sailing away, pushed southwards by the northern wind. The other boats were being frantically pushed into the waters, trying to follow Ishia. He stood on the stern, saying farewell to the crowd and promising to be back in a few days.

The powerful northern wind hurled the fishing boats southwards, rocking them and thrusting them agitatedly into the oncoming night. All of the disciples tried to steer, work the sails or bail out the boats, worrying and praying for their lives. Judas was the only one who showed no fear as he helped Cephas steer the rudder, knowing what Ishia was about to do.

"What is wrong with you, Judas? We are about to sink and you show no concern about our lives! Have you gone mad?" spoke Cephas in a challenging tone of voice.

"I care for everyone here; but I am not concerned about this particular storm I have full faith on My Lord. Now, let us concentrate on steering," answered Judas.

"What do you expect Him to do, order the storm to stop?"

"Exactly!"

"You must be mad! No one can stop a storm. We are all going to perish!"

"Have some faith in Him, Cephas. He truly is the Son of the Almighty Yahweh."

The boat rocked like a little toy as Cephas and Judas were hit by another wave of water.

"You should not mention His Name in vain. We are being punished for this!" uttered Cephas.

"I did not mention His Name in vain. I only said that Lord Ishia is the Only Son of the Almighty Yahweh. That is not in vain. It is the truth! And we are not being punished for anything. We are about to witness Our Lord's magnificence over nature."

"I hope that what you are saying is true, or this will be our final voyage to the bottom of Yam Kinneret."

Lord Ishia stood by the mast, looking towards Gadara. He stood calmly without holding on to anything, His body moved with the rocking of the boat as if He were glued onto the planks, totally unperturbed by the powerful squall.

"Look at Him. He is not normal. He is not a man. How is it possible for Him not be flung overboard when we have to hold on for dear life. Tell me, Judas for He calls you the messenger from the future. If you come from the future and know what is going to happen, then tell me if we will survive this terrible storm," begged Cephas.

"First of all, Lord Ishia is a man; and yet, He is the Son of God. Secondly, I do come from the future; and, as far as this storm goes, simply have a little faith in Him."

"It is hard to have faith when we are so close to death! And when will He stop this storm? Tell me, Judas. When?"

"I really do not know when. Concentrate on steering and we shall be fine."

Cephas stopped talking as he concentrated on steering with Judas; but the look on his face was a worried one. Judas estimated that they had been sailing for nearly one hour. Although, he knew that everyone was safe he had no idea when Lord Ishia would calm the storm. All of the disciples, on both boats, were afraid for their lives and held on for dear life. At least, one more hour had gone by and Lord Ishia had not yet calmed the storm. Judas looked around the mast; but He was not there. Frantically, he scanned the ship as he held on to the rudder, together with Cephas. Maybe, it was the wrong storm—storms were not uncommon on Yam Kinneret. Once again, he searched for Lord Ishia without success. As Judas kept on blinking to wash away the water from his eyes, he noticed that Lord Ishia was sleeping with His head on a cushion only two feet away. He had not noticed Him for he had been searching for Him around the mast. Judas was happy to see Him rest for He slept very little, spending most of His nights praying; however, he also had begun to worry about the storm.

"He has fallen asleep, Judas. We are going to sink!" exclaimed Cephas loudly.

Cephas' thundering voice woke Lord Ishia up; and, He sat up.

"Why did you wake me up, Cephas? I was taking a rest," whispered Ishia.

"My Lord, does it not worry You that we are about to sink. We are all going to drown. We are going to die. We can barely swim!" exclaimed Cephas.

Ishia got up and, without answering Cephas, stood facing north with His arms stretched out and His hands positioned to push. He began concentrating, as His hands seemed to push at the storm. He stood there for a moment; but, to Judas and the rest of the disciples that moment seemed to last forever. Suddenly, He cried out to the storm, "Peace!...Be still!"

Suddenly, the wind died down as the clouds were pushed southwards. The waters of the lake seemed calmer; and, the boats were not rocking any longer.

"Why are you afraid?" Ishia asked everyone, "You still do not believe in me?"

Everyone, including Judas, was shaken by that wondrous exhibition of heavenly power. Cephas whispered to Judas, "Who is He that even the wind and the waters obey His wishes?"

Once the boats reached the southern shore, east of Sennabris, the disciples secured the boats, as did the other fishermen, and then went around telling everyone to go to sleep for it was late and that their Lord was already sleeping. Without any complaints, everyone went to sleep for every man and woman was exhausted from the long battle against the storm and the constant fear of death.

It was early morning when Judas woke up, stood up, and stretched. Everyone was still sleeping except Lord Ishia, who was washing His face with the waters of Yam Kinneret. Judas got down from the boat without disturbing anyone and joined Ishia in washing up. He removed his outer clothing, following Lord Ishia's initiative, and waded until he reached the Lord. He was waste deep when he began to wash his face and neck. Ishia turned around and said, with a smile, "Good morning, my beloved friend! Did you sleep well?"

"I fell asleep from exhaustion! Last night I helped Cephas with the rudder. That storm was a powerful one. And, good morning to You, My Lord," replied Judas.

"Last night, for a moment I sensed that you, too, had lost faith in me, Judas."

"Only for a tiny moment, My Lord. It happened when You were sleeping, when I was not sure if last night's storm was going to be the one or not. You must forgive me, Lord, for losing faith for that little moment."

"There is nothing to forgive, my friend. It is not often that I calm down winds and storms. It was an experience even for me."

"I shall never forget it, My Lord…Lord, I have a favor to ask."

"You would like to be baptized again!"

"By you, My Lord. It would mean everything to me."

Picking up water with His cupped hands, Lord Ishia baptized Judas, solemnly uttering "I baptize you with this water that I purify for you so that it shall purify your body, your spirit, and your inner self."

"My Lord, My God!" whispered Judas.

"Go now and wake them up. I must see someone by the caves of Gadara."

Judas rushed back to the boats and gently began waking up everyone. Within minutes all the disciples and most people were up. Most of them took care of their needs, hiding behind bushes or rocks, and washed themselves in the waters of the lake. Judas found the idea of urinating or defecating in the open air very hard to accept. Ishia understood Judas' problem and had spoken to him more than once about it. The disciples did not understand Judas' finicky ways and they were at times annoyed by him. They called it cleansing; but their method was not clean at all. They used leaves, rocks, pieces of wood, and some even their robes or fingers to clean themselves. Paper would not be invented for many centuries to come. Seeing so many people cleansing themselves all at once was a messy and smelly testimony. People had to be careful where they stepped and most people smelled foully and were offensive to Judas. Lord Ishia had told Judas that this experience would only last for a few years for him; however, He had to endure it all His life. Also, He constantly taught His followers the importance of hygiene. Many people got sick because of their filth and many died of diseases because they would not or could not wash after cleansing themselves.

Judas rounded the rest of the disciples and tried to catch up with Ishia who had begun to walk towards the rocky hills of Gadara and Hippus. They came on a meadow, which was almost covered by a herd of swine, tended by several swineherds. Lord Ishia and Judas approached one of the swineherds while the rest of the disciples and people kept their distance. Hebrai believed that swine were unclean; however, gentiles raised them and ate them. Ishia had noticed some scabs on most of the pigs and He was concerned about the swineherds' health.

"Who is the owner of this herd, my good man?" asked Ishia.

The young man hid his face as he answered, "They belong to Yousef-al-Gader, a very rich man."

"Yousef of Gadara! Does he realize that his swine are infested with plague and hog cholera? And why do you hide your face, young man?" continued Ishia as Judas witnessed every spoken word.

"We are all covered with scabs, rabbi."

"All of the swineherds?"

"Yes, rabbi."

"Quickly, call all of the swineherds. I need to speak to all of you."

The young man ran to the other swineherds; and, together they began to walk towards Lord Ishia and Judas. The two dogs that followed the six men were also covered with sores and scabs. They stopped approximately ten cubits away, ashamed of their unhealthy state.

The young swineherd began, "Rabbi, we are all here."

Ishia studied them for a moment and then said, "Do you know who I am?"

They all shook their heads, as they whispered, "No, rabbi."

"I know who you are!" exclaimed a voice behind a large boulder, "You are Ishia, the son of the Highest God!" Then, he came forward and pleaded, "I beg You, do not punish me!"

"What is your name?" asked Ishia.

"Legion is my name, for we are many within this body," he said, falling on his knees. "Do not send us out of this country."

"He is possessed by demons, rabbi," spoke the young swineherd. "He lives in those caves. He is very dangerous."

"He does not look dangerous to me," replied Ishia and then faced the possessed man, who was still kneeling, "I order all of you to get out of this man."

"May we enter the swine, oh Ishia?" spoke another voice coming from the possessed man.

"You have my permission to enter all of the swine and the two dogs. Leave at once!" ordered Ishia.

The man fell down in a spasmodic attack. His body shot up and down in violent convulsions as dozens of screams escaped from his mouth.

"Do you believe that I can cure you?" Ishia asked the six swineherds.

The young swineherd emitted a cry of help as he fell on the ground while the five others stepped back in fear as they witnessed the possessed man bobbing uncontrollably and their friend crying in the dirt. Their steps suddenly turned into a run as they escaped from the scene. Their flight was followed by the unending screams and by a sudden rush of swine gone crazy. Hundreds of pigs and the two dogs scurried down the hills towards the cliffs overlooking Yam Kinneret. Nothing could stop them for the legion of unclean spirits had entered their plagued bodies, driving them towards the precipice to their death. By dozens, the swine and the two dogs took their uncontrollable turns over the cliffs. The other five swineherds ran towards Gadara, awestricken by what they had witnessed and fearful of the consequences of losing the huge herd of swine.

Meanwhile the man, which had been possessed by the legion of unclean spirits, had stopped his uncontrollable convulsions and rested on the ground. The young swineherd continued to stare at his arms and chest and kept running his hands on his face, incredulous of what had happened to him, to the possessed man, and to the herd. All of that was too much for anyone to take in such a short moment. How could a man have such incredible power? Who was he? His thoughts were arrested by his gentle yet powerful voice.

"Rise, young man. You are cured," He said. Then, He turned to the man who had been possessed and commanded, "Stand up, your spirit is free and clean."

The man who had been possessed got up in a kneeling position and kissed Ishia's feet, saying, "My Lord! Just say the word and I will do whatever You tell me to do. I will follow You anywhere, My Lord."

"My good man, go home to your family and tell them what I have done for you and that I have forgiven you of all your past sins. Go home and be a good son to your parents and a good husband to your wife. It has been a long time since they last saw you."

"My Lord, I would prefer to come with You."

"Have you no idea of the pain and suffering you have inflicted on your loved ones? I am giving you another chance to prove yourself that you can love them again," suggested Ishia.

"My lord, before I go, would it be all right with You if I stayed with You until You and Your followers leave this place?"

"When I and my friends sail away from here you will go back to your family."

"Thank you, My Lord, thank you!"

Ishia, then, turned around and approached the young swineherd and said," What is your name, young man?"

"Abu-al-Kursi, My Lord," he replied.

"Abu, from this moment on, you will follow me. You will take care of people instead of swine."

"I will follow You anywhere, My Lord!" exclaimed Abu-al-Kursi.

"Why him and not me, Lord?" asked the man who had been possessed.

"Abu is an orphan. You have a wife and parents who long for you. You must go back and start a new life and become a loving husband, a loving son, and when your wife bears your children you shall become a loving father. That is what I ask in return of what I have done for you. Promise me that you will do all that I ask."

"My Lord, it is so hard to be a good man."

"It will be harder if you follow me, Seth Bar-Oza. You must try again to be a good man. I am giving you this second chance and you must promise that you will give it your best effort."

"You knew my name all along. You are truly the Son of God and I promise to become a good man, My Lord."

Suddenly, from the direction of Gadara, angry voices reverberated from the valley over the eastern hills. From the sound of the cries it promised to be a large crowd. Abu, the swineherd, began to tremble with fear, knowing that Yousef-al-Gader, the owner of the swine was coming with an angry crowd from Gadara.

"My Lord, we must leave now. Those people are extremely angry and Yousef-al-Gader is not a very nice man. He is dangerous!" suggested Abu.

"We cannot allow men like Yousef-al-Gader oppress good people like you, Abu," said Ishia. "Even men like Yousef-al-Gader have a little goodness buried deep within their dark spirits. Do not fear him, Abu, for his tyranny thrives on people's fear."

Ishia stood tall, powerful yet gentle, with Judas and Abu by His sides. Seth and the rest of the disciples stood behind Him, feeling sheltered by their Lord. Suddenly, the voices grew louder as the angry crowd, led by the other swineherds and Yousef-al-Gader reached the top of the hill. Judas guessed the crowd to be no more than sixty people. They marched, with anger and vengeance regulating their every move and cry. The disciples stepped back a step or two, as did Abu. Only Judas stood his ground with Lord Ishia. The swineherds held their slingshots ready, while others were equipped with good size rocks for throwing.

The crowd stopped at approximately twenty cubits away, a perfect distance for throwing stones. One of the swineherds pointed at Ishia, exclaiming, "The tall one, master. He is the one!"

"Are you the one who caused all of my swine to drown?" asked a fat man, dressed in expensive clothes and adorned with gold necklaces and earrings.

"You must be Yousef-al-Gader, and the answer to your question is no," answered Ishia, while taking a few steps towards the crowd.

Several of them, including the swineherds, got into a throwing stance ready to make their first attack.

"Are you going to stone the Promised One!" exclaimed Seth Bar-Oza. "You imbeciles! We have been waiting all of our lives for the coming of the Mashìah; and, now that He is here you want to stone Him. Have you all gone mad?"

"Aren't you Seth the demoniac, called Legion?" asked Yousef-al-Gader.

"I was;" answered Seth, "but, thanks to My Lord, I am back to my old self. No more demons. They left my body and entered your sick swine. It was the demons who drowned your swine, not My Lord."

"My herd of swine died because of your lord; thus, he must pay for every single swine or he is punishable by death!" exclaimed Yousef.

"Does a person's life mean anything to you. Are a thousand swine worth more than a human life? Do you, Yousef-al-Gader, know who I am?" spoke Ishia.

"I do not care who you are!" replied Yousef. "I do not believe in your god; therefore I do not believe in you. You will have to pay for my entire herd."

"Do you have someone that you love, who has been afflicted with an incurable disease?" asked Ishia.

"Yes, I do…It is my son. He is very sick," whispered Yousef.

"He has been afflicted with the swine's disease," whispered Ishia.

"How can you possibly know that?" asked Yousef.

"If I cure your son, will his life be equal to all of your swine?"

"My son's life is worth much more than one thousand herds of swine, to say the least."

"Then, if I cure your son from this horrible disease and sure death what will you promise in return?" asked Ishia.

"If you can cure my son from this pestilence we shall consider ourselves even."

"That is not good enough."

"Nearly two thousand swine were lost and that is not enough!"

"A moment ago, you said that your son's life is worth much more than a thousand herds."

"Did I say that? What else do you demand in return?"

"Do you have slaves and servants?"

"Plenty of both!"

179

"I want you to promise, in front of all these people, that you will give them their freedom with one year salary."

"Have you gone mad?"

"Is your first-born's life worth all that I ask and more? Do you love him enough to give up your slaves and less than half of all your riches? In your eyes, is he not worth more than all of your riches?"

"Yes, he is. He is my own flesh and blood. I will still be a rich man after I free all of my slaves and servants; and, I will still be a rich man after I pay them a one-year salary to each one of them. Can you really save him, lord?"

"You still have some goodness deep in your heart, Yousef-al-Gader. Where is your son now?"

"Here, in the crowd," pointed Yousef; and, turning to the crowd, he cried, "Ybra-him, come forward, my son."

A young man of not more than seventeen years of age stepped out of the crowd and walked towards his father, dropping two rocks on the ground. His face, arms, and feet were covered with sores, as was the rest of his clothed body. He stood by his father, not knowing what would happen next.

"Yousef-al-Gader, do you believe that your son can be cured?" asked Ishia.

"Yes, because you cured Seth the demoniac and my swineherd, Abu-al-Kursi."

"What about you, Ybra-him, do you believe that you can be cured?"

"It is so hard for me to believe that I can be free of this plague, rabbi," answered Ybra-him.

"It is important that you believe, Ybra-him. Without your faith it is difficult to rid yourself of that foul sickness. You must believe if you really want to be cured."

Ybra-him fell down on his knees, begging, "Rabbi! Please, save me. I really believe you can save me. I will do anything in return."

Lord Ishia looked at Ybra-him and said, "Ybra-him, son of Yousef-al-Gader, you are cured!"

Suddenly, Ybra-him fell prostrate to the ground, facing Ishia. His father was alarmed by his son's total submission but Ishia motioned to him not to help his son.

Confused, but obedient, Yousef kept a distance from his son.

"Now, stand up Ybra-him! You are cured," ordered Ishia.

Slowly Ybra-him stood up, his dirty face was clear of any sore. He checked his arms and legs. They were clean of the sores. He pulled his robe down to his waist to reveal the sinewy body of a healthy young man. Yousef-al-Gader could not believe what he was seeing: his son in perfect health.

He fell on his knees and begged forgiveness, "My Lord, You are truly the Mashiah! You have given me my son back. I will keep my promises. I will free all of my slaves and servants and pay them each a year's salary for I have my son back. Come, My Lord. Come to my house for a great celebration. Come, You and all Your followers, and we shall feast to Your honor."

Some of the people in the crowd still held their rocks, waiting eagerly to stone Lord Ishia. Yousef saw this and tried to persuade them to put their stones down; however, many still wished to stone him for they had been promised a reward. Yousef promised to pay them; nevertheless, some of them, the bloodthirsty type, wished to carry out their agreement to stone Ishia of Nazerat. Yousef rushed back to Lord Ishia begging Him to leave.

"My Lord, I beg you to leave for Your own safety. This is all my fault. I hired those bad people to kill You. Please, forgive me, My Lord."

"You are forgiven, Yousef-al-Gader. I will leave now."

"Go, My Lord! I will hold them in place and I will keep my promises."

Ishia turned around, together with Judas, Abu, Seth, and all of His disciples, and began a quick-paced march down the foothills towards the shores of Yam Kinneret. As they marched they could hear Yousef's cries, "I will double what I had promised you. Halt! I will triple it. Yes, triple it! Are you all happy now, as you get richer I get poorer."

Judas looked at Ishia—a big smile covered His face. Judas smiled, too, happy to see Him smile. Most of the disciples were smiling as they heard Yousef's desperate cries of resignation. When

Ishia smiled, everyone would smile in return for He had the most infatuating smile Judas had ever seen on anyone. Knowing that He would be betrayed, tortured, and crucified He still managed to smile often enough, and sometimes even laugh. Often, the heavy burden and sorrow permeated through His defenses; and, on those occasions His countenance bore the excruciating pain of the whole world. During those sorrowful times, which were usually late at night while everyone slept, Judas would be watching over Him and at times trying to share that overwhelming anguish.

They reached the shore east of Sennabris, where an anxious crowd was impatiently waiting for Lord Ishia as they surrounded their two fishing boats and several other smaller ones. Quickly, they had learned of the spectacular miracles from Seth himself, who kept babbling about what had happened to him. Judas acted as Ishia's personal bodyguard, constantly looking for anyone who might want to harm Him. He could not let any harm come to Ishia for it might change the future of history. Events had to unfold accordingly and Judas was there to make sure they would. But, everyone needed to touch Him. Everyone needed His help. There were so many people that were sick, deformed, possessed, or had some horrible sickness. Judas had never seen so many sick people in all of his previous life. But he understood their need to touch Him. There were no real doctors, with the exception of Ishia, who was the greatest of all. He admired Ishia's love for the poor people, the sick, and the outcasts. He admired His patience, care, and love that He freely gave to anyone in need. He had been one of them: poor in spirit, dying from a horrible disease, and feeling like an outcast. What was going to happen to his daughter and his friends? Would they all soon die? Would everyone on earth die from nuclear cancer? He could not ever help them? A different earth, a healthy planet, and two millennia separated them from each other. Judas was awakened from his daydream by a sudden shove. It was an older woman with a desperate look on her face. She wanted to touch their Lord, to touch His hand, or even His robe. That would be enough to cure her hopeless disease. Judas recognizing that desperation took her hand and helped her towards Ishia. The Lord turned around as His eyes met with Judas' and He immediately took the older woman into a loving embrace, whispering something into her ear. He hugged her, as everyone watched in awe for no one, not even the other disciples, would have touched her. Her disease was extremely contagious. Yet, the Mashìah, the Son of God, in His unceasing love, had taken her into His embrace. The little time that He spent holding her seemed to last an eternity, as everyone watched in reverence. He gently kissed her cheeks and, finally, let her go. She thanked Him profusely as she kissed His hand for she was cured.

People chanted "Ishia of Nazerat, the Mashìah", as some fell on their knees. With all the cries and confusion, Ishia, Judas, and the rest of the disciples managed to embark the two fishing boats.

Ishia stood on the stern and spoke to the crowd. He told them to be loving and caring, and to share with their friends and even with their enemies. He told them to be good children, good parents, and good friends. He ended His sermon with a blessing and forgiveness for all their sins.

Finally, Seth spoke up, "My Lord, please, allow me to come with You."

"Go home, Seth, to your wife, to your parents and relatives. Tell them that I have cured you and forgiven all of your sins. Go, Seth, and be a loving son and husband."

"I will, My Lord, I will," answered Seth, resigned to go home, "and I will make sure that all of Decapolis will know what You have done, and who You are."

People began to push the boats out into the lake, pointing northwards. They sailed along the western coast, quickly passing by the shores of Sennabris. A gentle eastern wind pushed their sails along the western side of Yam Kinneret. They sailed by the fishing town of Ammathus when Cephas exclaimed, "My Lord, we will soon be by Tiberias. It is a wonderful city with beautiful buildings and Herod Antipas' palace. Would you like to stop there, for I know that You have never been there?"

"And I never will be there, Cephas. It disgusts me the way that Fox lives, in sin and in luxury, while people are starving and dying all over Hagalil. He is supposed to be their king, but in reality he is no better than a charlatan. No, Cephas, I will never enter that city. Let us sail to Magdala," replied Ishia.

"To Magdala! So be it, My lord," exclaimed Cephas.

The small fleet of fishing boats sailed gently northwestwards, straight to Magdala. After Tiberias, Magdala was the next most important town on the shores of Yam Kinneret, famous, throughout Galilee, Decapolis, and Philip, for its fish-curing industry. As the boats skimmed over the pebbly shore, the scent of the cured fish got stronger, overpowering all other scents. It was not a bad smell, once one got used to it. A young man, whose father owned a fish-curing house, came out with a large cured fish and offered it to Ishia. The Lord took the smoked-dried fish and thanked the young man. The young man bowed and thanked Him for accepting his fish. Ishia tore a piece and tasted it and passed the fish to Judas. It was salty but delicious! Judas tasted a small piece and passed the fish to Cephas. Every apostle had tasted the smoked fish and it had then reached the crowd. The people in the crowd tried to imitate Lord Ishia by taking only a small piece and sharing the rest, which permitted many in the crowd to taste the smoked fish.

As Ishia made His way into town, angry voices grew louder by the small town square. Several men, followed by an enraged mob, were dragging a young woman by her long hair. The woman, in her mid-twenties, was attractive, even though bruises clearly marked her face and neck. Two of the men pulled and shoved her until they reached the stony walls of the small square. She lay on the dirt as the two men walked back towards the mob, picking up stones on their way. Men and women, equally angry and equally armed with stones were ready to stone the young woman.

Ishia's pace grew slightly quicker, as He reached the bruised woman. He stood in the mob's way, looking majestic and calm. One of the men who had dragged the woman stepped forward ready to throw the rock.

"Move out of the way for we are ready to stone her," he shouted.

"For what reason do you want to stone her?" asked Ishia. But He did not get a reply as the man threw the stone at Ishia. Quicker than anyone had ever witnessed before Ishia caught the stone with His right hand and held it up, saying, "I had asked you the reason for your wanting to stone this woman; and, you try to stone me. Have I wronged you in any way?"

"You are blocking our way. She deserves to die!" the angry man shouted.

"For what reason does she deserve to die?" asked Ishia.

"She is a sinner. She is a prostitute," answered a woman.

"And according to the Laws of Moishe she must be stoned!" yelled another man.

"So, move out of our way so that we may do our job," screamed the angry man.

"If there is anyone among you who has never sinned I will move out of his way so that he may cast the first stone," spoke Ishia.

The mob stood there for a moment, frozen in their memories of wrongful deeds buried deep within the deepest crevasses of their brains. A man dropped his stones and left, with his head bowed low in shame. A second, and a third followed him. One by one, everyone left. Only the angry man remained, standing in a wide stance, ready to cast his second stone. His face was full of fury and venom.

"Are you the only one without sin?" spoke Ishia, breaking that moment of silence, "Is it possible that you have never sinned? Does not the fifth commandment say, 'Thou shalt not kill'! How many people have you stoned in your life? How many people have you killed?"

Finally, the angry young man's facial expressions changed from angry to confused, from lost to ashamed. Slowly, his fingers opened up letting go of the stone. He did not go away like the others; but he dropped on his knees, scraping them on the pebbles and rocks. He buried his face in his hands and began to cry like a child.

Ishia turned around and extended His right hand to the young woman, which she took with both of her hands and kissed it. He helped her up and comforted her in His loving embrace. She had never felt so loved and at peace with herself as she felt in His warm embrace. She stayed there, held by Him, and she wished that He would never let go of that wonderful hold. Still holding her, Ishia whispered, "I want you to forget all that you have done as I forgive you for all those iniquities. I want you to follow me and be with me and my friends for the rest of my days on this earth."

"Yes, My Lord. I will change my ways and I will be with You until I die."

The young woman was Miryam of Magdala, sometimes called the Magdalene, the most beautiful woman in that town. She had become very rich by prostituting her body to the richest men in Galilee and to others who came, by boat, from the other side of Yam Kinneret. Ishia and His disciples followed her to her house. She had servants and a lot of money secretly stashed away. She led Ishia and Judas into her private room and went immediately to one of its corners and, with a Roman stiletto, pried the corner floor stone that had been shaped to fit exactly into that space. Inside, a red stone layer formed almost a perfect cubical compartment of approximately one and a half cubits in dimension. A piece of fine red garment covered its bottom, holding several bags. She took all of the bags out of the secret cubicle and laid all nine on her bed. She untied them all, revealing a considerable fortune. One of the bags easily held over fifty precious stones. A second was filled with gold rings, earrings, necklaces and other jewels. Two other bags had been filled with gold coins of various origins. The last five bags were bigger and they held hundreds of shekels. Easily, there might have been a thousand of the silver Hebrai currency.

Cephas, who had followed them into Miryam's room, exclaimed, "She is as rich as Antipas!"

"Not quite!" said Judas "But she is a very rich woman Probably, the richest in all of Hagalil."

"It is all for Your cause," she whispered. "To buy food and clothes for You and Your disciples, for the poor that You care for. I will personally make sure that everyone has always two good meals each day."

"That is very generous of you, Miryam," spoke Ishia. "What about your servants?"

"They are free and I will give them this house and enough money to live comfortably for years to come. I do all of this for You, My Lord, because You have saved me from a sure death and You have cleansed my soul from all my sins. I want to dedicate the rest of my life to Your cause."

"And what cause is that, Miryam?" asked Ishia.

"The cause of true love, to love everyone, to care for others who are in need, and to be a good person for the rest of my life," she replied.

"You understand me so well, Miryam. Come, we must now leave. A matter of life and death awaits me in Kfar-Nahum."

Miryam the Magdalene willed her house and household furniture to her three servants and left them with three hundred shekels for food. Judas helped her to carry a wooden Roman chest, which held some of her clothes and the nine bags of money, jewelry, and gems. The rest of her clothes and sandals she gave to her three servants. She hugged and kissed them and wished them good luck, renouncing a life that had been extremely profitable but at times demoralizing and debasing.

The two fishing boats sailed northeastward to Kfar-Nahum, Ishia's new hometown. They sailed smoothly northeastwards without problems or incidents. As the two boats neared the shore of Kfar-Nahum a large multitude of people were anxiously awaiting the arrival of Lord Ishia, the Mashìah. Among the crowd were Miryam, His mother, Lydia and her mother and father, and Jairosh the rabbi of Kfar-Nahum. As Ishia's boat landed on the pebbly shore, it was evident that something was wrong for Jairosh the rabbi seemed troubled and His loved ones looked worried.

Ishia jumped off the boat, followed by Judas and the other disciples. Jairosh rushed at Him, fell down on his knees, and begged for help.

"What troubles you, my friend?" asked Ishia.

"My daughter, Rebekah, is dying, My Lord. Come to my house and save her with Your miraculous touch. I know that if You touch her she will be cured!" exclaimed Jairosh.

"Stand up and I will follow you to your house," answered Ishia, without embracing Lydia or His mother. Everyone understood the urgency of time.

Jairosh quickly led the way through the crowded streets of Kfar-Nahum as Ishia easily kept up with his fast pace, followed by His loved ones and the multitude of people, which grew bigger by every home they passed. The crowd had become so large that it had become almost impossible to pass through the narrow streets of Kfar-Nahum. Judas, Cephas, and the rest of the disciples were doing their best to make way for Ishia and Jairosh. The noise of the multitude made it very difficult to hear anything that anyone said.

A middle-aged woman had managed to reach Lord Ishia with the help of a few friends and relatives, who had made their way by shoving and pushing through the almost impassable crowd. As Ishia had come to a standstill, the woman touched His cloak with her deepest faith, healing her affliction almost instantly. Ishia turned around, feeling a great energy escaping Him, and asked, "Who touched me?"

Cephas answered, "My Lord, there are many people who have touched You for the multitude is great and everyone is pressing towards You."

"No, Cephas, this touch was different. Who touched my cloak?"

The woman fell down on her knees, trembling with fear, and answered, "It was I, My Lord. Please, forgive me. I have been suffering for the past twelve years from an unstoppable hemorrhage. I have seen dozens of so-called doctors and healers and no one has been able to end my pain. When I heard about You I pleaded with my family and friends to bring me here at Kfar-Nahum. We have been waiting here for many days, waiting for Your return. Once I was near You, I knew that I only had to touch Your cloak and I would be healed for You are the Son of the Almighty One."

The crowd was still silent from listening to the woman's story as Ishia spoke, "Daughter, your strong faith has saved you. You and your family and friends go in peace and enjoy a healthy life."

Jairosh was frantic, panicking for time lost, and was about to say something to Lord Ishia when three of his servants made their way to him. One of them, called Thomas, exclaimed, "Rabbi Jairosh, Rabbi Jairosh! Your daughter is dead. She is dead!"

"Let me pass immediately!" ordered Ishia to the crowd.

"For what reasons! You cannot help her now. She is dead! You do not need to trouble Rabbi Jairosh any longer!" exclaimed Thomas.

"How dare you speak to My Lord with such arrogance, you young fool!" replied Cephas. "Don't you know who He is?"

Ishia put His right hand on Jairosh's shoulder and said, "Do not be afraid, keep your faith strong for I know you believe in me."

"My Lord, I do believe in You. You are the Holy One, the Mashìah; but, my daughter is dead," cried Jairosh.

"Do not despair, my friend, for I am the Light and the Life. Your daughter's life depends on your faith in me. Let us now go to your house, my good friend."

Once they reached Rabbi Jairosh's house, Lord Ishia allowed only Jairosh, Judas, Cephas, his brother Yakov, and Yehohanan to enter it. Thomas was furious that he could not enter the house.

"Why can't I enter my master's house? I live here!" he shouted.

"Your lack of faith in My Lord is the reason that you cannot enter this house!" cried Judas, "You may come in when the rabbi's daughter is brought back to life."

"How could you be so sure that your lord can bring her back from the dead? Only the Almighty One can do so, if He wishes it," replied Thomas.

"He is the Only Begotten Son of the Almighty and His power comes directly from His Father. You must believe what I say," continued Judas.

"I will only believe when I see Rebekah alive, laughing, playing like she used to when she was alive."

"Then, you better prepare yourself for My Lord, Thomas," shouted Judas, shutting the door.

Judas followed Yehohanan into the young girl's bedroom. Jairosh held his wife, who cried hysterically as the lifeless body of their beautiful daughter lay on her bed.

Cephas and Yakov were trying to console the parents as Lord Ishia stared at the corpse.

"Do not despair, Rebekah is only asleep," whispered Ishia.

The mother became hysterical, switching from crying to laughing as if she had no control over her emotions. "She's dead!" she laughed. "Can't you see that she is dead!" she cried, "My beautiful Rebekah. She was only nine. Why Rebekah? Why not me?" She kept on and on, sometimes crying, sometimes laughing.

Her desperation did not seem to affect Lord Ishia's deep concentration. Slowly, He took Rebekah's right hand, gently holding it, and whispered to her, "Wake up, Rebekah, it is time to get up." His whisper was a command to her spirit, telling it to come back. And it did!

Rebekah gave a low moan as she opened her eyes and sat up. Her mother screamed her name with joy but was held back by rabbi Jairosh, who was in awe of Lord Ishia, the Only Son of the Almighty One.

"Rebekah, embrace your mother and father," He said. Then He spoke to everyone in the room, "Do not tell anyone what you have witnessed. If anyone asks, you may say that Rebekah was in a deep sleep. Now, you must ask one of your maids to prepare some food for Rebekah. Her body is greatly in need of nourishment."

Rabbi Jairosh knelt in front of Lord Ishia, thanking Him for his daughter's life, as his wife hugged Rebekah for dear life her body trembled from hysteria.

"Rabbi," spoke Ishia, "How long has your wife been suffering from hysteria?"

"As long as I have known her, My Lord," replied the rabbi.

Ishia quietly moved towards her and placed His hand on her forehead and camouflaged His intention by embracing her and her daughter. They hugged Him dearly in return as He concentrated on the mother's head. Suddenly, the rabbi's wife became composed and in complete control of herself. Once again, rabbi Jairosh was awestruck by Lord Ishia's heavenly power.

The rabbi went out of his daughter's bedroom and ordered his maids and servants to prepare a feast to celebrate the miracle of life. Upon hearing the rabbi's order, Judas went to open the door of the house to let in Miryam, Lydia and her mother and father, Miryam of Magdala, Thomas and the other two servants. Thomas was furious; however, Judas instructed him to be courteous and to believe in Lord Ishia. He did not bother to answer Judas and abruptly pushed his way in—he wanted to see for himself. He was flabbergasted at the sight of Rebekah eating a bowl of lentil soup. She had been dead. He was positive that her heart had stopped beating when he was sent to get his master, rabbi Jairosh.

"How can a man, made of flesh and blood, bring a person back from the dead? There are two possible answers to my question: one is that Ishia of Nazerat is truly the Promised One; and, two is that he receives his power from the Devil himself!" shouted Thomas.

Lydia and Miryam were offended by Thomas' remarks; but Cephas was quicker than anyone else in speaking, "Hush, you ungrateful wretch. Don't you know that you are in the presence of the Only Son of the Almighty One? His power comes directly from His Father, directly from heaven." Cephas pointed his index finger up. "You should be grateful for what He has done!"

"Thomas, go and help with the food. It is an order," commanded rabbi Jairosh.

"If you do not mind, rabbi, I would like Thomas by my side during this celebration," suggested Lord Ishia.

"Your wish is my command, My Lord!" exclaimed the rabbi.

Finally Ishia went up to Lydia and embraced her, kissing her gently. After embracing His mother, Linus and Lydia's parents, He remained by Lydia's side throughout the entire celebration. They sat together, with Thomas by His left. Yakov sat with his mother, Miryam. Judas sat between Miryam of Magdala and Yehohanan, Yakov and Cephas sat together with the other disciples. Rebekah sat between her mother and father. A lavish dinner was served with the rabbi's best wine.

"I would like to dedicate this celebration to My Lord, Ishia, the Only Son of the Most High. I thank Him for His love and for His gift of life. He has given my Rebekah a second chance in life and He has cured my wife. How can I possibly repay You, My Lord?" spoke rabbi Jairosh. "Name the price and I will gladly pay it. Anything You want, My Lord, just say the word."

"Thank you rabbi; but I do not need money or possessions. But, if it is possible, I would like this young man to follow me," answered Lord Ishia.

"Thomas?" asked the rabbi, "Of course, Thomas shall follow You, My Lord. Amen."

From that evening on, Thomas became one of Ishia's followers, daily witnessing His wondrous works, and his faith in Lord Ishia grew stronger with each day that came to pass.

Chapter 21

THE CHOSEN TWELVE AND THE TRANSFIGURATION

Ishia spent some time with His beloved Lydia, who was expecting their first child. Together, hand in hand, they walked along the pebbly shore of Kfar-Nahum. They were so much in love thought Judas, watching them from one of the fishing boats. He was so happy for both of them. Lydia was not yet big, but he knew that she was expecting. Ishia had told him about it. And He had been so excited in telling him that He would soon be a father. He watched them walk along the shore, at times getting their feet wet as the morning sun illumined every move they made. They were perfect for each other! But visions of His crucifixion haunted that perfect picture. Judas tried to shake it from his mind but failed. A vivid picture of His death, probably from the films he had seen as a young man, grew clearer in his mind, forcing itself to superimpose on the happy couple strolling along the shore of Yam Kinneret. Judas began to cry uncontrollably, his body shaking like the branch of a tree in the wind. Cephas came to him and asked why he was crying; but Judas did not answer as he continued on with his crying. Yehohanan, Yakov, and Andros came, trying to console him. Finally, Cephas was going to call Ishia but was stopped by Judas, who was still whimpering like a lost child. He told Cephas not to trouble His Lord for every moment He spent with

Lydia was precious for both of them. Cephas nodded but did not quite understand what Judas really meant.

Judas huddled in a corner of the boat, like a lost soul. The other disciples were concerned and did not know what to do. They had never seen Judas cry. Judas, the man of the future, whatever that meant, seemed to be always in control of any situation and seemed to know most of what was going to happen. That morning, he seemed lost and extremely sad. Maybe, he missed his world thought Yehohanan.

When Ishia and Lydia returned from their morning stroll, they found a sad-looking Judas, sitting on the deck by the stern. He stood up, trying to look normal; but the dried up beds of his rivulets of tears had streaked his countenance, clearly manifesting his sadness or sickness. Lydia asked him what was wrong. He partly lied when he told her he missed his world and his family. That was partly true but he had accepted that unconditionally. He knew he could never go back to the future. However, Ishia saw clearly through his facade and wished to have a private talk with him. Lydia graciously allowed them a private talk as she waited by the fishing boats.

"What troubles you, my dear friend?" asked Lord Ishia.

"As I said, My Lord, I miss my family and my friends," answered Judas.

"You are a good man, Judas, a loving husband and a loving father. One day you will see them again. However, I know that you are not telling me everything that is troubling you. Be candid with me. Are we not friends?"

"The best of friends, My Lord. I would sacrifice my life for You, My Lord, if it would be necessary for me to do so."

"Then tell me what is really troubling you, Judas."

"I cannot accept Your death by crucifixion. I am having a hard time with the vision of what will happen to You."

"Good Judas, I have the same difficulty in accepting death; however, through you I have found the strength to accept it."

"Through me, Lord?"

"Yes, my beloved friend, through you I have learned to accept it, even though it comes to haunt me in my dreams and in my prayers. I accept it for your sake and for the sake of mankind. You must be strong and you must do what is necessary when the time comes."

"I dread that moment, My Lord. I saw a vision of Your death as I watched You and Lydia walk along the shore. It took over my mind and I could not shake it off until I cried like a baby. The vision was terrifying, My Lord."

"You must stop thinking of it and enjoy whatever time we still have. Each day is precious and we must experience each day with whatever it brings us. Come, my good friend; but keep your vision to yourself. No one, except Commander Ghabriel and us know about what will happen to us. I will tell them on the night that I will be arrested."

"You mean on the night of my betrayal."

"Your so-called betrayal is not really a betrayal. You are caught in my world and you have a role to play. You will not betray me, Judas. You will guarantee that the words prophesied about my life here on this earth will come to pass. Your presence and your strength in what you have to do are pivotal to the success of my mission, to the success of My Father's Promise to mankind. You are an extremely bright man, the brightest I have encountered here on earth. Surely, you must understand that there is no going back in what we both have to do. You must understand the importance of your actions no matter what consequences follow."

"I do understand, My Lord; but it is still very painful."

"I know that pain and that fear. Try to forget it until the time comes. Now, we must go back, Lydia is anxiously waiting for us."

"Thank you, My Lord! I feel better already. I am fine now. Thank you for sharing my grief," said Judas, as both began to walk back towards the boats.

"I thank you, my friend, for sharing mine."

The following two weeks for Judas were spent in Kfar-Nahum in assisting Lord Ishia with His curing the sick and in helping the other disciples fishing to feed the constant crowds who came to see the Mashìah, the Son of God.

One early morning Judas was gently woken up by Ishia. It was still dark outside but the orange-pinkish rays of the hidden sun began to announce the early dawn of that warm day from behind the hills of Gaulanitis. Judas got up and helped Ishia in awakening the rest of the disciples. Some of them had complained that it was too early but Ishia explained that they had a long journey to make. It was time for Ishia to choose twelve of the disciples to be His apostles. He would test the chosen twelve by sending them on their first missions.

Having cleansed themselves, Ishia and His disciples were ready to begin their long journey to Har Tavor, which Ishia and Judas anxiously wanted to reach to rendezvous with Commander Ghabriel. Lydia and Miryam, Ishia's mother, knew about the journey Ishia and His disciples were about to begin; and, they had prepared breads, dried fish, and several skins of water for them. The journey to Har Tavor was going to be very meaningful to the disciples: twelve of them would be chosen as apostles; they would receive a special power and authority from Lord Ishia and Archangel (Commander) Ghabriel. That power and authority would enable the chosen twelve to fight evil and cure all sicknesses. Although most of the disciples knew the first nine among them who were undoubtedly to be chosen as apostles, they still hoped to be one of the other three apostles. Excitement and hope were manifested in all of the disciples' countenances even though they knew that Lord Ishia had the intention of reaching Har Tavor by the following day. Har Tavor was at least one hundred eighty stadia away and at five stadia per hour it would take thirty-six hours. That would be nearly impossible thought Judas, unless Ishia would keep a brisk pace at seven to eight stadia per hour. That would be possible. And it still would take twelve to thirteen hours per diem. The next two days were going to be tough for many of the disciples for some of them were not physically fit. If Matthias (Levi) were to be chosen as one of the twelve, his rotund body would have to shed some of that fat!

By the time Lord Ishia began His long march the morning sun was shining brightly over the hills of Gaulanitis and Batanaea. It was approximately six o'clock estimated Judas. He led them along the shore of Yam Kinneret, stopping only for a moment at Genne-Sareth. By mid-afternoon, they had reached Taricheae, where they stopped to rest and for a bite to eat. It was late afternoon when they reached the wadi, a couple of stadia north of Arbelah. Ishia had chosen the spot because of the water where they replenished their water skins. Also, they would be able to wash up in the morning. By dusk, most of the disciples were sleeping from exhaustion; thus, Ishia could not instruct them. He chose to pray away from everyone. Judas decided to give Him some privacy, thinking that Ishia must have had a lot on His mind. He watched Him from the corner of his right eye as He prayed by a large rock.

Judas woke up from Ishia's gentle pat and rubbed the sleep from his eyes. It was still dark, possibly five o'clock. Having washed his face and gargled some water, he helped Ishia to wake everyone up. They needed an early start to reach Har Tavor before dusk. The first rays of dawn had begun to slowly illuminate the eastern landscape with tints of a promising day. They traveled on the road to Nazerat most of the morning until they reached a smaller path to the left of the foothills of Har Tir'an. The smaller path led to the source of the northern Wadi Tavor. It was a bit past noon when Ishia and His disciples reached the source of the northern branch of the wadi. Everyone washed their sweat away and had a bite to eat, resting their weary feet by the water.

Ishia, Judas, and most of the disciples eagerly resumed the march. Even the small and rotund Matthias seemed eager and had given his best effort in keeping up with the leaner and faster walkers. Judas had been pleasantly surprised by his endurance and determination. By mid-afternoon the tired group was at the northern foothills of Har Tavor. Having, once again, refilled their water skins the disciples followed their quick-paced Mashìah up the northern slope of the mount. Ishia wanted to be on the flat top of the mountain before dusk. Judas followed a few feet away from His Lord. Most of the others tried to keep up with Ishia's pace. A few were at the tail of the long procession and their distances between each other seemed to get longer. By dusk, everyone was accounted for as they stood on Har Tavor gazing at the last images of the fertile Plain of Jezreel and Yam Kinneret. Even the slowest and the heaviest disciples had made it without any major incidents. Judas was glad that everyone had managed to reach the top of Har Tavor, where the rendezvous with Commander Ghabriel would take place that very night. Judas was too excited to feel his tired legs and went around like an ecstatic child at his birthday party, asking if everyone needed food or water. Only Ishia understood his excitement as all of the other disciples stared at his strange behavior and restlessness. Ishia smiled at Judas, sharing his expectations. The rendezvous was to take place at midnight.

Judas managed to convince Yakov, Ishia's brother, Yehohanan, and Andros to help gather some stones to make a large fire pit. Darkness was accompanied by a chill and most of the disciples were shivering from the penetrating cold. Lord Ishia was busy talking to some of the disciples, probably preparing them for the spectacular event, which would soon unfold. The four made a large fire pit by encircling a large natural hole in the rocky plateau with nearly two-dozen large rocks, forming a stony circle of nearly seven cubits in diameter. They had also gathered enough dried branches and leaves to build a bonfire. Judas built a small pyramid of kindling over dried leaves. From his worn-out GISA knapsack he took a waterproof matchbox, under the close scrutiny of his friends, who had always wondered on the contents of the strange sack. Judas took a match and struck it against the side of the tiny box with a strange writing and a flame burst, igniting the small pile of kindling. It was like magic for all the disciples that had witnessed the flame erupt from that tiny stick. He was truly the Angel from the Future thought many. Judas tried to explain that it was a simple match from the future. In vain, he tried to explain that there was no magic in the way he had started the fire. The four friends began to gently feed the small fire with the smaller branches. As the fire grew stronger, they piled the larger branches and pieces of dead tree trunks on it, creating a real bonfire. They all huddled around the fire to warm their tired and cold bodies. Even Lord Ishia came to warm up his hands and feet, remarking on the wonderful bonfire his four beloved friends had made.

"My beloved friends, as we enjoy this wonderful fire, I want to tell you the names of my chosen twelve. Choosing the twelve has not been an easy task for me and it has taken months of being close to all of you, experiencing daily events together. I equally care for all of you; and, I love you all, every single one of you, every single person on this earth. No matter how intelligent or simple you are, you are all equal in my eyes and in my Father's eyes. You are eighty-four in number and I have chosen you as my disciples. Your tasks will be equal, equally in their difficulties yet-to-be experienced. You, each one of you, I have chosen to represent me here on earth when the time comes for me to leave."

"Why would you leave us, My Lord!" interrupted Cephas.

"Within three years from now, I will leave this world to go back to My Father's world, Paradise. When that time comes…"

Judas gently stopped Cephas from interrupting again.

"Each one of you will travel throughout this world to instruct every man, woman, and child on what you will witness here this very night, and on what you have witnessed daily with me, and on what you will witness until the day comes when I must depart from this earth. Now, I must reveal the twelve among you that I have chosen, and the one who will represent me and become your leader when I am no longer on this earth."

Silence reigned over the group; and, only the crackling of the burning wood accompanied every word that their Lord spoke.

"The chosen twelve are: Cephas and Andros Bar-Jonah, Yakov and Yehohanan Bar-Zebedeus, Yakov Bar-Yousef, my half brother, Philip al-Beth-Saida, Nathanael Bar-Ptolemais of Qana, Thomas Didymus, Matthias Levi Bar-Alpheus, Thaddeus Yehuda Bar-Yakov, Shimon al-Kena'an, and last but not least, my beloved friend, the Angel from the Future, Judas Ish-Kerioth. The first to represent me when I leave will be Cephas Bar-Jonah and the last to represent me before I come back to this earth will be Judas, the Angel from the Future."

Judas stared in shock at Lord Ishia, not understanding the implications of becoming His last representative on earth. Ishia telepathically calmed Judas down, telling him that he would later explain his role as his last representative.

"And, now, each one of you, chosen twelve, will choose six other disciples to share your journey. They will assist you and learn from you as you have learned from me. Early tomorrow you will embark on your journeys as my representatives on this world."

Judas and the rest of the chosen twelve got up, congratulated each other and were congratulated by the other seventy-two. It was an emotional and exciting time for everyone, especially Thomas, Doubting Thomas. He had never expected to be chosen for he had given Lord Ishia such a tough time with his negativity and lack of faith. He wanted to know why he had been chosen when there were so many others who had greater faith in Lord Ishia.

"By the time I will be ready to leave this world, my Doubting Thomas, your faith will be so strong that no one will be able to take it away from you. Now, go and choose your six companions," replied Ishia.

As the flames of the bonfire receded, each chosen twelve worked hard in finding six other disciples to work with for their first mission. Judas had chosen Linus, Lydia's brother, Yehuda al-Kfar-Nahum, Abu-al-Kursi, the former swineherd, Manasheh, the young boy who had been cured by Ishia and his father, Henoch, and an older man named Shimon Bar-David. He motioned them to follow him towards a large oak. He sat down with his back to the trunk and asked his six disciples to sit. He told them about himself, his search for the Mashìah, and how Lord Ishia cured him of his incurable sickness; however, he did not mention anything from his other life from the future. In turn he asked each one to say something about himself and how each one had come to follow Lord Ishia, Son of the Most High. Judas knew Linus very well—they had become good friends since Yeriho. He also knew Abu-al-Kursi, young Manasheh and his father, Henoch.

Yehuda al-Kfar-Nahum was a young man of no more than twenty years old. He was born in the town of Kfar-Nahum, from a young Hebrew girl and a roman soldier. He never knew his father and his mother had tried her best to raise him. Sadly, his mother died when Yehuda was only six years old, leaving him with his uncle, who had sexually abused him for years until he got enough courage to run away. He had made his way to Thella, northwards on the Ha-Yarden, by the southern shore of Yam Hula, a much smaller lake than Yam Kinneret. There, he worked for a wonderful family of fishermen until he began to hear stories of the wonderful miracles of Ishia of Nazerat. He had decided to see for himself if the stories were true; and, of course, he had become a fervent disciple of Lord Ishia, the Mashìah.

Shimon Bar-David, at sixty-one years of age, was considered an old man. Most men did not reach past fifty. Life was tough and there were many dangers. Shimon had been waiting for the Mashìah all his life; and, he had been blessed by His presence and by the chance to follow Him. His children had all married and had left town; and, his wife, Yehudith, had died of a horrible sickness. Alone and lonely, he had decided to sell his home and search for the Mashìah.

Suddenly, Cephas broke the story with his powerful shout, calling everyone to go and listen to the Lord's message. Everyone got up and walked towards their Lord. He stood high on a rock as the chosen twelve and their seventy-two disciples stood all around Him.

"Please, sit down, my beloved friends. Tonight, anyone of you who has any energy left to stay up will witness the glory and power of My Father."

"We will all stay awake, My Lord!" exclaimed Cephas.

"Cephas, most of you are exhausted and the time to witness My Father's glory is not yet at hand. Most of you will be sleeping; but a few of you will witness His power and glory. Once you will have witnessed it," Ishia pointed up to the sky, "You will receive His power and authority over evil and the gift to heal the sick."

Everyone, including Judas was in awe at Lord Ishia's message, not fully understanding all its implications and consequences.

"Only when you will have witnessed My Father's power and glory will you begin to understand who I am. Tomorrow morning, each one of you that I have chosen, together with your chosen six disciples, will begin your first mission in my name. Each one of the twelve will choose a town, city, or village, which you have never visited and you will travel there, taking nothing for your journey. None of you will carry money, food, or extra clothing. You will not help yourself with a staff and you will not have a change of clothes. However, you will have the most powerful gifts that My Father can give you: authority over evil and the gift of healing. These two gifts will be your weapons to survive against evil and diseases; but these two gifts will not work without your unconditional faith in me, in My Father, and in yourselves. As you reach your destinations, stay where you are welcomed and fight evil and cure the sick in my name. If the place you have chosen does not welcome you, leave immediately and shake its dust from your sandals to witness your condemnation of that town. Now, each one of the chosen twelve gather your six disciples, discuss and choose your destination. Once we separate tomorrow, you will have six months of time to accomplish your first mission. Then, we will all meet again at my house in Kfar-Nahum," commanded Lord Ishia.

Without asking questions, heavy in thought of their mission, each apostle and six disciples found a private place to discuss their goal. Lord Ishia knelt on the rock He had stood on and began to pray. The commotion and disagreements some of the groups were experiencing did not seem to bother Him as His concentration grew deeper into a profound meditation; and, no one dared to break His prayer. Finally, every group had managed to come up with a town or village that had not been visited by each respective party. Exhausted by the long march, little sleep, and the hot fire, all of the apostles and disciples, with the exception of Judas, found a spot to rest.

Judas sat by the fire, fighting fatigue and rubbing his eyes to stay awake. His excitement was stronger than his exhaustion as he fought it with the little energy left in him. This rendezvous with Commander Ghabriel was pivotal regarding his future and the future of the chosen ones. He guarded the fire, the rest of the disciples, and His Lord. He was taking the responsibility to ensure that the rest of the apostles and disciples would bear witness to the power of Ishia's Father, Lord Yahweh of Paradise.

Judas sat by the fire, his eyes transfixed on his Meditating Lord. His countenance clearly manifested so much anguish and pain as tears formed rivulets from His eyes. Judas was concerned. Why was He crying? What pain was He experiencing in His solitude? Judas got up from the rock, which was warm from the fire, and tiptoed towards His Lord.

"Why do You cry, My Lord?" Judas whispered to Ishia for he did not want to wake up anyone.

"I cry for all the innocent people that will be slain, all the injustices that will be done, and all the lies that will be spoken in the next two millennia, all of them executed in my name. I cry often when those images of atrocities haunt my memory. The pain is too great for me to bear."

"I will gladly share some of that pain, My Lord."

"You already have had your share, my good friend. Your face bears the pain of all the suffering you and your friends have gone through during Armageddon. It will be because of you that I will give up my life for all the sins ever committed and that will be committed in the next two millennia."

"I am greatly troubled by what You have said, My Lord. Do you mean that I have to betray you?"

"No, my dearest friend, I do not mean that. I have been feeling that my dying might be in vain; but you have changed that feeling. Now, I know for sure that it will not be in vain because you will be there to amend all the wrong. You will be there to prepare for

201

my return. Knowing that you, Judas, will be welcoming me when I return makes my dying less painful."

"But, why must you die, My Lord?"

"In My Father's world, before the discovery of everlasting life, dying for a friend was the greatest gift anyone could give. My death will be my gift to mankind to show my love for everyone on earth. My resurrection will be the reminder of who I am."

"My Lord, I will always be by Your side, even at death. I will be beside You, on Your right hand side."

"I know, my friend, my beloved friend, Judas. And if my death were to be only for your friendship, it would be justified."

"There will be many good people who will live their lives according to Your teachings and die for You, My Lord. Your death will not be just for me; but it will be for the whole mankind."

"You are a true friend, Judas. You are the only one who fully understands my mission. Look at them—they sleep without any worries."

"Lord, there is a star traveling from the moon," Judas pointed out, staring at the vast darkness above them.

"It is Commander Ghabriel's ship. He will soon be here to demonstrate My Father's Power and Glory."

They both looked up, watching the star getting bigger as it got closer to earth.

"Shall I wake them up, My Lord?"

"No, my friend. My Father's Glory is not for everyone to see. Whoever wakes up shall witness His Power and Glory. Come, Judas, you will come up into Ghabriel's ship with me," spoke Ishia as he got up from the rock.

Judas followed Him to the bald rocky section of Har Tavor's top. The star had become Commander Ghabriel's starship. Its bright lights formed a circular geometric design, very much like a snowflake-shaped design within a circle. It was beautiful to see and anyone witnessing this spectacular display would definitely think of it as the star from heaven. The noise and wind grew stronger as the wonderful starship slowed down to a stop, hovering at about fifty feet from the rocky mesa. A slanted beam of light emitted from the center of the starship, reaching Ishia. Judas stood a few feet behind Him, eager to board Commander Ghabriel's wonderful spaceship. Ishia beckoned him to step on the wide beam, which would take them to the open hatch of the ship.

By now, Cephas, Yakov and Yehohanan Bar-Zebedeus had awakened by the powerful rush produced by the starship's arrival and had somnambulated towards their Lord. They witnessed their Lord, together with Eli-Yahw or Moishe, being taken into a bright cloud by a gigantic column of light. When their Lord reached the opening of the bright cloud, where the column of light came from, another person joined them, shaking hands and embracing them. The light became so bright that their Lord's face shone like the sun and His robe became whiter than snow. The two prophets, who must have been Eli-Yahw and Moishe, stood by His side, slightly behind Him. The three were speaking to each other.

"My Lord, it is wonderful for us to have witnessed your glory. If it is Your wish, allow us to set up three tents: one for You, one for Moishe, and one for Eli-Yahw," spoke Cephas, overwhelmed by his Lord's heavenly power.

A powerful voice, coming from the bright cloud, broke Cephas' offer, "This is my Only Beloved Son; and, I am proud of Him. Listen to Him for His words are Mine."

Cephas, Yakov, and Yehohanan fell on their knees, lowering their faces to the ground, afraid of the All-Powerful voice of Yahweh. They heard a noise like a powerful wind, which shook the trees around them. Their clothing flapped around their bodies and, then, everything was calm. They dared not look up, afraid of the Power of Yahweh, but a gentle touch to Cephas' shoulder startled him. It was His Lord; and, Judas stood behind Him.

"Stand up, my friends, and do not be afraid. Tell no one about what you have witnessed until the Son of Man will rise from death. Now, go back to sleep for tomorrow you will begin a long journey towards your first mission," revealed Lord Ishia.

Judas woke up early as the precocious hues from the orient impatiently waited to proclaim the glory of the new dawn. He searched around the sleeping bodies of his friends, looking for His Lord; but he could not find Him. He searched frantically on the rocky plateau only to find Him in deep meditation, sitting by the edge of the cliff. He approached Him slowly and carefully, trying his best not to make any noise that would disturb His Lord's meditation. Before

Judas could reach Him, Ishia gracefully got up and greeted him, "Good morning to you, Judas! You are up early. The sun has not yet shown its face; but judging by the warm colors emitting from the orient sky I can truly say that today will be a beautiful one.

"Good morning, My Lord! Yes, it looks like it is going to be a wonderful day; but..." answered Judas.

"You are not sure of yourself and of your mission," continued Ishia.

"Yes, My Lord, I am not sure of myself. I have doubts that I possess the gift of healing; and, if I do not have it my mission will be a failure," whispered Judas.

"My beloved friend, we have discussed this often enough during our travels. Each one of you has the power of healing. It is part of the human brain's healing dynamism. Every person has this gift, which was genetically given by My Father, and it has the power to combat any illness that enters the human body. This synergic force automatically heals illnesses, wounds, and foreign diseases that enter our human bodies. Of course, this power is stronger in some than others for it is directly influenced by each individual diet. The richer the diet, the stronger is the healing within each one of us. People with poor diets or lacking the proper nutrition will have weaker systems, allowing illnesses to take over. However, transferring the power to heal from oneself into another requires the belief of both parties. You, Judas, must believe in your own power and the sick persons must believe in you and their own inner power."

"I understand, Lord. But the power in me will be effective by my faith in You!"

"Your faith in me will never fail you, my beloved friend. You, Judas, are the only one who can conceptualize all of my teachings. Your mind is far more advanced than these simple fishermen; however, faith in my teaching, time, and experience will change all of them. Each one of them, at each respective time, will see the light that I bring to them. Come now; help me in waking them up. It is dawn and we all have long journeys ahead of us."

The sun's first rays gloriously illuminated the mountainous skyline of Yarden as Ishia and Judas walked back towards the sleeping group. Gently they proceeded in waking up each disciple and apostle. Once again, Lord Ishia instructed them on the powers of faith and of healing. He then began His descend of Har Tavor, followed by Judas and a long line of apostles and disciples. At the bottom of the mountain He embraced each one of them, wishing them a successful mission: to spread His good news and to cure the sick.

Judas and his six disciples chose to walk back with Lord Ishia until Kfar-Nahum. From there they would walk along the eastern shore of Yam Kinneret, and eventually reach Gadara, their chosen village for their mission.

Chapter 22

IN THE NAME OF ISHIA, THE MASHIAH

Judas, Linus, Yehuda al-Kfar-Nahum, Abu-al-Kursi, Shimon Bar-David, Manasheh Bar-Enoch and his father, Enoch, before leaving embraced their Lord, Miryam and Lydia, who was in her last stage of her pregnancy. The other eleven apostles and their respective six disciples had chosen Sepphoris, Scythopolis, Beth-She'arim, Usha, Ptolemais, Tyre, Meron, Thella, Caesarea Philippi, Shidon, and Damascus for their missions.

Having bidden farewell to everyone present at the house of their Lord, Judas and his six disciples began their journey to Gadara. Judas led the way towards Beth-Saida, their first stop, approximately thirty stadia away, a six-hour walk.

Four hours later, Judas and his six disciples stood by the west bank of the Ha-Yarden, the northern part of the river, which flowed from Lacus Semechonitis. Carefully, they crossed the sweet refreshing water of the sacred river and continued towards Beth-Saida, the hometown of Philip and of Shimon and Andros Bar-Jonah. Two hours later they reached Beth-Saida—it was mid-afternoon.

Along the shore Judas was recognized by a fisherman, named Yakov, who believed in Ishia the Mashìah. Yakov begged Judas and his six disciples to rest at his house and invited them to dine with his family. Yakov, his wife Hannah, his mother Sharah, and his eight children were ecstatic to have Judas and his disciples for dinner. Hannah had cooked freshly caught fish and delicious fresh bread, with olives cured in olive oil and wine vinegar. It was a simple but most delicious meal. Yakov even served wine from Arbelah, treating Judas as if he were the Mashìah. However, he understood that in Yakov's eyes he represented their Lord. Judas told them of their mission and Yakov asked him a favor: to cure his mother's constant headaches. Judas hesitated; but he remembered his mission and this would be a perfect time and place to test his healing power. Judas agreed as Yakov's big happy eyes smiled at the possibility that his mother's painful and constant headaches might be taken away from her head.

Old Sharah approached Judas as his disciples, Yakov, Hannah, and their eight children anxiously observed Judas' every move. Sharah was perhaps in her early sixties but looked much older, aged from her long life's travails. She had not had an easy life with an abusive husband and the duty to raise her ten children, of which Yakov had been the third. Raising six sons and four daughters was not an easy task. The loss of her husband, during a terrible storm on Yam Kinneret, was a blessing from heaven because there would be no more beatings. However, the loss of her two oldest sons, who were on the fishing boat with their father, was a tragedy for Sharah and her eight surviving children. Yakov had told Judas that the daily headaches had developed from the beatings his mother had received from her husband—he would slap and, at times, punch her head. She stood in front of wonderful Judas, who could have easily passed for a prophet or the mashiah himself. A little lady, slightly bent by the burden of a hard life, scarred by her husband's beatings, her heart broken by the loss of her two young and handsome sons.

"Please, sit down dear Sharah," whispered Judas with the gentlest tone, acquired by his own losses and sufferings from another life in another time. Also, living with Ishia had changed Judas into a gentler, more understanding, and loving human being. He laid his hands on Sharah's head, as she sat on a wooden bench by the table.

"Sharah, you must believe that you and I, together, can free your head from your terrible headaches. I know you really want to get rid of them; but, you must believe that I can cure you through the power of Our Lord Ishia, the Mashìah?"

"Yes, I believe in Lord Ishia the Mashìah, the Son of the Most High!" exclaimed Sharah.

"Do you believe that we, together, in His Name, can cast these awful headaches away, once and for all?" asked Judas.

"Yes, I really do believe that we can cast them away in His Holy Name."

"Then, in the name of Our Lord Ishia, the Mashìah, I order you, Sharah, to cast away the terrible pains that haunt your head and be free of them for the rest of your life!" exclaimed Judas, still holding her head with his two hands, praying with his eyes closed. Gently, Judas relaxed his hold and slowly he removed his hands from Sharah's head. He looked at her apprehensively. She looked confused, maybe lost. Minutes passed and Judas began to feel angst of failure and disappointment as he slowly walked out of Yakov's rustic stony abode. He sat, in the dark, on a stony bench by the front of the house, with his face buried in his hands.

Dreadful moments passed, which felt like an eternity within Judas, before Linus came out calling on Judas, "Judas! Judas! Quickly, come in. Come and see Sharah. I think she is cured."

Judas immediately stood up, rejuvenated by the positive news about Sharah, and followed Linus into the little house. Everyone stood happily around Sharah, smiling and taking turns hugging her. They all turned around as Judas reentered Yakov's warm and loving home. Sharah had the most wonderful smile, making her look a little younger, as she greeted Judas with open arms. She gratefully thanked him while holding him in a motherly embrace. Yakov and his family happily stared at Judas, waiting their turn to embrace him and thank him for curing their mother and grandmother. His disciples stood proudly and happy for Judas had worked his first miracle; and, they also waited to embrace him and congratulate him. Judas was very emotional, his lips trembling, his eyes gleaming with the wetness secreted by his lachrymal glands. He tried to hold his tears as one escaped from his right eye, hitting Sharah's gentle face.

That evening Yakov and Hannah served more wine and olives to celebrate their mother's cure and Judas' first miracle. They sipped on the semi-sweet wine of Arbelah, munched on the spiced olives, and talked about Lord Ishia, their Mashìah. They all celebrated until the first hour of the morning, until their eyes were laden with fatigue from the long day and all the emotion of the miraculous evening. Finally, having bidden each other good night, they all went to sleep.

The following morning, Sharah had prepared breakfast for Judas and his disciples.

The simple table was decorated with freshly baked bread, fruits, and freshly squeezed orange juice, a simple but healthy breakfast, which everyone enjoyed. Sharah had also prepared two loaves of bread, a small wheel of goat cheese, bananas, and oranges for Judas and his friends for their long march to Gadara.

Having embraced Sharah, Yakov, Hannah and their children, Judas, Linus, Yehuda al-Kfar-Nahum, Abu-al-Kursi, Shimon Bar-David, Enoch and his son, Manasheh Bar-Enoch, began their long walk along the eastern shore of Yam Kinneret. Yakov and his children followed them along the shore, frolicking with the gentle waves just like sandpipers, leaving their footprints only to be gently erased by each new disappearing wave. After several stadia they all bid each other farewell once again. Yakov and his children headed back north as Judas and his six disciples continued south towards Gergesa.

The late morning sun had become so hot that Judas decided to take a rest by the mouth of a small wadi. There they sat on some rocks and ate some bread, cheese, and fruits as their feet were cooled by the refreshing water of the tiny stream. It was Linus who broke the silence, "Dear Judas, how did you cure old Sharah's headaches?"

"I simply suggested to Sharah to get rid of her headaches by believing in the Name of Ishia, Our Mashìah!" exclaimed Judas.

"I know that, I witnessed your first miracle. But, I am trying to understand what went on inside Sharah's mind," continued Linus.

"The human brain has great powers: the power to fight most sicknesses; however, the sick person must believe in that power, and most of the times that power can be triggered by suggestion. Also, by invoking the name of Ishia stimulates believers like Sharah to fight the sickness that afflicts them."

"Are you saying that miracles are natural and can be controlled by anyone?" asked Linus, still somewhat unsatisfied with Judas' explanation.

"Miracles are complicated yet simple. Every day is a miracle—to wake up each morning and see the sun is a miracle. To be here with all of you is a miracle for me. To be alive and feel great about oneself is a miracle. Everything is possible if you really believe; but if you believe in Our Lord Ishia and in yourself the impossible can become possible."

Everyone was silent, ruminating on Judas' last explanation on miracles, even Judas himself. They continued southwards along the lakeshore, with the hills and mountains of Yarden by their left. It was a beautiful sunny day in Yarden for Judas and his six disciples.

Judas thought about his other world, two thousand years away. He missed his daughter very much. He still missed his wife, his son, and his parents, even though he knew they had died years ago. Their faces deeply photographed in the walls of the canyons of his memories. There had not been a day or night that he had not recalled those beautiful faces, which he loved so much. Although he missed his family whose features were sharply sculpted within his memories Judas knew that he would never see them again. He had resigned himself to fate and he would try to do his best with his new life as an apostle of His Savior.

Judas continued along the shore, followed by his men, recalling his loved ones and thinking about his new life. How could it be possible for him to be there in Yarden, in Hagalil, with the Only Son of Yahweh, with His Lord, Ishia of Nazerat? This had all been possible because of his old friend, Dr. Weinstein, and his wonderful invention. For Judas Dr. Weinstein had been the greatest inventor in the history of mankind. He had finally found His Mashìah because of his wonderful machine. And now, he was cured and healthy. Judas smiled as he wetted his feet with the waters of the Sea of Hagalil.

A despairing cry for help awakened Judas from his ambulating reverie. His dreamy eyes stared southwards along the shore, finally focusing on a few people approximately two stadia away. Judas began to run towards them, followed by his disciples. Young Manasheh and Linus easily passed him and outdistanced him as they ran full speed towards the hopeless cries. Within two minutes, Judas and his four older disciples saw Linus and Manasheh reaching the small crowd and then immediately removing their garments and quickly diving into the lake, swimming towards a floating body. By the time Judas and the elder disciples had reached the small crowd of people Linus and Manasheh had reached the floating body and were beginning to swim back, holding on to the body and making sure that the head was above the water.

"My sweet Esther, she's dead. Oh, woe to me, my angel is dead!" cried a woman, as she beat her breasts while a man held her tenderly. Both were crying.

"How long...ago...did your...daughter...drown?" asked Judas, reaching for breath.

"Why are you asking that? Can't you see how much pain we are in!" exclaimed the man as his wife continued her lamentation.

"Please, tell me how long? Maybe, I can still save her!" replied Judas.

"Are you Ishia of Nazerat?" asked a woman nearby.

"No, I am Judas, one of His apostles. How long as she been floating in the lake?" continued Judas with alarm.

"Only moments before those two brave young men got here," stated the man.

"Maybe, it is not too late to save her," declared Judas.

Everyone, including his four elder disciples incredulously stared at him as if he had blasphemed. Only the Mashìah had brought people back from the dead. They all stared at him with disbelief and some with contempt in their eyes. Their mood was instantly changed as Linus and Manasheh had reached the shore and were now carrying the body of young Esther. They gently laid her body down, using their robes to rest her head.

Immediately, Judas knelt beside Esther's body and placed his hand below her right lowest rib, just below her armpit and felt no movement, as he admired her beautiful face. She must have been in her mid-twenties and one of the most beautiful woman he had ever encountered; and, he was going to use any or all of the methods to resuscitate her. Quickly, Judas moved the bunched up robes forward underneath her shoulders as he gently dropped her head back. He got up and knelt at Esther's head with his knees beside her ears, grasping her wrists and placing her arms together across her chest. He rocked forward, putting pressure on Esther's arms as they pushed the lower part of her chest. Then he rocked backwards, lifting her arms in a circular fashion and then stretched them over her head as far as possible, as his torso leaned backwards. He repeated the strange rowing procedure several times without success under everyone's scrutinizing eyes. He could not give up! He quickly got up and knelt beside her head. Without wasting time he placed his mouth over Esther's beautiful lips, pinching her nose, and blew gently but constantly into her mouth. He saw her chest rise. Keeping his hands on her jaw and nose, he removed his mouth from hers and looked at her chest moving down, feeling the exhaled air on his ear. He repeated the strange kiss and stare every five-six seconds, counting in his head 'Thousand one, thousand two,…thousand six', continuing his mouth-to-mouth artificial respiration. Blowing and looking, blowing and looking, he continued without hesitation, concentrating every millisecond on resuscitating the beautiful Esther, as everyone stood around strangely staring at Judas kissing and looking at the dead body of beautiful Esther. Only the intermittent sobs of Esther's mother broke the silence of the crowd, which was getting larger by each second. Everyone wanted to see the strange man kissing the dead body of Esther as her parents and the six disciples had formed a protective circle around Judas and Esther's body. Linus had counted twenty-eight kisses before Esther moaned and vomited as Judas raised her torso up to allow easier breathing.

"ESTHER!" cried out her mother, "My beautiful daughter!" She embraced her.

Judas helped Esther stand up and for the first time noticed that she was blind. The crowd cheered for joy. Judas' disciples were astonished at his power. Judas gently led beautiful Esther towards the lake as her parents helped, fearful of the water. Judas stopped when the water had reached their waistline and he proceeded in washing the vomit from Esther's robe and face. Judas' disciples controlled the excited crowd, forbidding anyone to go into the lake for fear of another drowning. Most people did not know how to swim.

"You kissed me back to life," gently spoke Esther.

"It is called mouth-to-mouth resuscitation," volunteered Judas.

"It is the kiss of life!" exclaimed the father, "It is the kiss from the Lord Himself."

"It is just a method…" answered Judas.

"You have a beautiful kiss, my savior," whispered Esther into Judas' ear.

Judas looked back at the crowd, blushing from embarrassment.

"My name is Jared Bar-Yakov. This is my wife Deborah. Thank you for bringing my Esther back from the dead. Name anything that I own and it is yours."

"A bowl of soup and some bread for me and my disciples would be greatly appreciated," replied Judas.

Jared laughed, "Nonsense, a feast for you and your disciples to celebrate this wonderful miracle. Come, let us go to my house!" He waded between Judas and his daughter, holding both by their arms. His wife held the other side of Esther as they waded back to shore.

Judas' disciples came to embrace him, still mesmerized by his great miracle. Next to Lord Ishia, Judas was certainly the most powerful of His apostles. They followed Esther and her parents as the crowd cheered and spoke words of praise. *The kiss of life* seemed to be everyone's favorite phrase. Judas, his disciples, and the crowd followed the happy family to their house at the top of a hill on the northern outskirt of Gergesa.

Jared had a large house with guest rooms and a few servants, who quickly began to prepare a feast for Judas and his disciples. Roasted lamb and fish, fresh baked bread, olives and cheese, fruits, and wine were some of the food served by Jared's servants. Judas found out that Jared was a wealthy olive merchant. He owned a large olive orchard on the hills behind his house. His olives were harvested to be cured and to be pressed into olive oil. Jared's olive business was a family business, which had been found by Ybrahim Bar-Amalech, one of his ancestors.

Jared's wife, Deborah, had been infecund and after years of trying to have a baby she finally gave birth to a baby girl. She was named Esther after Jared's mother and she became the pupil of her father's eye. At the tender age of six, Esther lost her vision after a serious fall from an escarpment within his property. Healers tried every possible creams and pomades to no avail; thus, both parents accepted Esther's blindness as fate. They guarded her dearly all her life; and, although there had been a few suitors Esther had no intention to be married. Her wish was to remain with her parents, who loved her profoundly and were happy to have her at home and care for her needs. She was their only child and loved her the way she was, beautiful, blind, and as pure as the lilies of Hagalil.

As Judas ate, Esther sat beside him, enamored by what he had done and by his strange-but-charming accent. Jared and Deborah barely tasted the food, concentrating more on Judas than on the feast that had been prepared. They were studying him. They were studying the way he talked and the way he ate. They knew that Judas was a learned man with the most impeccable table manners. He spoke and ate like no one they had ever met and they liked the idea that their only daughter was falling madly in love with him. Judas spoke of His Lord, Ishia of Nazerat, the Mashìah. He spoke of His great miracles, of His mission on earth, and of the importance in believing that He was the Only Son of the Almighty Yahweh. Judas' disciples were busy eating and talking to several other guests, important people of Gergesa.

"Are you married, Judas?" asked Jared.

"I was! Both my wife and son died during a terrible war. I have a daughter, she is about five years younger than Esther."

"Where do you come from?" asked Deborah.

"From a far away land. You must cross the Mediterranean Sea and a greater sea to reach my country."

"Will you be going back to your homeland?" continued Jared.

"It is impossible for me to go back. There is no one that could possibly sail through the Atlantic Ocean. That is the name of the great sea, many times larger than the Mediterranean, which stands between my land and here. Also, there is a problem with time."

"Would it take too long to get there?" asked Jared.

"Yes, it would if any sailboat would be able to endure the Atlantic's storms," answered Judas, not wanting to try to explain the two millennia difference in time.

"My good friend, you are welcome to stay in my house as long as you want to and you may have anything that would please you. You have brought back my daughter from the dead!" exclaimed Jared.

"I do not wish for any worldly possessions and you have already given me and my disciples a wonderful feast. I thank you, Jared Bar-Yakov, Deborah, and beautiful Esther for your wonderful hospitality and delicious food and wine. However, tomorrow we must leave."

"Why must you leave, my savior?" asked Esther, perturbed by Judas' sudden decision to leave.

"I am on a mission, given to me by My Lord, Ishia of Nazerat. I must continue to Gadara, the goal of my trip."

"Will you not stay a few more days for Esther? You not only have brought her back from the dead but you have given her a new meaning to her life. You can be her teacher; and, I will pay you generously. Please stay with us…your presence brightens this house," begged Jared, as his disciples looked at him for his approval to stay longer.

Judas looked at his disciples' begging eyes—they were enjoying the delicious feast. He looked at Jared and Deborah and saw the eagerness in their face and then shifted his eyes to Esther's beautiful and innocent face, which was no more than a foot away from his, and he could not utter a negative answer to his host's expectation, "I will stay longer for Esther. I will teach her Lord Ishia's teachings. I will teach her about ancient history and beautiful stories that have been written; however, I do not wish to be paid for it. Your hospitality and daily victuals for me and my six disciples will be more than I could ever ask for my service," answered Judas.

Esther was so ecstatic that he hugged and kissed Judas on the cheek. His disciples and guests were extremely joyous, and Jared and Deborah beamed with happiness. It was Jared who broke the joyous laughter, "Another toast to Judas, my daughter's savior and teacher."

"To Judas!" everyone exclaimed with joy and drank more of the sweet red wine.

Gergesa, like Beth-Saida and Kfar-Nahum, was principally a fishing town; but there were several other businessmen like Jared: camel and horse traders, smiths, carpenters, masons, and a fishing boat builder. Jared proudly showed off his hometown, leading Judas and his disciples throughout its streets. Along the shore, it was evident from the smell that Gergesa was mostly a fishing town. Jared brought Judas and his men to the synagogue, where they met the rabbi and prayed for a while. Then, they followed Jared along the Wadi Samakh, which originated from the east side of Gergesa deep from the mountains of Hagolan. A path along the wadi led back to Jared's olive orchards.

Judas and his disciples dedicated the mornings to visiting Gergesa, helping the sick and the poor. Everyone in town loved them for their goodness and care they provided. Groups of people would gather to listen to Judas preaching the words of His Lord, Ishia of Nazerat, the Mashìah. Although Judas' accent was noticeable, his oratorical abilities were superior to most and he was able to attract a good crowd and their attention for hours. His knowledge of the human body was vast and was able to answer many questions about sicknesses and pain. Most of all, Judas surely had the gift of healing, which he had received from His Lord, and used it effectively. He cured many sick people in the name of Ishia of Nazerat, the Mashìah. His disciples were proud to be with Judas and learned so much from him. Every mid-afternoon Judas would help Esther to go up a small hill and sit under a great oak. There, protected in the shade, he would teach Esther about the ancient history of all great civilizations and would tell her wonderful stories about the great and famous people of the Old Testament. Judas welcomed his disciples and anyone from Jared's house to attend those late afternoon classes. However, after supper Esther would always ask for a private lesson from Judas. His disciples would happily oblige privacy for Judas and Esther and would gladly keep Jared company, sharing their daily experiences and some delicious wine.

Although blind, Esther would easily show Judas the way along the wadi up to the top of the hill. Being a true gentleman with genuine care, Judas would always hold Esther's hand, preventing many possible falls. Esther was deliriously in love with Judas, laughing at every time Judas would hold her from falling. Judas did not mind Esther's silliness. Actually, he enjoyed being with her and dreamt about her every night. Days passed. Weeks flew by and Judas could not bear to leave her for he had finally accepted the reality that he loved her dearly.

One evening, underneath the great oak tree, Esther declared her love for Judas.

"Judas! I love you," she spoke softly.

"My sweet Esther," replied Judas, "I love you very much."

Softly Judas kissed her beautiful full lips. Her lips burned like fire. He continued to kiss her as they both whispered tender words of love to each other. For the first time since he had lost his wife, Judas had romantically kissed another woman. He felt like a young man again. He was in love!

Judas could not fall asleep that night for he could not stop thinking about the beautiful Esther. The beautiful woman he had saved with mouth-to-mouth resuscitation was in love with him and he with her. He was being given a second chance in a second life so far removed in time and place from his first. He spent the entire night thinking about Esther, about Judith, about his children, Catherine and David, about Ishia, about what would Judith think, about what would his children think, about what would Ishia think! Finally, he fell asleep and dreamt about he and Esther being married by His Lord, Ishia. All the apostles and disciples were present. All of Ishia's followers were there; and, in that crowd, witnessing his marriage to Esther were also Judith, Catherine, David, his parents, Judith's family, all his colleagues, all his climbing friends, all the post-nuclear members of the Seneca Rocks Climbers. Everyone was there!

Judas woke up in a sweat. It was late morning. Everyone in Jared's house was anxiously waiting for him to get up. He washed his face, wishing for a toothbrush and the best toothpaste money could buy. He really missed brushing his teeth! He gargled some water and spit it out of the window into a bush. He went out of his room into the courtyard, where his disciples were eagerly waiting for him. A servant was also waiting for him with freshly squeezed orange juice, fresh bread and sweet dates. A healthy breakfast! Judas munched on the bread and dates, drank the rest of his juice and thanked the servant.

"Where is Esther?" asked Judas to his six disciples.

"She is with her parents in Gergesa. She went to buy material from Damascus," volunteered Linus.

"I see..." said Judas, "Follow me. I must share a secret and must ask your opinion on a very delicate subject."

The six followed him silently up the hill instead of the road to Gergesa.

"I, I...I'm having a difficult time with this," spoke Judas.

"It's about Esther? Isn't it?" asked old Shimon Bar-David.

"Yes, Shimon. It is about Esther," replied Judas.

"She loves you, Judas," continued old Shimon.

The rest were attentive and seemed to be extremely happy.

"Yes, Shimon. She does."

"And you love her!" exclaimed Shimon.

"How could you possibly know that?" asked Judas, in total shock that old Shimon knew his secret. He looked at the others. They were smiling at him. "Did you spy on me last evening?" he asked them.

"We would never do that, Judas. We have too much respect for you!" declared Yehuda al-Kfar-Nahum.

"Did you also know, Yehuda?" asked Judas.

"We all know, Judas," said Linus.

"Did Esther tell you?"

"No, but everyone can see that you and Esther are deeply in love," said Abu-al-Kursi, "Jared and Deborah have often talked about it. This is not a secret, Judas!"

"And I thought…"

"You thought no one else knew. It's written in your eyes, in your smile, in the way you attend to her, and in the way that she adores you, Judas. She lives for you, only for you!" exclaimed old Shimon.

"And the material from Damascus?" asked Judas.

"For a beautiful wedding tunic for Esther!" exclaimed young Manasheh.

"Oh, my…I must speak to her parents, today!" exclaimed Judas, "Tonight, after supper. I will propose after supper."

"I am certain that there will be excitement and joy in Jared's house tonight," proclaimed Enoch.

Everyone joyfully agreed and began to follow Judas down the path along the wadi. A path that he had walked on hundreds of times in the past four months, mostly with Esther, at times with his disciples, sometimes with Jared, and occasionally alone. He knew every step, every stone, every bush or tree along that path. At last, they were back at Jared's house. Judas went back to his room to think about what he was going to say. His six disciples waited in the courtyard, eagerly waiting for Jared, Deborah, and Esther to come home. They knew there would be a celebration that evening; and, they also knew that Jared would not spare anything to celebrate Judas' proposal to his beautiful daughter.

The sun was at midpoint in the sky. It was noon when Jared, his wife, and his daughter reached their home to find Judas' six disciples anxiously waiting in the courtyard.

"Is something wrong?" asked Jared, with a worried look in his face.

"No, nothing wrong, Jared; but, I think Judas would like to speak to you," replied old Shimon, "He is in his room."

Jared looked at his wife and then at his daughter. He smiled and quickly stepped up the staircase, which led to the bedrooms. He reached Judas' room and, without hesitation, knocked.

"Come in, the door is not bolted," Judas' voice seemed distant, muffled by the thick wooden door.

Jared pushed the door open and walked in, closing the door behind him. Judas stood pensively by the window. "Is anything wrong, my son?" asked Jared. Lately Jared had often called Judas son. Judas did not mind. Jared was very much like his father, happy and generous.

"No, Jared," sighed Judas, "But I must talk to you about Esther and I."

"Please, go on, my son."

"It is very difficult for me to say what I am about to say. So, please be patient with me."

"Take your time; and, I'm not in any hurry. You have my undivided attention!"

"Thank you, Jared, you are a very kind man. You know that I care very much for your daughter Esther; however, in the past few weeks my feelings towards her have grown immensely. I realize that I am sixteen years older than Esther—I'm not a young man anymore. I was once married with a family in another land far away. I am now a widower. I am not rich…and, I can't offer Esther a wealthy life that she so justly deserves. I have chosen to be a follower of Lord Ishia, the Mashiah; and, in doing so, I will follow Him everywhere He goes. That means that Esther must remain with you and Deborah at times for her safety…I love your daughter, Jared. If you are not pleased by this, I will leave this very instant. Please, try to understand my situation!" begged Judas.

"Not pleased! I have been waiting for this moment since your first evening in my house. I am the happiest father in the world because my beautiful daughter has found the most wonderful husband on this earth. You have my blessing, my son," exclaimed Jared, placing his hands on Judas' head, "And now, let me tell you something. My daughter comes with a very rich dowry; therefore, you will also be rich."

"It's not necessary, Jared. Your daughter is the richest treasure that I could receive in this world. Money and possessions are not important."

"You are wonderful and genuine, Judas; but, I insist in a dowry. I want my Esther to be comfortable. It's a father's wish. You understand?"

"Yes, I understand. But Jared, there is only one problem...I would like My Lord, Ishia to marry us in Kfar-Nahum."

"Then, we shall all sail to Kfar-Nahum for this wonderful wedding!" exclaimed Jared, "Come Judas, we must tell Esther and Deborah; and, we must make all the preparations to sail to Kfar-Nahum."

Judas followed Jared downstairs and into the courtyard, where everyone was eagerly waiting for them. Jarred told him to go on, lightly pushing him towards his daughter. Judas faced Esther. He gently took her right hand, knelt on his left knee, and whispered, "Esther, will you marry me?"

"Yes! Oh, yes, my love!" exclaimed Esther pulling him up to her as everyone shouted to kiss.

Judas kissed Esther and everyone came to hug them and to congratulate them.

That evening another celebration took place in Jared's house and it was as good as the previous one. Jared kept telling everyone present that the Lord had blessed him twofold: He had sent Judas to save his daughter and also to become his future son-in-law. The celebration went on through the early hours of the morning.

The next two days were spent in preparing for the trip to Kfar-Nahum and in purchasing gifts. Finally, on the third morning, Jared and his family and Judas and his disciples left the shore of Gergesa on a fishing boat and sailed northwest to Kfar-Nahum, leaving the servants in charge of the house.

Chapter 23

BIRTH AND DEATH

The gentle wind blew the sail of the rented fishing boat northwards. It was a perfect day for Judas as he held the beautiful Esther in his arms, gently whispering tender words of love and every detail of Yam Kinneret's spectacular view. He could not believe what fate had reserved for him: a second life as Lord Ishia's apostle and a second wife to begin a new family. It was late summer but he could not remember what day it was. He knew it was either the last day of August or the beginning of September. He was anxious to see His Lord again—he had missed Him dearly. He was also anxious to introduce Esther and her parents to Lord Ishia. He felt that the Lord would love Esther and her parents.

By mid-afternoon the fishing boat had reached the busy shores of Kfar-Nahum. There were dozens of fishing boats and smaller homemade vessels crowding the small port, making their landing very difficult. However, Adam, the fisherman, the owner of the boat, managed to steer it between two other fishing boats with barely two cubits space from each side. The voyage had taken a little longer because the wind had been extremely gentle; but everyone on board had enjoyed it. Jared was so happy that he gave Adam an extra silver shekel, thanking him for a marvelous and safe voyage. Adam and his son were grateful and helped Deborah and old Shimon to disembark while Judas took great care of Esther. Everyone bid farewell to the two fishermen and followed Linus and young Manasheh towards Lord Ishia and Lady Lydia's house.

As usual, a large crowd of sick people and homeless beggars sat around Lord Ishia's house, waiting to be fed and cured. And, as usual, several Pharishaiya, stood nearby commenting about anything that Lord Ishia would do. They looked more like black vultures waiting to attack their Lord. Judas led the way through the crowd until they reached Lord Ishia. He was in the garden, which looked more like a temporary hospital, curing each sick that wished to be cured.

He stood up, tall and handsome, and turning around He said, "Welcome home, my dear Judas. Linus, Shimon, Yehuda, Abu, Enoch, and young Manasheh." He hugged each one.

"My Lord, I would like to introduce my bride-to-be, Esther!" exclaimed Judas, "And, these are her parents, Deborah and Jared."

Lord Ishia greeted them with a warm and loving embrace, welcoming them to His house. He then told Judas to go in and introduce them to Lydia and to His mother, Miryam, and to the other women who constantly helped in preparing meals for the hungry, and the homeless.

While Judas went inside, holding Esther's hand, leading his future in-laws into the kitchen, his six disciples remained with Lord Ishia, assisting Him with the crowd of sick and starving people. Within minutes, Judas was back beside His Lord.

"Forgive me, My Lord, I never reached Gadara," whispered Judas.

"It was fate that you did not, my friend; and, it was fate that you brought back Esther from the dead," spoke Lord Ishia.

"My Lord, I simply used mouth-to-mouth resuscitation to revive her."

"Do not underestimate what you have done, Judas. Linus told me about old Sharah and all the sick people that you cured in Gergesa. All that you have accomplished in the past few months clearly show that you believe and that very belief empowers you to do great works."

"My Lord!"

"I am proud of your work, Judas. Come, I need assistance. This crowd is very demanding."

Judas spent the rest of the afternoon beside His Lord helping and curing the sick. The two worked together like two old partners, performing wondrous works under hundreds of mesmerized eyes.

That evening, before supper, Lord Ishia met with Judas and Esther in the garden. The crowd had dispersed, leaving only a few beggars asleep near the entrance of the house. "My beloved friends," He said, "I am so happy for both of you. Esther, you have found a bright, honest, generous, and loving man in my good friend, Judas. And Judas, you have found a beautiful, bright, and pure lady to share the rest of your life, here in Hagalil."

"My Lord, we would both like to be married by You. Would You grant us this favor?" asked Judas.

"It will be an honor to marry you and Esther, my beloved friend," answered Ishia.

"However, I wish to give you both a very special gift. It will be my wedding gift to both of you...Come close to me Esther," He gently commanded.

Esther stepped closer as Judas guided her close to His Lord. Ishia gently placed His thumbs over Esther's eyelids and extended all of His fingers on her temple and began to concentrate. Judas realized that it was going to be the gift of sight and he was speechless as he watched His Lord perform a real miracle on the woman he loved. The few minutes that it took for Lord Ishia to perform that miracle seemed to last an eternity as Judas watched in awe.

"Come and take my place, Judas. Stand facing Esther," gently commanded Ishia.

Judas stepped where Lord Ishia had stood as He had stepped out of the way. Watching them facing each other, He said, "Now, open your eyes, sweet Esther, and behold your man, Judas."

Slowly, her eyelids opened and her eyes began to focus on Judas' gentle and kind face. "Judas, I can see you," she cried as she gently held Judas' face, caressing his cheeks, his nose, his lips, and his chin.

"Thank you, My Lord! You have given us the greatest wedding gift, Esther's sight!" exclaimed Judas, "How can we ever thank You, My Lord?"

"With your friendship and your love," whispered Ishia.

Esther stepped towards the Lord and hugged Him dearly, saying, "Thank You, My Lord. You are truly the Only Son of the Almighty. You are My Savior!"

"Let us go inside, everyone is waiting for us," suggested Ishia.

They followed Him into the house, where everyone was eagerly waiting. It was Esther who spoke first, still trying to adjust to the different colors and trying to match the faces of the people she had met, "I can see, I can see again. Lord Ishia has given me the gift of sight."

Everyone was overjoyed and everyone hugged Esther, Judas, and Lord Ishia. Esther's parents were forever grateful and could not stop thanking the Lord. Finally, they sat for supper and Lord Ishia blessed their food. Esther and Deborah helped Miryam, Lydia, and the other women serving the food. They talked about the wedding and Lydia's pregnancy. Judas and Esther would be married that very week by their Lord. Lydia was expecting to give birth within two weeks. It was going to be a fine month that September!

It was the first Thursday of September, of the year 31 A.D., the day of Judas and Esther's wedding. None of the other apostles had yet returned; so, it was going to be a smaller celebration. Augustus Horatius and his wife Miryam, the parents of Linus and Lydia, were present. Augustus, dressed in a rich Roman tunic, looked more than a centurion. Lady Miryam, the Lord's mother, Esther and Sarah, Cephas' wife and mother-in-law had been busy all morning preparing a feast. The beautiful Mary of Magdala was also helping in the kitchen. Lydia was seated nearby, strictly ordered by everyone to rest and not to exert herself. Linus, Manasheh, Enoch, Yehuda and Abu-al-Kursi were helping to set the table and in preparing some of the goods that Jared and Deborah had bought in Kfar-Nahum's market.

Finally, by mid-afternoon, Lord Ishia married Judas and Esther. Augustus and his wife, Miryam, were the witnesses. A delicious feast followed Lord Ishia's sacred ceremony. Judas felt like the luckiest man on earth! He had been given a second chance to have a family. He felt privileged to marry such a beautiful woman and to have their Lord Ishia actually consecrate their marriage. The feast lasted past midnight and the poor people who had remained by the Lord's house had been invited to share the meal and some wine.

That night, Judas and Esther consummated their marriage. Judas had long forgotten how wonderful the touch of a woman had been.

The second day after Judas and Esther's marriage, Lady Lydia gave birth to a beautiful healthy baby boy. The birth went smoothly without complication. Lord Ishia was ecstatic with Lydia and their son. Lydia chose the name Jesus Justus, the Roman name for Ishia the Just. Ishia happily accepted Lydia's choice and He stayed constantly with them, admiring both, holding them, and whispering His Love for them. For the following week, Lord Ishia was a busy father and husband, full of devotion and love for them.

On Tuesday, September 25th, 31 A.D., after a four-day ride, a Roman messenger reached Kfar-Nahum. He gave the message to Augustus Horatius, which he promptly read. His expression was one of sorrow; and, then anger took over his countenance. Yehohanan the Baptist, Lord Ishia's cousin had been imprisoned at Machaerus by Herod. That previous Friday, September 21st, during his birthday's celebrations, Herod had ordered the Baptist to be decapitated to please his unlawful wife, Herodias, the lawful wife of his brother Philip.

Augustus Horatius himself went to Lord Ishia to tell Him about the death of Yehohanan the Baptist. Ishia was deeply saddened by the news and He began to plan for a trip to Qumeran.

Chapter 24

YEHOHANAN'S HEAD

Wednesday, September 26, 31 A.D.

Leaving Kfar-Nahum was very difficult for both Lord Ishia and Judas. Lord Ishia did not wish to leave Lydia and their baby boy; and, Judas was enjoying his second marriage to the beautiful Esther. Nevertheless, both felt obliged to visit Qumeran to pay a visit at the Baptist's tomb. Esther had decided to help Lydia and Mother Miryam with baby Jesus while her parents would travel back to Gergesa. Jared had left enough gold and silver pieces for Esther and Judas to last them a lifetime.

Having hugged and kissed their loved ones, Ishia and Judas began their journey with Jared Bar-Yakov and Deborah aboard their rented fishing boat. They would sail south to Sennabris, where they would begin their long journey to Qumeran. Augustus had volunteered two horses to expedite their trip, which Ishia had gratefully accepted. Ishia's concern was that Yehohanan's head might have not been buried together with his body; and, He was going to make sure that his burial had been properly attended to.

They sailed all day, arriving at Sennabris by night. Lord Ishia did not wish to be recognized by anyone in order to speed up the trip. All four supped together in a quiet corner of an inn and they shared a room together. Their horses were being tended by the innkeeper's son, inside a small walled garden beside the inn. Keeping His head hooded with His robe, Lord Ishia managed not to be recognized by anyone.

The following morning Lord Ishia and Judas got up very early before dawn and left after bidding farewell to Jared and Deborah, who would themselves leave within a couple of hours. They left without eating, with only a loaf of bread that Deborah had insisted in buying for them the previous night. They trotted out of Sennabris and finally began to gallop on the west bank of the Ha-Yarden, following along the sacred river. It was nearly seven hundred stadia to Qumeran and Lord Ishia wished to reach it by the following evening, which meant to constantly travel throughout the two days with frequent stops to rest and water the horses.

Stopping every two hours to water their horses, Lord Ishia and Judas reached the mouth of Wadi Abu Sidra by dusk. To their right were the foothills of Samaria. Lord Ishia told Judas that the wadi was midpoint from Sennabris to Qumeran. There they rested and ate some more bread, washing it down with the cool water of the wadi. The horses were grazing on a small meadow speckled with flowers and would drink from the cool wadi from time to time. After a couple of hours, Judas tied the horses to a nearby bush where they continued eating. Having prayed, Lord Ishia wished Judas a good rest. Both fell asleep, exhausted from their long journey on horseback.

Lord Ishia's gentle touch on Judas' right shoulder was enough to wake him up. Judas always slept on his left side and was an extremely light sleeper. Most of the times Judas would get up by himself; however, on that morning Judas would have slept an extra hour before opening his eyes. It was still dark and the stars shone brightly, illuminating the pitch-black sky.

"Good morning, Judas. It is time to get up. We must reach Qumeran before dusk," whispered the Lord.

"Good morning, My Lord. It is very early, isn't it?" asked Judas.

"About an hour before the first rays of dawn. We must be ready to leave within the hour for I would like to reach Mesad Hasidim before dusk," replied Ishia.

Judas got up and went to the wadi to wash up. The horses neighed as Judas passed by to check if they were still there. Having relieved himself behind a bush, he reached the wadi and began to wash away the sleep from his eyes.

Having watered the horses, Lord Ishia and Judas walked them along the bank of the Ha-Yarden. That area was too rocky and Lord Ishia did not want to chance any possible accident with the horses. The terrain was too unpredictable and it was still dark! Finally, the first rays of the sun began to illumine the east side of the hills, permitting them to ride their horses.

Ishia and Judas galloped their mounts along the northern section of the Vale of Aulon; and, it was still midmorning when they reached the mouth of Nahal Tirza, a good size stream that originated north of Shekhem by the northwest side of Jebel Tammun, a mountain in Shomeron. There, they ate a few morsels of bread and drank from the cool waters of Nahal Tirza. Judas had tied the horses on a small tree by the bank of the cool stream, permitting them to drink and eat some grass growing by the water. Having rested for a good half-hour, they crossed the stream at a shallower point and resumed their gentle but steady gallop on the northern Wilderness of Yehuda. The sun was midpoint in the September sky as they reached the mouth of the Wadi Mallaha, which evoked memories of Lord Ishia saving Augustus Horatius and his men from the angry attack of Yehuda Bar-Abbas and his brigands. Once again they rested, allowing the horses to refresh themselves in the waters of the wadi. Judas went up to the horses and washed their sides with the water from the wadi, cooling them from the strong midday sun.

Ishia and Judas continued along the western bank of the Ha-Yarden, which bisected the Desert of Yehuda. It took less than two hours to reach Bet-ha'Arava, their last stop along the Ha-Yarden, the place where Lord Ishia had been baptized by the Baptist. While Judas watered the horses, Lord Ishia prayed by the boulder, which Yehohanan had used to stand on when preaching to the crowds. Tears flowed down Ishia's face. Tears for the death of His cousin, Yehohanan the Baptist. At least one hour went by and Lord Ishia was still praying. Judas had cooled down the horses with the sacred waters of the Ha-Yarden and had found a small shady spot for them. There he waited, protected from the heat by the shadow of the rocky bluff.

Finally, Lord Ishia joined him and together they led the horses over the promontory, into the heart of the Wilderness of Yehuda. It did not take long for them to reach the salty shore of Yam Ha-Melah, also known as the Dead Sea or Salty Sea. They continued along the shore until they reached the Wadi Qumeran by the tenth hour of the day. More than two hours still remained before dusk as they entered the gate of Mesad Hasidim.

The middle-aged monk whom Judas had left in charge of his Judas-One and his flashlight greeted them, still mourning Yehohanan's death. The entire population of Mesad Hasidim was mourning his death, each day praying and fasting until dusk. Led by the guardian monk, Lord Ishia and Judas joined the mourning monks in the main hall of the monastery. Judas and Lord Ishia stood out from the monks clothed in black for they wore white. Some of the monks looked insulted that they were not wearing black clothing.

Ishia broke the cold reception by saying, "A dark shadow has shrouded my heart. You may neither be angry nor insulted with me because I do not wear black. My clothes do not mourn for me for my body and my spirit mourn the death of Yehohanan, my cousin. No greater sorrow can be found than the one I carry within my heart, within my spirit, and within my mind. Yehohanan was not only my cousin but he was also my baptist and friend. Where is he buried that I may see him?"

An older monk answered, "Lord Ishia, the sacred body of Yehohanan lies in the main cave, directly above the Wadi Qumeran. It has been sealed and it cannot be opened. It would be sacrilegious to open it!"

"And it would be more sacrilegious if Yehohanan's body was not completely buried!" exclaimed Lord Ishia.

"What do you mean by that, Lord Ishia?" asked the old monk.

"Since I heard of Yehohanan's death I have been having horrible dreams and I am here to verify what I saw in my dreams," answered Ishia.

"What was the vision of your dreams, Lord?" asked the old monk, trembling in fear.

"In my dreams, Yehohanan's decapitated head spoke to me. He told me that his head wished to be buried with his body!"

Cries of desperation emanated from the group in black. Judas then understood Lord Ishia's need to see the Baptist's body as soon as possible.

"You were not able to bring back Yehohanan's head?" asked Ishia, upset at the entire group, "His headless body is inside the main cave, isn't it?"

"Yes, Lord," whispered the old monk. "We were only able to get his body from Herod. When we asked for his head he became insane, screaming at us to take the Baptist's body and to leave. He threatened us with the same punishment. We left in fear. Please, understand! We were all afraid to suffer the same consequences. Heavy-heartedly, we took his headless body and came back to bury him. Since it happened we haven't stopped mourning for him, Lord!"

"I understand your fears! What I need to know is where could Yehohanan's head be found so that I may bring it back and bury it with his body?" asked Ishia.

"Lord, people say that Herodias keeps it inside an oil vase in a corner of her chamber at Herod's fortress in Herodium," volunteered the guardian monk.

"Please, Lord, do not go there!" exclaimed the old monk, "I fear for your life and it will soon be dusk and the beginning of Shabbas!"

"Thank you for your concern, my friend, but I cannot rest and even Shabbas can wait until Yehohanan's head rejoins his body. Judas we must leave now!" exclaimed Ishia.

"My Lord, it will be dusk within two hours!" protested Judas.

"Rest, Lord Ishia, and you can leave in the morning," suggested the old monk.

"Time is precious, my good friends. I must leave now. Judas we will need your flashlight; it will save us," cried out Ishia.

"I have guarded the sacred light with my life," spoke the guardian monk, excited that he could be of help, "I would like to come with you, Lord!"

"You have been chosen to guard the throne of time, good friend!"

"Yes, Lord! I will guard it for *the Angel from the Future*. My name, Lord, is Moishe Bar-Abel. Here is the sacred light, My Lord," he exclaimed.

"Thank you, Moishe. You are a good man and a great keeper," said Ishia, "I need one more favor from you, my friend."

"Name it and it shall be done, Lord."

"I need a sack and some linen to wrap the holy head of our beloved Yehohanan."

Moishe Bar-Abel bowed and excused himself, moving as quickly as possible, fully understanding the urgency of time. He returned within moments with several cubits of white linen, the type used to wrap a dead body for burial, and a sack made of hemp. He gave them to Lord Ishia, placing the folded linen neatly into the sack.

"We will be back by morning," promised Ishia, "With Yehohanan's head."

"May the Lord, Our Creator, be with you!" exclaimed the old monk.

"He is within me!" replied Ishia.

Lord Ishia departed in a hurry with Judas trying to keep up with His urgent speed. Moishe ran ahead to prepare their horses. Without wasting time, they mounted their horses and galloped westwards along the Wadi Qumeran in the heart of the Wilderness of Yehuda. Ishia turned left along the Wadi Sekhakha and Judas followed Him until they had reached the fortress of Sekhakha. At Sekhakha, Judas followed Ishia southwestwards to Herodium, zigzagging along wadis and valleys. Ishia knew exactly where to go for He had spent much time in the Wilderness of Yehuda. Dusk made it difficult to gallop and Ishia slowed down his horse to a walk. Judas followed along, not daring to ask for a small stop. There was no time for a rest!

Finally, Ishia stopped his horse and turned on the flashlight for it had become too dark. They rode for several more hours following the small-but-powerful beam of light until they reached Herodium, Herod's fortress and palace, built on an artificial cone-shaped hill. Flickers of lights emanating from oil lamps and torches illuminated the upper two floors of the fortress and its tower. The main entrance, with its long staircase was heavily guarded and Ishia chose to leave the horses by a stone rampart at the bottom of the hillock. Judas gave the horses some water from his cupped hands and then tied the reins around a large rock. He then removed the one hundred foot long 6mm climbing rope and placed it around his neck and right shoulder.

"What is your plan, Lord?" asked Judas.

"My first plan was to go through the main entrance and demand to speak to Herod Antipas."

"My Lord, they will kill us!"

"My second plan was to climb the hill and then the tower. Enter the fortress, find Herodias' chamber and take Yehohanan's head back to his tomb."

"What if a guard discovers us?"

"I have thought about that, Judas. I can order them to be silent and still. I know my powers and I do not wish to abuse any of them and I do not wish to hurt anyone, even Herod's henchmen; but I came here to take Yehohanan's head back to where it belongs. I have no choice, my good friend!"

"I will be by Your side, My Lord!"

"I know you will, my beloved friend, Judas. First, you must remove your boots. Silence is imperative," whispered Ishia while He removed His sandals.

Quietly, the two men climbed the round-pyramid-like hill until they reached the stone walls of the circular fortress. Ishia gently moved towards his right into the second corner formed by the wall of a smaller tower and the wall of the fortress. Ishia had chosen that corner because there were no signs of guards, while three guards were visible on the main tower.

Judas studied the corner for a moment. The angle was slightly more than a right angle because of the curvature of the tower; but, the stone blocks were slightly bigger than a cubit in height with enough space, in between, to fit your fingers for a fingernail hold. He gently unraveled his 6mm purple climbing rope and tied one end around his waist three times with a bowline knot. He whispered in Ishia's ear that he would climb first and then belay him up, using a column on the upper floor of the tower. He also instructed the Lord to tie the end of the rope around his waist once he had reached the top floor. Ishia nodded and whispered that He would cushion his landing if Judas should fall. Judas smiled and turned to face the corner.

The climb was not too high, twenty cubits at the very most before he would reach the base of the columns. He was going to climb the corner much like a chimney-climb, using both feet and fingertips. He reached high with his right hand, brushing loose mortar and dust that had accumulated between the blocks, and followed with his left hand, stepping up with his left foot and then his right. Slowly but quietly he escalated the first six rows of stone blocks ending at a small window-like opening. He quietly looked into the dark room, which seemed to be empty, and then mantled the ledge of the opening with his left foot and pushed his body straight up. He continued on a wide stance, each foot on opposite walls, climbing the corner of the fortress block by block. He reached the second porthole and heard someone snoring. He decided to stay away from that ledge, using a much harder move, grasping the top of a block with his fingernails. Within a minute longer he had reached the base of the corner column. Grabbing wide, he grasped the first two bases of the circular colonnade, which held the upper chamber of the tower. He mantled the ledge with his right foot and pushed his body up. He had made it! He looked around the chamber, which seemed to be more of a large balcony than a room, and saw no one.

Judas untied the rope from his waist, placed it around the column and began to take up the slack of the rope until he felt Lord Ishia's weight. He passed the rope around his hips and took a firm stance to butt-belay Lord Ishia up the corner. Ishia had tied Himself when Judas had reached the first porthole and had watched Judas' technique in climbing the corner. Judas gave three gentle tugs, the signal to begin climbing, and Lord Ishia began to climb. Judas watched Him, ready to brake if He should fall. However, Ishia climbed steadily, using the same technique as Judas, with an agility of a seasoned rock climber. He kept away from the portholes and was careful not to make the slightest noise or sound. He reached the colonnade within a few minutes. They both untied their respective end of the rope and Judas proceeded in rearranging it.

Lord Ishia led the way down a stone staircase, which ended into a large columned hall. The hall, lightly illumined by four oil lamps, was empty! At one end of the hall was an elevated throne, Herod's. It must have been past midnight for everyone seemed to be asleep, except for a few guards at the entrance and on the main tower. Suddenly, they heard footsteps coming up from the long staircase at the fortress' entrance. Both hid behind columns. The guard reached the main hall and began to walk towards them. The guard was probably going to sleep when Ishia moved around the column as he passed by. Placing one hand on his mouth and one hand on his temple, Lord Ishia tranquilized the guard. He did not let go of him as if He was searching for something within the guard's mind. Gently, Ishia placed him in a seated position with his back resting on the column's base.

"Follow me, Judas. I know where the chamber of Herodias is located," He whispered on Judas' ear.

Judas nodded, still mesmerized by Lord Ishia's power, and began to follow Him. He tried to step like Ishia, without making a sound. He followed Him through a columned entrance, which led to a circular corridor. They stopped by a richly carved double oak door, Herodias' chamber. Ishia gently pushed the door but it would not open for it was bolted on the inside. He looked at Judas and motioned to him to be silent and to wait for Him. He then faced the door and began to concentrate. Slowly, He stepped through the door, leaving Judas in shock. Within seconds, one of the doors opened gently without making a sound. It was Ishia! Judas was still in shock by what he had witnessed and Ishia had to gently pull him into the chamber. A huge richly carved oak bed stood at their right. A silky-like canopy to keep insects outside enshrouded the bed. There were two large windows on the outer wall. A chaise longue faced a standing copper mirror on the left. A lighted oil lamp gave a gentle glow to the chamber, enough to look around. Ishia quietly closed the door, bolting it. Inside the canopy two people were asleep, Herod Antipas and Herodias.

Ishia quietly moved to a corner, looking for the oil vase with Yehohanan's head, but returned to Judas. He searched the other corners without luck. There was neither a jar nor a vase. Only a commode with a marble top stood on the right side of the bed. Lord Ishia faced the commode and tried to open it. It was locked!

Suddenly, one of the persons sleeping sat up and said, "You need this key to open that commode. Who are you?"

It was Herodias and she had a key tied to her wrist.

"It is not important who I am. I have come to take the Baptist's head!" said Ishia.

"Like a thief in the night! Tell me who you are before I scream for the guards!" she exclaimed. Herod was still deeply asleep from too much drinking.

Ishia turned on the flashlight at her face illuminating a beautiful but evil woman. The beam of light had frightened her. "Are you an angel?" she whispered in fear.

"I do not wish to harm you, Herodias, even though you deserve punishment for the evil deed you and Antipas have committed. Yehohanan's head belongs with his body, in his tomb. This is a grave sin you are still committing, by keeping his holy head in an oil vase like a trophy. Open this door before My Father's Wrath descends on this fortress and destroys everyone!" ordered Lord Ishia, with total control.

"I will open the commode and you may take the Baptist's head; but, do not hurt me!" she exclaimed.

"You will not be harmed. I give you my word," answered Ishia.

She got off her bed and opened the commode with her key. Antipas continued to snore during the entire event. Lord Ishia gently wrapped Yehohanan's head with the white linen and placed it inside the sack and tied it. Herodias pulled a stiletto, which had been hidden by the bedpost and was about to strike Lord Ishia's back. Judas moved forward to stop her but Ishia quickly turned around and grabbed her wrist while holding the sack with his right hand. Judas immediately took the stiletto away.

"You are worse than a viper, Herodias. You are more evil than the plague. No harm will come to you now for my word is sacred. However, Antipas will not rule for much longer. His power will be stripped away by Rome and you will be no better than a rich harlot without a soul. That will be your punishment for all the evil deeds you have done. And now, I command you to go back to bed and weep in silence. That is all I ask," commanded Ishia.

Herodias went back to bed, whimpering like a poor unfortunate victim.

Lord Ishia moved quickly out of the chamber and into the main hall, as Judas silently followed him up the staircase to the columned balcony of the second tower. The guards could still be heard from the main tower. As silent as the night, Judas wrapped the rope around a column, allowing equal lengths of the rope quietly down. He wrapped both sides of the rope around his hip and slowly rappelled down to the same corner they had climbed. Ishia, like an expert, butt-rappelled down in seconds. Judas pulled the rope down and quickly rearranged it in a neat circle, tied it and placed it back into his knapsack. They descended the hillock in zigzag fashion to slow them down from gaining too much speed. They reached the horses in minutes. The entire mission at Herodium had taken less than half hour.

They walked their horses for nearly three stadia before they began a gentle trot around a group of hills. By the second hour of the following day, Lord Ishia and Judas were back at Mesad Hasidim with the holy head of Yehohanan the Baptist.

Everyone cried upon seeing their leader's head. Lord Ishia gave his blessings and led the mourning group of monks to Yehohanan's tomb, on the top of the canyon. Yehohanan's head, wrapped in fresh white linen was placed on top of the shoulders of his wrapped body. The entrance was sealed once again with a huge stone and everyone marched back to the monastery.

Everyone begged Lord Ishia and Judas to stay, but He was too eager to go back to Kfar-Nahum and see his baby boy and beautiful wife, as was Judas. Moishe promised to guard the throne of time with his life. Judas decided to leave his flashlight with Moishe once again as a reward and as power. The flashlight was regarded as holy light from the angel from the future. The monks gave Ishia and Judas two breads, some cheese, olives, and dates for their trip back home. They each embraced Lord Ishia and Judas and promised to pray for a safe journey back to Kfar-Nahum.

Waving good-bye, Ishia and Judas began a slower and more peaceful journey northwards along the valley of the Ha-Yarden. Ishia asked Judas not to tell anyone what he had seen at Herodium. Judas promised, trying to understand how was it possible for a person to go through a door. As they traveled north, Judas could not stop thinking about it. Finally, on the third day, he remembered Dr. Weinstein's words: when you reach the speed of light you and everything inside Judas-One will turn into light. It was then that Judas understood. Lord Ishia had the power to be light: to disintegrate and reintegrate at will. Judas understood a few of the powers that Lord Ishia had demonstrated. He could not conceive the rest of the powers that were present in Lord Ishia's brain.

Chapter 25

WALKING ON WATER

It was early November, in the year 31 A.D. and the weather had cooled down in Kfar-Nahum. The temperature was still pleasant but the sun was not as powerful as in the summer months. It was perfect weather for sailing and fishing. Cephas had missed fishing. After all he was a fisherman. All the apostles and disciples had come back to Kfar-Nahum to report to their Lord, telling Him many adventures and stories. Each night, after supper, each apostle retold his stories of his group's travels. Some had been successful in preaching and curing the sick while others did not seem to yet have the gift of healing. Some told adventurous happenings and others told of their misfortunes. When it came to Judas, the other apostles did not believe that he had brought Esther back from the dead. In vain, he tried to explain that what he had done could be done by anyone. That he could teach them three different methods of resuscitating a person that had drowned. They were disgusted by his false pretense to be a savior. Only Ishia and His Father could bring anyone from the dead. It took Ishia Himself to explain to them what Judas had done. Still, they found it hard to believe.

Finally, Cephas exclaimed, "Lord, let's go sailing. I haven't sailed since early spring. And, I cannot take the crowd that gathers in front of your house every morning. Please, My Lord, I am in pain!"

Everyone laughed.

"All right Cephas, let us go fishing for we are short of food to feed the crowd," said Ishia. "However, I must first tell the ladies that we are leaving."

When Lord Ishia returned everyone got up and followed Cephas, even Ishia. They reached the shore where the two boats were docked and realized that there would not be enough place for everyone. There were other fishermen who gladly volunteered the use of their boats if they could keep half the catch. Cephas was trying to bargain them down to a quarter of the catch; but Lord Ishia agreed to half.

"My Lord!" exclaimed Cephas, "We could have had three fourths of each catch."

"Would you have been contended with only a quarter of the catch if it had been your boat, my dear Cephas?" asked the Lord.

Cephas lowered his head, disappointed.

"Come on, Cephas, be happy. We are going fishing!" exclaimed his brother, Andros Bar-Jonah.

Cheerfully, like a big child, Cephas helped Andros and Judas to ready their boat, while Nathanael and Philip helped Yakov and Yehohanan Bar-Zebedeus with theirs.

The other apostles and several disciples were helping the fishermen who owned the other six boats.

Lord Ishia asked the fishermen to first bring all His apostles and disciples to Genne-Sareth, a fishing village southwest of Kfar-Nahum. Once all of the disciples would be ashore with Him, they could sail their boat for a great catch. They all agreed for Lord Ishia's words were sacred and always honored. The eight fishing boats, heavily loaded with twelve apostles, seventy-two disciples, and the Mashìah, Himself, sailed towards Genne-Sareth. Within an hour, they would reach the pebbly shores of that fishing village for it was not far from Kfar-Nahum. Meanwhile, over a thousand people were running along the western shore of Yam Kinneret, waving and calling their Mashìah.

As the fishing boats reached the shore of Genne-sareth thousands of people were eagerly waiting for their Mashìah. The clamor that arose from that crowd frightened Cephas so much that he exclaimed, "My Lord, I wanted to get away from the crowds but we are sailing to a larger and noisier one. Maybe, we should sail east towards Gergesa. It is quieter there!"

"Do not be afraid, Cephas. Judas, and all the disciples will get off with me. You and the rest of my apostles will help those fishermen with their catch. Once your boats are filled with fish, come back to Genne-Sareth to cook our share for those people," said Lord Ishia.

"But, My Lord, with the rest of the crowd coming from Kfar-Nahum there will be well over five thousand people, maybe six or seven thousand. How can we catch so many fish, Lord?" asked Cephas.

"Have you so easily forgotten your last big catch, Cephas?" asked Ishia.

"No, My Lord, but it is a lot of work to clean all that fish and then cook it!" answered Cephas.

"I know, my friend, it is a lot of work; but, this time you have so many helpers and your disciples will take care of the cooking. And look at all those people. They have traveled so far to see me; and, most of them are poor and hungry. Your work will mean so much to me, to them, and to My Father. You will be rewarded for your good deeds Cephas, and so will everyone else."

"I will do it with all my heart, My Lord!" exclaimed Cephas.

"We will be by the stream, Nahal 'Ammud, north of Genne-Sareth."

Judas smiled for he knew that Cephas was slowly changing into a great man with a big heart full of love. He just needed the Lord to awaken that love that was hidden within his heart. Judas disembarked the boat with Lord Ishia, as did all the disciples. The eight fishing boats began to turn around sailing away from the shore.

Suddenly Cephas turned around and yelled, "Where should we fish, Lord?"

"Cast your nets when you see a large fish jump out of the water on your way to Gergesa. There, you will fill all eight boats. We will wait for you at the mouth of the stream," instructed Lord Ishia.

As the eight fishing boats sailed away, the disciples began to make way through the crowd for their Lord. *Mashìah, Lord Ishia, Ishia of Nazerat, Nazarene, Christos*, and *My Lord* were uttered by thousands of people. Everyone wanted to touch Him, but Judas and the disciples kept the crowd apart for fear of being crushed. Finally Lord Ishia raised His hands, which seemed to appease the huge crowd, which kept getting larger as the people who had walked and had ran from Kfar-Nahum had reached the northern outskirts of Genne-Sareth.

"Why do you seek me, my friends?" asked Ishia.

"We have been searching for you since Yehohanan's death, My Lord," spoke a young man. "He told us that you are the Mashìah, Lord. And, I also know that you are the Son of the Almighty?"

"How can you be so sure that I am he?" asked Ishia.

"I was present when Yehohanan baptized you in the sacred waters of the Ha-Yarden and I witnessed the power of Your Father descending from the heavens and His Spirit encircling your sacred head, My Lord!" exclaimed the young man.

The crowd cried, praising Lord Ishia, the Mashìah.

"My friends, I know you have traveled far and most of you are hungry for food and for my word. I do not want anyone hurt. Follow me without hurting anyone and I will speak to you while my apostles are fishing so that everyone will eat. Each one of you will be given a turn to be close to me. Now, move gently for I see old people that need help. If you see someone beside you who needs help, be his guide, her helper, be her brother or sister. Come, follow me and take care of each other."

As Ishia walked northwards to the stream, young people were helping the older ones and the sick. Everyone seemed to be concerned about others. The disciples and Judas were helping, showing care and so much love. Slowly, the large crowd moved out of Genne-Sareth, over the northern hills into the valley of Nahal 'Ammud. There, they sat by the slopes of the hills next to the stream, as Lord Ishia stood on a large rock with Judas by his side. The Lord raised His hands and, once again, there was a silence. It was unthinkable that He could appease such a large crowd simply by raising His hands!

His voice was gentle yet powerful enough to be heard by everyone, "My good friends, you have come so far to see me and to listen to my words. I will be brief with my words for I would like to spend some time with each and every one of you. My disciples will be gathering dry branches and kindling to cook the fish that will be caught by my apostles. Through My Father, who is in Paradise, I was born on this earth to show you the way to Him. I come in peace, and my mission is one of peace. Not only must you obey the ten commandments that My Father gave Moishe and to all the people of this earth; but, you must also obey my only commandment: to love everyone. When I say you must love everyone it should not make a difference if the color of his skin is different from yours. It should not make a difference if he is rich or poor, healthy or sick, sane or crazy, handsome or ugly, man or woman, young or old, your friend or enemy, Hebrew or Philistine. Every one of these is a child of My Father. And, in His eyes they are all beautiful. Love will conquer all. If you love your enemies, eventually they will become your best friends. I would like each one of you to shake hands and embrace the people next to you and continue to do so until everyone has felt some of your love. That is all I have to tell you today. I will begin to receive each and everyone of you and when you have seen me, find some new friends and discuss what I have just told you!"

Ishia got down from the rock and began to embrace every single person in a long line, which kept getting longer and winding as more people queued, waiting for their turn to touch Him. Judas stood by Lord Ishia's right, helping the lame and the sick, and ensuring His safety. One by one, young and old, man and woman, rich and poor, white and black, healthy and sick, He embraced them all with such fervor and love. He cured anyone that was sick or lame. He showed love with everyone, even with the most hideous and grotesque. The Lord was truly a perfect example of the love He had spoken about.

By the time He had seen everyone and performed such wondrous works of healing, the disciples had collected twelve huge piles of branches, driftwood, and kindling and had built twelve fire pits surrounded by rocks. Judas helped each group to start their fire. The disciples were ready to cook when shouts of excitement began to grow in the crowd as the eight sailboats had reached the mouth of the stream. The boats were pulled ashore on the south side of the stream and the apostles asked their disciples for help with the catch. Each boat was loaded with fish, caught from the middle of Yam Kinneret, halfway to Gergesa. The other fishermen were excited about their catch and were extremely generous in sharing it with the crowd.

The smell of cooked fish breezed through the foothills and shore as the large crowd began to form twelve huge lines. Continuously, the disciples served the different people in their line. Some disciples, in each group, would continue to feed their respective fires with more wood. Some would serve the already-cooked fish, and others would place more fish on the fire. Each one received a fish as their meal and used the water of the stream to drink. After feeding over five thousand people each cooking pit still had a basketful of fish leftover. The crowd was instructed by the apostles and disciples to relieve themselves around the hills and away from the stream for fear of contamination. They were also instructed to wash their hands and faces with the water of the lake. The water of the stream was to be used only for drinking.

The crowd was satisfied with the food and awed by the miracles of Lord Ishia. Finally, it was almost dusk and Lord Ishia instructed his apostles and some of the disciples to sail to Beth-Saida. But Cephas exclaimed, "What about You, My Lord, will You not sail with us?"

"Go ahead, my friends, while I take a little time to dismiss these people. Judas and I will join you soon," spoke Ishia.

"My Lord, it is getting dark. How will you be able to find us in the dark and who will provide you with a boat? The other fishermen have all gone back to Kfar-Nahum," asked young Yehohanan, the son of Zebedeus.

"Do not concern yourself for me, Yehohanan. I will join you before you reach Beth-Saida. Now go for it is getting dark."

Cephas and Yehohanan lit their oil lamps at the stems of their boats to better see ahead of them. All of the apostles, except Judas, and with a few disciples, including Linus and young Manasheh embarked the two boats, after having pushed them into the shallow water of Yam Kinneret. Concerned about their Lord and Judas, they waived and began to sail northeast towards Beth-Saida.

Lord Ishia spoke to the crowd and thanked them for coming to see him. He also instructed the rest of the disciples to keep the fires going for the night and to share the rest of the fish with anyone who wished more. He told them to sleep there for the night and that he would meet them at Kfar-Nahum the following day. Once again, he recommended the disciples to be caring leaders, and to assist anyone who was in need of help. At dawn, they were to lead the crowd to Kfar-Nahum.

Having bid everyone a good and peaceful night, Ishia and Judas crossed the stream and slowly disappeared in the darkness.

Judas followed Ishia up to the top of the hill. There He prayed by a tree as Judas knelt beside Him, also trying to pray. No matter how hard Judas tried to pray he found it difficult to do so. Instead he worried how they were going to rejoin the others. It was pitch black and one could not see in front of him. How and when were they going to reach them?

Finally, Ishia spoke to Judas, "Why do you worry so much, my friend?"

"Lord, it is too late to find a boat. And look where they have reached; they are at least one fourth of the way to Beth-Saida!" exclaimed Judas, looking at the two flickering oil lamps on the boats on a sea of darkness.

"Judas, I have kept you because you may be the only one that can succeed with me in what we are about to do."

"And what might that be, Lord?'

"We will walk there."

"I can run, My Lord, but my right knee is problematic, and it is nearly one hundred stadia to Beth-Saida. Even running, it will take most of the night to get there. I do not know if my right knee can take all that?"

"I was not talking about walking along the shore, Judas. We will join them on the lake," explained Ishia.

"My Lord, I cannot walk on water and I cannot swim that far. I am only a fair swimmer."

"Judas, you remember when I walked through the door at Herodium?"

"Yes, Lord. I cannot stop thinking about it."

"Well, you can do that, too."

"Lord, I am not You."

"When you crossed two millennia with your time machine, you and your machine became light."

"Yes, Lord, but that is not the same."

"Judas, in your brain, in the right hemisphere, there is a small section that controls the very essence of lightness. It can order every single cell in your body to become light and be able to walk through doors or walk on water. That same part can be controlled."

"My Lord, I do not think that my brain is as developed as Yours. I am only using a fraction of my brain while You are using all of it."

"Judas, I can stimulate that part of your brain so that you may experience walking on water or going through a door. Your brain is much more advanced and developed than the others; and, you can comprehend the possibilities that lie inside your brain. You have two millennia of development within it."

"Would you really do that for me, Lord?'

"Gladly, Judas, but your faith must be pure."

"I believe You can do anything, My Lord!"

"But you must also believe that with time you will also be able to do anything, my dear friend."

"I do believe, Lord!"

"Then, with your permission I will awaken that power within you."

"I am ready, Lord."

Facing Judas, Ishia touched the right section of his head, between the ear and the eye, concentrating with His Almighty powers of suggestion. Minutes passed before Ishia removed His fingers from Judas' right side of the brain.

"Let us go now, it is time," commanded Ishia.

Judas followed Him down the slope without any problems. They stopped by the shore. Judas was silently looking at the dark water of Yam Kinneret. The light breeze had developed into a wind.

"Think only positively. Do not have any doubt whatsoever. Take a moment to free your mind and have only one thought, to walk on water."

"Will you hold my hand, Lord?"

"If that makes it easier for you, I will gladly hold it."

"If you hold my hand, Lord, I know I can do it!"

"Then, let us walk, Judas," commanded Ishia as He took Judas' left hand.

Ishia took his first step and Judas followed, keeping his eyes shut. They continued walking on the water at a great speed.

Meanwhile the wind had become powerful but it had no effect on them.

The two fishing boats were in trouble and were not going anywhere for the wind was against them. It did not take long for Ishia and Judas to reach them. Someone screamed in fear when he saw the two ghost-like figures nearby; and, everyone thought they were ghosts.

"Do not be afraid. It is I and Judas!" exclaimed Ishia.

Everyone marveled at what they saw.

"Lord," spoke Cephas, "I, too, would like to walk on water. Tell me to come to you and I will do it!"

"Cephas, come to me, my beloved friend."

Immediately, without hesitation, Cephas began walking towards Ishia and Judas. He took several steps before realizing how strong the wind and the waves were. At once he sank into the water and began swimming for dear life, screaming, "Save me, Lord, I am drowning!"

Without wasting any time, Ishia and Judas helped Cephas into the boat and then both climbed in. Both Ishia and Judas radiated an aura that was actually seen by the rest of the apostles and disciples. Ishia then calmed down the wind and sat next to Cephas. All, even Judas, fell on their knees in adoration.

"Indeed, You are the Only Son of the Almighty Yahweh, My Lord!" exclaimed Judas, followed by everyone else.

"Let us sail back to Genne-Sareth. Tomorrow afternoon we will sail back to Kfar-Nahum," suggested Ishia.

The following morning, more people had reached Genne-Sareth bringing their sick and wanting to see the Mashìah. Lord Ishia cured all the sick that morning. By early afternoon, He and His apostles sailed the two boats back to Kfar-Nahum.

Chapter 26

THE RICH YOUNG MAN

It was good to be back home! Lord Ishia's home had also become Judas' home; and, its grounds had become all of the apostles' and disciples' home. Even though there was so much work for the women, they never complained about it. Even Judas' Esther had joined the other women in the kitchen, around the house, and at the market: cooking, cleaning, washing, and shopping. It was a full-time job. However, the women in Lord Ishia's house were respected as equal and deeply loved by everyone, especially by Lord Ishia, Himself.

One early mid-November morning, in 31 A.D., while Lord Ishia was teaching His apostles and disciples, a group of Pharishaiya and Tsadduqim infiltrated through the crowd, which was allowed to listen to His teachings, and pushed their way up to where He was sitting.

"If you truly are the Son of Our Almighty Father, then show us a sign from the heavens," demanded a Pharish.

"It is easy to predict if it is going to be a nice day tomorrow or if it will rain. Anyone can do that by looking at the western sky before dusk or by looking at it at dawn. It is easy to read the sky and predict the weather; but, you, Pharishaiya and Tsadduqim, cannot read the signs of the times! You demand a sign but you do not deserve to know it. Look at these poor people. They can tell the signs of times because they see them through me. They come to me with open hearts and minds. Your hearts and minds are heavily clouded by greed and corruption and that is why you ask for you cannot see the signs. You are blinded by evil and jealousy and the only sign I will give you is the sign of Jonas. Now leave, you are bothering me!" answered Lord Ishia.

Infuriated by His words, the Pharishaiya and Tsadduqim left, creating a commotion by shoving people along their way.

"All of you are far richer than those black vultures for you are here searching for the truth while their only concern is to be stumbling stones in my way. I am the Truth and the Light. I was sent by My Father to show you how to live and to illumine your way. He who believes in me and loves everyone shall be rewarded at the end of the road of life."

As He spoke, four servants made the way for their young master. When they reached the Lord, one of the servants introduced his master, "Lord, this is my master, Ybrahim Bar-Yakov, the richest man of Chorazin."

A richly dressed young man, twenty years of age, cleanly shaven and with a short Roman-style haircut, wearing several earrings on both ears and rings on each finger with three gold necklaces adorning his upper chest and a ring in his nose, walked up to Lord Ishia.

Matthias Levi Bar-Alpheus, one of Ishia's apostles and former tax collector, approached the Lord and whispered into His ear, "Lord, this young man is a rich libertine. As the rumor goes, Lord, he likes both men and women."

"Let us not prejudge the young man, everyone has sinned at one time or another," Ishia whispered back to Matthias Levi; and then, He spoke to the young man from Chorazin, "What do you seek from me, Ybrahim Bar-Yakov?"

"I have heard so much about you, Lord," declared Ybrahim.

"What have you heard about me, Ybrahim?"

"That you are the Son of the Most Holy and that you are the Mashiah. Are you?" asked the rich young man.

"It is not for me to tell you who I am. It is up to you to believe or not to. All of these people believe in me by my actions and not because I told them so. What do you believe, Ybrahim Bar-Yakov?"

"I want to believe in you, Lord. I want to be one of your disciples. Is that possible, Lord?"

"Anything is possible, Ybrahim. It is all up to you."

"If it is up to me, Lord, I want to be your disciple; and, I want to begin as soon as possible!" exclaimed the rich young man. "Tell me what I have to do, Lord."

"Firstly, you must be willing to remove all of your jewelry, sell them, and distribute the money among the poorest of this crowd. Can you do that, Ybrahim?"

"I suppose I could remove all my rings, earrings, and necklaces and sell them. They are of the finest gold and will bring over a thousand shekels for the poor. I will do it, Lord; but, please, would you explain why it is necessary to sell all of this jewelry?" asked the young man.

"Look at my twelve apostles and my seventy-two disciples. They wear no earrings, nor do they wear necklaces or rings on their fingers with the exception of the married men. They may wear a simple wedding band to symbolize their sacred union with their wives for marriage is sacred in the Eyes of My Father. The human body is also sacred in the Eyes of My Father and it should not be pierced, mutilated, or tattooed."

"I can live without all of these, Lord. I will sell them and distribute to the poor the shekels that I will receive in exchange. Then, Lord will I be able to be your disciple?"

"Secondly, Ybrahim, you must free your servants and slaves and sell all of your worldly possessions and share all of that money with all the poor people in Chorazin. Thirdly, you must give up your sexual desires and purify your body so that when you meet the right woman you may join her in holy matrimony. If you can do that, Ybrahim, I will gladly accept you as one of my disciples."

"Lord, you ask too much of me. I cannot sell my palace and free all my servants and slaves. My father worked all his life to gain all those riches that he has left me. And Lord, it is impossible for me to give up sexual pleasures. The urge is too powerful. It is too difficult for me to follow you, Lord. It is too difficult to give up all that you ask. I am sorry, Lord. I must now go," said the rich young man sorrowfully. He then bowed and turned around with disappointment in his eyes, following his servants as they made way for him through the crowd.

"It is easier for a camel to go through a needle's eye than for rich men to go into My Father's Kingdom. It is useless to amass a fortune and not share it. That is greed and false power. How can any rich man not share with his poor fellow men? How can anyone stand the sight of a hungry person and devour enough food for ten. I tell you, my good friends, you are far richer than the richest man on earth for your pure hearts, spirits, and minds are richer in My Father's Eyes than all the gold of the world. As long as I am here on earth, anyone is welcome to share the daily food that we can provide. When I leave this earth to go back to My Father, I will hope that my apostles and disciples and their children and descendants will continue to share what mother earth will give us…"

"Master, Master, I beg you to cure my son for he is my only son," cried a voice from the crowd, interrupting Lord Ishia's sermon.

"Who cries so painfully for my help. Let the man step forward," commanded Ishia, disturbed by the man's interruption.

The crowd made way for the man and a young boy, not yet ten years old. Before they could reach the Lord the boy was thrown to the ground as if by an invisible force, bruising his back and arms. Suddenly, his body began convulsing, his mouth foaming and screaming the foulest language ever heard.

"Lord, I asked some of your disciples to cast his demon out, but they could not. I beg you, Lord, help my only son," begged the man.

"Linus, Judas, help that man bring his son to me," demanded Ishia.

Promptly Judas and Linus helped the man carry the convulsing boy to Him. As gently as they could they placed him down as his body continued to kick wildly on the ground and as his mouth spewed forth more insults.

"Silence! I order you to be silent and still in the Name of My Father," ordered Lord Ishia.

The young boy stopped convulsing and yelling, his body lay still as a corpse on the ground.

"Now, get up Yoakim, son of Yshak, and go to your father. Never again shall demons enter your body!"

The young boy ran to his father and embraced him.

"How did you know our names, Lord? You are truly the Only Son of the Most High!" exclaimed Yshak, falling down on his knees and praising the Lord. Everyone marveled at Lord Ishia's power. The crowd remained there all day long until they began to smell the baking loaves of bread that Lady Miryam, the beautiful Lydia, Esther, Miryam of Magdala, Esther and Sarah, and the other women had been kneading all morning long. They baked hundreds of loaves and sliced them so that everyone could have a good slice of the freshly baked bread. The crowd kept Lord Ishia, his apostles and disciples always busy and the women were always cooking for the poor and the hungry. They had all accepted their new way of life: to care for, share with, and love everyone that came hungry and thirsty for the Lord.

Chapter 27

TO YERUSHALAYIM BY PERAEA

On a December morning, in 31 A.D., Judas was watering the small persimmon trees that had grown from the seeds of the fruit given to him by Commander Ghabriel. Only two had grown out of several seeds; and, whenever possible Judas would water them and fertilize them with camel manure. Whenever he was gone, Mother Miryam took care of them, together with a vast garden of fig trees, olive trees, pomegranate trees, bushes of various nuts, peas, and grapevines. Judas was tying the tiny persimmon trees to two straight branches he had cut to guide their growth. The tiny trees were already over two cubits in height and with the proper care they might grow enough to bear their first fruits the following fall. Kfar-Nahum's winter was not really a cold season. It was cool but not cold and most plants did very well through the cooler winter months. Nevertheless, it had already snowed on top of Jebel Hermon for its height was well over six thousand cubits. However, Kfar-Nahum always did seem to have warmer days in winter for Yam Kinneret was nearly five hundred cubits below sea level. As Judas cared for the young persimmon trees and thought about the snow on Jebel Hermon, which he did not miss at all, Cephas had come to call him.

"Judas, the Lord is planning a trip to Yerushalayim! We are all excited. Come, He wants to speak to us," announced Cephas, excitedly.

"I will be there in a moment, Cephas. Let me finish tying these beautiful persimmons."

"Why do you waste your time with those little saplings? There is so much to prepare for the big trip."

"Dear Cephas, do you have any idea from where the seeds of these persimmons have come from?"

"No, not really! How should I know and what difference does it make where they come from?"

"A world of difference, Cephas, for their seeds come from Paradise, from Lord Ishia's Father Himself."

"I find that difficult to believe, Judas. Now, come! Do not keep the Lord waiting for you," exclaimed Cephas.

"You are right, Cephas!" agreed Judas, finishing his last knot, "But, if you do not believe me about the persimmon seeds, ask the Lord Himself and you shall know the truth. I do not lie, my friend."

Judas followed Cephas inside the house, where the rest of the apostles were already waiting for their Lord to announce His plan about a trip to the holy city of Yerushalayim. Cephas went directly towards Lord Ishia with the intention of asking Him about the persimmon seeds; but he did not have time to ask his question for the Lord was ready with the answer.

"Yes, my beloved friend, Judas speaks the truth. Those persimmon seeds had originated from Paradise, from My Father Himself," explained Lord Ishia.

Cephas fell on his knees, affirming his belief, "My Lord, forgive my lack of trust in Judas. You are truly Krystos, the Mashìah, the Only Son of Our Almighty Father!"

"Cephas, your faith is becoming stronger by the day and upon you, Cephas, I will build my temple. On the second feast of Pesach, yet to come, I, the Son of Man will be arrested by the high priests of Yerushalayim. They will allow the Romans to beat me and crucify me on a wooden cross. On the third day, I will rise again in the Glory of My Father."

"My Lord," spoke Cephas, heavy-heartedly by this announcement, "Why must you die? Shall not the angels come down from the heavens and protect You, the Only Son of the Most High?"

"Cephas, I was born on this earth to show everyone the way to live by loving everyone. The ultimate gift anyone can give for his friends is life itself. I will die for you, my beloved friends, and for everyone else that shall ever be born until the end of times. My sacrifice will light the way for all of you. But do not be afraid for on the third day of my death, the angels will come down and I will resurrect from death. That will be the final proof of who I am," answered Ishia. "I beseech you all not to tell anyone what I have told you. Do not tell Lydia, neither my mother nor any of the women for they will suffer greatly if they find out...Now, let us get ready for our journey to Yerushalayim. We will march to Beth-Saida, through Philip, Hippus, Gadara, Peraea, and Yeriho. Come, gather your disciples for we shall be leaving within the hour."

The women had already prepared three dozen loaves of olive bread and two sacks of dried figs for they had known of Ishia's decision the previous day. Judas rushed to Esther, embracing her and telling her how much he would miss her. During the past three months, they had been trying hard to conceive a baby. Judas was hoping that the previous night's attempt would be fruitful. Esther told him not to worry—she was in good hands with Mother Miryam, the beautiful Lydia, all of the other women, and beautiful baby Jesus Justus. He agreed with her as he hugged her and gently kissed her delicious lips.

The eleven apostles and seventy-two disciples followed Lord Ishia and Judas, the angel from the future, to Beth-Saida. There, they made a brief stop for some water from a well and went directly to Yakov and Hannah's house. Cephas and Andros Bar-Jonah and Yakov and Yehohanan Bar-Zebedeus knew them very well. He was a fisherman just like them. Sharah was thrilled to see Judas and his disciples again and they were honored to have Lord Ishia, the Mashiah, in their humble home. Yakov and Hannah's eight children were drawn directly to the Lord and sat beside Him and by His feet. Ishia sat the two youngest on His knees and kissed their rosy cheeks.

"Do not pester the Lord," said Thomas Didymus to the eight children. "Go and play outside."

"They are not bothering me, Thomas," exclaimed the Lord angrily, "And you must not bother them for My Father's Kingdom is theirs. And as long as anyone does not become innocent, like these children, he will not enter My Father's Kingdom." He continued to hug them and kiss them as if they were His own children.

"My Lord, my wife, Hannah and my mother would like to cook for you and your disciples. We do not have much; but, whatever we have we are willing to share," said Yakov, "Also, you can all spend the night here and around my house. It will be an honor for me and my family to have you sleep in our humble house, My Lord."

"To the first offer, I must decline for we have much more food and we would like to share some of it with you. To the second offer, we would very much appreciate resting around your house. However, let me warn you, Yakov: we will leave very early tomorrow morning. By dawn I would like to be on the way to Gergesa," answered Lord Ishia.

"Thank you, My Lord, for your kindness and for choosing to rest in my humble house!" exclaimed Yakov.

"You have wonderful children, Yakov and Hannah. You are good parents for they are good children, full of love and respect... Judas, Cephas, let us share the rest of the olive bread and dried figs with this wonderful and loving family."

Cephas and Judas, together with Hannah and old Sharah, cut up twelve loaves of the delicious olive bread and a full sack of dried figs. Yakov insisted on sharing his last jar of wine and Lord Ishia accepted his offer. They all shared the wine from the same terracotta cups. Everyone enjoyed the olive bread, dried figs, and the Arbelah wine, feeling very much like a big family.

After the delicious but humble supper, Lord Ishia led everyone in front of the stone house and looking into the heavens He began to speak, "I give thanks to You, My Father, Lord of this Universe, from having hidden the truth from learned and prudent men; but You have chosen to reveal it to these little ones and to these good people." Then He said to everyone, "Everything has been given to me by My Father. No one knows who the Son is except the Father, and who the Father is except the Son. I choose all of you to know that I am His Son. Blessed are your eyes for they see what they see. Many kings and holy men have desired to see what you see, but they have not seen it; and, they have desired to hear my words but have not heard them. You are all chosen for I see the goodness in each one of you."

Thomas Didymus asked, "Even me, My Lord?"

"Of course, Thomas! Deep within you lies an ocean of goodness," replied Ishia.

He continued His sermon on the importance of love towards everyone on earth, including the enemy. He spoke about returning to a life of innocence. He spoke about helping the sick, feeding the poor, loving the unwanted and the hopeless, and even the untouchables.

That night everyone slept under the stars, bundled up with their winter robes, and warmed up by the bonfire that some of the apostles had made with all the branches and driftwood they had managed to gather. The nights were rather cool and, at times, even cold.

Yakov hardly slept, thinking how lucky they were to be with the Lord, the Mashìah; and, he knew when Lord Ishia had awakened. He had seen Him go to the shore and wash up. Gently he woke up every one of his children and his wife and mother for they had begged him to do so. Slowly, Judas woke up and within minutes everyone got up. Each one went towards the hills to relieve oneself; and, then each one washed up with the cool December water of Yam Kinneret.

Lord Ishia, Judas, and every apostle and disciple hugged Yakov and his family and began their march towards Gergesa. It was still dark outside!

The first rays of dawn shone over the hills of Hippus, filtering through the gentle waves of the cool December water of Yam Kinneret, giving a semblance of an enchanting rippling cadence.

What a beautiful day it was going to be! Cool and sunny. A perfect day for traveling thought Judas as he followed the quick-paced footsteps of Lord Ishia. The other apostles and disciples would try their best to keep up with the quick march, especially the younger ones. However, from time to time, the Lord would stop to allow everyone to catch up with Him. He was indefatigable! He could walk for days.

By mid-morning, they had walked half the way to Gergesa. Lord Ishia saw that His older disciples needed a break and something to eat. There, they broke their fast using the rest of the bread and dried figs. They had just enough for a good slice of bread and two dried figs each. It was good enough to hold their stomachs until they would get to Gergesa. While everyone slowly nibbled at their bread and figs, Judas asked Him permission to go ahead of them to announce to Jared and Deborah that the Lord and His apostles and disciples were coming. This would allow them to prepare a good supper for everyone. The Lord agreed and Judas chose Linus to accompany him to Gergesa.

While everyone was still eating and resting, Judas and Linus began a fast walk towards Jared's house. Hopefully, they would reach it by early afternoon. As the two waved good-bye, Lord Ishia explained what Judas and Linus were about to do. Everyone seemed pleased and thought very well of Judas. He was a kind and understanding man.

Jared and Deborah were pleasantly surprised to see their son-in-law and young Linus. Judas explained what was about to take place. Jared was joyful and honored to hear that the Lord Himself would be visiting their house. Quickly, they gathered their servants and cooks and began to prepare a feast. Two servants were given orders to buy a boatful of fish. Others were decorating the tables— more tables had been rented from neighbors for the occasion. More wine was purchased. The cooks and Deborah were preparing plenty of fresh bread, hummus, and several dishes of cured olives, spiced with the finest spices available. Fresh olive oil was poured into beautiful decanters, ready to be served together with lemon slices over the hummus. One of the cooks was preparing delicious sweets made of dates, nuts, and honey, wrapped by the finest dough. Judas and Linus' mouths were watering from the aromas emanating from Deborah's brick ovens. It was going to be truly a feast!

It was the end of the afternoon when Judas spied Yehohanan and young Manasheh walking beside Lord Ishia while the rest were trying very hard to keep up with them. It was young Manasheh who was leading the way for he was very familiar with the area. Judas, Linus, and Jared went to welcome the Lord and the rest of His chosen ones.

Jared and Deborah were genuine believers in the Lord for they had the greatest proof: Judas, one of His apostles, had resurrected Esther and then she had been given her sight back by the Lord Himself. They firmly believed that Lord Ishia was the Only Son of the Most High and the prophesied Mashìah. The feast they were giving on His honor was done with love and care for they felt blessed by His presence and by the presence of Judas and the rest. His apostles and disciples had all become holy men and some had the power of healing, which had been awakened by the Lord. That evening, Jared and Deborah, their cooks and servants had been perfect hosts to the holy group. Jared had gone through the trouble of hiring three musicians, who sang King David's psalms and great ballads of ancient Hebrew heroes. It had been a perfect supper for everyone, giving them a chance to rest, relax and enjoy good food and delicious wine. What a treat! Lord Ishia thanked Jared and Deborah for their love and kindness, praising them for their unshakeable faith in Him. He also thanked Judas and Linus for their thoughtfulness.

That night, Lord Ishia and the Apostles slept on real beds, while the disciples lay down on every possible space available, using their winter robes as covers. Everyone slept like a baby after such a feast.

The following morning Jared and Deborah treated everyone to freshly-baked banana bread, dates, nuts, fresh fruits, and freshly squeezed orange juice for breakfast. Also, Jared's cooks and servants had been busy baking enough bread and sweet pastries for them to last for a few days. Once again, Lord Ishia blessed Jared, Deborah, and their household for the warmest welcome and the delicious food they had received from them. It took almost an hour before they were on their way for everyone, beginning with Lord Ishia, hugged Jared, Deborah, their servants and cooks good-bye.

Lord Ishia guided the group to Hippos, where they stopped for a break and some food. Several beggars joined them for a late lunch and the Lord healed several sick people. They continued on along the valley, up a small mountain and down the Mezar Valley, where the Nahal Mezar flowed into the Nahal Yarmouk. By the time they had reached the Mezar Valley it was dusk. They camped by the gentle and cool water of the Mezar stream. The valley was warmer and, with two bonfires, the night was perfect for a good rest. Abu-al-Kursi knew that area very well for he had worked for Yousef-al-Gader, guarding his herd of swine for nearly four years. He retold stories that had taken place in the mountains of Gadara and along the Yarmouk Valley. Finally, he retold the story of how he had witnessed the most fascinating miracle ever performed by their Lord: when He had ordered the demons that had possessed Seth Bar-Oza for years to enter the sick swine, which drove the herd over the cliffs into Yam

Kinneret. Also, he recounted how the Lord had saved him and how he had been chosen to follow Him.

In the morning, after washing up in the cool Nahal Mezar, they followed the stream until it joined with the Yarmouk river. They followed the Nahal Yarmouk, which emptied into the Ha-Yarden, until they reached the road to Gadara. They bypassed the village of Emmatha and by mid-afternoon, Lord Ishia and His followers had reached Gadara. Several people recognized Abu and ran to tell Yousef-al-Gader. As Ishia and His followers marched into the town square a large crowd led by Yousef-al-Gader and his son, Ybra-him, met them. Seth Bar-Oza was pushing his way through the crowd for he had wanted to welcome the Lord to Gadara. Yousef, Ybra-him, and Seth welcomed their Lord and Savior into their town. They embraced Abu as if he were a brother. Yousef proudly invited the Lord and His chosen men to his villa.

While they sipped warm wine, for it was colder in Gadara because of its elevation, Yousef's cooks and paid servants were preparing a feast. Judas was fascinated by the welcome they were getting everywhere they had been. Everyone wanted to be near the Lord. Yousef, Ybra-him, Seth, his wife and children sat near the Lord. Yousef's wife, Meron, was a sweet lady who kept coming with more hot wine for everyone. The house, which had been modeled after a Sicilian villa, had a large walled garden, where most of the apostles and disciples were resting. The crowd outside congested the entrance to the house, making it almost impossible for anyone to enter or exit it. A blind man led by a young girl was desperately trying to see the Mashìah, hoping for a miracle; but the crowd was so thick that there was no space to get by. People would not budge and the commotion made it difficult for anyone to hear the desperate cries of the young girl and of the blind man.

Nevertheless, Lord Ishia's ultra sensitive ears heard their cries of desperation and resignation. He asked Seth, "Seth, would you be so kind as to allow a blind man and a young girl to enter the house. I fear that the crowd is blocking the entrance. Would you do that for me, good Seth?"

"My Lord, it would be a great honor for me to do anything for You," exclaimed Seth, excited that the Lord Himself had asked him for help. "I will go immediately."

Seth excused himself and went out of the dining room, down the main hall towards the door. He quickly opened the door and raised his two hands and kept them up until the crowd's clamor subsided to whispers. He instructed the crowd to make a passage to the door for the Mashìah desired to see a blind man and a young girl. The crowd, out of curiosity, managed to split into two, creating a small path leading to the door. A blind man led by the young girl finally appeared at the beginning of the path.

"Come!" he exclaimed. "The Lord is waiting for you."

"It is Moishe, the blind man, and his daughter, Eva," cried a voice.

"Lucky Moishe!" cried another, as the two walked up to the door.

Seth let the two in and shut the heavy door, under much protest from the crowd. He guided the two down the main hall into the dining room and up to where the Lord was seated. The girl fearfully looked around, studying all the strange faces.

"Do not be afraid, my child," spoke the Lord, with a tender and caring tone that reassured the young girl. "Come closer. Bring your father to me."

Slowly, Eva led her blind father by the hand reaching Lord Ishia, who had stood up. He seemed like a giant to her but the love radiating from His face comforted her and she felt secure near Him.

"You have brought your father to me, my sweet child. You wish for him to see you. Do you believe that I can cure him?"

Eva nodded.

Lord Ishiah bent down and whispered something into her ear. By this time, all the apostles and disciples had gathered around to witness another wondrous work by their Lord. Lord Ishia picked her up and stood her on a bench so that her face was at the same level of her father. Eva, following His instructions, dipped her ten fingers inside the Lord's warm wine and wiped the wine on her father's eyes. Everyone stood there, mystified as the blind man began to open his eyelids and focus on his wonderful daughter for the first time in his life.

Moishe had lost his sight before Eva was born. He had had a degenerative vision since his childhood, and as a young man his vision was so poor that he could only see shadow-like figures of people at a close range. His wife had miscarried twice before Eva's birth and she had died giving birth to her. Moishe's mother, Ada, had raised her grandchild as her own. Ada had been waiting for the Mashìah all her life and she had taught young Eva to believe in Him. When Ada and Eva had heard that the Mashìah was in Gadara, the One that had cured Seth and Ybra-him, she quickly had taken her father's hand and guided him to Yousef-al-Gader's big house. Eva's faith was pure and invulnerable and Lord Ishia had seen that from the very beginning. Her little desperate cries were also full of that belief that her grandmother had instilled within her.

Moishe's eyes began to cry as he embraced his beautiful Eva, and she joined him in tears of joy. Then, she turned around and hugged Ishia, kissing His cheeks. That was her way of thanking Him for curing her father.

Ishia hugged her back and held her as He spoke, "Do you all see this beautiful child. Her innocence and her faith are so unshakeable that she cured her father through me. If anyone of you can acquire such innocence and such faith you will be able to do wondrous deeds in my name." He hugged her again and kissed her forehead, and then spoke again, "Dear Moishe, your daughter's faith in me has cured your blindness. Stay with us for supper for I am sure that Yousef would enjoy your presence. Everyone here can learn so much from Eva's virtues. Her spirit, her heart, and her mind are purer than the whitest lilies that grow in the valleys of Hagalil."

The supper at Yousef-al-Gader's house had been a feast and everyone slept deeply that night.

The following morning Lord Ishia was ready to go on south towards Peraea. Yousef tried in vain to convince the Lord to stay for a few more days at his house; however, he managed to give Him enough supplies to last a few days for His whole entourage. Lord Ishia, Judas, Abu, and everyone else thanked Yousef and his family for their generosity and kindness. Yousef had become the kindest man in Gadara—that in itself was a great miracle.

For the next two days Ishia and His followers traveled through the northwestern section of Decapolis, entered Peraea, and camped on a valley outside the northern outskirts of Pehel. They remained in the mountainous region of Gilead for several days. One night, a light snowfall dusted the mountains of Gilead; and, although it had been a cold morning everyone enjoyed scraping the little snow that had fallen and had delighted in a snowball fight, behaving like little children. Even Lord Ishia Himself had joined in the frolicking, bringing back memories of childhood. They remained in Peraea, along the northern bank of Nahal Yaboq, for several days. The water of the Yaboq River was refreshing, originating from the eastern mountains of Gilead. The cool water was great for drinking and washing up but too cool for bathing. The northern bank was steep, forming a canyon; but its caves were good shelters for the holy group. The fires they had built in each cave gave them enough warmth during the night that it was actually pleasant. They remained there until Lord Ishia announced that it was time to move on.

Ishia led the group westward along the canyon of the Nahal Yaboq; and, many times Judas had used his climbing rope to help some of the apostles and disciples up or down difficult passages, especially when they reached the Ha-Yarden Valley, which dropped over five hundred cubits below sea level. Judas' rope was a lifesaver for many older followers. Both Lord Ishia and Judas led the way and, at times, Judas body-belayed some of the older disciples down. He was the last one to descend, waiting for everyone to reach the valley. Many of them thanked Judas for his help and great knowledge in climbing and descending steep passages.

Traveling through the colder mountains of Gilead had been an experience for most of them. They had reached the low valley of the Ha-Yarden and the sun's rays were much warmer, forcing most to remove their winter robes. The sand was warm and the water, although cool, was much warmer than the water of the Yaboq. Everyone, following Lord Ishia's and Judas' example, removed most of their clothing and bathed in the holy water of the river. Many of the disciples and a few apostles were baptized by Ishia. It was a sacred day for everyone. After the baptism, Lord Ishia led them across a shallower section of the river across to Yehuda. He reached a small-secluded plateau on the west bank of the river; and, there He showed them how to meditate and concentrate. The entire day was one of fasting and purifying one's spirit and mind. That night they shared the little food they had managed to save. They went to sleep, tired from the long march and from the day of meditation.

Lord Ishia knew that it was possible to reach Yeriho in one full day at a quick pace; but, He also saw that some of His men, especially the elders, were tired and hungry. He decided to take two days to reach Yeriho. Each day, they meandered along the valley, eating flowers, berries, and persimmons. Finally, on the second day, by mid-afternoon, they entered the gate of Yeriho.

Linus went directly to his old house, followed by the rest, touching the walls of the garden and the studded oak door brought back memories of his childhood. Another Roman officer and his family were living there and he did not dare to knock. It was Ishia's hand that woke him from his reverie.

"Come, Linus. Do not dwell in the past. Think about today! Where can we eat, everyone seems to be famished?" said Ishia.

"Lord, there is an inn on the city square, but it does not have a good reputation. Too many drunkards and prostitutes! But the food is good and the wine is tolerable."

"Then, lead on, good Linus for they seem to be extremely hungry."

Linus led the way to the inn. It was the same malodorous inn that Judas had decided against when he and Ishia had come to Yeriho together. It had been the right decision for Judas had found Lydia asking for help. He remembered running to the synagogue to get the Lord. He also remembered when the Lord told him that the mother was already dead. Little did he know what Lord Ishia could do! The inn had the same smell as last time.

"Lord, are you sure you want to enter such a lowly place?" asked Judas.

"Judas, do not judge the place by the pungent smell of cheap wine. The food is decent and most of them are hungry," replied the Lord.

"Lord, do we have enough money? I have two golden denarii and ten silver ones," volunteered Judas. "Esther gave them to me for the trip."

"Judas, that is more than enough. One golden denarius equals twenty-five silver ones. And I am positive that many disciples have a few coins. Come, let us enter."

The acrid smell of cheap wine did not seem to bother Ishia or most of the followers, with the exception of Thomas and a few others who were offended by the smell and decided to remain in the town square. The innkeeper and his wife were roasting mutton and had made fresh hummus and bread. The Lord was contended with a bit of hummus and bread, while everyone else had ordered roasted sheep. The inn had been empty because it was still too early for supper; but it was then filled by Lord Ishia and His men. They sipped on the cheap wine, which was slightly acrid and stout, nevertheless potable; and, they munched on olives, bread and hummus. The innkeeper and his wife began to serve slices of already cooked meat and within the hour everyone was served. The mutton had been spiced and it tasted good, especially because most of them had been starving. Finally, Thomas and the other men ventured in and also enjoyed some of the mutton and cheap wine. Judas decided to pay with his two gold denarii and he was pleasantly surprised to have received nine silver denarii in change. The innkeeper had charged a silver denarius for every two people and Lord Ishia's meal had been free. Judas happily gave the men two more silver denarii for good service. The innkeeper and his wife were happy and wished everyone a safe journey to the holy city. They managed to leave before the local customers were beginning to enter the inn for supper. That night Ishia and His men slept outside the walls of Yeriho.

As they were about to leave Yeriho, a blind beggar called Shimon Bar-Timeush, who was sitting by the road to Yerushalayim, had heard that Ishia of Nazerat was passing through and he cried at Him, "Ishia, Son of David, have mercy on this blind wretched man."

Many people in the crowd told him to be silent. Some were downright angry with him for being so insolent. Who was he to cry the Lord's name? He was nothing but a blind, dirty, stupid beggar.

Infuriated by the insults, Bar-Thimeush cried even louder, "Son of David, Son of David, HELP ME!"

Ishia clearly heard him and ordered him to come forward. The same people that were trying to silence him were now telling him to get up for Ishia of Nazerat had asked for him to come forward. Bar-Thimeush threw down his cloak and jumped up and he was led to Lord Ishia.

"What do you seek from me, Bar-Thimeush?" asked Ishia.

"Rabbi, I would like to see You for You are the Mashìah!" exclaimed Shimon.

Ishia touched his eyes with His fingertips, saying, "Behold, Shimon Bar-Thimeush, the Son of the Father."

Shimon opened his eyes, focusing up on Ishia's face. He kissed His hand, wetting it with his tears, "My Lord, You are truly the Son of the Most High. Thank You, thank You!"

"Your faith, Shimon, has cured you."

Shimon Bar-Thimeush stayed with the crowd, following Him all the way to Beth-Ananiah and Yerushalayim.

Two days later, traveling through the hills of Yehuda, the group reached the house of Eleazar, Martha, and Miryam, in the tiny village of Beth-Ananiah. The road from Yeriho to Yerushalahim circled the base of the ridge of Har Ha-Zetim, called Mons Olivae by the Romans.

Eleazar and his two sisters greeted Ishia like a king, welcoming Him into their house and making everyone comfortable. Miryam sat by the Lord's feet, hugging His legs and kissing His shins. Martha was busy preparing food and wine. Most of Ishia's followers were admiring the view of Yerushalayim.

"See how my sister loves You, My Lord. She would make a great wife, full of love and devotion," said Eleazar.

"I am already married, good Eleazar," whispered Ishia into his ear, "And I am already father of a handsome boy. Do not say anything to Miryam. Wait until I am gone to tell her these news."

"Congratulations, My Lord! She must be a wonderful woman," whispered Eleazar.

"Thank you, beloved friend…You must understand that Miryam and Martha are like sisters to me and you are my brother, Eleazar."

"Yes, we are!" exclaimed Eleazar, smiling, fully understanding the reason why Ishia could never marry Miryam or Martha.

Martha came back with drinks and food, complaining, "My Lord, tell her to help me. I need help to serve all these people."

"Martha, dear Martha, always troubling yourself about pleasing me. Do not trouble yourself, sit down by my side," answered the Lord.

"Lord, I cannot sit down until everyone is served."

"Miryam has chosen to stay by me; and, you cannot take that away from her. There will be plenty of time for you to serve many friends to come; but, there is very little time that I can stay here…Judas, would you and a few others, please, help Martha for she is overwhelmed with work!"

"Gladly, My Lord!" replied Judas, "Come Linus, Cephas, Yehohanan, let us help Martha."

Everyone enjoyed Martha's food and drinks; and, everyone enjoyed Eleazar and Miryam's friendship. The two sisters and brother loved the Lord like their own brother. It felt good to be with them and their genuine show of love for their Lord. Eleazar had offered his house to the Lord and the apostles. The disciples could sleep anywhere they could find space or in their wonderful garden, which went all the way up to the foot of Har Ha-Zetim. There, a grotto was used as a family mausoleum. Their parents, grandparents, and several generations of ancestors were buried there on stone shelves that had been built for their family. The entrance was sealed with a stone slab which had been sculpted in a circle in order to facilitate moving it whenever necessary.

Lord Ishia accepted their genuine offer to stay for several nights. At dawn, each day, they would walk to the holy city, which was a short walk from Beth-Ananiah. From Eleazar's house, one had a beautiful view of the east section of the city. From the Monument of Jannaeus to the Fortress of Antonia, from the Temple and its square to the tombs of Abshalom, of Bene-Hezir, and of Zechariah all the way down to the Qidron Valley, one could scan the entire eastern section of Yerushalayim. What a wonderful view! A perfect place to have a house!

The following morning, having broken the fast, Ishia of Nazerat, followed by Eleazar, Miryam, Martha, all His apostles and disciples, walked down to the Qidron Valley up the path that led to the Gate of Essenes. Through the centuries, the entire city of Yerushalayim had been built on a plateau and had been fortified by a turreted wall, surrounded by valleys and beautiful gardens. It was truly a spectacular city! The few that had never seen the holy city were truly impressed by its majesty. As the group walked up the road towards the Gate of Essenes more people joined them as they found out that their tall leader was Ishia of Nazerat. There were two Roman guards at the sides of the gate and the walls were crowded with beggars and pilgrims. Ishia entered the gate, followed by the long cortege of followers and sightseers.

Ishia stopped by the rose garden, which stood to the left of Ha-Shiloah, to smell the wonderful roses. The rose garden was filled with a great variety of colored roses and their perfume was wonderful.

By the time Ishia had reached the Wailing Walls of the Temple, that section of the city was congested with several thousand people. The square by the town hall was so crowded that it was impossible to get through. Some Roman guards were worried by a possible revolt, but they felt reassured when they were told that it was Ishia of Nazerat, a great holy man. They did not mention the word *Mashìah* for it meant redeemer and that meant a revolt.

Ishia entered the temple square through an archway. He went directly to the Temple to pray. By the time He came out of the Temple, its square was filled with people. He spoke to them about His commandment of love. That if they would love both friends and enemies and respect everyone there would not be war. There would be peace and friendship. That every person, no matter what color or religion or where he came from, would become a brother or sister for every single person on earth was a child of the Father. They listened to Him, taking in whatever He had to say. However, the Pharishaiya and Tsadduqim throughout the crowd were calling Him a blasphemer and a liar. Although, Ishia's enemies tried very hard to get Him into cornered situations He would always exit in style. That day, however, the apostles and disciples had to make a path for Ishia through the vast crowd, shoving Pharishaiya, Tsadduqim, and scribes along the way. This incident infuriated them and they immediately reported it to Yoseph Kaiaphas and the San-hedrin. Gratus, the Procurator of Yehuda, had appointed Kaiaphas high priest of Yerushalayim in 18 A.D.

That afternoon, Kaiaphas and the San-hedrin ended their meeting early for it was Friday and the Shabbat would soon begin. They, however, voted to keep constant spies following Ishia of Nazerat.

That evening they ate the Shabbat supper at Eleazar's house, enjoying the company of Miryam and Martha, who clearly were both in love with the Lord. Eleazar felt sick after supper and decided to retire early to bed, giving a chance to his body to recuperate from that illness. Miryam and Martha stayed very close to the Lord, demonstrating much love and tenderness.

The following morning, the Feast of Dedication, Ishia had wanted to go to the Temple to pray. The apostles and their disciples followed Him, while Miryam and Martha remained home to care for Eleazar, who still felt sick. Once again, Ishia led His men along the Qidron Valley and up the southern Gate of Essenes. A cold breeze forced the apostles and disciples to cover their faces with their winter robes.

As they walked up the path, the apostles stopped by a blind beggar, who sat on a rock by the road. Yakov Bar-Zebedeus asked the blind man when had he lost his vision? The man told Yakov that he had been born blind.

"Lord, who has sinned against the Father for this man to have been born blind, his parents or he?" asked Yakov.

"Neither he nor his parents have sinned for this man to have been born blind. He was born blind so that I could give him sight. I must do my work as long as it is day for I am the light that shines in darkness. It will be day as long as I am on this earth. When I leave this earth darkness will take over," answered Lord Ishia. He then spat on the dry soil several times and mixed His saliva with the soil and took some in His palm. He divided the wet clay into two small lumps and plastered them over the blind's eyes, saying, "Yakov, take this man to the pool of Ha-Shiloah and let him wash the clay off his eyes. We will meet you there."

Ishia continued along the path into the gate towards Ha-Shiloah. There, they met an excited Yakov and the former blind beggar, who was not blind anymore. Quickly, Ishia continued on towards the Temple as everyone tried to keep up with His quick pace. There were other people around the pool who knew the blind man and asked him if he was the blind beggar who begged by the Gate of Essenes.

"Not any longer!" he replied. "I can see now."

"You look like him, but I do not think you are that blind beggar!" exclaimed another beggar.

"I am he, but I am no longer blind!" exclaimed the cured man.

"How did you manage to open your eyes, for they had been shut since I can remember?" questioned another man.

"Ishia of Nazerat put wet clay on my eyes and told me to wash the clay off in this pool. When I washed the clay off, my eyes began to open and I was able to see. Were you not here witnessing what I just told you?" asked the cured man.

"Yes, but I was not looking at you. I was talking with my friend. And, by the way, how did you manage to get here from the gate without any help?" asked the same man.

"The Nazarene told one of His men to take me here."

"Quickly, let us go to the Temple. Everyone should know about this!" exclaimed the man.

The small group of beggars moved along the same path towards the Temple, telling everyone they encountered about the miracle. Before they could reach the Temple, the small group met two Pharishaiya who were going to the Temple for their Shabbat prayers; and, they told them the story about the blind beggar.

"Is this true?" asked one of the Pharishaiya.

"Yes, it is the truth!" exclaimed the cured man. "I can see. Yerushalayim is so beautiful. So many things to see!"

"Come along, we must speak to the high priests about it," ordered one of the Pharishaiya, grabbing the cured man's elbow.

The group kept getting larger and by the time they reached the old Dung Gate of the ancient inner wall, several other Pharishaiya and Tsadduqim had joined the group.

"What is all the excitement?" asked a short, fat Tsadduqim.

"Ishia of Nazerat has cured this beggar. He was blind from birth! It is Shabbat and the Feast of Dedication. Any holy man would not dare lift a finger on this day. The Nazarene is not from the Most High for he does not keep the Shabbat!" exclaimed the Pharish who held the cured beggar.

"I hear what you say," answered an old Pharish, "But if Ishia of Nazerat were a sinner, how is it possible that he could do such wondrous works?"

"Then, this man is a liar. He was never blind. There are beggars who fake blindness to make a living!" exclaimed the Pharish, still firmly holding the beggar by his elbow.

"You should ask my parents about my blindness. They will tell you the truth," spoke the cured beggar.

"Where do your parents live?" asked the old Pharish, whose name was Youseph A'Ramathayim.

"In the eleventh house past the rose garden," answered the cured man.

"Let us go there," ordered Youseph A'Ramathayim. "His parents will surely know their own son!"

The group turned around and headed south towards the Gate of Essenes and turned right on the street where the rose garden began. The former blind beggar stopped for a moment to look at all the different color roses.

"I had no idea that roses came in so many colors!" exclaimed the cured man.

Everyone looked at him for he was genuinely surprised by the colors.

The group, led by old Youseph, reached the eleventh house, a small one-floor house, with a dirt floor. Poor people! Thought Youseph. The cured man's parents, an elderly couple, came out to see what was all the commotion in front of their humble little house.

"Is this your son?" asked the Pharish, still holding him tightly by the elbow.

"Yes! He is our son. Has he done something wrong?" asked the old father.

Before anyone could answer the old man, the cured son freed himself from the unbeliever dressed in black and hugged his father and mother, exclaiming, "Father, mother, I can see you!"

"This is our son. He was born blind; but, how is it possible that he can now see, and who cured him?" asked his father, happily but fearful that his family would not be allowed to enter their synagogue again. The poor people had been warned by the high priests not to acknowledge Ishia of Nazerat as the Mashiah. They had been told that anyone who would do so would be barred from the Temple and from any synagogues. "My son is old enough to speak for himself. We are grateful that he has been cured!"

"You must thank the Almighty, not the Nazarene. He is a blasphemer and a sinner!" exclaimed the same Pharish that had held him.

"I do not know that Ishia of Nazerat is a sinner. I only know that I have been blind for twenty-nine years but I can now see. This is the most wonderful day of my life!" exclaimed the cured man.

"What did the Nazarene do? How did he open your eyes?" asked the angry Pharish.

"I have told you already and I have repeated it a few times! Why do you want me to repeat it again," answered the cured man, angrily. "Maybe, you are interested in becoming his disciples?" He continued, mocking them.

"You are his disciple. We are disciples of Moishe. We know that the Almighty spoke to Moishe and gave him His Commandments. We know nothing of the Nazarene and where he comes from!" exclaimed another Pharish.

"You do not know where he is from, yet you know that he opened my eyes. Ishia of Nazerat is a man of God and He has His powers for He lives according to His will. Never have I heard anyone that could open the eyes of a man born blind. Only the true Mashìah could have given me sight!" he exclaimed.

"You, that were born blind out of sin, are trying to teach us!" shouted the man who had held his elbow. "Go away before we have you arrested, blasphemer!"

The cured man ran away towards the Temple, chased by the Pharishaiya and the Tsadduqim.

Youseph A'Ramathayim stayed with the old couple, reassuring them that no harm would come to their son and to forgive the others for their disgraceful words and accusations. He then left them, walking back towards the Temple.

The cured blind man, whose name was Yehuda Bar-Aaron, reached Ishia of Nazerat by the Wailing Wall, which was crowded with people honoring the holy Shabbat. "Lord," he spoke, breathing heavily from running," they are chasing me…The Pharishaiya and the Tsadduqim…They do not believe in you…They are your enemies!"

"I know that, Yehuda, but I am not interested in their trickeries. Do you believe in the Son of Man?" asked the Lord.

"Lord, tell me who it is that I may believe in him."

"You are looking at him and he is speaking to you."

"I believe in You, Ishia of Nazerat!" uttered Yehuda, dropping on his knees. "You are my savior and the Chosen One, the Mashìah!"

"I have come to this earth to light your way. But I also have come to judge, so that blind men may see and some that see may become blind!" exclaimed Ishia.

"Surely, we are not blind!" exclaimed some Pharishaiya who had heard him.

"If you were blind you would not be guilty; but, you are guilty for you see and yet do not believe."

Offended, all the Pharishaiya left and entered the Temple.

Lord Ishia continued to preach to his followers and to the crowd, which was multiplying by the second, "In all seriousness, I say to you that anyone who does not go into the sheep pen through its gate but breaks in is a thief and an outlaw. Only the shepherd enters through the gate. The gatekeeper knows him and allows him to enter. The sheep recognize his voice and obey his commands. He leads the way and the sheep follow him because they know his voice and trust him. If it were a stranger, the sheep would never follow him; instead, they would run away because they would not recognize his voice."

"Lord, we do not understand the meaning of your parable," spoke Cephas.

"Permit me to explain it in a more personal manner. I am the gate to Paradise. All others who have come before me and who will come after me are thieves and outlaws, but you have not noticed them and will not. I am the gate and anyone who enters through my name will be safe. He will be free to go in and out and be able to find what he really needs. Thieves come for the purpose to steal, kill, and annihilate. I have come to this earth to give life to the fullest. I am your good shepherd and I am willing to die to save you. A hired hand will not die for you; he will run away and abandon the sheep when he sees the wolf. He has no concern for the sheep because they do not belong to him. I am your good shepherd and I know my sheep. I know you just as the Father knows me, and I will die for you. There are other sheep that do not belong with this fold, and I am also their shepherd and they will listen to me because they will recognize my voice. The Father loves me for I am His only son. He loves me for I will die for you so that I may conquer death and live again. I will die of my own free will; and, as I have the power to die for you I also have the power to resurrect from death. This is my mission on this earth which has been given to me by my Father."

"He is mad!" exclaimed a scribe.

"Do not listen to him for he is possessed by the devil!" exclaimed a Pharish.

"If My Lord were possessed by the devil," yelled Judas, "Would He be able to cure the blind, to cure the sick, to bring the dead back to life? He is the Only Son of Yahweh! He is the Mashìah, you blind fools!"

"Blasphemer! You are a blasphemer just like your master!" exclaimed a Tsadduqim.

"My Lord, we should enter the Temple before it is too late. I fear that there will be trouble today," whispered Judas to His Lord.

"You are right, Judas. We have very little time before the Temple guards will be searching for me. However, we do have enough time to enter the Temple before we must flee," agreed Ishia.

The apostles began to make way for their Lord; and, the disciples formed two columns, keeping the crowd in place as Ishia of Nazerat entered the Temple archway.

They reached the Portico of Shelomo, where the crowd pressing around Him forced Him to stop.

"Do not keep us in suspense any longer, Ishia of Nazerat!" exclaimed a man. "If you are the Mashìah, tell us now!"

"TELL US!" roared the crowd.

"I have told you many times through the works I do; but, still you do not believe in me. The works I perform I do all in My Father's name. The works are my witnesses and yet you do not believe because you are not my sheep. The sheep that are mine listen to my voice. They know me and I know them. I give them everlasting life and they will never be lost; and, no thief will ever steal them away from me for I protect them. I am willing to die for them. My Father who has given me this power is the greatest of this universe. My Father and I are One!" answered the Lord.

Many present found stones, and picking them up they got ready to throw.

"I have done so many good works for you, and everyone of them was done in My Father's name. For which ones are you going to stone me?" asked Ishia.

"We are going to stone you for blaspheming not for your works!" answered some.

"You're a man, not god!" exclaimed others.

"If the judges of old were called gods, even though some were unfaithful to the Father. The Law uses the word gods for those holy men and you cannot reject the Law. But you call me a blasphemer even though I am the Son of the Father. You are the blasphemers for I am His Son and you refuse to believe it. Even if you refuse to believe in me, you must believe in the works that I do; then, you will surely know that My Father's Blood flows in me and I in My Father's Blood."

Most people were confused and knew that Ishia of Nazerat had done great and wondrous works. But the Pharishaiya, the Tsadduqim, and the scribes wanted him to be arrested. Suddenly, the Temple guards were coming to arrest Him, but the crowd was blocking their way. Judas, the rest of the apostles and all the disciples forced their way out, protecting their Lord.

Quickly, Ishia moved along the street that led to the Gate of Essenes, followed by His men. Before the Temple guards were at the gate, Ishia and His followers were already on the road that led to the Wilderness of Yehuda. When they reached the top of the mountain, which faced Yerushalayim, Ishia stopped and looked back at the holy city. It looked spectacular in that sunny but cold winter day. The crowd following the Temple guards was reentering the city.

"Sorrow will come to you, my beautiful Yerushalayim for you have rejected me. Your Temple shall be destroyed and you shall be sacked and burnt many times over. At the very end, fire from the sky shall engulf you in total destruction!" exclaimed Ishia with deep sorrow in His heart and mind.

Ishia led His followers to the Ha-Yarden and crossed it to the east bank, where they remained for several days. Lord Ishia cured and baptized thousands who believed in Him and taught them His commandment of love.

Chapter 28

RESURRECTING ELEAZAR

A week had passed since their escape from the Temple guards. Ishia explained to His apostles that it was not the right time for Him to be arrested. I will not let anyone arrest You, My Lord? Had declared Cephas. One more time, Ishia explained His mission on earth to them. It was difficult for them to understand why should their Lord, the Mashìah, be arrested, beaten, and put to death.

Judas was the only one who understood. But then, he too came from another world, two millennia into the future. He knew that there would be no escape for His Lord; and, that there would be no escape for him in playing the role of His betrayer. His Lord was counting on him. On his knowledge of what would happen. On his knowing that there would be no escape from the fate that linked his role with the last few years of Lord Ishia's life on planet earth. These thoughts shot through Judas' mind, sharp as swords, as dusk was closing in another miraculous day with the Sanctus Christus Himself. Judas pondered on his luck every night—to be living with Ishia of Nazerat, the Holy Mashìah, the Only Begotten Son of Yahweh, every day of their last years, to be His best friend, His trusted friend, His betrayer! Judas cried for there was no escape from his duty. No escape from the painful role he had to portray. He wiped his tears upon hearing the sound of a galloping horse approaching their camp along the east bank of the Ha-Yarden, by the Wadi Abu Gharaba.

A young man, in his twenties, jumped off his steed, and ran towards Lord Ishia. It was Nathanael, Eleazar's trusted servant. He knelt in front of the Lord and recited his message to Him, "My Lord, Eleazar, the friend You love like your own brother is extremely ill. He is about to die, My Lord! Please, Lord, tomorrow you may have my horse so that you will reach my master's house before noon. Miryam and Martha beg You to come and save their brother!"

"Dear Nathanael, tomorrow morning you shall go back to your masters' house and let them know that I will be there on the third day after you arrive," replied the Lord.

"My Lord, he will surely die before then!"

"Do not despair, Nathanael, for through Eleazar's death the Son of God shall be glorified."

Everyone, except Judas, was puzzled by the lack of interest their Lord was showing towards one of His best friends. However, no one dared tried to convince Him to leave early next morning. They had seen their Lord perform too many marvelous acts to tell Him what to do in this delicate situation. The Lord worked in mysterious ways, always demonstrating who He really was, the Only Son of Yahweh.

The following morning, Nathanael left early to bring his masters the news about Lord Ishia's arrival.

One hour before the dawn of the second morning after Nathanael had left Lord Ishia woke everyone up, announcing that it was time to leave for Beth-Ananiah. No one complained because everyone knew it was a solid two-day walk to reach their friends' house. Also, most were anxious to get there to see what their Lord would do to cure Eleazar. Judas, who knew exactly what would happen, never spoke a word to anyone. However, Cephas and a few other apostles and disciples were fearful and concerned about returning to Yehuda.

"Lord," spoke Cephas, "Why do you want to go back to Yehuda? Only a few days ago the Yehudi wanted to stone You and the Temple guards wanted to arrest You!"

"Dear Cephas, always worrying. Do not worry, my friend. We can walk the twelve hours of the day. We will rest at night. I will not ask you to walk during the night for it is dangerous without light. We will be there by tomorrow afternoon. Meanwhile, our friend,

Eleazar is resting. Tomorrow, when we get there I will wake him up."

"Lord," replied Cephas, "If he is resting, surely he will get better."

"Good Cephas, our friend Eleazar is dead. He died yesterday in his sleep, before dawn. And I am glad that I was not there because I want all of you to believe in who I am, the Son of the Father. Now, let us leave."

"Let us go and die with Him," whispered Thomas Didymus to Cephas, "For if the Yehudi kill Him, I do not want to live without Him."

For two days they followed their Lord on the road to Yerushalayim, along wadis and over hills. The first night they slept in two caves along the cliffs of Nahal Og. They reached Beth-Ananiah by early afternoon of the second day of the march.

Their friends' house was full of people paying their condolences to Miryam and Martha. When the two sisters heard that Ishia of Nazerat was approaching their house, Martha went out to meet Him. Miryam remained sitting shibah inside the house, still upset with Ishia for not coming sooner.

Martha greeted Him outside the village, kissing His cheeks. She was still crying as she whispered in a sorrowful tone, "My Lord, You are too late. Three days too late. If You would have been here, my brother would not have died."

"It still would have been too late. Eleazar died hours before Nathanael reached your house," replied Ishia. "However, your brother will rise again!"

Shocked by His knowledge about her brother's death, Martha cried, "I know he will rise again on the last day. He will rise again with everyone!"

"I am the Resurrection, Martha! Anyone that believes in me will live on even when he dies; and, if anyone believes in me when he is alive he will never die. Do you believe this, dear Martha?"

"I believe in You, My Lord. I believe that You are the Holy Mashìah, the Only Son of God, the promised One born on this earth!" exclaimed Martha. "Lord, I will run to call Miryam!"

She ran ahead as Ishia and His entourage walked up the path that led to Beth-Ananiah on the slope of Har Ha-Zetim.

Martha recomposed herself as she entered her house and walking up to her sister she whispered in her ear, "Our Lord has arrived. He is waiting for you outside the village. He wishes to see you."

Miryam quickly got up and ran out of her house and down the road to the entrance of the village. The Yehudi that were visiting followed her. When she saw Ishia, she threw herself at His feet, crying, "You are too late, My Lord! Eleazar is dead! Oh, he is dead! If You had been here, My Sweet Lord, he would not have died! Oh, help me with my pain, My Lord Ishia! Help me!" Her tears flowed into rivulets, down her cheeks, onto His weary feet.

The Yehudi who had followed her were also crying for they loved the sisters and had loved Eleazar. They were their best friends in Yerushalayim and its surrounding villages.

Ishia was so deeply moved by Miryam's tears and her friends' love for her that He helped her up and hugged her with so much love. He asked, "Where is he buried?" as tears dropped from His eyes.

"See how much he loved Eleazar!" exclaimed an elder Yehudi.

"Yes, but if he loved him so much why did he not prevent his death? He was able to open the blind beggar's eyes," uttered a woman.

"He is buried in our family tomb, my Lord," whispered Miryam.

Ishia took Miryam by her hand and walked past their garden by the foot of the mount, where the tomb stood. Everyone followed. A circular slab blocked the entrance to the cave.

"Judas, Cephas, choose a few more men to remove the rock from the entrance," He ordered, His cheeks still wet with tears.

"My Lord, his body will smell. It has been four days since Eleazar died," said Martha, confused by the Lord's command.

"Martha, if you believe in me you will see the glory of My Father through me!" He exclaimed.

Judas, Cephas, Yehohanan, and Linus pushed the stone, rolling it against the rocky foot of the mount. A rotting stench emanated from the sepulcher. The four stepped back covering their mouths and noses.

Lord Ishia stepped forward seemingly undisturbed by the foul smell, and entered the tomb. His voice echoed back out, "I thank You, Father, for hearing my request. I truly know that You always listen to me; but, I ask You this special favor for the sake of all these people that I care for and love so much, so that they may truly believe that I was sent by You to this earth…Eleazar, my beloved friend, stand up! It is I, Ishia. Stand and come to me!"

Outside, everyone, except Judas, did not know what to expect. Suddenly, Lord Ishia appeared at the entrance helping the bandaged Eleazar to walk.

"Quickly, remove his bandages so that he may breathe and walk!" ordered Ishia.

Miryam and Martha rushed to their brother, hugging him and removing his bandages. Eleazar was in a stupor, slowly coming back to life. But he was alive, resurrected by their Lord. Everyone dropped on their knees, for they had witnessed the glory of God through His Only Son, Ishia.

Most of the Yehudi visiting Martha and Miryam believed in Ishia, after witnessing Eleazar's resurrection; but, a few of them went to tell the Pharishaiya about what they had seen. They told Kaiaphas, the high priest. Quickly he called a meeting of the San-hedrin.

Kaiaphas began the meeting by announcing, "This quick meeting that I called is concerning the Nazarene. This man is working miracles throughout Yehuda, Hagalil, Ha-Yarden, and everywhere he goes. Thousands of people believe that he is the holy Mashìah because of all the wondrous signs that seem to follow him. This man worries me. What are we going to do?"

"He is a blasphemer! He thinks he is the Mashìah, the Son of God!" exclaimed one of the Pharish.

"And what if he is the true Mashìah, the Son promised to us by God Himself? Will we completely disregard his powers because we are too blind to read the signs!" exclaimed Youseph A'Ramathayim.

There was a rebuttal between most of the Pharishaiya and Tsadduqim and a few members of the San-hedrin, who sided with Youseph and Nikotheimos, another Pharishaiya who secretly admired Ishia of Nazerat.

"I am not going to miss this opportunity if he is truly the Mashìah. I am too old to disregard the signs that follow him everywhere he goes. You must open up your minds and interpret his wondrous acts. This man has never wronged anyone; but he has healed hundreds, thousands of people. He has done things that are not of this earth. And, now he has raised Eleazar from the dead. I knew Eleazar. He was a friend and I was at his burial. Now you tell me that Ishia of Nazerat has resurrected him! What other proof do you need?" lectured Youseph A'Ramathayim.

"I had no idea you felt so strongly about the Nazarene! What do you suggest, my good friend? I value your answer," answered Kaiaphas.

"Let him go in peace. Meanwhile, we should have some of our younger members follow him wherever he goes and report to us periodically for if he is the promised Mashìah, it is our duty to welcome him as our spiritual leader," suggested Youseph.

"I see!" remarked Kaiaphas, disturbed by his old friend's belief. "We will have several of our men follow him and report to us every month. Does this please you, Youseph, my friend?"

"That is fine, Lord Kaiaphas," uttered Youseph, concerned with Kaiaphas' zeal and ruthlessness.

The short meeting was concluded and two young Pharishaiya, two Tsadduqim and a scribe were chosen to spy on Ishia of Nazerat.

Both Nikotheimos and Youseph A'Ramathayim went directly to Eleazar's house to verify his resurrection. At seeing his good friend, Eleazar, alive, Youseph knew that Lord Ishia was the true Mashìah. Both of them asked to see Ishia of Nazarene to warn Him about the spies that the San-hedrin had sent to follow Him. Unfortunately, Eleazar's savior had left in a hurry, promising to come back to see him and his two wonderful sisters the next time He would visit the holy city. Youseph and Nikotheimos spent several hours conversing with Eleazar, along with other Yehudi still present. Miryam and Martha, still excited by their Lord's greatest miracle, were preparing food and drinks to celebrate their brother's resurrection. The atmosphere in Eleazar's house was one of joy and celebration. Youseph was happy for Eleazar; but he was still remembering his friend's funeral that he had attended the previous week. Puzzled yet beginning to see a clearer picture, Youseph

A'Ramathayim finally came to a personal resolution: Ishia of Nazerat was the true Mashìah, the Promised Son of their God, Yahweh.

Chapter 29

BACK TO HAGALIL THROUGH SHOMERON

Ishia had left Eleazar, Miryam, and Martha because He feared the possibility of being arrested. He could not take that chance for it was not His time to die. He promised to return in autumn, during the Feast of the Tabernacles. His friends had understood His concern and had wished Him a safe and good journey back to His family, in Kfar-Nahum, giving Him some provisions to last a few days for the entire group.

Four days later, Ishia and His followers had reached Har Gerizim, in Shomeron. That night they camped at the foothills of that mountain, sleeping around a bonfire they had made. The following morning they came to the village of Sychara, which stood in the valley between Har Gerizim and Har 'Eval. The road forked and the city of Neapolis was only five stadia away by taking the left road, while Sychara was only a few hundred cubits ahead. The apostles and disciples decided to go to Neapolis to buy some provisions for they had exhausted the food given to them. They would rejoin their Lord by the *Well of Yakov*, beside the land that Yakov had given to his son, Youseph.

It was noon when Ishia reached the well; but He had no means to draw water from it. He sat down with His back against the well and patiently waited, as He watched a woman with a water jug on her head approaching the ancient watering hole. When the woman reached the well, He told her, "Please, give me a drink of water."

"How is it possible that a Yehudi like you is asking a Shomeroni for a drink?" asked the woman, surprised. "Yehudi do not talk to Shomeroni, especially women!"

"If only you would realize who I am and what gift My Father would grant you," replied Ishia, "If you would have asked for a drink He would have given you the water of life."

"Sir, you do not have a jug; and, the well is deep, as you can see. And tell me, how or where can you get this water of life? Do you pretend to be greater than our patriarch, Yakov, who dug this well and used this water for himself, his family, and his cattle?" spoke the woman with pride.

"Anyone who drinks the water of this well will soon be thirsty again; but, anyone who drinks the water from my well, will be quenched forever. The water I give to anyone will become an eternal fountain of life within him or her."

"Sir, please, give me some of your water, so that my thirst will be quenched forever and I will never need to come to this well again!" exclaimed the Shomeroni woman.

"Go home and tell your husband to come back here with you," ordered Ishia.

"I am not married," she replied.

"You have spoken the truth, for although you have previously had five husbands, the man you live with now is not married to you."

"Are you a prophet, Sir?" asked the woman. "You do not think that Yerushalayim is the only place to glorify the Lord, for we have been praying to Him on Har Gerizim since our forefathers built a holy temple on its top."

"Woman, believe me, it is time that you will not worship the Father on this mountain nor in Yerushalayim. You pray to the unknown. The Yehudi pray for a savior. But the hour is here for true believers to worship the Father with their spirit, with truth in their mind, and with their heart."

"We, Shomeroni, are also waiting for our savior, the Mashìah. He will reveal everything to us when He comes!" exclaimed the woman.

"I am the one that you have been waiting for. I tell you this because I come not only for the Yehudi, but also for the Shomeroni. I come for the whole world," He announced.

The apostles and disciples were coming back from Neapolis when they witnessed their Lord speaking to a Shomeroni woman by the Well of Yakov. Suddenly, the woman placed her water jar near Lord Ishia and ran to her village, Sychara. The apostles and disciples were shocked to see their Lord speaking to a Shomeroni, and a woman! Yehudi did not lower themselves to speak to a Shomeroni. That is the way it was! However, no one questioned their Lord for doing that, for He always had a good reason for anything He chose to do.

The Shomeroni woman had reached her village and had announced to everyone that the Holy Mashìah, the Promised One, was by the Well of Yakov. She told them that He knew everything about her and that He had revealed Himself to her. Immediately, every person in that village followed the woman to the well.

Cephas offered food to his Lord, "Have something to eat, My Lord."

"I have eaten My Father's food," He answered.

"Did that woman give you food, Lord?" asked Cephas.

"No, Cephas! My food is to fulfill My Father's mission. As the saying goes: there are still four months of growth; and, then comes the harvest! I tell you all to look for I am the harvest. All of you who reap will gather fruits of everlasting life. As the ancient prophets have sown you all shall reap the harvest, and I am the harvest. You are the lucky ones for you shall reap what the ancient ones have sown."

As Ishia was giving His message to His apostles, hundreds of Shomeroni, young and old, had arrived with the woman. They begged Him to stay in Sychara, offering a place for Lord Ishia of Nazerat and for all His followers. Ishia accepted and stayed two days curing anyone that was sick. Sick people from Neapolis had also come to be cured. He cured everyone and preached His commandment to them, to love Yahweh, His Father, to obey His laws and to love everyone, friends and enemies. The Shomeroni felt blessed by the presence of the Holy Mashìah in their land of Shomeron.

As Ishia and His men were departing for Hagalil an old man from Sychara exclaimed, "We believe in You, My Lord, for we have witnessed Your wonder that has been given to You by Your Father. You are truly the Savior of the whole world."

The apostles and disciples traveled for six more days, bypassing Nazerat for Ishia would never return to that town. They reached Qana, where the Lord's wedding had taken place and where He had changed water into the most delicious wine, and stopped by the synagogue to pray. An officer of the royal court happened to be in Qana, whose son was dying in Kfar-Nahum. The officer ran towards Ishia.

"Sir, please come to my house in Kfar-Nahum. I know that you also live there and I know that you can cure my son. I have horses, sir! Please, come with me before my son dies," begged the officer.

"Do you know who I am?" asked Ishia.

"People say you are the Promised One, the Mashìah."

"What do you believe?"

"Such wondrous things you have done can only come from God the Father Himself. I believe, sir, that you are His Son!"

"Your faith, my good man, has saved your son. Go home, your son will get better."

Having thanked Him, the officer and his men galloped away towards Yam Kinneret. The following morning, before they reached Kfar-Nahum, the officer and his men were met by two of his servants bringing good news of his son.

"When did he get better?" asked the officer.

"Yesterday, sir!" replied a servant.

"At what hour?"

"On the seventh hour of the day, sir."

That was the exact time that Ishia of Nazerat had told him that his son was better. From that day on, that officer, his family and all his servants believed in the Lord as the Holy Mashìah.

Three days later Ishia and His followers entered Kfar-Nahum. Lydia and their beautiful baby boy were thrilled to see Him again. Judas was ecstatic to see his Esther and extremely joyous to hear that she was expecting a child. Lydia told Ishia that a Shomeroni man named Eleazar had brought a gift for Lord Ishia, his savior. The gift was heavily wrapped in white linen. Judas remembered Eleazar, from Shomeron, whose deep wounds had been miraculously cured by His Lord. Judas and the rest waited until their Lord had unwrapped the gift. It was a beautiful silver goblet with a golden image of the Lord. Under the image the name of Ishia, 𐤉𐤔𐤏𐤉, had been inscribed in Aramaic. Judas inspected the simple but beautiful silver goblet with Ishia's image and name in gold bas-relief. He could hardly believe that he was staring at the Holy Grail itself. Ishia was deeply moved by the beautiful gift from the Shomeroni silversmith, Eleazar.

Ishia and His apostles spent the rest of the winter in Kfar-Nahum, enjoying the company of their spouses, families, and friends. Pesach was celebrated at Ishia's house, crowded with all the apostles and their families, all of their disciples and friends. Ishia recited the Haggadah. It was wonderful to hear His beautiful voice tell the ancient story of the Exodus from Egypt.

Once the Pesach holiday had been celebrated, the apostles and their disciples followed their Lord to Gush Halav in Upper Hagalil and up to Qedesh. At Qedesh, they climbed Hare Ramim, the mountains which overlook the Valley of Hulah. Ishia spent a few days there teaching His followers how to pray, how to cleanse themselves, including how to take care of their teeth. Most of them had bad teeth for they did not know how to take care of them. Ishia showed them how to clean in between their teeth with a splinter of wood and how to keep them shiny by using a piece of soft leather. He taught them *hygieine techne,* the art of cleanliness. Once again, He told them about His mission on earth: to teach them about love and to die for their sins.

"Why must You die, My Lord?" asked Cephas once again.

"I must die for all of you and for every person who will be born in this planet, for death is the ultimate sacrifice I can make for you to show you how much I love all of you; and, only through death shall I come back from its darkness for I am the Light, the Son of My Father," replied Ishia.

Ishia showed them the power of the mind and told them that the mind could do wonderful things: things that are impossible could become possible with the power of the mind. The power had to be awakened for it was there all the time, placed there by His Father at the beginning. Judas fully understood the Lord; but it would take years before the rest would finally realize the meaning of those words.

From Qedesh they traveled into Tayr and up the Phoenician coast to Shidon. While traveling from Tayr to Shidon they encountered a Syrio-Phoenician lady, who had come to meet the Lord after having heard that He was traveling towards Shidon. She begged Ishia to go to her place to cure her daughter, who was possessed by an unclean spirit. Ishia told her that her daughter had been cured because of her faith in Him. She went home to find her daughter cured from the evil possession.

From Shidon they crossed the smaller Ha-Yarden, near its source, and went into Syria, Gaulanitis, and Batanaea, curing the sick along the way. When they reached northern Decapolis a large crowd blocked their way. The curious crowd had brought a deaf and dumb begging the Lord to cure him. Ishia spit on His fingers and placed the spit into the man's ears and touched his tongue with the spit. Ishia, with His hands stretched to the sky, sighed "Eph-pheta!"

A moment passed and the man began to speak clearly, using the language correctly. He also could hear for he answered many questions asked by people he had known all his life. How could that be possible? That man had been deaf and dumb since birth! They began to chant praise about Ishia of Nazerat, the Mashìah. The crowd followed them everywhere, getting larger from town to town. Ishia continued to work miracles, compelling unbelievers to believe. From Dium to Abila, and from Abila to Gadara, Ishia circled back to the southern shores of Yam Kinneret.

Several fishermen, who knew the Lord, gave Ishia and all His men a ride in their fishing boats all the way to Beth-Saida. From Beth-Saida they traveled north along the east bank of the Ha-Yarden up to Caesarea Philippi. There they visited the high cliffs, where there is a cave dedicated to Pan and many niches had been carved to hold statues of nymphs. It was on those cliffs that Lord Ishia officially declared Cephas to be His first successor and leader of His followers once He would leave this world. After several days in Caesarea Philippi, performing many more miracles, Ishia led His followers back to Kfar-Nahum. It was the end of summer of the year 32 A.D.

Chapter 30

INCOGNITO

Lucius Aelius Sejanus, captain of the guards of Emperor Tiberius Claudius Nero, had enjoyed power for years. Emperor Tiberius had named Sejanus as ruler of Rome during his retirement on the island of Capreae. Tiberius had problems with the Roman senate and chose to escape to a beautiful island leaving the captain of his personal guards in charge of the empire. Sejanus had appointed Pontius Pilatus as Procurator of Yehuda, Shomeron, and Idumea. Youseph Kaiaphas had been appointed high priest of Yerushalayim by Gratus, the former Procurator of Yehuda. Sejanus had been good to the rulers of Yehuda, Shomeron, Hagalil, Gaulanitis, and the surrounding provinces; however, his penchant thirst for ultimate power had led him to have several members of the royal family put to death. No one was going to stand in his way towards becoming emperor. Unfortunately for Sejanus, Tiberius found out his schemes and ordered his death. Sejanus was assassinated and Tiberius returned to rule the empire for six more years.

News of the death of Lucius Aelius Sejanus reached Hagalil, Yehuda, and the other provinces. King Herod Antipas, his brother, King Philip, Pontius Pilatus, and Youseph Kaiaphas all felt insecure of their posts. They would do anything for Rome in order to remain in power. However, small groups of rebels felt it was an opportune time to revolt against the Romans and drive them out of their land. One of these rebels was Yeshua Bar-Abbas, the very same person that

Ishia had stopped from murdering Augustus Horatius and his men. Bar-Abbas was planning a revolt during the Feast of Tabernacles, Succot, which would take place during early autumn.

Ishia had enjoyed the roles as husband and father, spending time with Lydia and little Jesus Justus. He loved them dearly and the time He spent with them was important and precious. He had told His son the wonderful stories of ancient heroes from around the world. However, the apostles and disciples grew restless and all, except Judas, wished to go back to Yerushalayim to celebrate Succot. Most men from all the states of Yisrael would make a pilgrimage to the holy city of Yerushalayim during Succot. The roads leading to Yerushalayim would be crowded with Hebrai coming from near and afar. Ishia told them to go to the holy city, like all good Hebrai, and make their pilgrimage during the month of Succot.

The scorching hot days had disappeared with the summer; and, autumn had brought mellower sunny days with gentle breezes blowing northwards along the great Valley of Ha-Yarden. Autumn in Kfar-Nahum was wonderful! The apostles and all of the disciples had left for Yerushalayim passing through Tiberias on the western shore of Yam Kinneret. From Tiberias they traveled to Beth-She'an or Scythopolis, as the gentiles called it. From Beth-She'an they would travel to Shalem, where they would cross the Ha-Yarden and travel through the foothills of the mountains of 'Ammon and cross the holy river again to reach Bet-ha'Arava. They would rest there for it had been Yehohanan the Baptist's favorite spot by the Ha-Yarden. From Bet-ha'Arava they would travel across the desert to Yerushalayim.

Lord Ishia and Judas had left two days later and had caught up with His apostles and disciples at Bet-ha'Arava. Ishia stayed away from His followers and had covered most of His face with His robe while Judas had worn his hood to keep from being recognized. Along the way, Ishia had talked to Judas about the next Pesach and the role He would play. Judas begged Ishia if it were possible to change His role during Pesach; but, He told him that it had all been planned millennia before. All the great prophets had predicted what was going to happen during the following Pesach. A profound melancholy had taken over Judas, saddened by his fateful role.

"Do not dwell on it, my beloved friend, for it will surely sadden this holy pilgrimage," said Ishia. "Enjoy this day for once it is over, it will be gone forever. Enjoy each day that I am here with you for my time is getting closer by each moment."

"Lord, I have often seen You in so much pain. It must be terrifying for You to know all that is to happen."

"It saddens me to have to do it all over again!"

"What do you mean, My Lord?"

"Next Pesach will not be the first time that I will die for my people."

"I do not understand, Lord."

"I have gone through what I will go through on this earth several times in similar worlds. It is my role as the Son and I accept it although it is so difficult to do. So, my friend, you will play your role only once. Now, let us not dwell on this subject for it is painful even to talk about it. However, let us enjoy each day that we are alive and together."

For a while they sat in silence; and, silence turned into a long meditation.

(Thursday, September 11, 32 A.D.)

The following morning, Ishia and Judas left Bet-ha'Arava before dawn on the road to Yerushalayim. The rest of the apostles and their disciples were still sleeping and by the time they would all wake up Ishia and Judas would have traveled at least forty stadia. Judas had become accustomed to the Lord's quick pace. It was going to be a full day of marching along the dry wadis of the Midbar Yehuda for Ishia's intentions were to reach Eleazar's house at Beth-Ananiah by dusk. It would take two days for the apostles and disciples to reach Yerushalayim. Several of them were older and could not keep up with a quick-paced march all day long.

Judas was exhausted by the time he and Lord Ishia reached Eleazar's house. It was the first hour of the evening and it had taken them sixteen hours of fast walking, taking only four small breaks eating a little bread and some water. At first, Martha and Miryam did not recognize them for it was dark outside and their faces were still covered. As soon as Ishia uncovered His face, they shouted His name with joy and showered Him with hugs and kisses. Eleazar came to see what the commotion was all about and he was ecstatic to see his savior, hugging Him with such fervor and love. Judas was treated in a similar fashion as he was almost smothered with hugs and kisses. Eleazar was in excellent health. He had regained a healthy color and the weight he had lost.

Lord Ishia and Judas were given the royal treatment with a spread of food and honeyed wine. As they munched and sipped the sweet wine, Eleazar told them about his experiences with people who knew that he had been dead. He told everyone that Ishia of Nazerat, the Holy Mashìah, was truly the Only Son of God for He had resurrected him from death itself. Even the Pharishaiya and the Tsadduqim could not say much to that for Eleazar was living proof of the power of their Lord. That evening, Lord Ishia and Judas slept like babies, their bodies exhausted by the long walk and pacified by the good food and honeyed wine.

(Friday, September 12, 32 A.D.)

The celebration of the New Year had ended and early that morning all Hebrai would continue their fast and pray all day for forgiveness. It was Yom Kippur, the Day of Atonement, the most solemn day for all Yehudi and all other Hebrai, no matter where they were. It was a day of fasting and prayer. Without speaking a word, Ishia woke up early to cleanse Himself. Judas, Eleazar, Martha, and Miryam also woke up and washed up. They followed Him up Har Ha-Zetim until they reached the top of the mountain. Without saying a word to each other the four joined their Lord in deep prayer. The previous evening, Ishia had told them that He would prefer to pray on the top of Mount of Olives instead of the Temple. There would not be any privacy in the Temple for thousands of pilgrims had come to Yerushalayim to celebrate the New Year, Yom Kippur, and Succot. After a full day of prayer, Ishia stood up and began to descend the mount, followed by Judas, Martha, Miryam, and Eleazar. Their fast ended with some delicious food the sisters had prepared the previous night.

Ishia and Judas spent the following four days helping Eleazar built a booth for the Feast of Succot. Using a pile of poles, kept especially for building a booth, they built a shelter, tying them together with twine and covering the roof with fresh branches. It was big enough for a dozen people to eat and sleep in it. Each family or house would build a booth. The building of the booths symbolized the nomadic life of the Hebrai during the years spent in the Wilderness of Sinai after the Exodus from Egypt. Enterprising young men were already selling small branches of myrtle, citron, willow, and palm, which were used by everyone in ritual waving at each other during the feast. Miryam had already snapped several branches from their citron and myrtle bushes and a few long branches from their willow tree. She had carefully tied five bouquets, each containing a sample of the three plants. The palm trees were too tall for Miryam to climb. Ishia had looked at Judas and he had immediately understood. Judas offered to climb one of the palm trees and cut one of its branches so that Miryam could cut it into smaller sections to complete her bouquets. Judas easily climbed the palm tree and cut one of its branches with a knife that Miryam had given him. She kissed his cheek happily, thanking him for his bravery, and proceeded to finish the five bouquets, which now contained a sample of each of the four plants.

During those four days, Eleazar had suggested to visit the Temple but Ishia had declined the offer. "Why not, My Lord?" had asked Eleazar.

"The Temple has become a market!" He had exclaimed. "It is supposed to be a house of prayer, My Father's House; but it has become a den for business and thieves."

"True, My Lord," had whispered Eleazar sadly, "True."

"However, tomorrow we shall go there to pray!" exclaimed Ishia.

A smile reassured the pensive Eleazar. Miryam came into the booth and gave each one a bouquet of the four symbolic plants, which they would bring to the Temple.

(Wednesday, September 17, 32 A.D.)
(First day of Succot)

Ishia, Judas, and Eleazar took their bouquets of branches to the Temple, followed by Miryam and Martha, as was the custom.

Ishia and Judas kept their faces hidden for safety sake. They entered Yerushalayim by the Sheepgate, near the pool the Hebrai called Beth-Saida. A multitude of people crowded the five porticoes by the pool. Some had stepped into the water, anxiously waiting for *the Angel of the Lord* to stir the water so that they may be cured. That was the belief about the Beth-Saida pool. Ishia had stopped to look at a paralyzed man, lying on a pallet. No one seemed to care about him or to place him into the water. Ishia whispered something to Judas. Judas went to the paralyzed man and whispered Ishia's message into his ear.

They had to make their way through the crowds to reach the Wailing Wall, the western wall of the Temple. Yerushalayim was crowded with thousands of pilgrims, all waving their aromatic branches in honor of the Feast of Succot. Ishia, Judas, and Eleazar walked up the ramp that led through the Temple archway, while Miryam and Martha remained by the square facing the Temple.

Ishia and Judas hid their faces and turned away from Eleazar when Youseph A'Ramathayim came to talk to him. Youseph took Eleazar by the arm and led him into the Temple. Ishia and Judas followed them as Eleazar kept turning his head to see if they were still there. Ishia kept in total silence, hidden in a corner of the great Temple. Judas recognized the apostles and disciples who prayed silently on the other side. Most of them had managed to find palm and citron branches, which they held reverently. Finally, Eleazar rejoined the Lord and Judas. The three walked out of the Temple walls without any incident. Roman guards were standing by every strategic point of the city, expecting trouble or a possible revolt.

During Thursday and Friday mornings, Ishia returned to the Temple through the Gate of Essenes with Judas and Eleazar, always holding the bouquets and waving them at everyone. Each time, Ishia and Judas hid their faces from everyone, keeping their identity and presence a secret.

(Shabbat, September 20, 32 A.D.)
(Fourth day of Succot)

Miryam and Martha joined the Lord, Judas, and Eleazar on the Shabbat morning of the feast, enjoying waving the fragrant bouquets at any citizen or pilgrim, who responded in kindness by waving theirs in return. Once again, Ishia led them to the Sheepgate by Beth-Saida. The paralyzed man was there, lying on his pallet, while many beggars and poor people were by the pool, wetting their legs and arms. The paralyzed man recognized Judas and cried, "Master!"

Ishia and Judas walked up to him. Ishia asked him, "Do you want to get well?"

"No one wants to help me get into the water when it is stirred. Everybody keeps getting in front of me. Would you help me to get into the water, Master?" cried the crippled man.

"Stand up, my good man, pick up your bed and walk to the water," ordered Ishia.

The paralytic looked at the tall man but could not see his face for it was covered with his robe. Slowly, he got up for the first time in thirty-eight years and began to pick up his pallet and wobbled to the pool. People who had seen him often enough moved out of his way in shock. How was it possible? How could he walk with his tiny atrophied muscles, which could barely hold his bones together? But he did walk to the water, down the steps, submerging himself into the water. At the other end of the pool stood Lord Ishia, together with Judas, Eleazar, and his pretty sisters. Ishia put His hand into the water and stirred it in a circular fashion until it formed a rippling current, which rushed towards the former paralytic. The current hit the former paralytic, forcing him to step back and regain his stance. Suddenly, a vitality shone throughout his slim body and he felt young again. He looked at the tall stranger and cried out, "Thank you, Lord!"

The tall stranger turned around and quickly made his way towards the Temple, keeping his identity a secret to the crowd.

The cured paralytic was smiling, even laughing, and his shuffle was almost a dance of joy. He picked up his pallet and walked towards the direction the tall stranger had disappeared into. The streets were crowded with people, all dressed in their festive garments and all carrying their fragrant branches, waving them and greeting friends, acquaintances, neighbors, and even total strangers. Yerushalayim was crowded because it was a special day, the Shabbat of Succot. Carrying a homemade bed was not easy in that crowd and the former paralytic was having some trouble making his way towards the temple, sometimes bumping the front of his pallet into people's behinds. As he searched for the tall stranger, his pallet hit a fat Pharish's posterior.

The fat man dressed in black turned around and cried out, "Watch where you are going, you blind fool!" And, when he realized that the man who had bumped him was dripping wet and carrying a worn out pallet he screamed, "Do you not know that today is not only a Shabbat but the Shabbat of Succot. Shame on you! Do you not know that you cannot carry your pallet today? You are breaking the law of Moishe."

"But, sir! The tall man who cured my paralysis told me to stand up from my bed and to take it and carry it. You see, I have been lying on this bed for thirty-eight years!" exclaimed the cured man.

"Who is the tall man who ordered you to carry your bed? And how did he cure you?" asked another Pharish.

"I do not know the man. His face was covered with his robe. I have seen him go into this direction," pointed the man.

"He must be by the Temple. Listen, put your bed down beside this wall and come with us," ordered the fat Pharish.

"But someone might take my bed!" exclaimed the cured man.

"No one will dare steal your stinking bed. Look at it. It is filthy and torn, and it is probably infested with bedbugs," said the other Pharish. "Now, put it down and come with us. I am ordering you to do so!"

Silently, the man placed his worn out bed beside a wall and followed the two Pharishaiya towards the Temple, constantly looking back to see if anyone would steal his bed. To his surprise, most people moved away from the filthy bed as they passed by. They reached the temple, followed by a crowd, interested to see what would happen. The square facing the Wailing Wall was crowded with people and as the two Pharishaiya looked up towards the Temple they saw the tall stranger, together with two men, entering the archway. They tried to push their way through the crowd, which was walking up the ramp but people pushed back and began to shout at them.

Finally, the two Pharishaiya and the drenched man made it through the archway and, once again, caught a glimpse of the tall man entering the Temple with his two friends. Quickly, they pushed their way until they, too, entered the sacred Temple. The cured paralytic was left behind as the two Pharishaiya pushed their way in.

Suddenly, Ishia stood in front of the man and said, "Now that you are cured, take good care of yourself. Obey the commandments and learn to love everyone. If you do so no harm will come to you." Ishia lowered His robe from His face and smiled at the man.

"Lord, it is You!" cried the man, recognizing that it was Ishia of Nazerat. Before he could say anything else, Ishia disappeared into the crowd.

The cured man found the two Pharishaiya and told them that one who cured him had been Ishia of Nazerat, the Holy Mashìah.

The fat Pharish screamed out, "How dare he cure you on the Shabbat of Succot? How dare he order you to carry your infested bed? He is not the Mashìah! He is the devil himself!"

"Whom are you speaking of?" asked a Tsadduqim next to the fat man.

"Ishia of Nazerat! The devil Himself!" exclaimed the fat man.

The apostles and disciples who were in the Temple turned around but did not dare defend their Lord for they were afraid of the possible consequences. Judas, who had heard everything turned around, screaming, "How dare you speak of My Lord in that foul manner. Are you too blind to recognize that He truly is the Holy Mashìah!"

"Are you one of his followers?" asked a man.

"Not only am I one of His followers, but I am also one of His best friends!"

"Then you know that he does not observe the holy Shabbat!" exclaimed the man.

Ishia uncovered His head and face and spoke out, "My Father never stops working, and I go on working for I am My Father's Son."

"BLASPHEMER!!" yelled several men.

"He thinks he is the Son of God!" cried another.

Finally, the apostles and disciples took courage and made a circle around their Lord, ready to protect Him.

"In all reverence of this holy feast," cried out Ishia, "I cannot do anything by myself. I can only do My Father's work for whatever He does, I also do. My Father loves me and reveals everything to me. Through Him I will do great things that will amaze you. My Father raises the dead and gives them a new life. Likewise I give life to anyone I choose to. My Father judges no one for He has given me the power to do so, that you may honor me as you honor My Father. Whoever among you that refuses to honor me refuses to honor My Father. Truly, I tell you, whoever believes in what I say and believes in My Father who sent me shall have eternal life. Those who believe will be spared judgment. The hour has come for anyone who is dead within himself and recognizes the voice of the Son of God shall live. My Father is the creator of man on this earth and He has given me that same power. His sacred blood flows in my veins and He has appointed me supreme judge."

Many listening were in total shock.

"Do not be shocked at what I tell you," He continued. "I do not act by myself, I have orders from My Father to judge; and, I will judge justly because I will please My Father and I will do His Will. I will not be my own witness! You sent messengers to Yehohanan and he was my witness and his testimony is binding. I am not saying this for my sake but for the sake of your salvation. Yehohanan was a light in this world of darkness and you were happy to see his brightness. But, my word is greater than Yehohanan's. The works that My Father has given me to do are the evidence that I am the Son of the Father. He is my Witness! You have never heard His Voice, nor have you seen His Figure, and His Words are lost to you because you do not believe that He has sent me to do His Work. You all have studied the scriptures believing that His Words will give you eternal life. These very scriptures speak of me and you refuse me. I do not need your approval. I know that deep within you there is no love of God. I have come in His Name and you refuse to believe me; but you accept others that do not come in His Name. How can you possibly believe when I see you looking at each other for approval, completely disregarding my approval? You are not concerned with my approval, even though it comes from Yahweh Himself. I will not accuse you before My Father. Moishe shall be your accuser for you place your hopes in him. And, if you truly believe in Moishe you would believe in me. But how can you believe in me when you do not even believe in His scriptures."

Ishia's rhetoric enraged most Yehudi that they began screaming for his blood. For his death! Many were trying to get to him but the apostles and disciples forced their way out of the Temple, running down the ramp towards the Gate of Essenes. The crowd frantically ran after them, gone crazy with suspicion and hatred. Suddenly, a group of Yehudi took their swords, which had been hidden underneath their robes and attacked several Roman soldiers, killing three of them. Ishia turned around and stopped, as did everyone else. As He looked back, He recognized Yeshua Bar-Abbas, the rebel leader. He was being held by two Roman soldiers who had managed to arrest him. Like a terrifying deja vu, Ishia and His followers ran out of the gate, down the ramp, and made their way into the Wadi Qidron.

Having said a quick farewell to Eleazar, Ishia and His followers quickly made their way through the northern section of the Midbar Yehuda. After four days of traveling, they reached the southern lands of Shomeron, stopping at the village of Efrayim. There, they remained for several days. Lord Ishia cured any Shomeroni who came to Him. Saddened that His own people wanted His death, Ishia gladly cured all the Shomeroni that came to Him asking to be cured. Their belief was pure and their reward was great.

Chapter 31

THE LAST PESACH

From Efrayim Ishia led His followers back to Hagalil, stopping at Sychara and at the city of Shomeron, where He thanked Eleazar, the silversmith, for his wonderful gift. Eleazar was so excited by the Lord's visit that he celebrated the occasion with a feast in honor of his Savior. From Shomeron they traveled to Ginnat, where the people refused entrance to the Lord. He promised to come back to that town to give them another chance to welcome Him. The Lord stopped at Nain, where He was greeted like a king. No one from Nain would ever forget what Ishia of Nazerat had done. From Nain they traveled to Tiberias and continued along the shore until the group reached Kfar-Nahum.

Matthias Levi Bar-Alpheus had often complained about too much walking. Being short and rotund made it difficult for Matthias to move at the same speed of the rest of the group. Also, he was constantly sweating. As they reached Kfar-Nahum he said, "Lord, I think I have walked enough to last me a lifetime. Next time I think I will use a horse."

"Matthias, walking is great for the whole body," said the Lord. "It exercises the entire body and all its organs. Walking is to the body what praying is to the spirit. Never stop walking, Matthias! Look at yourself. You have lost some weight because of all the walking you have done. Walking keeps you young and it regenerates vigor within your body. Never stop walking, I say to all of you!"

There were only six months left before the next Pesach and Ishia wished to enjoy as much of that time as possible with His loved ones. He remained in Kfar-Nahum, enjoying the company of Lydia and their little boy. Esther, Judas' wife had given birth to a healthy baby boy and had named him Judas the Younger, after the man she loved. Gentle, kind, and generous Judas. Her savior! Together, Ishia and Judas spent many hours each day with their families. The rest of the apostles and disciples were enjoying their rest, totally oblivious to what would soon happen to their Lord and Judas. They also enjoyed their families and loved ones. The winter of 32 A.D. was a time of rest. The group had relished vintaging and tasting the fresh wine in October. Following the vintage, everyone enjoyed the delicious persimmons harvested during November and early December. Persimmons were Hagalil's favorite fruit. Persimmons were found everywhere throughout Hagalil, some growing wild. Probably, many of those wild persimmon trees had grown from persimmon pits that people had spat out. Hagalil was rich with persimmons, figs, grapes, dates, and nuts; and, it was popular to decorate tables with baskets of those fruits and nuts.

During those winter months, there were many people that were brought to Lord Ishia to be cured. They were cured because they wanted to be cured and believed in His powers. January and February went by and spring was beginning to show its face. Ishia knew that His time was close at hand. He had a heart-to-heart talk with Judas away from the rest of the apostles and disciples. Judas could not hold back his tears as visions of His betrayal, of Ishia's horrifying crucifixion, and of his own death oscillated deeply within his brain. As he approached the others, several asked why he had been crying. All he could utter was *it is the end*, adding more perplexity to their ignorance of what would soon unfold, which would affect each and every one them for the rest of their lives.

Ishia summoned His father-in-law, Augustus Horatius, and explained to him what was about to happen. Augustus volunteered himself and his men to protect Him; but, Ishia told him that what was about to happen was part of His Father's Plan. Augustus was disturbed by His Lord's fateful end. Ishia told him that His death was out of His love for the whole mankind, and that on the third day after His death He would come back to life. The reason for having summoned Augustus was to ask him to take care of Lydia, His son, Esther, and Judas' son. As soon as He would be dead he should take them, together with his family, to Massilia, across the Mare Nostrum. There they would be safe from the high priests, from the Pharishaiya, and from the Romans, for their intention would be to exterminate His family and followers. Ishia's half brother, Yakov Bar-Youseph, would be coming along. He would instruct him to do so on the last day. Augustus promised Ishia that he would follow His wish and protect their loved ones with his own life. Augustus hugged Ishia and told Him that he would take all their loved ones to Yerushalayim. His wife had a friend there, a widow, who also believed in Him. She would be happy to keep them for a few days. Augustus would travel by horse-drawn cart and with a Roman escort to protect the women and the two babies.

Ishia and Judas both tried to explain to Lydia and Esther what was about to happen, which resulted in their breaking down and crying. They did not and could not understand Ishia's mission. Why did He have to die? What about all His great works? Did they not count? What about their son? What about them? Ishia told them of Augustus' plan and promised them that both He and Judas would visit them in Massilia. That promise seemed to pacify their fears and pain. Both women knew that Ishia's words were sacred. They embraced and shared the last few hours of the last day of February together, strolling by the shore, together with their baby boys.

(Sunday, March 1, 33 A.D.)

On the second hour of the day, after making their last farewell, Ishia, Judas, the apostles, the disciples, and all the members of their families began their long journey on foot, along the western shore of Yam Kinneret. Miryam, Ishia and Yakov's mother would travel with Lydia, Esther, and their two boys. They would leave on Wednesday and reach Yerushalayim before Ishia and His followers. Dolorous by His knowledge of what was about to happen, Ishia's pace was moderate at the very most; but His stamina was inexhaustible. It was early afternoon when the large group reached Genne-Sareth and Lord Ishia stopped only for a little water. He told everyone to take a little break and eat something while He would pray underneath a tree. Judas wetted his lips and joined the Lord in prayer.

The group resumed the march with more people following Him, reaching Magdala by dusk. At Magdala He was welcomed as the Mashìah, which seemed to raise His spirit up. Judas even noticed a smile on His face as the people of Magdala showered Him with praise and gratitude. Ishia had cured many people in that fishing town and they would never forget who He was. That night they rested in Magdala, where many houses opened their doors to Ishia and His followers and their families, sharing their food and space with them.

(Monday, March 2, 33 A.D.)

At the first rays of the sun that filtered through the mountaintops of Hagolan, Ishia resumed His march towards His death. More people, from Magdala, who were going to make a pilgrimage to the Temple of Yerushalayim in celebration of Pesach, joined His group. Most of them were young men and a few women with their older children. He led them all the way to Qana, where He was welcomed by the townspeople. The Rabbi, an older man, who had witnessed one of His miracle in his own synagogue had invited Him to speak. Graciously, He accepted and spoke to them about love. That love would conquer all. That He loved them all. The little synagogue was filled to capacity with hundreds of people surrounding the building as they tried to listen to His message. Qana had been blessed for the Lord had been married there and He had, more than once, revisited that beautiful town on the foothills of Har 'Azmon.

Ishia's followers had multiplied and it took that large crowd two full days to reach Ginnat. The Lord had made a promise to give the town of Ginnat a second chance to welcome Him. As the group reached the outskirts of that town, ten lepers were coming to greet Him. The people of Ginnat had sent the ten lepers to greet Him, hoping that He and His followers would go away. They had no intention to share their food, wine, and houses with vagabonds. The apostles and all the followers came to a stop, fearful of the lepers approaching them.

"Ishia! Master! Have pity on us, Lord!" exclaimed the lepers.

Ishia continued on until He was at an arm's length from them. He asked, "What do you seek from me?"

"Cure us, Lord!" exclaimed one.

"Have pity on us, Holy Mashìah!" uttered another.

"Are you from Ginnat?" asked Ishia.

"No, Lord, but we have heard that you were coming this way and we rushed here; but, the townspeople did not want us to come in," answered a leper.

"Do you know why they refuse anyone to enter their town?" asked Ishia.

"Lord, they do not want to share their food and houses with anyone," answered a woman in the group.

"Do they not know who I am?" asked the Lord.

"They do not believe that you are the Mashìah, Lord!" answered another.

"Then all of you go back and tell them who I am."

They all turned around and began to walk back towards Ginnat, but before they could reach the entrance their skin had been cleansed and purified by the Lord Himself. Nine of them went on to tell the people of Ginnat what the Lord had done. However, one of them had gone back to the Lord to thank Him. Ishia told him that not only his body had been purified but also his soul. The man begged Him to follow Him and Ishia welcomed him like a brother.

The townspeople upon finding out that Ishia of Nazerat had cured all ten ran after Him trying to invite Him to stay in their town.

The Lord answered, "Now that you have witnessed my power you ask me to stay in your town. Will I be able to bring my twelve apostles in your town?"

"We will gladly accommodate them, Lord. Please, come!" pleaded a fat and bald middle-aged man.

"Can my seventy-two disciples and their families and the families of some of my apostles join us and share your food with them?" asked the Lord.

The townspeople looked at each other and agreed, "They are many, but we will manage to give them some food," spoke a woman.

"What about the rest of my followers," asked Ishia, "They too need food and shelter."

"You ask too much, Lord. There are a few thousand people following you, and they will surely clean us up. We will have nothing left by the time they all eat. Please, Lord, you and your apostles, your disciples, and their families are welcome. The rest can wait outside," spoke the fat, bald man.

"Woe unto you, people of Ginnat, for you are selfish and stingy. All of those people, each one of them is my brother or sister, and you have refused them. I shall never enter your town for your hearts are untrue. Twice you have refused my people and me. You shall never get a third chance," spoke Ishia. He then turned around and left with His people towards the Valley of the Ha-Yarden.

(Saturday, March 7, 33 A.D.)

It was noon when Ishia and thousands of followers reached the spot where the Wadi Yabis empties into the Ha-Yarden. It was one of Ishia's favorite camping spot. Some of the people had begun to complain that it was Shabbat and they had no temple or synagogue to pray in.

"I am the Temple for the Blood of My Father runs through my veins. The Ha-Yarden is a temple for I am here. You do not need columned temples made out of chiseled blocks of stone. See these stones by the river—those stones can be a temple. Your hearts can be temples where My Father would gladly reside. Each day can be a Shabbat within your hearts. If two or more of you meet in my name and truly love and respect each other like loving brothers and sisters you have a temple," declared Ishia. "Now, if anyone of you has never been baptized by Yehohanan or by me and wishes to be baptized with the sacred water of the Ha-Yarden come to me and I will cleanse your spirits!"

One by one, thousands of men, women, and children lined up to be baptized by the Lord. At dusk, He was still baptizing people in the name of His Father. That night, they slept by the west bank of the river around several bonfires they had made for the nights were still cool.

That evening Ishia called His twelve apostles and for the third time He announced His fate, "We will reach Yerushalayim in seven days. Everything that has been prophesied by Yesha 'Yahu and other great prophets about the Son of Man will come to pass. Betrayed by my own people, I will be delivered to the Romans to be spat on, mistreated, mocked; and, after scourging me they will nail me on the wooden cross that I will be forced to carry. On the third day I will resurrect from death."

"My Lord," cried Cephas, "What are you saying? Talking about death? These people want You as their King. You are their Savior!"

"Cephas, you have not yet understood my mission. Only Judas knows and understands my pain for my pain will also be his pain," answered Ishia.

"We will die with you, Lord," spoke Thomas. "We will fight the Romans by your side. We will fight like the heroes of old."

Most of the apostles agreed with Thomas; but Ishia cried out, "You have not understood my message. Although I have the power to destroy this earth, I did not come here to fight anyone. I come here in peace. My mission is to teach you how to be a loving people for love will conquer all, even the Romans."

"Why must you die, Lord? It is not necessary for you to die!" exclaimed Yakov, the Lord's half brother.

"Dear brother, dying for someone is the ultimate show of love. My death is for the love I share with all of you and with every person that shall be born on this earth. I die for you, so that you all may be reborn through my death. But do not fear, on the third day after I die I will come back to see you. I will be with you for a little while more..."

"And then, Lord?" asked Yehohanan.

"I will go back to My Father."

"Where, Lord?" continued Yehohanan.

"In another world called Paradise."

"I want to come with you, Lord, so that I may see the Father!" exclaimed Cephas.

"It is not time for any of you to see My Father. Cephas, you must remain here to lead my people. All of you will spread my word around this world, until everyone has heard my message. I put all of you in charge of that mission. You, Cephas, shall be the first leader; and, you, Judas, shall be the last."

"Lord," cried Judas, "How is it possible for me to go back to the future. I have been here with You over three years, Lord!"

"Three years! Seven days! Is there a difference?" answered Ishia. "Time is relative for true time does not really exist!"

Judas pondered on the deep meaning of what His Lord had just revealed to him. How was he going to get back? Would Judas-One work? Would he see his daughter and friends again? Those questions and more stirred within Judas' brain for most of the night until he fell asleep from fatigue.

The next morning, they crossed the Ha-Yarden to Peraea and wandered along the foothills of the Ammonite mountains for four days, finally arriving at the Wadi Abu Gharaba, which faced Bet-ha'Arava across the Ha-Yarden. Ishia crossed the river wishing to sleep at Bet-ha'Arava for it had been the place where He had been baptized by Yehohanan the Baptist. Bet-ha'Arava always stirred visions of the fearless Yehohanan in Ishia's deep memories. Yehohanan had been a just man, always preaching the truth, fearing no consequences; and, it had been his spoken truth, which had eventually caused his arrest and death. He missed him dearly!

(Thursday, March 12, 33 A.D.)

The sun was still hidden on the other side of the mountains of Ammon when Ishia woke up. Judas, being an extremely light sleeper, got up and followed Him to the river where He was washing away the night's sleep from His eyes.

"Good morning, Lord!" Judas broke the silence.

"Good morning, beloved Judas. You did not need to wake up so early. I had wanted to pray before we leave for Yeriho," whispered Ishia with sadness in His voice.

"What is it, My Lord?" asked Judas, knowing precisely why He was so sad.

"Good Judas, I wish I did not have to go through this agony once again; and, I wish you did not have to do what you must do...But there is no escape from the fateful event that will soon unfold. My fears are rooted from my human nature; and, as a man I, too, fear death. However, as the Son of Yahweh, I welcome death for only by embracing it will I resurrect with My Father's Glory."

"I am afraid, Lord. I am afraid to betray You; and, I am afraid to die," whispered Judas.

"Do you believe in me? Do you have complete trust in me?"

"I believe in You, My Lord. I trust in You more than anything else in this universe; but, it is impossible not to be afraid," continued Judas. "As You said, fear is part of being human."

"Then, do what you must do and everything will come to pass as it was prophesied. You will conquer death and your body shall shine like the light from My Father's Glory," promised Ishia. "Now, let us go to Yeriho. We shall sleep in a villa tonight."

"Whose villa, My Lord?"

"A very rich man's. An old tax collector."

Judas tried to remember his name but it was hidden deeply in a crevasse of his memories. He followed Ishia up the bank where everyone was still sleeping. Thousands of bodies slept on the sandy, rocky surface of 'Arvot Yeriho. The fires had been reduced to smoking gray ashes, still hot from hours of burning. Gently, Ishia and Judas touched the apostles to wake them up. In turn, they gently awoke their disciples, who took their turns in awakening the thousands of followers and pilgrims.

The sun was peeking over the mountains of Ammon by the time everyone had been awakened. The Lord gave them an hour to wash up before they would march for Yeriho.

It was mid-afternoon when Ishia entered through the gate of Yeriho. A fragrant breeze came through the cedars and eucalyptus trees, giving the town an aromatic scent. The tumult arising from the chanting crowd brought out the entire population of Yeriho. The streets had become so crowded that people could not move. A short but richly dressed citizen of Yeriho wanted to get a glimpse of Ishia, the Mashiah. He gave a young man a silver shekel to help him up a branch of a sycamore tree so that he would be able to see the Son of God pass by. When Ishia reached the spot where the sycamore tree was He stopped and looked up at the small rich man who sat on one of its branches.

"Get down, Zacchaeus! Quickly, for today I shall stay at your house," exclaimed the Lord.

"Immediately, My Lord!" responded Zacchaeus, jumping down from the sycamore tree. Many in the crowd began to complain about the Nazarene's choice of company for Zacchaeus was a tax collector and a sinner. Offended, Zacchaeus parried their insults by saying, "Lord, I am willing to donate half of all I own to the poor; and, I promise to pay back fourfold to anyone I have cheated."

"Dear Zacchaeus, today you have saved yourself. I have come to search and save you because you were lost; and, you, also, are a child of My Father. Come, let us go, my brother," declared Ishia, placing His hand on the little man's shoulder.

Happy as a child, Zacchaeus led the Lord and His apostles and disciples to his house, where his servants prepared a feast in honor of Ishia of Nazerat.

(Friday, March 13, 33 A.D.)

It was impossible to fast walk for the crowd had multiplied into tens of thousands. Ishia knew that morning that walking to Beth-Ananiah from Zacchaeus' house would take two days. There were so many people who wanted to walk with Him. He simply could not have left in the middle of the night. That would have been inconsiderate for most of those people had walked for days to be with Him. He could not have abandoned them when they were showing so much devotion and faith. He led them up and down the arid hills of the Wilderness of Yehuda as His apostles and disciples helped to control the huge multitude of people. At times the crowd would cover two entire hills and the valley in between them. Ishia's followers did their best to model care and genuine brotherhood by helping the elder, younger children, and anyone feeling ill.

At dusk, Ishia preached a sermon on the importance of caring for each other and sharing whatever little food with their immediate neighbor. For the first time, most of those people celebrated the beginning of Shabbat in the open air; and, their Mashìah blessed them and their simple meal, which consisted mainly of old bread and water. That night, everyone slept in the open around several bonfires, which kept them warm from the cool desert night.

Vincent L. Di Paolo

(Saturday, March 14, 33 A.D.)
(Last Shabbat before Pesach)

Ishia reached Bet-Ananiah by the tenth hour of the day, hoping to find a little privacy at Eleazar's house; instead, his friend's house was filled with Yehudi, including a few Pharishaiya and Tsadduqim. Among them were Nicotheimus and Youseph A'Ramathayim, who had come to warn their friend Eleazar of what Kaiaphas and the rest of the Pharishaiya had decided at the last meeting of the San-hedrin.

Eleazar was pleasantly surprised by his savior's visit. Space was made at the table for the Lord and His apostles. The disciples stayed outside, preaching to the crowd, which had been divided into groups. From the village to several stadia away, every possible open space along the eastern foothills of Har Ha-Zetim was occupied by the great multitude. When Martha heard Ishia's voice she immediately came to embrace Him, kissing Him repeatedly on the cheeks. Everyone wondered why Miryam had not come out to greet their Lord; however, Ishia knew very well why she was late in coming to greet Him. Ishia sat down as Martha came back with honeyed wine for Him and the twelve apostles. They sat close together around the table while some stood around, crowding the room. No one wished to leave for all present, including the few Pharishaiya, believed Ishia to be the Holy Mashiah, the Krystos, the Only Son of the Almighty Yahweh. Each one yearned to be with Him and to listen to His angelic voice, to look at His loving face, to witness the Almighty Power that radiated around Him. It was electrifying, to say the least. Yet, through all of His beatitudes a glint of sorrow filtered from His gorgeous eyes and peaceful countenance. Only Judas knew the reason for His Lord's sadness and the massive burden that weighed His spirit down.

It was at that very moment that the lovely Miryam entered the room carrying a decanter of very expensive perfumed ointment. She walked up to the Lord and poured a few drops on His forehead, gently smearing it with her fingertips. She, then, knelt down by His feet and poured some of the aromatic ointment on His feet and proceeded to wipe them with her hair.

"I believe that is the most expensive aromatic oil anyone can purchase!" exclaimed one of the Pharishaiya.

"It can easily be sold for, at least, three hundred denarii!" added Matthias Levi Bar-Alpheus.

"We can give that money to the poor!" continued Judas.

"Do not castigate Miryam," interjected Ishia. "She has purchased this fine ointment for my body for the day that you shall bury me. You will always have the poor to help; but, you will not have me for much longer."

"My Lord, do not speak of death," cried Cephas, "You are the Son of God!"

"I am also the Son of Man," answered Ishia, "And as the Son of Man, I will soon be betrayed and put to death. On the third day after my death as a man I will resurrect in the Glory of My Father. Only then will some of you truly believe in me."

"Lord, we all believe in You!" exclaimed Thomas Didymus.

"Thomas, your faith has grown greatly since we first met; but, when you will see me dead, hanging on two pieces of wood, your faith will dwindle to no more than a doubt," sadly responded Ishia.

"My Lord and my brother," spoke Yakov, the Lord's half brother, "There are tens of thousands of people outside who will welcome you as their new king into the holy city. Why speak of death now?"

"Dear Yakov," answered Ishia, "That same crowd will soon condemn me. They will soon forget all that I have done, and they will choose a brigand over me. Despite what will soon happen, that crowd will serve to fulfill the prophesies of Yesha 'Yahu by welcoming me as King of Yisrael into Yerushalayim. But, do not despair, for on the third day after I die I will be back in the Power and Glory of My Father."

No one spoke! Silence reigned and everyone stood still as Ishia's prophetic words resonated in each and everyone's mind. Only Miryam dared to kiss the Lord's feet, which perfumed with the sweet scent of the aromatic ointment. It was Ishia Himself who broke the silence, "Why the gloomy faces? I am alive with you. Let us enjoy the day and the joy you bring by being here with me. Let us drink to our friendship and to the love we share."

They drank to Ishia's toast and ate the Shabbat meal that Martha, Miryam, and their servants had prepared. They enjoyed each other's company sharing wonderful stories they had experienced. Ishia seemed to be happy, relishing that precious moment. That night, the village of Bet-Ananiah and the entire eastern foothills of Har Ha-Zetim were filled with tens of thousands of sleeping bodies, resting from the long arduous journey they had made with Ishia of Nazerat, the Mashìah.

(Sunday, March 15, 33 A.D.)

Har Ha-Zetim was resplendent as the first morning sunrays rose above the hills of Yehuda. The people who woke up first witnessed the splendor and the beauty of that day, a wonderful sunny morning, a perfect day to welcome Ishia of Nazerat, the Holy Mashìah, as their new King of the Yehudi and of all Yisrael. As they woke up, people realized the magnitude of that morning. The crowd stretched from the outskirts of Bet-Ananiah all the way to the neighboring village of Bet-Phage. As thousands woke up on that glorious morning, their tumultuous cries of joy reverberated over the mountains and were heard in the city of Yerushalayim. The lucky ones who had slept on Eleazar's land were the first to see their Lord come out of Eleazar's house. The cries of "The Lord is awake!" traveled all around, from mouth to mouth, like a rippling wave, reaching everyone within moments. Ishia managed a smile, which was immediately received by cries of *Hosh 'ah nna*, which spread like wildfire among the vast crowd.

The apostles, Eleazar, Martha, Miryam and the other guests, awakened by the joyous clamor, joined their Lord in front of the house. With the exception of Judas, all of Ishia's apostles and disciples were overwhelmed by the crowd's show of joy and devotion towards their Lord. Only Ishia and Judas understood the deep meaning of their cries. *Hosh 'ah nna* was not a simple save us now; on the contrary, the crowd was asking the Mashìah to save them from the Roman rule. Ishia's words from the previous evening clearly haunted Judas' memory, "That same crowd will soon condemn me.

They will soon forget all that I have done, and they will choose a brigand over me." Ishia's smile petered out.

"My Lord," spoke Cephas, "See how much they love you!"

Ishia, realizing the precious little time that was left, asked Cephas for a favor, "Cephas, take your brother with you up to Bet-Phage. Opposite the town there is a tiny village with only a few houses. Outside the third house you will find a colt, tethered to a post. I want you to untie and bring that colt to me so that I may ride her. If anyone asks you why you are taking that colt away, tell him that Ishia of Nazerat needs it and that it will soon be brought back to him."

"Lord!" exclaimed Cephas. "They are welcoming you as their king. We should get a horse for you, not a young donkey!"

"A white horse, Lord!" continued Andros. "You will enter Yerushalayim like a king!"

"It has to be a colt!" exclaimed Judas, "It was prophesied by Zachariah that the Lord should enter Yerushalayim riding on a colt."

"Judas is correct," agreed Ishia. "Cephas and Andros, fetch me that colt for Zachariah's prophecy has to be fulfilled. Please, be as quick as possible for there is very little time left."

"We will go immediately, Lord!" exclaimed Cephas.

The two brothers made their way through the crowd without stopping. It took a while to reach Bet-Phage for the crowd reached past that town. They crossed a small path, west of the town, where stood a small cluster of houses. By the third house, a young donkey grazed on a patch of grass; it was tied by a long hemp rope to a post. They approached the colt and began to untie it from the post.

A man came out of the third house, upset at Cephas and Andros, yelling, "Why are you stealing my colt? Who are you?"

"My good man," answered Cephas, "My name is Cephas Bar-Jonah, and this is my brother Andros. Our Lord, Ishia of Nazerat, has sent us. He needs this colt to enter Yerushalayim. Do not worry, we will bring it back later this morning."

"Please, take it. It is an honor that my colt will carry the Holy Mashìah into Yerushalayim. We have all been anxiously waiting for Him so that we may welcome Him as our King," replied the man.

"We will bring her back, fed and groomed!" exclaimed Andros.

Excited, the man ran inside to tell his wife about their colt.

As Cephas and Andros made their way through the crowd, guiding and pulling the frightened colt, they observed thousands of people holding olive and palm branches, and various types of flowers they had managed to pick. The branches and flowers were to be used in welcoming their Lord into Yerushalayim.

Cephas and Andros proudly approached their Lord, pulling the young donkey. Cephas took off his cloak, folded it evenly and placed on the colt's back. Ishia stepped to the side of the colt and gently sat on it. Cephas took the rope and led the colt, carrying Ishia, along the path around the base of Har Ha-Zetim. The apostles, Eleazar, Martha, Miryam, Youseph, Nikotheimus, and the disciples walked along both sides of their Lord, protecting Him from the joyous crowd. "Hosh 'ah nna", "Ishia of Nazerat", "The Mashìah", "Son of David", "Son of God" and other cries of praise were constantly chanted. Some placed their cloaks and robes on the road while others decorated the path with flowers and branches.

By the time the joyful multitude reached *Sha'ar Haarayot*, the Lion's Gate, it had doubled, making it almost impossible for everyone to pass through the gate. Cephas and the rest of the apostles led the colt into the holy city and up onto the large Temple plaza.

Kaiaphas, along with a group of Pharishaiya, watched the long and joyful procession become the largest crowd they had ever witnessed in Yerushalayim. Looking at the Praetorium, they saw hundreds of Roman soldiers getting ready for a possible battle or confrontation. They saw the procurator of Yehuda, Pontius Pilatus, standing on the southeastern tower of the fortress together with several Roman officers.

Pontius and his officers attentively scrutinized every move of the acclaimed Mashìah. What Kaiaphas did not know was that centurion Augustus Horatius was one of the officers present, who had spoken to Pontius about Ishia of Nazerat's peaceful mission. Besides, how could a man peacefully riding a young donkey be the leader of rebels? Impossible! That man was a holy man. He had heard from many sources, including Augustus Horatius, that he was a great healer. Pontius' fears subsided. He sipped on a cup of Marsala, a sweet wine from Sicilia, and enjoyed the spectacle.

On the western section of the city, atop the northern turret of Herod's palace, Herod Antipas and his unlawful wife, Herodias, watched the largest crowd they had ever witnessed entering the holy city. The population of Yerushalayim had easily doubled and possibly tripled. Both Herod and Kaiaphas feared the worst. A revolt! There were more than enough people to easily overtake the Roman garrison. Even if the Yehudi would win, Herod and Kaiaphas knew that Rome would send an army to destroy the entire city. Their fears intensified as Ishia dismounted the colt and began to upset the tables of the moneychangers with such fury and anger that most merchants hid in fear. He freed all the doves and lamb, overthrowing any table along His way.

"This temple," He cried, "Was built to honor My Father! My Father's house is a house of prayer; but you have turned it into a market. You are conducting business, cheating people, in My Father's house. Take your money, your tables, and your booths and leave this holy place."

Some of the apostles and disciples joined in, helping their Lord to rid of the merchants. Meanwhile Cephas told two of his disciples to bring back the colt to its owner, ordering them to feed it and groom it before returning it.

Kaiaphas, afraid of the possible consequences that the Nazarene's actions might bring, immediately sent two Pharishaiya to fetch every member of the San-hedrin for a prompt meeting concerning Ishia of Nazerat.

Ishia knew exactly what He had done. He had always wanted to clear the Temple; but He also knew the exact consequences of His action. He knew that Kaiaphas and the San-hedrin would hold a meeting and vote on His immediate arrest. This had been the opportune moment for Him to take such a drastic action. This would surely guarantee His arrest, which would speed up His death before Pesach. His time was now so close that He could sense everything that was going to happen. It scared Ishia, the man. Ishia, as the Son of Man, would love to please His people by bringing the ruthless Roman power down to its knees, not only in Yisrael but also throughout the entire Roman Empire. He simply had to order Commander Ghabriel to attack strategic cities and points throughout the empire. Commander Ghabriel had enough space shuttles with firing power of such great destruction that the total defeat of the empire could be orchestrated in a single day. This thought entered His human mind; instead, His pure divine mind was unaffected by the weakness of His human nature. Without a second consideration, He canceled that weak thought from His holistic intellect, forbidding it to ever enter it again. Never would He allow His mind to entertain such weakness. Once again, this time on planet Earth, He would offer His human body as the sacrificial lamb for the sake of all mankind. This painful sacrifice looked weak and senseless in the human eye; still, He hoped that His teachings about love and its ultimate sacrifice of life itself would one day find the strength and the power it held deeply within.

"Lord," cried Cephas, "We must leave immediately. You have angered the high priests. Surely, they will order an immediate arrest of You and of us."

"Do you fear being arrested, Cephas?" asked Ishia.

"Why should anyone be arrested, Lord?" replied Cephas. "If we leave now, we shall escape being arrested!"

"At this very moment, Kaiaphas has sent his messengers to look for every member of the San-hedrin for a judgment meeting on me. We still have an hour before they meet and make their decision. I wish to spend this hour in the Temple, now that it is clean of impurities. Come, Cephas! Come Judas, Yakov, everyone! Come into My Father's Temple."

Ishia made His way into the Holy Temple dedicated to His Father, followed by His apostles, disciples, followers, and Pharishaiya and Tsadduqim present.

An older Pharish barked, "By what authority have you done such a horrible deed? Those were honest Yehudi trying to earn a living!"

Ishia replied, "Permit me to ask you one question. If you answer my question I will tell you by whose authority I cleansed this temple. Now answer this question: did Yehohanan's baptism come from God or from man?"

The old Pharish argued with other Pharishaiya and Tsadduqim who were present. A high priest whispered among the religious group, "If we say that Yehohanan's baptism came from the Almighty, he will ask why we refused to believe in him. If we dare say that his baptism came from man, the entire nation of Yehuda will revolt against us for they all believe that Yehohanan was a great prophet. What answer shall we give? He has trapped us. What shall we answer? He waits for our answer."

"Tell him that we do not know," whispered the old Pharish.

"Sir," answered the high priest, as a messenger reached the religious group, "We really do not know the answer to your question!"

"Then, I shall not tell you by whose authority I cleansed this Holy Temple. But I can tell you, by the same authority, that you have been called for an immediate meeting to make a judgment on me," responded Ishia.

Perturbed by his great knowledge, the high priest, the elder Pharish, and two other members of the San-hedrin left for their meeting.

Other Pharishaiya and henchmen of Herod Antipas quickly formulated a trap for the Nazarene. An Herodian henchman asked him, "Sir, we know of your honesty and of your fearlessness. We know that you do not fear the rulers of this city and of this nation; and, we also know that you honestly teach the way of God. Should we, Yehudi, be paying taxes to Caesar or not? Should we pay these taxes or maybe not?"

"Why are you trying to trap me?" answered Ishia, clearly seeing through their deceit. "If you have a denarius, let me see it."

The henchmen, who carried a leather purse fixed into his belt, took a denarius and gave it to Ishia.

Ishia looked at the coin and asked, "Whose head is imprinted on this coin? Whose name does it bear?"

Everyone quietly waited for the answer that most already knew. They kept their silence for many knew that Ishia of Nazerat had a special message hidden in His simple question.

"Rabbi, that is evident. It is the emperor's head whose name is Tiberius Caesar," answered the henchmen, smiling that he knew the answer to such an easy question.

"Then, pay the taxes to Caesar for these coins belong to him; but, pay back to God what belongs to God."

Ishia's answer was a shocking surprise! It brought everyone back to the reality of being a Yehudi under the Roman rule. Yet, many of them still wanted to trap him with a deceitful question. A Tsadduqim, who firmly believed that he knew the Laws of Moishe and who did not believe in resurrection, asked him, "Rabbi, Moishe wrote that if a man dies leaving his wife without child, his brother should marry her so that they may continue the man's lineage. Once there lived seven brothers, rabbi. The oldest married a young lady; but, he died, leaving her without children."

Everyone quietly listened to the new deceptive question, which might trap Ishia of Nazerat, as the apostles and disciples grew restless and worried as time flew by.

"The second brother, rabbi," continued the meretricious Tsadduqim, "Married the widow. Unfortunately, he also died, leaving her without child. To make the story short, rabbi, the third, fourth, fifth, sixth, and seventh brother each married the widow in turn, each one leaving her without children;" he smiled. "And, unfortunately, she died, too! At resurrection time, rabbi, when everyone supposedly will rise again, who shall be her husband since all seven had been married to her?"

"That is a good one!" exclaimed a Pharish, with a wicked smile, thinking that this would be the question that would expose his imposture.

"Obviously, young man, you do not understand the scriptures nor do you understand the power of My Father. About resurrection, have you ever read the passage when God spoke to Moishe, saying, "I am the God of Ybrahim, the God of Yshak, and the God of Yakov. My Father is God of the living, not of the dead. You, my young man, are greatly mistaken. Now, you must listen to me for it is time for the Son of Man to be glorified. Verily, I tell you, when a grain of wheat falls on the ground it is still a grain of wheat; but, if it dies, it gives birth to many new grains. Any one of you who loves his life in this world loses it; on the other hand, any one of you who despises his life in this world will live forever. If you chose to follow me be prepared to die in my name, for through your ultimate sacrifice you shall live forever. Now, my spirit is perturbed for it is my hour. This very moment, they have judged me; but it is for this very judgment that I have reached this hour. Sentence has been passed on me. It is time to defeat death itself for when I am resurrected, everyone shall come to me."

None, except Judas, understood the meaning of Ishia's words. The crowd began to grow restless for nothing was happening. Their Mashìah was not leading them against the Romans. Was he really the Mashìah? Or was he a charlatan? Already, they had forgotten the great deeds He had done. They were blinded by their own selfish needs and desires. Their hearts had hardened!

"Father," cried out Ishia, His arms raised upwards, "My life for Your Glory!"

Immediately, Ishia began to move out of the temple, followed by His apostles and disciples. The crowd, disillusioned by His lack of leadership needed to fight the Romans, became agitated. Ishia and His men disappeared into the crowd, leaving the temple square as the temple guards came out with precise orders to arrest Ishia of Nazerat and any of His followers. The immense crowd became a lynching mob, ready to kill the very man they had greeted and welcomed as their Mashìah.

Through the same gate He had gloriously entered that morning, Ishia had escaped through it in a hurry. He could not be caught yet. He still needed to see His loved ones and spend a few days with them. He still needed to instruct His apostles. To make sure that Judas would play his role for His sake. Quickly, He moved, as swift as the wind up to the Garden of Gat-shemanim. There, He stopped to rest, waiting for all His followers to catch up with Him.

At Eleazar's house, Ishia met Martha and Miryam. They were still waiting for their brother and were beginning to get worried. Ishia and Judas comforted them while the rest stood outside, guarding the house and watching for any conspicuous person approaching the valley. For the time being, all the commotion seemed to be restricted within Yerushalayim. Young Yehohanan spotted three men leaving the city in a hurry through the Lion's Gate and walking down the steps, which led to the road to Yeriho. Yehohanan went running back to Cephas, who stood by the house, to tell him of the three men who were moving towards Bet-Ananiah.

Cephas and Yehohanan ran ahead to intercept the three men before they might reach Eleazar's house. When both apostles reached the top of the mount, they relaxed their guard for they were able to recognize the three men. They were Eleazar and his two Pharishaiya friends, Youseph A'Ramathayim and Nikotheimus. They resolutely walked up the hill. However, as they got closer their faces distinctly bore the fateful look of apprehension. They both ran down to meet them and learn about the situation in Yerushalayim.

Eleazar saw Cephas and Yehohanan coming towards them and decided to run up to meet them to tell them about the Sen-hadrin's decision about Ishia of Nazerat.

"Where is My Lord?" cried Eleazar.

"At your house! Your sisters have been worried about you!" exclaimed Cephas.

"Our Lord is in danger. We are all in danger. There is a warrant to arrest Our Lord and any of His followers," cried Eleazar.

"Cephas...Cephas..." cried Youseph unable to speak, winded by the upward run, "I come...directly...from the...San-hedrin. We had a quick meeting,...where the Lord was condemned...by His actions and words...There is an immediate warrant for His arrest... and a reward of one hundred silver denarii...will be given to anyone who will reveal His hiding place. Also, there is a warrant for your arrests and for the arrest of any of His followers."

"We must take Our Lord back to Hagalil this very moment!" exclaimed Yehohanan. "He will be safe there."

"We will join you," said Nikotheimus, "For I fear they might find out that we, too, believe in Ishia of Nazerat as the Mashìah, the Only Son of God."

The five men rushed towards Eleazar's house without wasting time for they all felt its importance. As they quickly walked along they instructed any disciple or apostle they encountered to leave their guard posts and follow them to see their Lord. By the time they reached Eleazar's house every apostle and disciple knew of the dangerous situation that loomed over them.

Without hesitation, Eleazar opened the oak door to his house and walked in to find Ishia sitting by the table consoling Martha and Miryam.

"Lord, You must leave this very moment," he exclaimed as Martha and Miryam ran to embrace him. "There is a warrant for Your arrest and a one hundred silver denarii reward for anyone that will lead the temple guards to You. Also, there is a warrant for the arrest of any of us that believe in You."

"This is true, My Lord!" cried Youseph. "Nikotheimus and I come directly from that meeting. Kaiaphas fears for his position and he is willing to sacrifice You, my Lord, to save his neck. We were opposed to this sacrilegious decision; unfortunately, we were a small minority. Most members of the San-hedrin think You are a madman and a charlatan. We are regretful, Lord, about this decision!"

"Lord," continued Nikotheimus, "Youseph and I have enough money to pay for transportation and living for all of us and your families to Caesarea Maritima. There, we will board a ship to Massilia, where we could live safely until all of this fades away."

"I am moved by your concern and care, Nikotheimus; nevertheless, I do not have a choice in this situation," sighed Ishia. "I cannot leave; and, tonight, Judas and I must return to Yerushalayim to be with our families."

"You cannot go back to Yerushalayim, Lord," cried Cephas. "You will be arrested. We will all be arrested."

"Cephas," murmured Ishia, "You do not remember my warnings. Three times I have told you that my mission on this earth is to fulfill My Father's Wish: to die for all of mankind. I will be the sacrificial lamb for this Pesach. Before this coming Shabbat, I will be arrested, judged, beaten and put to death. Kaiaphas wishes to eat his Shabbat supper and celebrate this Pesach without trouble. He has planned to dispose of me before the beginning of Shabbat."

"But why, My Lord?" asked Thomas. "I really do not understand why You must die! It does not make any sense to me."

"Man, through the millennia, has forgotten the true meaning of love. My Father's Ten Commandments have constantly been broken. Hatred for each other, jealousy of each other, and the wish to annihilate the enemy, which is anyone who is not your kind, has become the way of thinking and the way of life," whispered Ishia as everyone attentively listened. "I was born from the Sacred Seed of My Father, which was implanted into the womb of my earthly mother, to show you and all mankind that it is time to change this hatred into love. Love shall conquer all with time. My mission is to show you how to care for each other, to love one another as true brothers and sisters, to treat everyone equally and with kindness, rich or poor, friends or enemies. In Paradise, my Father's world, before life became eternal, to give up one's life for someone else was the ultimate demonstration of love."

"But, Lord, you do not have to die for us," cried Yakov, His half brother. "We all know the love You have for us!"

"Yakov, my brother," He replied, "If I do not die, men will not believe in me in the future. But if I die for all mankind until the end of time, men shall believe in my sacrifice."

"How will they believe in You, Lord?" asked Cephas. "If You die, You will be forgotten in the future."

"This coming Friday, I will die for all mankind; however, on the third morning, I will defeat darkness and I will come back to see you. Then, I will instruct all of you on how to bring my message to every man and woman of this world. And your children's children shall continue to bring my message until everyone that will be born on this earth shall know of my sacrifice. All of you shall be witnesses to my resurrection, which will give life to your words. Then all shall know the purpose of my sacrifice. Before I leave to go back to My Father, you will all receive His Power. Only then will you fully understand what I have been telling you and only then will you have the fortitude to go and conquer the entire world in my name."

"Even Rome, Lord?" asked Thaddeus.

"Especially Rome!" exclaimed Ishia. "With time and your own sacrifices the power of Rome will bend under your gentle love. Cephas, Rome shall become the center of my people, and you shall be the one to go there to preach my message. Now, Yakov, Judas, Linus and I must go to Yerushalayim to be with our families. You will all be safe here for tonight. Early tomorrow morning, Cephas, Yakov and Yehohanan Bar-Zebedeus will go to Yerushalayim. Cover your faces not to be recognized. Go to the dyers' quarter, where you will see a man carrying a jug of water. Follow that man to a house. Tell the owner of the house that I, Ishia of Nazerat, will need the upper room of his house to celebrate Pesach. He will show you the room and you shall prepare it for this coming Thursday, the first day of Pesach. We will all meet there by the twelfth hour of the day to celebrate Pesach together."

"Lord," spoke Youseph, "The house you speak of is near Kaiaphas' palace. That will be a very dangerous place to meet."

"On the contrary, Youseph," replied Ishia, "That will be the safest place for no one will be looking there. They will search everywhere else but there. Dear Youseph, may I ask a favor?"

"Name it, My Lord. It will be an honor for me to serve You."

"Will you oversee my burial, Youseph?" asked the Lord. "I know that you own a family tomb outside Yerushalayim."

"Oh Lord, this is painful to acknowledge; but, it shall be done," responded Youseph. "And, I will take care of your family, Lord. I shall take them to Massilia."

"Thank you, Youseph!" said Ishia. "My brother, Yakov, and Centurion Augustus Horatius will join you there. I will see you there on the third day after. We will celebrate Pesach together."

"What about us?" asked Cephas, offended that he was not included in the plan.

"I will see you soon after, Cephas. Do not worry—I will not abandon you. Now, I must leave. All of you will be safe here for tonight. Help each other. Yakov, Judas, and Linus will come with me tonight. We will meet on the twelfth hour on Thursday to celebrate the first day of Pesach."

Ishia hugged Miryam, Martha, Eleazar, Youseph, Nikotheimus, Cephas, and the rest of his followers. He, then, left with His half brother, Yakov, and with Judas, and Linus. The four walked down the Qidron Valley and up to the Gate of Essenes.

Two Roman guards guarded the gate. Both Yakov and Judas were afraid to be discovered and arrested. Linus seemed to be in a daze, blinding his fear.

"Do not fear, my friends," whispered Ishia. "Follow me and do not utter a word."

As if they had been invisible, the four friends entered Yerushalayim without being recognized or questioned. Ishia knew His way around even in the dark, leading Yakov, Judas, and Linus through the narrow streets of the city and, then, along the wall of the City of David. Voices of temple guards were heard everywhere searching for the Nazarene; but Ishia led the way without ever encountering a single guard. They entered the old city, which had been King David's capital, and walked to its center, stopping in front of an old, but well-kept stone house. Ishia knocked on the heavy oak door as Yakov, Judas, and Linus looked around the old street.

Augustus Horatius opened the door with a *gladius* on hand. He happily hugged Ishia, his son, Yakov, and Judas into the house, bolting the door behind them. The house belonged to a dear friend of his wife's family, Sepphorah Bat-Ybrahim, a widow and a believer in Ishia as the Holy Mashìah.

Ishia hugged Lydia while holding their baby, kissing their faces. Likewise, Judas hugged and kissed Esther and baby Judas. Miryam, the Lord's mother hugged Yakov, then Ishia, Judas, and Linus. Augustus' wife hugged her son as tears washed down her face. They all shared a warm and emotional embrace, happy to be together after such a painful and worrisome day. Ishia thanked Sepphorah for her kindness and love she had shared with His family. It was an honor for Sepphorah to have such loving and wonderful guests. Her house was their house as long as they needed it. And their company was a blessing to her lonely life, especially the two infants. She loved them as if they were her own grandchildren. Ishia recognized in Sepphorah the kind of love He had been preaching to His people and was grateful for all she had done.

During the following three days Ishia and Judas enjoyed their families, spending every moment with them, playing with their wonderful boys in the small inner courtyard of the house. Only Augustus Horatius, his wife, Miryam, and Sepphorah went out to purchase a lamb for the upcoming Feast of Pesach. They would consume the meat during the next three days. They enjoyed each other's company during those three days. Ishia ate only bread, vegetables, and fruit, with a little wine. He would not taste the meat for it reminded Him of His own fate: He would be the sacrificial Lamb of His last Pesach.

(Thursday, March 19, 33 A.D.)

For Ishia and Judas, bidding their last farewell to their loved ones was a very painful thing to do, fully knowing that they would both die. Judas had decided that he would die beside His Lord. Yakov followed them towards the southwest section of the city, where the rest of the apostles would be waiting for them to celebrate the commencement of Pesach. Only Ishia and Judas really knew that it would be the final meal they would share with the rest of the chosen twelve. Quietly, Judas and Yakov followed their Lord along the narrow streets of Yerushalayim until they reached King David's Tomb, which stood facing Kaiaphas' palace. The house, whose second floor had been rented, stood a few blocks away from the high priest's palace.

Judas stopped suddenly as fear itself had paralyzed him.

Ishia turned around and said, "Good Judas, do not be afraid. Tonight, you do what you must do."

Judas answered, "Lord, I am so afraid. I fear that I cannot do what I am expected to do."

"What are you talking about, Judas?" asked Yakov. "We are about to celebrate Pesach. Why do you speak of fear?"

"Judas fears for me, Yakov," replied Ishia.

"Why should he fear for you, the Mashiah, the Son of the Most Holy?" continued Yakov.

"Yakov, my brother. Tomorrow, I will be the Sacrificial Lamb for all My Father's children."

"I do not understand about you as the sacrificial lamb!" exclaimed Yakov.

"Tonight, I will explain everything during the Pesach supper. Come, Judas. There is little time left to do what we both must do. We, both, have no choice about what we must do. You and I were preordained to be sacrificed and to be resurrected by the will of My Father. We must fulfill His Words, lest my mission fail. Come! Let us go. Everyone is waiting."

Cephas was waiting for Lord Ishia, hiding behind the locked door, looking out for Him through a spy hole in the door. When he saw His Lord approaching, followed by Judas and His half-brother, Yakov, he opened the door and greeted Him by kissing His cheeks. He led the way upstairs to a large room, where three long tables and several benches had been arranged to accommodate all the apostles and the most important disciples. A sculpted wooden chair had been placed in the middle of the main table for their Lord. The three tables had been covered with white linens and had been set with earthen plates and cups. The silver goblet made by Eleazar, the Shomeroni, stood next to the plate for their Lord. All the apostles, the selected disciples, and several of their women stood up as Ishia entered the banquet room. Each one greeted Him with the customary hug and kisses on the cheeks.

Finally, they all sat on their respective places as Cephas showed each one where to sit, reserving the spaces next to Ishia for himself and Judas. The women were busy preparing the food and wine on a counter by the wall. The walls were made of stone with large wooden beams holding up the roof. The Lord got up from His chair and went to the counter where the women were busily preparing the Pesach meal. Everyone's eyes followed every move He made. He removed His cloak and wrapped a towel He had taken from the counter around His waist. He took a large wooden basin and poured water into it and brought it to His apostles. He knelt by Yehohanan's feet and began to wash them. The young apostle began to protest but Lord Ishia continued washing his feet with a melancholic look on His face. He continued washing each apostle's feet, finally reaching Cephas.

"I will not let You wash my feet, Lord!" exclaimed Cephas.

"Cephas, at this moment you do not understand why I must wash your feet. One day, you will look back and you will realize why?" replied the Lord.

"I will never allow You to wash my filthy feet, Lord. I should be washing Yours, Lord!" continued Cephas.

"If you do not allow me to wash your feet, Cephas, there will be no partnership between you and I."

"Then, My Lord, wash my feet, my hands, my head, and any part of me that You think should be cleansed," cried out Cephas.

"Do you all understand the meaning of what I have done to you? You call me Lord and Master; and, I am. I am the Son of the Father and I wash your feet. You should follow my example and wash each other's feet. What I am about to tell you is so that you will know and believe that I am His Son," Ishia said, pointing up with His index finger. "Whoever welcomes me welcomes My Father for I am His Messenger. Do you understand what I have just told you?"

Everyone nodded, although many did not really understand the implications of His sacred words.

"Lord," cried out Cephas, "I will always welcome You as the Son of the Almighty!"

"Cephas, Cephas, my hardheaded Cephas, I fear that you may not keep that promise," answered Ishia.

"What do you mean, My Lord? I don't understand why You are saying that?" asked Cephas, disturbed by the Lord's disbelief in his declaration of faith in Him.

Lord Ishia looked troubled. He sat down between Cephas and Judas, as if an enormous weight had just forced Him down. Judas looked at Him, fully understanding what Lord Ishia was about to announce. Judas' face showed so much pain that he could not control the tears that ran down his cheeks. Wiping his tears, he whispered on Ishia's left ear, "My Lord, is there any other way for me to fulfill my obligation to Your mission?"

Ishia turned gently, facing His beloved friend, Judas; and, with the saddest look on His beautiful face, He whispered, "No, my good friend, there is no other way." He then looked at everyone and stated, "I must now tell you this before it is too late. One of you, this very night will betray me."

Every apostle and woman present looked at each other, wondering who could possibly betray their Lord. Pain and confusion reigned on each follower's countenance.

Seeing through their newly found anguish, Lord Ishia said, "My beloved friends, the person who will betray me tonight does not have any choice. He must betray me and he must do it soon, before it is too late."

"My Lord, I really do not understand what is going on!" cried Cephas.

"My betrayal, death and resurrection were prophesied by many prophets. Even King David foretold what is about to happen to me in his psalms. There is no escape for me, Cephas; and, there is no escape for the one who must betray me."

"No matter what is written in the scriptures, Lord, I would never betray you," cried Cephas.

"In my betrayal, true friendship is found in my betrayer!"

"How is it possible, Lord, for a true friend to betray You? Certainly, a true friend would never betray You, My Lord. I would never betray You, Lord, and I consider myself a true friend," answered Cephas.

"You and Judas are my most beloved friends, Cephas," whispered Ishia.

"Is it Judas, Lord? Shall I strike him down before he betrays You, Lord?"

"You would hurt Judas? Do you not love him like your own brother? Cephas, you truly do not understand the sacrifice that I must suffer for all mankind. And, you do not understand the anguish Judas must experience in betraying me!" Ishia whispered in Cephas' ear.

"Why are you trying to defend him when he is about to betray You, Lord?" retorted Cephas angrily.

"He has no choice. He is destined to betray me so that the prophecies written about me will come to pass; but, you, Cephas, have a choice."

"I told You, Lord, that I would never betray You! I will suffer and die with You!" exclaimed Cephas.

"My beloved friend, this very night, before the cock crows twice you will deny that you even know me, not once, but three times. And, once I am gone from this world, you will deny me again."

"I rather die than reject You, My Lord!" continued Cephas, upset by the accusations.

"It is time!" whispered Ishia to Judas. "Go, my friend, and do what you must do quickly before it is too late."

"My Lord, I wanted to share Your bread and wine before I go," cried Judas.

Ishia took unleavened bread and broke it, dipped it in a wine and olive oil mixture and gave it to Judas, saying, "This bread represents my body, which will be sacrificed for all of you. Remember me every time you share bread!" Ishia passed pieces of unleavened bread to everyone.

Judas ate his piece, feeling blessed in being allowed to eat the very bread of life.

Ishia took the silver goblet, handcrafted by Eleazar the Shomeroni, which was filled with honeyed red wine, and lifted it up and exclaimed, "Take this Pesach wine and share it among you. This wine represents my blood, which will flow for you tomorrow. Every time you share a cup of wine, remember me." He passed the silver goblet to Judas.

Judas held the precious goblet with both hands, savoring that most special moment, knowing very well of all the future battles that would be fought in the search of that gorgeous and precious artifact. He sipped the sweet wine and passed it to Cephas, who had a killer look in his eyes. Judas stood up, whispered his love and devotion and kissed Ishia on the cheek.

"Go, my friend for it is getting late. I will be on the Mount of Olives, praying and waiting for you," whispered Ishia.

Judas turned and quickly left, hiding his tears, down the darkened steps, which led to the outside door. The door of no return! The door of sorrow!

He stood outside that door, his legs paralyzed by what he was expected to do. His brain was mush, unable to think. His heart was heavy, beating hard and fast like a long-distance runner. Judas' heart was broken! How was he expected to do that treacherous act that would damn him for eternity? How? Why? He looked up at the night sky and shook his fist. Is this Your Plan? He thought. How could You promise Your own Son to be sacrificed like a Pesach Lamb? And why have I been chosen as the betrayer? He thought: he would be damned if he decided not to betray the Lord; and, he would surely be damned if he did.

Judas gathered whatever little strength he had left within him and moved his right leg towards Kaiaphas' house. His left leg followed, then his right. His first few steps were staggered and unnatural. Finally, he began to walk rapidly, realizing the precious time he had wasted. The high priest's house was close by. He stopped, once again petrified by his fateful role. Once again gathering his strength, Judas went up the steps of Kaiaphas' house. He knocked on the door. A temple guard opened it and Judas walked in.

Chapter 32

THE PASSION, CRUCIFIXION, AND DEATH

(Friday, March 20, 33 A.D.)

After His last Pesach with the rest of His apostles, Ishia had led them down to the Valley of Qidron and up to one of His favorite places, the Garden of Gat-shemanim at Har Ha-Zetim, the Mount of Olives. It was midnight when Ishia and His eleven apostles reached the garden. It was peaceful there; and, a little time was left before Judas would come with Kaiaphas' temple guards to arrest Him.

"Stay near me while I pray to My Father," whispered Ishia to His apostles. He walked to a large rock and knelt down to pray.

The apostles soon fell asleep, tired from the long day and from worrying about their Lord's strange Pesach. Never had any one of them ever experienced such a Pesach supper.

"Abba, if You wish, take this sacrifice away from me. Abba, the pain in my heart is so heavy; but, I will serve Your Will, not mine," Ishia prayed to his Father.

A tall hooded figure gently walked up to Ishia and with his right hand he touched Ishia's right shoulder. He whispered, "Be strong, my Lord, on this last day of Your mission as a man."

Unperturbed, Ishia turned His head and responded, "It is you, Ghabriel, my mentor. As a man, what I fear the most is death, the end of my life as a human being."

The apostles kept on sleeping, their brains groggy from the long day and sweet Pesach wine, totally undisturbed by the eventful conversation taking place beside them.

"Through death, my Lord, the ultimate sacrifice You shall make for Your people, a new life shall come forth. You will be resurrected, my Lord, with a new body, a glorified body that shall never die."

"Death still frightens me, dear Ghabriel; but more than my death I fear for Judas I fear that he is in so much pain about his role that he will kill himself soon after he delivers me to Kaiaphas."

"I will remain in the garden to witness Your arrest and immediately thereafter I will follow Judas. Lord Yahweh's plan is that he be crucified beside You."

"Will he be also resurrected with me?"

"That is not part of Your Father's plan, my Lord."

"Ghabriel, you know that the plan has changed. You know that Judas comes from the future and to his people he must return. My Father's plan cannot be entirely fulfilled unless he goes back to his people and time. He will be my last representative and his mission will be to prepare all survivors for my return."

"Your wish, my Lord, is Your Father's wish. It shall be fulfilled. Judas shall also be resurrected."

"And his body glorified as I have promised him."

"Your will be done, my Lord."

"Thank you, Ghabriel. This means a lot to me."

"My Lord, I am your humble servant."

"You are my teacher, Ghabriel, my mentor."

"I thank you, Lord. It is time now. I hear footsteps in the valley. They will be here shortly. Be strong, my Lord. I will be constantly near You and I will take care of Judas."

Ishia stood up and embraced Ghabriel. He whispered in his ear, "Your presence, my lifelong friend, has given me the strength to finish my mission. You have been my light from my conception, throughout my life, in my death, and forever in my new life to come. My Father knew best in choosing you, Ghabriel."

"Thank You, my Lord. I must now go for I hear them ascending the slope. My spirit will be constantly with You, my Lord."

As quietly as he had come, Ghabriel disappeared in the woods of the garden.

Ishia walked to His sleeping apostles and shook Cephas, saying "Wake up, they are here to arrest me. Wake up and go, you must not be taken prisoners along with me."

Cephas woke up, confused, still flustered by the day's event and wine, "Who is coming, Lord?"

Before Ishia had time to answer, Judas, followed by a group of armed temple guards, approached Him. Judas walked up to His Lord and embraced Him, kissing Him on the cheek. "My kiss is the signal, my Lord," he whispered.

"With a kiss you must betray me, Judas. Thank you for your help, dearest friend," answered Ishia.

Judas did not have a chance to speak as the armed temple guards quickly moved in and began to tie Ishia's hands. As quick as the guards, Cephas drew his sword, which hang by his side, hidden by his robe, and struck the guard that was about to tie His Lord, severing his right ear. The other guards were ready for a fight to avenge their wounded comrade, Malchus.

Before Cephas' attack on the guard might turn into an affray Ishia immediately picked the bloody severed ear and firmly spoke, "Put your sword away, Cephas. Do you want to annul my mission assigned to me by My Father!" He placed some of His saliva on the severed part of the ear and gently placed it back on the wounded guard's right side, saying, "Heal, Malchus. Do not allow any of your comrades arrest my apostles. Let them go! It is not them that you seek. I have seen all of you at the Temple; and, never did you try to stop me or arrest me. But, it is your time to fulfill the sacred scriptures that foretell my mission. It is the beginning of darkness!"

Mesmerized by the miracle, Malchus and his comrades seemed to be frozen, staring at the Lord. Cephas and the rest of the apostles quickly ran away, fearing that they also might be arrested. Judas stood by with his head abased as tears dropped like rivulets down his face, wetting his beard and neck. It was Ishia Himself who broke the silence, "And now, finish your work."

Malchus was still mesmerized and too busy checking his right ear, which seemed to be solidly attached to the right side of his head. It was his comrades who continued tying Ishia's hands together with a rope. However, they proceeded to do it so gently, still in awe of what he had done to Malchus' ear.

As they led Ishia of Nazerat out of the garden Judas exclaimed, "Please, do not hurt my Lord!" Judas followed them without realizing that someone was following him.

(2:00 a.m.)

Ishia stood in front of the house of Eleazar Annas, a high priest and Kaiaphas' father-in-law. Malchus was confused and he asked his comrades, "Why have we brought the Nazarene here. Should we not be at Lord Kaiaphas' house?"

"Malchus, the blow on your ear must have dulled your senses. Kaiaphas would be furious if we should disturb him at such hour. He wakes up one hour before dawn. Besides, old Annas wanted to see for himself if the Nazarene is possibly the Mashiah," answered another guard.

One of the guards knocked at Annas' large wooden door. A servant opened the door letting the group inside the courtyard. Young Yehohanan Bar-Zebedeus managed to get into the courtyard for he knew the lady servant while Cephas waited outside the walls. They had followed their Lord, hoping to free Him. Yehohanan begged the servant to let his friend in. She had agreed; and, as she opened the door to let Cephas in she thought she recognized him.

"Are you not one of the Nazarene's followers?" she asked Cephas.

"Definitely, I am not!" exclaimed Cephas, trying to protect himself from a possible arrest, as he walked into the courtyard.

Two of the guards had started a fire for it was a cool night and everyone stood around the fire, warming themselves. Cephas and Yehohanan stood around the fire, hoping to hear anything that would concern their Lord. Lord Ishia stood quietly by the wall with two guards by His sides. One of the servants had gone to call the old high priest, Eleazar Annas.

Temple, I will let him go free. Now, I must go back to sleep. I need to rest. Tomorrow is a very important day! Go now. I will see you at the Temple."

"You do not understand, we have made a serious mistake!" exclaimed Judas.

"Oh, I understand perfectly. You have made the mistake, not I. Now, get out of my house before I have you arrested. You are nothing but a nuisance. Get out!"

Judas, already depressed and heartbroken, reached the very bottom of his spirit. This last label, nuisance, brought him down to the very lowest of existence. Head bowed down, he left the palace somnambulating his way into the narrow streets of the sacred city. Ghabriel followed him at a distance, never losing sight of him. Judas reached the Gate of Essenes, walking out of the city, down into the Valley of Hinnom. He reached a tree with a large branch protruding at a height of six cubits and proceeded to remove the rope that encircled his waist thrice. He easily climbed the tree and sat on the large branch as he tied the rope around it and then around his neck.

Ghabriel moved swiftly under the branch, catching Judas' legs as he jumped down.

"Let me go!" he yelled in mortal pain.

"Judas, my good friend, you cannot end your life this way," spoke Ghabriel.

"Who are you? Do I know you?" he asked, his voice strained from the deep pain within his heart and spirit.

"Judas, it is I, Ghabriel."

"Ghabriel! I have done a terrible thing. I have betrayed our Lord. I am a traitor. Let me die!"

"First of all, you have not betrayed our Lord. He has often spoken to you about your role in His mission. Secondly, you will not die by hanging yourself."

"Tell me then, how shall I die? Tell me, Ghabriel, for I cannot live any longer. My heart is broken forever. I cannot bear to live."

"You shall die today, crucified next to our Lord, and you shall rise from death together with Him. That is His wish; and, His will is my command."

"Yes, I shall die next to Him, and experience the excruciating pain that He will go through. It is the least I can do. But, you spoke about life after death."

"His wish is that you will be resurrected with Him. He has very special plans for you. Now, remove the rope from your neck. We need to get you arrested and crucified with out Lord."

Ghabriel helped Judas down and, then, embraced him. He whispered to Judas, "You are hurting for what you have done; but, you had no choice. You are part of the plan. You will have time to heal after we resurrect you with our Lord. Let us go back to Yerushalayim. Time is quickly passing."

Together, Ghabriel and Judas walked back to the city, towards the Temple, where fate awaited them.

(4:00 a.m.)

Cephas and Yehohanan kept their silence, fearful that they too would be arrested. It was not easy to be silent as they listened at the guards and servants insult their Lord, spit at Him, and even punch His sacred face and chest. Cephas could not take their abuse any longer. He stood up and walked towards the guards, ready to fight.

"Aren't you one of his followers?" asked one of the guards.

At that moment, a rooster crew!

"No, you are mistaking!" exclaimed Cephas as he was caught off guard.

"Hold it!" exclaimed another, "You are the one who wounded my cousin, Malchus. You are from Hagalil. You are one of his men."

"No, you are making a big mistake. Let me go!" exclaimed Cephas as he moved towards the entrance door. For a moment, his eyes met with His Lord's. The saddest eyes he had ever seen! He quickly opened the wooden door and left the high priest's house.

As he turned the corner of the narrow street a rooster crowed for the second time. It was then that Cephas remembered His Lord's words, 'My beloved friend, this very night, before the cock crows twice you will deny that you even know me, not once, but three times. And, once I am gone from this world, you will deny me again.' Those fateful words and the sorrowful look in His Lord's eyes reverberated within the deepest chasms of his memory as Cephas wept bitterly for his cowardly rejections.

(5:00 a.m.)

The early morning sunrays had not yet broken the dark veil of that ominous night. Although it seemed like the beginning of a normal Pesach only a handful of people really knew the unforgettable events that would come to pass on that prophetic day. Two of those who knew were Ghabriel and Judas who waited for their Lord to be led to the Temple, where the San-hedrin was about to meet.

Pilgrims who had come to the Temple ran by the main archway to see the captured Ishia of Nazerat coming, tied up like a criminal. They were the same people who had welcomed Him as the Mashìah the week before. Now, they mocked Him and laughed at Him as He walked through the archway into the Temple Square. Ghabriel consoled Judas as he cried at the sight of their Lord.

Ishia was taken into the meeting hall of the Temple, where the San-hedrin was impatiently waiting for Him. Apart from Youseph A'Ramathayim and Nikotheimus the rest of the San-hedrin wanted to get rid of Ishia of Nazerat once and for all. And they had all the intention of accomplishing that goal that very morning. He stood in front of the San-hedrin, facing the high priest, Youseph Kaiaphas, the appointed spiritual leader of the Yehudi. Everyone was silently staring at the Nazarene. Was he the promised Mashìah or was he another charlatan magician? That was the question in most members' minds.

Finally, Kaiaphas broke the silence with a question, "Are you the Mashìah?"

Ishia knew very well that Kaiaphas had asked a trick question. He knew very well that the political connotation of the word Mashìah was the 'anointed one' or king, which meant treason against Roma. The spiritual meaning of Mashìah was 'the Son of God', which meant blasphemy against God. Kaiaphas had taken time to prepare such a trap of a question.

"If I do tell you that I am, you will not believe me. If I ask you a question, you will not truly answer it. If I ask you to free me, you will not let me go. However, I am here because I must obey my Father's Will. I serve my Father, while you serve the Roman Empire and money," replied Ishia.

Kaiaphas tried to keep his cool; but, what the Nazarene had just said had hit the reality of his existence and he would not show his anger and discomfort.

"We have heard him say that he would destroy this Sacred Temple and rebuilt it in three days!" exclaimed one of the Pharishaiya.

"That's right! Everyone has heard him say that!" continued another member of the San-hedrin.

"What do you have to say to that?" asked Kaiaphas. "Those are damning accusations against you."

Ishia stood erect but silent.

"Lord Kaiaphas," expressed Nikotheimus, "I am positive that Ishia of Nazerat did not mean this Temple when He said that. As you know that temple can also mean spirit, the individual temple where the Most High can dwell in."

"Nikotheimus, I am well aware of the double meaning of the word temple;" retorted Kaiaphas, "therefore, make your point clearer."

"Lord Kaiaphas," answered Youseph A'Ramathayim, trying to contain his anger towards the high priest. "When Ishia of Nazerat spoke those words He clearly pointed to His heart, meaning His inner temple, His spirit."

"Yes, but that is your interpretation and Nikotheimus'!" exclaimed Kaiaphas, "It is definitely not my interpretation, nor of any other member of the San-hedrin. And, I have often heard that both of you sympathize with this blasphemous Nazarene."

"How can we be sure that Ishia of Nazerat is not the true Mashìah, the very Son of the Most High? And, if He is, we are ready to have Him killed by the Romans!" exclaimed Youseph A'Ramathayim.

"Well, if you feel so strong about this, I will ask him one more time if he truly is the Mashìah!" yelled Kaiaphas. "Let us see if this Nazarene has the little courage that it takes to answer this simple question." Turning to Ishia, the high priest continued, "Are you the Mashiah, the Son of the Most High?"

"I am," answered Ishia, "And you will see this man seating at the right side of My Father and riding with the clouds of Paradise."

"You have heard the blasphemy!" cried Kaiaphas, standing up and tearing his tunic from his chest, "What is your verdict?"

"Death to the blasphemer!" shouted a few.

Some stood up and spat at him to show their disgust of his pretentious, blasphemous claim.

The guards punched him and shoved him around as most jeered him and accused him of blasphemy.

Only Youseph A'Ramathayim and Nikotheimus kept silent, praying for their Lord.

"Take him to Pontius Pilatus!" ordered Kaiaphas to the members of the San-hedrin. "Make sure he will be put to death this very morning. Do not come back here with him. This matter is urgent—you must take care of it immediately."

The guards pulled Ishia away from the meeting room. All the members of the San-hedrin followed them. Only Kaiaphas remained, seated at his high chair.

(6:00 a.m.)

"What is the commotion, Marcus?" asked Pilatus to one of his centurions.

"It is the San-hedrin, sir," responded Marcus, "With some temple guards, bringing us a prisoner."

"Oh, why do they bother me at such ungodly hour with one of their own. This is not my problem!" exclaimed Pilatus furiously. "Well, let them in, Marcus!"

"Sir, they will not enter the Praetorium."

"And, why not?"

"Sir, you know very well that it is their Pesach," answered the centurion. "They would become unclean if they enter here; and, they would not be able to eat their Pesach supper. We must go out to them."

Since Sejanus' death, Pontius Pilatus did not feel as powerful as he used to. He now had no choice but to please these people in order to secure his post.

"Unclean!" he ejaculated, "Have you smelled these people, Marcus? They are unclean! They do not wash or bathe regularly and they dare call the Praetorium unclean. Oh, I am sick and tired of these people. Seven years at this post and three more years to serve before I retire, Marcus. Ah, let us see what these dogs want." Pilatus got up from his desk and followed Marcus and two of his guards outside the Praetorium.

Pilatus and his men stood at the top of the staircase, staring down at the group, mostly Pharishaiya and Tsadduqim, all dressed in black like vultures. He looked at the tall man, with his hands tied in front of him, and could not imagine what the gentle-looking Yehudi could have done.

"Why do you bring me this man so early at such a blessed morning?" asked Pilatus sarcastically.

"We would not have brought him to you if he were not a criminal!" replied one of the Pharishaiya.

"Then, why don't you judge him yourselves, through your San-hedrin?" continued Pilatus.

"We, the San-hedrin, are not allowed to condemn anyone to death," answered another member.

"You!" cried Pilatus to Ishia, pointing his finger at him, "Come up. Come, come!"

Ishia walked up the steps reaching the top and stood a few feet away from Pilatus, Marcus, and the two soldiers.

Pilatus studies him for a moment. Then, he asked, "They say you are king of the Yehudi. Are you? Are you their king?"

Ishia softly answered in perfect Latin, "*A temetipso hoc dicis, an alii dixerunt tibi de me?* (Do you ask this yourself, or have others told you regarding me?)"

"Impressive!" exclaimed Pilatus, "A learned man who speaks my language! *Numquid ego Iudaeus sum?* (Am I a Jew?) *Gens tua et pontifices tradiderunt te mihi. Quid fecisti?* (Your own people and priests have betrayed you. What have you done?)"

"*Regnum meum non est de hoc mundo,* (My kingdom is not of this world,)" answered Ishia. "*Si ex hoc mundo esset regnum meum, ministri mei utique decertarent, ut non traderer Iudaeis; nunc autem regnum meum non est hinc.* (If my kingdom were of this world my servants would have fought for me and would have stopped my surrendering to the Jews; hence, my kingdom is not of this nature.)"

"*Ergo rex es tu?* (Then, you are a king?)" asked Pilatus.

"*Tu dicis quia rex sum ego,* (You yourself say that I am king,)" continued Ishia. "*Ego in hoc natus sum et ad hoc veni in mundum, ut testimonium perhibeam veritati; omnis qui est ex veritate audit vocem meam.* (For this I was born and for this I came to this world: to give testimony to the truth; and, all who believe in the truth listen to what I say.)"

"*Ah, veritas*! The truth!" exclaimed Pilatus. "I wish I knew the truth. But, I believe you, my good man. For that is what I see in front of me, a good man. I do not believe them!" He pointed at the crowd. "They lie; and, they are blood-thirsty for your blood. So, my good man, I cannot judge you. You have not done anything wrong." Pilatus turned to the crowd and declared, "I find this man innocent. I cannot judge him!"

"He is arousing the people of Yehuda," screamed a Pharish, "with his sermons and magic tricks. He is warping the minds of all Yisrael, from Hagalil, where he comes from, to Yehuda!"

"If he is from Hagalil," declared Pilatus, "then you should take him to Herodes. He is king of Hagalil. He is staying at his palace for Pesach."

Pilatus, Marcus, and the two guards went back into the Praetorium, leaving Ishia standing on top of the stairs. Two temple guards quickly ascended the stairs to bring him down.

The guards, the San-hedrin, and the crowd, agitated by their unsuccessful attempt in having the Nazarene judged by the Romans pushed Ishia along the narrow street leading to Herod's palace.

The crowd reached the palace in very little time; and, their tumult pressured Herod's guards to open the huge steel-reinforced doors, which led to the front courtyard. The guards allowed only the prisoner, the temple guards, and the members of the San-hedrin to enter the courtyard. The mob remained outside, shouting and threatening, creating a fracas. One of the guards went to inform Herod Antipas that the San-hedrin was outside with Ishia of Nazerat.

He returned smiling, telling that Herod was anxious to finally meet Ishia of Nazerat, the Mashìah, the Krystos.

Herod sat by his throne on a dais, still eating some of his breakfast. Herodias, his second wife, sat by his side. Salome, Herodias' daughter, and a few of his ministers sat at a lower platform in the royal hall of the palace.

The Temple guards shoved Ishia forward until He stood by the step of the first raised floor. The San-hedrin members and the guards stood back, silently waiting for King Herod to speak.

"Welcome, Ishia of Nazerat!" began Herod Antipas. "You have become a legend. I have heard of so many stories about you. You have done so many miracles, healed so many people. I am so excited to finally meet you. I hear that the San-hedrin has brought you before Pontius, that Roman pig; and, he has sent you to me. I am delighted that he did so. I can finally witness some of your magic.

"I heard that you changed water into the most exquisite wine ever savored in the world. We have this pitcher of water for you to change it into that wine. I just can't wait. Guard, untie him!"

One of Herod's guards went to untie Ishia, which alarmed the members of the San-hedrin. Nevertheless, the guard freed Ishia.

"Come Ishia of Nazerat. Do your magic; and, I will also believe in you," murmured Herod.

Ishia stood still, unmoved by Herod's request.

"I see," spoke Herod, "You are still upset by Yehohanan's death. I am too. I haven't been able to sleep without the help of wine and elixirs. You must forgive me for I was intoxicated that evening by Sicilian wine and Salome's seductive dance. Come Ishia and show me this wonderful magic."

Ishia did not move nor speak. He stood erect, looking at Herodias.

"He is looking at me!" exclaimed Herodias to Antipas. "He scares me, my love. He is the man who entered my bolted chamber at Herodium and took the Baptist's head."

"It was you that night!" exclaimed Antipas. "This is so intriguing. Herodium is impregnable! The main entrance was heavily guarded; and, guards were patrolling everywhere. How did you get in? Only a true magician could have entered my fortress. Change this water into that delicious wine and I will make you magician and healer of my kingdom."

Ishia remained silence, with the slightest hint of a smile upon His countenance.

"Oh, you refuse to speak to me! Why are you still so upset at your cousin's death? Look at me, I suffer too for that fateful night," whispered Antipas. He paused for a moment, with his head down, thinking of what to say next. He continued by saying, "You preach forgiveness. Forgive me for your cousin's death. Can't you see how much I suffer? Speak to me!…You are not like your cousin at all. He spoke to me. He preached sermons to me. He was exciting; but you are boring. You stand there like a statue, without action, without saying a word. You bore me."

"Love," whispered Herodias into Herod's ear, "Have his head cut off, too."

"Oh, no!" he exclaimed, terrified at the thought, "I cannot do that again. Guards, remove this boring Nazarene from my sight. Bring him back to Pontius with this message."

One of Herod's ministers went up to the dais to write Herod's message to Pontius Pilatus.

"Dearest Pontius, we have been apart too long," began Herod. "I would like to renew our friendship. You, your lovely family, and your highest officers are invited to a Pesach supper, tonight at my palace. I am sending the Nazarene back to you. He is boring. He is no fun. Your judgment on him will be mine. Your dearest friend, Herod Antipas."

The guards were ready to go back to Pilatus, when Herod stood up, shouting, "Wait! I must give the Nazarene something." He took off his expensive red cloak and stepped down to place it around Ishia. "They say you are king of the Yehudi! You see! I am the real King of Yehuda. So, I am giving you my kingly cloak so you can feel my power. AH! AH! AH!" he mocked him as everyone joined in the laugh. "Take him away, now. This has tired me. I need rest this morning."

The guards took Ishia back to Pontius Pilatus, followed by the San-hedrin and a larger mob.

(8:00 a.m.)

The crowd numbered by the thousands by the second hour of the day, pushing behind the San-hedrin and the guards, who in turn pushed Ishia towards the Praetorium. The plaza, which stood by the Praetorium and the Temple, was filled to capacity. People were everywhere, climbing walls and trees, excited that something big was going to happen.

Pontius Pilatus came out, with Marcus, two other centurions and most of their soldiers, who quickly took their positions, ready to control the crowd.

Herod's guard ran up the steps to give the Roman governor the message from his king. Pontius unrolled the papyrus and read the message, which had been written in Latin.

"Splendid!" he exclaimed, "It is all up to me, Marcus. These people are so weak. They have no backbone. They have put me in a tough situation, Marcus. What shall I do?"

"Have him flogged and released!" suggested Marcus.

"Earlier this morning, you brought this man on the charge of blasphemy and pretending to be king!" Pontius addressed the members of the San-hedrin. "And now, you have brought him back to me after having been seen by Herod Antipas, the King of Yehuda. As I have told you earlier, I find Ishia of Nazerat innocent of your accusations. But, to please you, I will have him flogged. Sixty blows shall be administered by two of my soldiers. That is more than sufficient to satisfy your accusations. Guards! Take him into the courtyard and administer sixty lashes. Use the flagrum, it will make lasting impressions."

The flagrum was a short Roman whip, with two leather lines attached to tiny barbells made of lead. Each blow would leave two double wounds on any prisoner.

Several Roman soldiers took Ishia through the door, which led to the courtyard of the Fortress Antonia. The crowd was very agitated but the Roman soldiers kept control of the situation. Judas followed Ghabriel through the crowd towards the side of the fortress. Judas needed to be in there with His Lord. They finally reached the door, which was guarded by four Roman soldiers.

"How do I get in there, Ghabriel?" asked a worried Judas.

"Say something nasty in Latin to the soldier by the door," suggested Ghabriel.

"How will that get me into the courtyard?" asked Judas.

"You distract them while I will open the door. It will only take me a moment," suggested Ghabriel.

Judas walked up to the soldier who stood directly in front of the door and desperately tried to recall some of the Latin he had learned long ago. He recalled the phrase *cave canem,* which meant 'beware of the dog'. He quickly made up an offensive phrase and yelled at the soldier, "*Mater tua canem est!* (Your mother is a dog!)"

The soldier was quick to respond with a blow of his shield on Judas' face as he screamed, "*Canis Iudaeus!* (Jewish dog!)"

It took that moment of distraction for Ghabriel to open the door. Swifter than the wind, he shoved the guard with one hand and grabbed Judas with the other. The guard was propelled onto another guard by the superior force of Ghabriel as he pulled Judas into the courtyard, shutting the heavy wooden door behind them. Ghabriel executed all of that in one swift movement. At the other end of the courtyard, Lord Ishia had been tied to a pillar, fastened to two thick iron rings protruding off the pillar. The guards were taking their turns with their *flagra* whipping Lord Ishia's naked back. Every hit produced blood flowing from the two barbell-shaped cuts. His back was bloodied and each new stroke brought forth new blood.

"What do we do?" quickly asked Judas.

"I cannot be seen, my friend;" explained Ghabriel, "But, you must go and stop one of them."

"They will arrest me and flog me!" whispered Judas.

"Exactly!" answered Ghabriel, "But you must move fast, the guards are opening the door. Go, my friend, keep company with Our Lord at His time of death. I will see you again, Judas. You can count on me!"

After a quick embrace, Judas ran to one of the Roman soldiers and grabbed his wrist, whose hand held the flagrum, stopping his next blow. Judas cried out, "That is my Lord you are hitting."

As this happened, two of the guards had opened the door and had come running towards Judas. The two soldiers grabbed Judas; but he succeeded kicking one of them away. The soldier who had been stopped by Judas came back with a blow of his flagrum on

Judas' head, knocking him out. He dropped to the ground, blood emanating from his forehead.

"What is the trouble?" asked Marcus, who had come to inspect the whipping.

"This *Iudaeus* hit me and managed to open the door!" exclaimed the Roman soldier, "It was so fast that no one really saw how he did it. One thing I know for sure, Centurion, is that this man is one of his followers and had the intention of freeing the Nazarene."

"Tie him on the other side of the pillar and give him twenty lashes!" ordered Marcus.

One of the soldiers came back with a bucket of filthy water and threw it at Judas' face. Judas opened his eyes: his vision was blurred. He had a terrible headache. He licked his lips, tasting the sweet blood that kept flowing from his wound. Two guards grabbed him and brutally stood him up and tied him up on the other side of the pillar. His eyes were now only two or three *pollicis* from his Lord's face.

"My beloved friend, Judas!" whispered Ishia, "You are here with me."

"Forgive me, Lord, for what I have done!" whispered Judas.

"You are the only brave friend who could have done what you did," continued Ishia as the whipping resumed. Ishia was silent, keeping the pain within Himself.

"AAHHH!" screamed Judas as the first blow hit his naked back. "Help me, Lord. Help AAHHH! me to be like you. It is so painful, Lord AAHHH!"

"Scream inside yourself, Judas. Scream within your spirit; but do not utter in pain. That gives them more strength for the following blows."

Judas followed his Lord's suggestion, screaming only in his mind. His lips opened at each blow of the Roman whip; however, no sound came out. Judas and his Lord continued to be flogged until the sixty and twenty blows had been administered. The two roman soldiers came to untie them as the two prisoners' backs ached from the rawness of the wounds and from the blood that flowed from them. Instantly, Judas dropped to the ground from the pain of the wounds and from exhaustion. Somehow, Lord Ishia managed to remain standing, wavering at every small step He took. One of the Romans had made a cap from the thin and thorny branches of the *etabuh*, a lote bush that grew by the wall of the fortress. Lote bushes were everywhere in Yehuda. He walked towards the Nazarene holding the thorny cap and a cane. Two other soldiers grabbed Ishia and sat Him on a block of stone by the wall. The soldier holding the thorny cap placed it on Ishia's head and beat it into His skin with the cane.

"Just to make sure it doesn't fall!" laughed the Roman soldier. "A king needs his crown!"

All the soldiers joined in the laugh as the soldier continued to beat the thorny cap onto Ishia's head. Whether it was voluntarily or by chance one of the blows landed on Ishia's right cheek, another landed on His nose, breaking it. Two other blows landed on His lower lip and on the left cheek. His face began to swell from the blows and was covered with blood that flowed down from His head from the many holes caused by the long thorns. Judas watched all this from the ground, unable to move. Finally the Roman soldiers stopped hitting, spitting, and mocking Him.

Gathering His strength, Ishia stood up and slowly, one step at the time, walked to the stairs. Step by step, He climbed them without falling, reaching the elevated platform of the fortress. The Roman soldiers had never seen such willpower in any one of their prisoners. Usually, most prisoners would drop to the ground and remain there for a while after twenty lashes from the flagrum. The Nazarene had received sixty and had been badly beaten with the cane and a crown of thorns had been pounded into His skull. Truly, He was not an ordinary man!

Ishia stood in front of Pontius Pilatus and his centurions. The few followers of the Nazarene, mostly women, cried at the sight of their bloodied and badly beaten Lord. The rest of the crowd laughed and cheered.

"*Ecce homo!* (Here is the man!)" exclaimed Pilatus. "Are you now satisfied?"

"CRUCIFY HIM! CRUCIFY HIM!" shouted the crowd, instigated by the Pharishaiya and the members of the San-hedrin.

"Look at him!" answered Pilatus. "He is no threat to you. Take him and crucify him yourselves: I find no case against him!"

"He has broken our law!" exclaimed a Pharish. "And the penalty is death for he claims to be the Son of God."

Pontius turned to Ishia and said, "If you are not from this world, where do you come from?"

Ishia stood silent.

"Talk to me!" he exploded. "Don't you know I have the power to free you or to have you crucified?"

"I come from Paradise, where My Father reigns," whispered Ishia. "There you would have no power over me! Whatever power you have has been granted to you by My Father. He has granted power to any king of this earth."

Pontius ruminated over what the Nazarene had just told him. What a strange man. Not scared of death! Unlike any other man he had ever met in his life. He wanted so much to free this man.

"Sir!" Marcus exclaimed, breaking his thought. "There is a Pesach custom of releasing a prisoner for this special holiday."

"Yes, I know, Marcus!" answered Pontius. "But, I fear that most of this mob would like me to release the rebel, Yeshua Bar-Abbas. That is one man I would not like to free!"

"Sir, the Nazarene has many secret followers," continued Marcus. "Surely, they would like to see their Mashìah freed."

"It is a chance, Marcus, that I fear we must take!" said Pontius. "We will allow the crowd to make the choice. I will personally wash my hands on the fate of this man. Marcus, have a basin of water and a towel brought to me."

Ishia looked at Pontius' eyes with disapproval on his cowardly symbolic gesture he was about to make.

"Caius," called Marcus to one of his soldier, "Bring fresh water and a clean towel for the procurator. Hurry!"

"Crucify him!" shouted some people in the crowd.

"*Silentium!* (Silence!)" shouted Pontius. *"Ecce Rex Iudaeorum!* (Behold the King of the Jews!)"

"Caesar is our king!" shouted some.

"If you free him you will be betraying Caesar, our King!" shouted a Pharish.

"If the Nazarene is our king," cried another, "Then what is Caesar to us?"

Pontius Pilatus feared for his position. Surely, freeing this man would surely end his career. Caius was ready with a copper basin of clear water. He dipped his hands into the water, exclaiming,

"I wash my hands to the fate of this man. I will not be responsible for his death." He took the towel and, wiping his hands, he continued, "It is a custom of this state that a prisoner be released once a year on the morning of the Pesach celebration. We have two prisoners, one of which you may chose to be released. We have a Yeshua Bar-Abbas, a rebel and a murderer; and, in front of you stands Ishia of Nazerat, a holy man, a healer. Which of these two men do you, the people of Yehuda, want me to release?"

"FREE BAR-ABBAS! BAR-ABBAS!" shouted the crowd.

"Ishia of Nazerat! Free Ishia!" shouted a few.

"FREE BAR-ABBAS! WE WANT BAR-ABBAS!" cried the majority.

Pontius called Marcus and whispered to his ear, "Bring out Bar-Abbas."

When Marcus and two guards returned with Yeshua Bar-Abbas most of the crowd went wild screaming for his release.

"If you want me to release Bar-Abbas," cried out Pontius, "What do I do with Ishia called the Mashìah?"

"CRUCIFY HIM!" responded the crowd, muffling the few cries for Ishia.

"What has he done that you all scream for his death?" asked the procurator.

"CRUCIFY HIM! CRUCIFY HIM!" was the answer.

"This is your wish!" cried Pontius. "I am innocent of the blood of this man."

"He is bleeding from your whipping!" cried a Pharish.

"May his death be on us and on our children!" shouted another.

"So be it! Release the rebel!" cried Pontius to the guards. "Get the Nazarene ready for crucifixion." He turned to the mob and his final words to them were, "May his blood be on you and on your children!" He turned to Marcus and gave him full power to proceed with the crucifixion. Pontius Pilatus retired to his room, disgusted and defeated by the angry and unreasonable mob.

Yeshua Bar-Abbas stopped in front of Ishia. "You!" he cried, "The man who stopped my attack on the centurion. How ironic? You saved a few Romans and those same Romans condemn you to death."

"Move on!" shouted one of the guards. "You are free."

"Yes, I am!" cried Bar-Abbas. "I am free!"

The crowd cheered as Bar-Abbas jumped down instead of walking down the steps.

Marcus ordered some of his soldiers to get two *patibula* (crossbeams) ready for the Nazarene and the thief. He told them to work quickly—he wanted to finish as quickly as possible. He needed to bathe and change for Herod's supper.

"Sir," spoke one of the soldiers, "We will need three *patibula*. Remember the man who received twenty lashes with the Nazarene?"

"Release him!" answered Marcus. "He received enough punishment for what he did!"

"Sir, he is asking to be crucified with his Lord."

"What is going on with these people?" shouted Marcus. "I will speak to him myself."

Marcus walked towards Judas and said, "You are free to go!"

"Please, sir, let me die beside my Lord," begged Judas, barely standing.

"Why do you want to die when I am giving you your freedom?"

"I cannot live without my Lord. I beg you, once again, to let me be crucified beside my Lord."

"I will grant your wish; but I am not responsible for your death. The responsibility lies on you for you have begged me twice to die with your Lord."

"Not you, nor any of your men are to be blamed for my death," cried Judas.

"Very well!" exclaimed Marcus. Then, turning to his men he shouted, "Prepare three *patibula*. We have a new customer!"

All the soldiers laughed.

The soldiers brought three crossbeams out. The chiseled beams were nearly five cubits in length and weighed approximately eighty librae each. The three crossbeams were placed on the three men's shoulders and their arms were tied to them with hemp ropes.

A soldier walked up to Marcus and announced, "Sir, the procurator wishes that this sign be nailed on top of the Nazarene's head."

On the board was written "*Hic est Iesus Rex Iudaeorum.*" The message *This is Jesus King of the Jews* was also written in Aramaic and in Greek, in smaller letters beneath the larger Latin inscription.

"Make sure that it is nailed above the Nazarene's head. Pilatus feels very strong about this sign!" ordered Marcus.

"It shall be done, sir!" replied the soldier.

"Felix and Horatius, bring three *sedili* (pegs), three *suppedanea* (footrests), and plenty of nails and ropes!" ordered the centurion. "Everyone ready! Keep the mob away and against the walls until we get to Gulgoleth!"

(9:00 a.m.)

Gulgoleth, the Mound of Skulls, was approximately three stadia away, a walk that would take about half hour under normal conditions. However, there was nothing normal on that unforgettable day. Ishia had been beaten to a pulp and was barely walking with a heavy crossbeam tied on His shoulders and arms. Judas seemed to have regained a little strength and he was able to carry his load. The thief was not having any trouble for he was in the best shape of the three condemned men. The crowd was agitated. There were rebels with Bar-Abbas whose goal was to kill a few Romans. There were Pharishaiya, Tsadduqim, and members of the San-hedrin whose goal was to assure the Nazarene's death. There were a few followers of Ishia, mostly women, who had no power over what was happening but prayed that their Lord might make all of that horrible ordeal go away and come out of it victorious as He had often done. The rest of the crowd was there for excitement and amusement. Therefore it was going to be a slower and more painful walk to Gulgoleth.

The centurion led twelve soldiers and the three condemned men out of the Praetorium. As soon as two soldiers opened the main gate, six soldiers shoved the crowd back with their lances, making way for the three doomed men. There were cries of desperation from the women. There were cries of condemnation and mockery from many. Some, like Youseph A'Ramathayim and Nikotheimus, were in too much shock to even utter a cry. Ishia stared at them for a moment and then continued the walk along the rocky and bumpy road to

Gulgoleth. Judas followed, keeping his head down, not wanting to be seen or recognized. The thief moved along, stopping only when the small procession would come to a halt.

Ishia was having a difficult time as the rough crossbeam scraped and pressed into His open wounds. His face was in so much pain: His cheeks and lower lip were blue and swollen from the blows; His broken nose had swelled at the center; and, His head hurt from the many thorns imbedded into His scalp and from the people shouting at Him. His vision was blurred as sweat and blood mixed into His eyes. His bare feet were bleeding and swollen from cuts He had incurred since the time of His arrest. He was exhausted from not having rested or slept through the night. Suddenly, He stubbed His right big toe on a rock, nearly breaking it, and fell to the ground. He brought His right side down, stopping a deadly fall; however, the weight of the beam brought Him face down and pinned His chest to the ground. One of the soldiers whipped Him, telling Him to get up. Ishia used the right side of the beam and His knees to get up.

Different people kept taunting Him, asking Him to save Himself if He were truly the Mashìah. Others laughed at Him with disdain. Suddenly, a friendly faced appeared in front of Him—it was Verenike, one of His followers. She was crying as she held a white handkerchief over His face, absorbing most of the blood and sweat. A soldier pushed her away as she guarded the cloth with dear life.

Ishia continued slowly along the bumpy and rocky road, which led downhill away from the city. Once again, He fell. This time He was unable to use any side of the beam, hitting the ground with His chest, scraping it on the rocky dirt road. More cuts. More pain. More blood flowed from His chest! A muscular black man from the crowd helped Him to get up. A soldier pushed him back with his lance; but the black stranger showed no fear. The stranger continued to make his way along the crowd.

Exhausted and badly cut, Ishia fell a third time. People laughed at Him. A few cried. Once again, the black stranger stepped in only to be stopped by the same soldier. He begged to carry the beam for the Holy One. Marcus agreed, giving permission to Shimon from Cyrenaica, a North African Roman province, to untie the Nazarene. He untied the Lord's arms in the gentlest way and helped Him to get up. The fall had cut Ishia's knees, and front torso.

"Thank you, Shimon," whispered Ishia.

"My Lord!" cried Shimon as tears swelled in his big eyes, dropping to the ground like heavy rain, "What have they done to You?" He picked up the beam, placed it over his shoulder, and slowly followed his Lord. Shimon was the father of Alexandros and Rufus, two young followers of Ishia of Nazerat. Shimon was also a believer that Ishia was the Mashìah, the Son of God.

Finally, after passing through the Gennath Gate, the three condemned men reached Gulgoleth, where a framework of *pali* (large posts) had been permanently fixed at the top of the hillock for the sole purpose of crucifying rebels and enemies of Rome. As soon as Shimon dropped the *patibulum* on the rocky mound two soldiers shoved him back towards the crowd. Two other soldiers grabbed Judas and the thief and threw them to the ground. Both landed on the crossbeams that they were tied to, hurting their shoulders and heads. They screamed in agony as more blood trickled down their backs. Without wasting time, Ishia was once again tied to His *patibulum*. Immediately, the soldier with the nails placed a long and thick iron nail at the beginning of Ishia's right wrist, on the line next to the ridge of His upper palm and hit it with his hammer, breaking the flesh and entering into the tiny gap that was formed by the four bones of His palm.

"Abba!" cried Ishia.

A second blow forced the nail through the wrist, forcing that small gap to widen, pushing the four bones out of their normal places. Blood squirted from Ishia'a wrist as He grimaced from the agonizing pain shooting through His right wrist, His back arching to take in some of that excruciating agony. A third blow pinned His right wrist into the crossbeam. The soldier expertly secured the nail deep within the wood with a fourth blow.

"Abba!" continued Ishia.

The soldier repeated the four blows on His left wrist, driving the second nail into the other side of the beam. A rope was tied around the center of the crossbeam and pulled over the center of the standing framework.

"The king gets the center!" cried the same soldier, wiping Ishia's blood from his arms.

Ishia's body was slowly raised, tied and nailed on His crossbeam, as four soldiers pulled Him up until the center of the beam met with the chiseled hollow on the center post. A soldier on a ladder guided the crossbeam into the chiseled groove and proceeded to nail into place using two long nails.

As His hanging body pulled Him down, Ishia continued His cry, "Abba, forgive them for they do not know what they are doing."

Judas was nailed into his crossbeam in the same fashion, uttering the most agonizing cries with each blow of the hammer. Within moments, his body was being raised as His Lord's feet were being nailed together over the *suppedaneum*. The soldier drove the single and long nail through the space between Ishia's second and third toe bones. As Judas' feet were also being nailed over his respective *suppedaneum* the thief was being nailed into his crossbeam. His screams were louder and longer than Judas'. The soldiers worked like clockwork and within a few more moments the thief was also being raised onto his post.

(10:00 a.m.)

The three crucified men were now on their proper crosses: Ishia was on a *crux immissa* at the center; Judas was on a *crux commissa* by Ishia's right; and, the thief was on Ishia's left, also on a *crux commissa*. A soldier, on a ladder, was nailing the sign over Ishia's head.

One of the leaders of the San-hedrin, a Pharish, yelled out, "Why have you placed such a sign over the Nazarene? He is not the king of the Yehudi!"

"Silence, you black vulture!" exclaimed Marcus. "What Pilatus has written he has written; and, it will stay there! Now back off, you are becoming a nuisance."

"You cannot speak to me that way!" exclaimed the Pharish. "I am..."

"I don't care who you are!" screamed Marcus, disgusted by their disgraceful persistence. "To me you will not be anything but a black vulture. Now, back off before I will need to use something to shut that vile mouth of yours."

Angry and hurt, the Pharish moved back into the crowd and began to instigate some of the men near him.

"How are you going to destroy the sacred Temple and rebuild it in three days, Ishia of Nazerat?" yelled one of the men.

"You have saved so many," screamed another. "Why don't you now save yourself?"

"He can't save himself!" yelled another man. "Can't you see he is nailed and tied to his cross?"

Many laughed, finding the last condemnation amusing.

"If he is the king of the Yehudi, he should come down and take over Yehuda!" exclaimed yet another.

"If you are really the Son of God," said the crucified thief, "Then, save us and yourself."

"My Lord," whispered Judas, "Do not listen to any of them. They are poison!"

"My friend, Judas!" cried back Ishia. "I forgive them, for they really do not know what they are saying."

"This is so painful, my Lord!" exclaimed Judas.

"It will not be too much longer, my beloved friend, Judas!" whispered Ishia. "Soon you will be with me, together with my angels, and on the third day you will be resurrected with me. And, your body will be glorified...It will live forever."

"My Lord, my God!" whispered Judas.

The crowd continued taunting the Nazarene.

The crucified three kept switching their position, sometimes raising their bodies by pushing on their *suppedanea* and at times by sagging their bodies and resting on their footrests. Either way was painful! When they pushed on their footrests it would reduce the weight and pain on their wrists; however, their legs would cramp up. As they sagged their body to alleviate the leg cramps, the pressure would go back on their wrists and arms and they experienced breathing difficulties, which would eventually lead to asphyxiation. The three dying men kept alternating their positions to prolong the last few hours of their lives.

As the three condemned men tried to survive their last hours, some of the Roman soldiers played for the Nazarene's robe and thorny crown with their die.

Marcus finally allowed Miryam, Ishia's mother, and a few friends to come forward to see her son. Young Yehohanan held His Lord's mother from falling. She was in a state of shock, not quite understanding the events, which had led to her son's arrest, flogging, and crucifixion. She thought that people loved her son for all the miracles and cures He had performed to help them. Miryam of Magdala was there with several other women.

Ishia looked down and said to His young apostle and mother, "Yehohanan, take care of your mother...Mother, take care of Yehohanan, your new son."

All the women began to cry upon hearing their Lord's voice.

Hiding by the walls of the city was Cephas crying at the horrifying spectacle he had witnessed, the crucifixion of his Lord. He was too scared to go through the crowd and get close to his dying Lord. He did not want to be crucified like Judas!

(12:00, noon)

By then, the sun had warmed up the day, beating on the nearly naked bodies of the crucified men. Sweat mixed with blood ran down their bodies, especially Ishia's, who had been severely beaten.

Suddenly, a gigantic dark cloud moved over the entire area, enshrouding the entire city of Yerushalayim and its surrounding villages. The gargantuan black cloud blocked the sun, bringing darkness to the area. The most awesome noise that any of them had ever heard emitted from the black cloud. Instantaneously, it began to pour heavy rain. Thunder and lightning struck different parts of the city. The temperature dropped to a cool and refreshing downpour for the dying three. The crowd dispersed in fear, running for their lives. Only two of the San-hedrin remained: Youseph A'Ramathayim and Nikotheimus. They joined the brave followers who stood by their Lord's mother. A few daring people remained by the city walls, hoping that God would descend from that awesome cloud and save His Son. The members of the San-hedrin had ran into the Temple when the earth began to shake, where everyone witnessed the veil of the *qodesh haqqodashim* splitting apart as if the Hands of the Almighty Himself had torn it out of anger.

Even the Romans were afraid.

"He truly must be the Son of God!" exclaimed Marcus, questioning his own meaningless Roman beliefs.

"*Eli, Eli, lama sabachtani!* cried Ishia towards the sky.

The heavy rain continued on Yerushalayim and its surroundings.

"He is calling Elishah!" exclaimed a man.

"He feels abandoned by God!" exclaimed another.

Only Judas really knew that Ishia was not calling Elishah, nor did He feel abandoned by His Father. Judas knew that his Lord was uttering the first verse of Psalm Twenty-two. He turned towards his Lord and he could barely hear Him whisper the rest of the psalm.

"…So far from my invocation, from the utterances of my cry? Oh, My Father, I cry out this day and you do not answer me; there will be no relief for me during this tenebrous night. Yet you sit on your Holy Throne, oh Glory of Yisrael! The great fathers had faith in You; they believed in You and You delivered them," whispered Ishia, "But I am a maggot, not a man; ridiculed by many and despised by my people. All who see me laugh at me; mocking me with their parted lips, wagging their heads at me. They say, 'He trusted His Father; let Him deliver him; let Him rescue him if He loves him.' Father, you have been my way since my conception, my guardian while I drank from my mother's breast. To you I belonged since birth for you were My Father while I grew within my mother's womb.

"Do not leave me for I am in agony; stay by my side for there is no one to comfort me. I am surrounded by bullocks, the powerful bulls of Bashan. They scream at me like voracious and roaring lions.

"My body has lost all its blood and water; all my bones are in agonizing pain. My heart feels like wax melting within my chest. My throat is so dry that it feels like baked clay, and my tongue is glued to my palate; You have sent me to my death.

"Truly, I am surrounded by angry dogs, a mob of sinners have enclosed me; they have pierced my hands and my feet; I am so dehydrated that I can count all my bones. They stare and laugh at me, rejoicing; they divide my clothes among themselves and cast their die over my cloak.

"But You, My Lord and Father, stay by me; and now, be my help. Save my lonely spirit from the fangs of these wild dogs. Free me from the lion's jaws; save my worthless life from the horns of these bullocks.

"Eli, I announce your Holy Name to my brothers; I will praise You among the crowds." Ishia raised his head, looking towards the crowd by the city walls, and cried out, "Any one of you who fear My Father, the Lord, glorify Him; all children of Yakov glorify Him; worship Him all you children of Yisrael. For He has not rejected nor scorned the outcasts in their misery, nor did He turn away from them. However, He heard their cries of misery. I will praise You, Father, among the crowds; I will fulfill my sacred mission You have bestowed upon me among those who fear You. The poor shall be satiated; the seekers of the Lord shall glorify You, Father. If you, my brothers, do this, your hearts will be forever merry.

"The entire earth shall remember and seek You, Father; and all families from every nation shall worship Your Name. For You, My Lord and Father, are All Powerful, the Ruler of all nations. To You, alone, shall all pray before they sleep; and all who die will follow Your Will. And through You my spirit shall live. Teach all future generations about the Lord so that His justice be known by them."

Judas gently turned to his Lord with his last ounce of strength left within him and whispered, "To you my Lord, I entrust my spirit!" His eyelids heavy with mortal pain shut down, his heart gave up as his lungs collapsed through asphyxiation.

Tears rolled down Ishia's eyes as He saw His beloved friend die. Judas had stuck with Him till the end!

"And now, Father, into your hands I entrust my spirit," whispered Ishia. He then cried out, "I am thirsty!"

Marcus ordered one of his soldiers, "Dip the sponge into the wine mix and give it to the holy man!"

The soldier took the sponge and placed into the bowl of wine and water, allowing it to absorb the mix. He took his lance and speared the soaking sponge and brought it up to Ishia's lips.

He tasted it but refused to absorb the liquid from the sponge. "It is bitter!" whispered Ishia, "...Father, my mission is accomplished." His head bowed, his eyes closed as he gave up his spirit to his Father.

(3:00 p.m.)

It was the ninth hour of the day. The ultimate sacrifice had been performed by the greatest man that had ever lived on earth. The dark and ominous black cloud moved away, picking up great speed as if the most powerful wind ever was behind it. Once again, the sun shone brightly in the western sky as the water began to evaporate from the wet soil.

"Pierce the Nazarene's heart, but do not break his shins!" ordered Marcus.

"And the other two?" asked the soldier.

"Break their shins! That should be sufficient."

A soldier took the large hammer and followed his centurion's command by breaking Judas' shins and then the thief's.

The same soldier who had lifted his lance with the sponge up to the Nazarene's lips removed the sponge from it. With the same lance he speared the Nazarene underneath His left armpit. The blade entered between the fifth and sixth ribs piercing His heart. Whatever blood was left in His heart came out mixed with whatever little fluids remained within His body.

The women broke out in cries of desperation. Their Mashìah was dead! Yehohanan held his mother tenderly as her cries of hopelessness and total abandonment ravaged her beautiful and delicate heart.

Youseph A'Ramathayim and Nikotheimus, carrying two folded white linens, approached the sorrowful group and offered their prayers and love for the loss of the great Ishia, their Mashìah. Youseph had a written letter from Pontius Pilatus, which gave him permission to take down their Lord's body and that of Judas to be properly buried.

"Why do you bother with the traitor?" asked Yehohanan angrily.

"Judas was the Lord's friend! Ishia loved him like a brother!" exclaimed Youseph.

"He betrayed Him!"

"We are not sure if he did. However, the Lord Himself asked me personally to take care of this matter and…" spoke Youseph.

"Of taking care of Judas? How did He know that Judas would also be crucified?" asked Yehohanan.

"It's a mystery; but I am honoring His wish. It is only just that we honor Him," suggested Youseph. "I have our family tomb in the garden before the North Gate. It is not far and we are here to help."

Youseph showed the paper to the centurion, which he promptly acknowledged upon seeing Pontius' signature. He ordered his men to bring the bodies of the Nazarene and His follower down. With ladders and ropes they lowered the body of their Lord down. Miryam, His mother, held His emaciated and dehydrated body in her arms kissing It and washing It with her tears.

Judas' body was also lowered by the soldiers. Youseph paid some of the soldiers to help them carry the bodies to his family tomb, which was about one hundred paces away.

Youseph's family tomb was a deep grotto with a carved entrance. A staircase had been carved out of the stony hill, leading to a room, large enough to accommodate several bodies. Two stone altars had been cut for Youseph and his wife. However, the altars were to be used for their Lord's body and that of Judas.

The women took charge of wrapping the Lord's body; however, Youseph and Nikotheimus prepared Judas' body for the women refused to touch it, still placing all the blame on him for what had happened on that sacred day. There were two white linens. It was obvious that Youseph had thought about it and had bought the linens well in advance for it was Pesach.

The women took the longer *sindon*, made of a rich material that had been weaved into a herringbone pattern, which was nearly ten cubits long and two and a half cubits wide, and neatly placed half of it over the long stone slab, which was four and a half cubits long. Youseph, Yehohanan, Nikotheimus, and two women gently lifted the body of their Lord and placed It on the half of the shroud that covered the stone slab. His body nearly covered the length of the stone! Lovingly, they crossed His right hand over His naked private parts and lay His left hand over His right wrist, tying them together with a narrow strip of linen. His feet were placed together and gently tied with another strip of linen. Nikotheimus took two *leptonis* (coins minted under Pontius Pilatus) and covered Ishia's eyelids. Then a thin *sudarium*, a fine veil, was gently placed over His sacred face.

Then, Miryam of Magdala which held the rest of the long sindon, gently folded it over His head and face and together with the wife of Cleophas stretched the rest over His body and feet, and tucked the rest underneath His feet.

The same procedure was repeated for Judas; however, it was quickly done without the care and tenderness they had showed for their Lord's body. The women would return on the morrow following the Shabbat to anoint the Lord's body with myrrh and aromatic aloes that Miryam, Eleazar's sister, had bought for Him.

When the three men and the five women came out of the tomb, three Roman soldiers were waiting for them.

"Why are you back?" asked Youseph.

"We were ordered by the procurator himself to seal and guard the tomb!" exclaimed one of them.

"What for?" asked Youseph. "He is dead. He is no threat to anyone!"

"It was the leaders of the San-hedrin who requested this and paid us to guard it for three days," volunteered the second guard. "They think that his followers will come and take the body away and claim that he has come back from the dead."

"That is preposterous!" exclaimed Nikotheimus. "Well, since you are here will you help us to seal the entrance?"

"That is our job!" exclaimed the third.

Together, the three men, the three Romans and even two of the women slowly rolled the heavy round slab that would seal the tomb. As soon as the stone fell into the groove of the entrance it set and could not be budged.

"It will take more than four men to pull that stone away!" exclaimed the first soldier.

"Or an elephant!" laughed the second.

"Do not worry," said the third. "We will guard it with our lives. No one will remove this stone."

The three men and the five women went away from the tomb towards the North Gate. They were all going to Youseph's house, where Lydia and young Ishia were waiting for them. Linus, Esther and her baby, Augustus and Miryam, and other friends were all there. There they would be together on that ominous day in the history of mankind.

Chapter 33

THE RESURRECTION AND THE LIGHT

Saturday, March 21, 33 A.D.
(1:00 a.m.)

Two of the three Roman guards were in a deep sleep, intoxicated by the sweet wine brought by the tall stranger. Never in their lives had they tasted anything as wonderful as that red wine. The third guard sat by a rock, trying to stay awake; but he was having a difficult time doing that as his eyes struggled to stay open. The same tall stranger, followed by three other tall men, carrying strange-looking bags, approached the drugged guard.

"He must have drank less than the others," whispered the tall hooded man to the other hooded men, "Or maybe he has a stronger metabolism. Nevertheless, he will fall asleep within minutes, even if he had a mouthful of the wine."

"Who...goes...there?" slurred the guard.

"It is I, Ghabriel," answered the tall man.

"The...best...wine," were his last words before the guard fell into a deep sleep.

Ghabriel caught the guard, stopping him from falling into the rocky ground, and laid him down gently beside the stone.

The entire city slept on that unforgettable night, most of them drunken by their honeyed pesach wine, as Ghabriel and three of his men gently rolled the heavy stone which blocked the entrance to the tomb.

One of the men took out a small conical-shaped device from a pocket. By turning it, the small device emitted a most powerful light, which illumined the entire tomb. When all three men had stepped down the tomb, Ghabriel rolled back the stone from the inside without any effort.

"We have four hours to revive Lord Ishia's and Judas' bodies," announced Ghabriel. "We need to work efficiently and be gone before the early sun's rays. The guards will sleep longer than that; but, I feel that some of the members of the San-hedrin might be here early in the morning to see that the stone is in its place and that at least one of the guards is awake."

"Lord Ishia is extremely dehydrated," informed Sha-el, lifting the sindon up. "He will need a total blood infusion. I will need to rebuild His heart first before we can infuse Him. His heart has been pierced. Joel, you will work on His skin. Every wound must be repaired and be readied for tomorrow's procedure. You can begin by using the electro-suture on every cut and scrape. However, you must not touch the wounds on His wrists, on His feet, and the lance wound under His armpit. That was Lord Ishia's wish. I must now check Judas' body."

As Joel began with the electro-suture, repairing every microscopic section of each wound or cut, the chief physician went to inspect Judas' body. Ghabriel and Daniel had already uncovered Judas' body and were inspecting him.

"Judas' body is in better shape. It has, by far, less cuts and wounds," explained Ghabriel. "However, both of his tibiae have been broken. Daniel and I can repair the bones and wounds while Lord Ishia's body requires your talent, Sha-el. There is no better physician than you in this galaxy. Only you can assure the resurrection of our Lord."

The tomb was brighter than any surgery room of earth's future. The machinery they were using was the most advanced. It would take man at least two millennia before inventing anything close to what they had. And even then, their machinery would be clumsy and gigantic in comparison.

(2:00 a.m.)

Sha-el had repaired Lord Ishia's heart and had begun the blood and oxygen infusion. Joel was already working the wounds on His back. Ghabriel and Daniel had restructured Judas' tibiae with a skeletal cell stimulator. Both machines worked under the same principle: to accelerate cellular division and restoration. This process also accelerated rehabilitation: within two to three days both men could be up walking and running within a week. Ghabriel and Daniel began working on Judas' wounds while Sha-el inspected Judas' legs.

By the end of the second hour, both bodies were ready for electro-impulses of their brains and hearts. Under normal circumstances, the electro-impulse initiator would be applied two or three times on the *locus coeruleus*, in the brainstem, to reactivate the chemical, norepinephrine (noradrenaline), resulting in a chemical brainstorm that would stimulate the activity of acetylcholine and other neurotransmitters. An immediate injection of liquid vitamin-Bs would trigger a micro-galactic storm propelling the chemical acetylcholine to travel to the heart and reactivate its function, pumping the blood and oxygen throughout the body resulting in the respiratory function of the pulmonary system. Within moments all the neurotransmitters would be working, reactivating the memory network and the functions of all systems throughout the entire body. A second injection of a liquid mixture of all the other necessary vitamins would revitalize their bodies.

(3:00 a.m.)

Lord Ishia and Judas' bodies were free of all wounds and cuts, with the exceptions of the nail wounds and the deep cut between the Lord's fifth and sixth left ribs. Those wounds were disinfected and dressed with ultra-sterile padding. Both bodies had been infused with O-Rh negative blood and oxygen. Through a previous testing, they had found out that Judas had the same rare and holy blood as Ishia. The very same blood that the Almighty Yahweh and several other important Paradisian families had, including Ghabriel's!

Twelve hours had passed since Lord Ishia's body had expired and estimating from previous resuscitations, Sha-el thought it would take several attempts to reactivate His body. Having located his Lord's *locus coeruleus*, Sha-el proceeded to perform the first application with the electro-impulse initiator. To his surprise and to the others' amazement, Ishia's heart began to pump its newly acquired blood and oxygen. Considering the condition that His body had been and nearly a total loss of blood, Ishia's superior brain and body had been resuscitated immediately with the first application. Ishia was truly like His Father, Lord Yahweh. It was the first experience of such a miracle for Ghabriel, Sha-el and the two other Paradisians.

Happily, Sha-el injected Lord Ishia with a third injection, which was filled with all the nutrients for the following twenty-four hours and a double dosage of a somniferous sedative that would permit Him to rest and allow all the nutrients and vitamins do their work.

With Judas's body, it took Sha-el six applications to his *locus coeruleus* with the electro-impulse initiator. It was that sixth application which began Judas' heart. After the third injection, the four Paradisians felt at ease for having accomplished that most significant and delicate part of their earthly mission, the resurrection of their Lord and of their friend, Judas.

Sha-el and Joel would remain inside the tomb, using extremely subdued and localized light, to monitor the next twenty-four hours, which were crucial to the lives of their Lord and Judas. Ghabriel and Daniel would return during the following night, after completing another important part of their earthly mission. It was a little after four past midnight when Ghabriel and Daniel rolled the stone back to its exact place, noticing that the three Roman guards were still deeply asleep like babies. The somniferous wine would loose its effect within an hour, allowing them to wake up by dawn.

(5:00 a.m.)

Swiftly, Ghabriel and Daniel reached Sepphorah Bat-Ybrahim's house. Although Ghabriel did not have a key he quickly unlocked the door. Both men entered, locking the door behind them. They reached Augustus and Miryam's room and woke them up gently. Within moments, everyone in the house had been awakened with the exception of the two infants. It was better that they slept. All their precious possessions had been packed, including Lord Ishia's silver goblet, the Shomeroni goldsmith's gift. They all thanked and embraced Sepphorah for her hospitality, kindness, and love. They would miss her very much.

Ghabriel, Daniel, Augustus, and Linus carried the heavier bags. Miryam, the Lord's mother, and Miryam, Augustus' wife, both carried smaller bags. Lydia carried Ishia Justus and Esther carried baby Judas. Both infants were bundled against the cool night. Briskly, they all followed the two tall men through the streets of Yerushalayim without ever encountering a soldier or guard. Everyone was sleeping, including the two guards at the Gate of Essenes. It was still dark when the group reached the Valley of Hinnom, where a strange and large silvery object stood on its four legs. With the exception of their Lord's mother, everyone else was terrified by the strange round metallic object, which was wider than most houses.

"Do not be afraid," spoke Miryam, the Lord's mother. "Ghabriel is the messenger of the Almighty Lord. He is here to help us. Do not fear what you do not understand!"

"Come, dear friends," whispered Ghabriel. "This very morning you will be in Massilia, far away from all this."

"How is that possible?" exclaimed Augustus Horatius. "It takes at least two weeks of rough sailing from Caesarea Palaestinae to Massilia, stopping only in major ports. And we are so far away from the port of Caesarea!"

"Dear Augustus, this morning, you will all be flying faster than the swiftest hawk. We will reach the outskirts of Massilia as the first rays of dawn will appear in the eastern sky;" explained Ghabriel. "And, Yakov, the Lord's half brother, and Yousef A'Ramathayim are inside the shuttle with my men. They will join us for Massilia."

"This is so difficult to comprehend!" exclaimed Augustus.

"I understand;" answered Ghabriel, "But, do not be afraid! We need to move before dawn. Time is of extreme importance. Come do not fear!"

The group fearfully followed the two Paradisians up to the shuttle. The large round metallic object seemed to have neither windows nor doors. Augustus dared to touch the brilliant polished metal. Never had he seen a metal so polished and so brilliant.

To their surprise and fear, an entrance suddenly appeared with a beam of bright light emitting from it, reaching the ground. Ghabriel and Daniel helped them, guiding them up the beam which miraculously carried them into the vessel without having to climb or walk. Inside, they were received by Youseph and Yakov who seemed at ease, without fear. Strange but beautiful chairs stood in semi-circular fashion facing four other larger but similar chairs. Three other men were present, strangely dressed in the whitest of white garments, which clung to their bodies like skin. They too were cleanly shaved like Ghabriel and Daniel. The five Paradisians helped everyone in sitting down and arranging safety harnesses which imprisoned them to their seats. The two infants, who had awakened were given a delicious drink to pacify them for a little while and were placed in two special chairs, which curved around their bodies like a shell. The two infants did not cry and were smiling. This reassured the frightened earthlings.

The five tall men were also seated and strapped to their seat. Ghabriel broke the silence, "Begin gently, Daniel; we do not want to alarm the infants or any of our friends."

Gently, with a hissing noise like the wind, the shuttle retracted its legs and began to climb up. Suddenly, windows miraculously appeared all around the chamber revealing the walls of Yerushalayim getting away from them. Instantly, the holy city shrank before their eyes as they soared up into the sky, finally disappearing below the clouds. Within moments, the shuttle had reached the *Mare Internum* (Mediterranean Sea). The lanterns from the earliest fishing boats were visible off the coast, flickering like fireflies in the last hour of the night.

It was still dark when the shuttle came to a stop in midair, high above the port of Massilia. Augustus who knew the distance from Yerushalayim and Massilia was flabbergasted at the speed of the heavenly vessel. Who was his son-in-law? If people like Ghabriel and his men had the means to fly at such unthinkable speed they probably had the power to destroy the entire Roman Empire in less than a day; and, they served Ishia. He truly was the Son of the Almighty God, Yahweh.

The shuttle descended straight down above the highland east of Massilia, hovering above a flat surface of the hills. The hissing sound was heard again as the shuttle equalized its four legs allowing it to settle parallel to the small plateau. Everyone followed Ghabriel and Daniel out of the circular vessel, except the three men, in white, who would guard the precious flying ship. Once outside the vessel, Augustus commented on the beauty and purity of the whitish metal, noticing that it had become one solid piece again. The windows, the light beam, and the entrance had all disappeared.

Ghabriel led those earthlings he had come to love for they were all so very much like the children Lord Yahweh had originally intended to evolve from His creations, loving people. From Miryam, the purest and most loving young lady he had found and chosen to be the mother of His Lord's Son, to the Roman centurion, Augustus Horatius, who had fought many battles and killed many enemies yet remained with a heart full of love and tenderness, to the Pharishaiya and elder member of the San-hedrin, Youseph A'Ramathayim, who had recognized Ishia as the true Mashiah through his gentle eyes and heart. He led them all down a path that descended towards the eastern outskirts of Massilia. The first rays of that holy Shabbat made their descend a little easier. It was the beginning of the first hour when they reached a large Roman villa with a stone wall surrounding the large piece of land it had been built on. It had a vineyard and an orchard with various fruit trees, which had begun to bloom. A piece of land had been prepared for a vegetable garden. There was a stable, with cows, horses, sheep, ducks, and chickens.

As they entered the fortified gate, an aroma of fresh bread and sweet desserts flowed from its kitchen. Everyone seemed to appreciate that welcoming scent.

"Who are the lucky people who own this beautiful villa?" exclaimed Esther.

"You all are," answered Ghabriel. "This will be your home from now on. I purchased this villa with Augustus' money. It is the safest home around. The people that have been working here, preparing to welcome our Lord's family and friends, are also Yehudi who have been living here for generations. They have heard of all the wonderful stories about our Lord and they believe that He is their long-awaited Mashìah. They are eager to work for you and feel very lucky to serve the Holy Mashìah's family."

"We do not need servants!" exclaimed Miryam, the Lord's mother. "They will be our friends and members of our family."

"They will be delighted to hear that," responded Ghabriel.

Everyone settled in the roomy villa after a hearty breakfast of freshly baked goods and sweet milk milked from their cows that very morning. There was also a bathroom with a large hot bath whose waters were warmed by the hot air coming from the brick oven underneath it. Beside the garden there was a well for fresh potable water. It was a beautiful home to raise the two boys and the perfect place to continue Lord Ishia's teaching.

Ghabriel and Daniel stayed until late afternoon, helping them to choose their rooms according to each one's needs. Ghabriel told them to be happy for he would bring their Lord and Judas on the following morning, just like he had promised them. Some still were fearful that the resurrection might not happen for they had witnessed their Lord die on the cross and a soldier piercing His heart with a lance. Ghabriel reassured them that Lord Ishia and Judas would be visiting them on the morrow. He and Daniel embraced each one and left on the same path that they had descended.

The shuttle could be seen from the villa as it climbed straight into the heavens, shrinking into a shiny star, and suddenly disappearing into the southern sky just like a shooting star. How many of the shooting stars he had seen were flying vessels of the Almighty Yahweh thought Augustus as he stared into the southern sky above the Mare Internum? The Roman gods were powerless in comparison to the True God! The Roman gods were nothing but statues he thought.

(12:00-midnight)

Ghabriel and Daniel approached the A'Ramathayim family tomb that was still guarded by three Roman guards. The round stone still blocked the entrance to the tomb and the subdued light being used by Sha-el was too weak to filter through. From the outside no one could have noticed anything different with the tomb. Two of the guards were sleeping while the third Roman stood in front of the stone that blocked the entrance. Swifter than a cheetah Ghabriel moved towards the guard, immediately immobilizing him with a touch to his neck. Gently, he laid the guard's body down and applied the fumes to his nostrils from a tiny vial. He approached the two sleeping guards and also let the fumes emitting from the vial enter into their nostrils. The induced coma-like state would last three hours. They would need to use that time to help Lord Ishia and Judas out of the tomb and remove any trace, leaving only their shrouds with Joel and Daniel in the tomb. They would announce the resurrection of their Lord to the devout women who would be coming to anoint the Lord's body at the first hour of the morrow.

Ghabriel easily rolled the large stone to the side and went down the steps leading to the grotto. Daniel replaced the stone from the inside with the same ease that Ghabriel had used to move it and followed him down.

Sha-el and Joel were both awake, knowing that Ghabriel and Daniel had returned from their important trip. They noticed that both Lord Ishia and Judas had been cleanly shaven of their beards. They looked much younger without their beards and their bodies had been cleansed with a solution. Their breathing was near normal and some color had returned to their skin.

"How are they doing?" asked Ghabriel.

"Lord Ishia is ready to be awaken;" answered Sha-el, "But, I fear that Judas needs more rest. His heartbeat has been irregular while Lord Ishia's has been constant."

"Would two more hours help?" asked Ghabriel.

"A little!" answered Sha-el. "We might need to carry him on the retractable litter. He needs all the rest he can get. How far is the shuttle, Commander?"

"Not too far," answered Ghabriel, "About three stadia away at the very most. We could not land in the quarry—the guard would have seen the shuttle."

The four began to pack their equipment and extended the litter into its full size. Judas was carefully placed on the litter, still being monitored by Joel. Sha-el gently woke up Lord Ishia from His much-needed sleep by touching His forehead with the tip of his fingers while telepathically asking Him to wake up.

Sunday, March 22, 33 A.D.
(1:00 a.m.)

Lord Ishia slowly opened his eyes, slowly focusing into Sha-el's face. Smiling, Ishia whispered, "Sha-el."

"Yes, my Lord!" whispered Sha-el. "You are back from the dead. You are alive!"

Ghabriel, Daniel, and Joel joined Sha-el in welcoming their Lord back from His most painful death. All four smiled back at Him, welcoming Him back.

"I saw My Father!" whispered Ishia. "Judas was also there. Is he alive?"

"Yes, my Lord;" replied Ghabriel, "But, he needs more sleep."

"Where is my family?"

"They are all safe in Massilia," answered Ghabriel. "We will be going there so that they may see You. How do You feel, my Lord? Are You able to stand?"

"I believe I can," replied Ishia. "It might take a few moments to regain my balance." He felt His face with His fingers and exclaimed, "You have shaven me!"

"Yes, Lord," replied Ghabriel, "You now look exactly like Lord Yahweh."

"Help me to get up, Ghabriel," whispered Ishia. "I long to see my family."

Ghabriel helped his Lord to stand up. He took a few paces around the stone altar He had been laid to rest, holding to it with one hand. Within moments, Ishia felt good enough to leave the tomb. Sha-el helped the Lord with a new white robe and new sandals while Daniel placed a white linen over Judas, gently tucking it in below his chest.

Ghabriel went to roll the stone so that Daniel and Joel could leave the tomb with the floating litter, carrying the sleeping Judas. Sha-el walked behind Lord Ishia with care, helping Him up the few steps. Once outside the tomb, Ghabriel walked beside Ishia for the ground was uneven and rocky; however, his Lord knew every little rock or depression along the walk towards the shuttle. Not once did He falter or hesitate. It was as if He was walking on air.

Lord Ishia was the first to be welcomed into the shuttle by the three men. Daniel and Joel followed Him into the space vessel guiding the floating litter with the sleeping Judas. They immediately came out and went back with Ghabriel to the tomb.

Outside the tomb, the three guards slept deeply. Ghabriel would take back the rest of the medical equipment, leaving Joel and Daniel in the tomb. They would greet anyone that would show up early that morning. Only a few necessities and the powerful conical light were left with them. On the two flat stones rested the two sindons, with their respective images of the bodies they had recently held. Ghabriel wished Joel and Daniel good luck and planned to meet them at Eleazar's house on the third hour of the day. He knew that Joel and Daniel could easily take care of themselves even against a dozen armed men. Their superior powers and fighting skills made them the perfect men for that part of the mission.

(3:00 a.m.)

The shuttle gently landed on the small plateau overlooking Massilia as the town rested under a starry sky. Not a soul was awake when they reached the villa. Ghabriel directed Lord Ishia to Lydia's chamber, while the others placed Judas in the large dining room, where they would wait until morning.

Lord Ishia quietly entered His lady's room. Lydia was sleeping on a large bed with their beautiful boy sleeping beside her. He looked at them. They were so beautiful! So pure! So full of love! He wanted so much to hug them; but, He knew how tired they must have been. He knelt beside her and whispered ever so gently to her, "I love you, Lydia. I love you, my sweet baby Jesus."

"I love you!" she replied in her sleep, deep within the dream He had entered.

Carefully, without waking them up, He kissed them. There was a chaise in the room. He decided it would be best to wait the few hours left before dawn resting on the chaise. The chaise was

371

comfortable; but, He could not go back to sleep. He felt His arms, His face, and His chest. All the scars were gone except the wound on His side, which was bandaged up, and the nail wounds on His wrists and feet, which had also been dressed by Sha-el. He smiled. He was alive and with His loved ones!

Yerushalayim
(6:00 a.m.)

It was still dark when Miryam of Magdala, Martha and Miryam, sisters of Eleazar of Bet-Ananiah, reached the Gennath Gate, which led to the mound called Gulgoleth and to the tomb. Miryam of Bet-Ananiah carried the amphora filled with myrrh and aromatic aloes that she had purchased to anoint her Lord. Now, she would use that perfumed oil to anoint and cleanse His dead body.

The three women reached the tomb as the very first rays of that sacred morning flickered over the walls of the city. A light as bright as the sun shone through the open tomb, revealing the rolled entrance stone and the three Roman guards in a deep sleep.

Miryam of Magdala dropped the linen she was carrying and ran to wake up the guards. "Wake up! Wake up!" she cried. "Someone has taken our Lord away!"

The guards slowly got up, rubbing the sleep from their eyes.

"Look," continued the Magdalene, "The stone has been moved!"

"What is that light?" asked one soldier, shielding his eyes with his arm.

"We must go in to see if the bodies are still in there," said the second soldier.

"I am afraid!" cried the third. "I have never seen a light as bright as this. What forces could be inside the tomb?"

"We are going in," said the Magdalene, "With or without you!"

"Come on, Remus," said the first soldier, "It is our duty to verify if the bodies are in the tomb or not. We are being paid for this."

Reluctantly, the guards followed the three women down the illumined steps. The light became brighter inside the tomb. It was so bright that it blinded them. As they blocked the bright light with their hands they all could see a vision of two tall angels, all dressed in white, standing beside the rectangular stone that had held their Lord's body. Their faces were clean, with no beards, and the light shone around them like a bright star. The Roman guards were frozen with fear; and, the three women were speechless and in awe for they had never seen such glory and beauty before.

It was Joel who broke the revered silence, "Do not be afraid! You are looking for Lord Ishia, the Son of Lord Yahweh. He is not here for He has risen from the dead. Go and tell His disciples for He has risen as He had told them. Tell them that He will meet them at Bet-ha'Arava by the Ha-Yarden on the Shabbat morning of the following week."

The three women left while the three soldiers stood still, frozen by fear and by a powerful voice in their brain telling them not to move.

"Now, it is your turn to leave," Joel ordered the soldiers. "Go to the San-hedrin and tell them what you have seen."

The three soldiers stumbled out of the tomb and ran towards the Fortress Antonia.

(7:00 a.m.)

Cephas followed Yehohanan as swiftly as he could. However, his younger friend was outdistancing him for he was much younger and leaner than he. The other apostles were too scared to go outside their hiding place and had not believed the women's story. As the two dearest apostles of their Mashìah ran as quickly as their bodies permitted them their Lord's promise reechoed in their minds, "On the third day, I will resurrect in the Glory of My Father."

Yehohanan reached the open tomb first. He noticed that the stone had been moved to the side and there was no one around. He turned around when he heard someone approaching. It was Cephas and he was out of breath.

373

"Wait!" blurted out Cephas, bending down and resting his hands on his knees. "Please…wait for…me!"

Yehohanan impatiently waited for Cephas to regain his normal breathing. "Come on, Cephas!" he said excitedly, "I cannot wait any longer."

Finally, Cephas placed his hand on the young man's shoulder, pushing him to go on. Yehohanan trembled as he descended the stairs to the grotto. Cephas followed him. There was no bright light. There were no angels in white. And there were no bodies. No Ishia! No Judas! Only their shrouds had been left, neatly folded on their respective rocks. Yehohanan took the shroud that had held his Lord. The blood and sweat stains of His Lord had seeped through the cloth, leaving an imprint of the front and back of their Lord. He held it to his chest preciously and then kissed it. He would not touch Judas' shroud and neither would Cephas. In their minds, Judas had betrayed their Lord; and, they were still upset that he had been buried in the same tomb as their Lord.

Yehohanan, still holding the sacred imprint tightly, began to walk back at a brisk pace.

"Slow down, Yehohanan!" cried Cephas. "There is no rush now. He is alive!"

Yehohanan stopped, waiting for the older Cephas to catch up with him. Together they walked towards the Gennath Gate. Before they could enter it, a rowdy group of Pharishaiya and Tsadduqim were quickly coming their way. There was no time to hide.

"Ah!" cried one of the religious men, pointing his finger at Yehohanan and Cephas, "There come two of his disciples."

"What have you done?" cried another, "You have stolen the Nazarene's body and now you have come back for his sindon!"

Yehohanan and Cephas, fearing for their lives turned around and ran down the valley, circling the southwestern section of the city, running along the Valley of Hinnom. Panting, they reached the Gate of Essenes, having circled half of Yerushalayim. The group sent by the San-hedrin had not bothered to follow them. They were only interested in inspecting the tomb themselves.

Massilia
(7:00 a.m.)

Little Jesus had awakened Lydia who had noticed the stranger seating on the chaise, thinking that it was one of Ghabriel's men who had been left to guard her. As she cleared the sleep from her eyes and sat up, she noticed that his hands and feet were bandaged and he was smiling at them. He stood up and walked to her side of the bed.

"Do you not recognize me, my beautiful Lydia," He whispered.

"Ishia!" she exclaimed, embracing Him, "You are alive, my love! Little Jesus, come to hug your abba."

Little Jesus crawled to them as they cuddled Him into their loving embrace.

"Let me look at you!" exclaimed Lydia. "You look so much younger without a beard. You are so handsome, so beautiful, my love!"

Ishia kissed them both, holding them close to His heart for He knew that soon He would leave them to go to His Father. He held them tightly kissing their beautiful faces. "My beautiful Lydia," he whispered, "My wonderful little boy!"

The delicious aroma of the freshly baked goods drew everyone out of their sleeping chambers and into the dining room where Lord Ishia was embraced by all His loved ones and by His new followers. Judas was awake but weak; however, everyone, especially Esther, was delighted to learn that he would soon be walking around. Ishia and all His loved ones, which included the people working at the villa, enjoyed a delicious breakfast together, savoring the good food, fresh milk, and the love they had for each other.

Yerushalayim
(8:00 a.m.)

"In the Name of Our Lord, Ishia, the Mashìah," exclaimed Cephas, "I tell you that He is alive!"

"Have you seen Him?" asked Nathanael Bar-Ptolemais, "Have you spoken with Him?"

"No, but I know that He is alive, I tell you!" answered Cephas.

"We have heard the same story from the women," cried Andros. "Have you become like them, believing in fancy tales, full of emotions and wishful thinking."

"Look at His Sindon! Is this wishful thinking!" exclaimed Yehohanan. "I found it neatly folded on top of the stone we laid Him on."

"Someone could have stolen His body," said his brother, Yakov Bar-Zebedeus.

"And, would that abductor have taken his time to fold His Sacred Sindon so neatly?" insisted Yehohanan. "No, my brother, He was not abducted. He has risen. He has defeated death itself! He truly is the only Son of God!"

"How could the two of you be so sure?" asked Thomas Didymus.

"Why can you not believe, Thomas?" retorted Yehohanan. "Why must you always doubt?"

"Because He was crucified and a Roman soldier pierced His heart!" exclaimed Thomas. "And, once your heart is pierced you are dead. Forever!"

"What about Eleazar?" asked Cephas.

"I do not know," cried Thomas. "I just do not know what happened with Eleazar neither with my master's daughter. Maybe they were not really dead."

"What would it take for you to believe, Thomas?" asked Yehohanan.

"If only I could see Him and touch His wounds," exclaimed Thomas, "then I would surely believe that He is alive."

Suddenly, inside the dark and bolted secret room, a gentle voice whispered, "Peace be with all of you."

"Who opened the door to this stranger?" cried out Cephas.

"No one opened the door after you came back," replied Andros.

"Who let this stranger in?" panicked Thomas. "The San-hedrin is still looking for us. Surely we will be next if we have another traitor in the group."

"Thomas, Thomas, you have such little faith," said the stranger, pulling His robe to the side, manifesting the gash that had pierced His heart. "Come Thomas and place your fingers inside my wound so that you may also believe that I am alive."

Thomas Didymus fell on his knees crying like a baby. The rest followed his example by also kneeling in devotion.

"Forgive me, My Lord!" cried Thomas. "I am not worthy to be one of your apostles."

"Now you believe, Thomas, because you have seen me," said the Lord. "Fortunate will be those who will believe in me without ever seeing me. Now, get up, Thomas and give me an embrace."

Thomas slowly got up and gently embraced his Lord, fearful of touching His wound. One by one, each one of the eleven embraced Lord Ishia.

He spoke to them for a little while, telling them to meet Him at Bet-ha'Arava on the following Shabbat morning. There He would spend some time with them before He would leave this earth to go back to His Father. As His apostles questioned each other about their Lord's departure to His Father He inconspicuously left their hideout without opening the heavily bolted door. In vain they searched for Him, knowing that the door had never been opened. Finally all present realized the divinity of Ishia of Nazerat.

Imwas
(4:00 p.m.)

Yakov Cleophas and Theudas Ephrayim, two disciples of the Lord, had been walking and talking since that morning on the road west of Yerushalayim. They were approaching the village of Imwas when a tall hooded man came to them from behind. The two disciples stopped to see if it was a soldier or a spy. They kept their heads down, hiding their faces, in fear of being recognized.

"What is the subject of your discussion?" asked the stranger.

"You must be the only one coming from Yerushalayim who does not know the horrible things that have happened these past three days!" exclaimed Yakov Cleophas.

"What horrible things?" asked the stranger.

"I see that you are not a Yehudi for you are clean shaven," continued Yakov. "Are you a Graikos, stranger, that you have not heard about Ishia of Nazerat?"

"What about Ishia of Nazerat?" asked the stranger as the three men resumed their walk.

"He was the Mashìah," answered Yakov. "He was a great prophet. He did wonderful things and was the best orator I have ever heard."

"Kaiaphas, the high priest, and the San-hedrin had Him arrested and delivered to the Romans!" exclaimed Theudas. "They beat Him and scourged Him and, then, they crucified Him. They buried Him in a tomb which belongs to a member of the San-hedrin, Youseph A'Ramathayim, an elder Pharish who has suddenly disappeared along with a few others."

"Please, go on," said the stranger.

"We all hoped that Ishia of Nazerat would have freed Ysrael from the Romans!" exclaimed Yakov. "But, that was not to be! However, early this morning, some of our women went to the tomb to anoint His body. Instead of finding His body, they found two angels, surrounded by a bright light, who told them that Ishia of Nazerat was alive."

"Then, two of His most beloved apostles went to see for themselves," continued Theudas, "Only to find an empty tomb without angels and no shining light. On their way back, they were confronted with members of the San-hedrin. They ran for their lives, barely escaping their wrath."

"Is that why you are running away?" asked the stranger.

"What would you have done in our place?" retorted Theudas.

"You fools!" exclaimed the stranger. "Have you not read the scriptures? Moishe, King David, Yesha-Yahu and other prophets foretold of His betrayal, His passion and crucifixion, and of His resurrection of the dead!"

"Then, you believe in Him as the Holy Mashìah!" exclaimed Yakov.

"We are at Imwas," said the stranger. "Farewell! I must continue on."

"Please," begged Yakov, "Dine with us."

"Please, stay with us!" exclaimed Theudas. "It is a pleasure to hear you speak. You have so much knowledge to share."

"Very well," answered the stranger, "I will dine with you."

The three men entered a small inn in the village of Imwas. The owner immediately served them a small loaf of freshly baked bread and a pitcher of cool water.

When the stranger picked up the loaf to break it, Yakov and Theudas noticed the nail wounds above His palms.

"Whenever you are two or more, do this in memory of me," whispered the stranger as he gave them each a piece of the bread.

"It is You, Lord!" said Yakov.

"Forgive us, Lord," cried Theudas, "For not believing in You."

"Tomorrow, go back to Yerushalayim to rejoin the others. Stay with them," instructed the Lord, "And, I will soon see you again."

The two bowed their heads in reverence as their Lord spoke. When they looked up to Him He was gone. They looked around the small inn but their Lord was not there. Immediately, they got up, paid for the bread and water, which they took with them, and went back to Yerushalayim in a hurry.

Lord Ishia spent those few-but-precious days with His family and friends at Massilia. Judas was walking again and enjoying those specials days with his family and loved ones. Together, they took morning strolls along the beautiful little beaches hidden by the rocky shores of Southern Gallia. Judas would build sand fortresses and castles for their infant boys. The salty water would sting the wounds on their feet as they waded along the blue waters of the enchanting coastline of Massilia, holding hands with their beautiful wives and children. The memories of those days would be eternally infused in Ishia and Judas' brains. They enjoyed that week with their families, stretching the hours of each day, under the watchful eyes of Ghabriel and his men who hid behind the rocks and caves along the shore. Ghabriel gave them the privacy they needed with their loved ones but was always present to ensure their safety. Lydia, Esther, and the boys never knew that they were always protected by Ghabriel and his men.

Once again, Lord Ishia explained to Judas their inexorable fates: that Ishia would soon leave to be with His Father; and, that Judas would be going back to the future to prepare for Ishia's second coming. Both Lydia and Esther had accepted those fates knowing that their respective husbands were extraordinary men with the grandest missions to accomplish. Lydia and Esther's upbringing had prepared them for any fatalistic possibility in their lives, living in a time and world where death itself was always unpredictable. However, it was Judas who was torn apart between staying with Esther and little Judas and going back to his loving Catherine. He loved them all with the deepest love he could possibly ever manifest. Once again, Ishia explained to him that there was no choice. Everything had been planned. Judas needed to be back into the future to become His last *apostolos* on earth and to prepare every living person for His return. Judas again had difficulty understanding how would it be possible to go back in time after more than three years. How would it be possible for Judas-1 to work again when it had been programmed for only seven days? Once again, Ishia explained to him the concept of a universe where time was relative to each world and space. He explained to him that a thousand earth years was very little time in the lives of Paradisians. Once again, He explained to Judas that Ghabriel had been on earth with His Father ten millennia ago. Ghabriel had come back to earth on the mission to conceive Ishia's birth with His Father's seeds, remaining there for forty years without aging. Ishia remembered Ghabriel when He was just a child. Ghabriel still looked the same: young, powerful, and ageless. And now, they too had the same power of time. Both Ishia and Judas would never age. A gift of eternity from His Father!

Judas took all that in, finally accepting his fate.

Ishia explained that Joel and Daniel would remain on earth to ensure that their loved ones would always be protected and that both boys would become great men for Gallia and that their bloodline would be continued for the next two millennia. Joel and Daniel would rejoin Judas in the future to help him prepare Ishia's return.

The following Shabbat morning, Ishia, Judas, Yakov, Ghabriel, Joel, and Daniel were ready to rendezvous with all of Ishia's followers at Bet-ha'Arava.

Bet-ha'Arava
Saturday, March 28, 33 A.D.
(9:00 a.m.)

"It is already the third hour of the day!" exclaimed a young disciple. "Are you sure that you have seen Him?"

"You should not speak!" cried Cephas. "Not only have we seen Him and spoken to Him; but He has promised us. The Son of the Almighty Yahweh has promised us that He would come back to see us, here at Bet-ha'Arava, this very morning. Do not be impatient, young Avel!"

"I, too doubted His resurrection!" said Thomas, "But, when He asked me to put my fingers inside His wound, I fell on my knees and cried like a baby! I know that He is about to arrive. I can feel it!"

A silvery cloud came from the sky, descended towards them, and finally hovered a few hundred cubits above their heads. Everyone fell down on their knees on the sandy soil, some prostrated, in total adoration. The resurrected Lord appeared in all His glory, descending in a column of light. Two angels followed Him down the column of light. Finally, two other men came after the two angels. All of them were dressed in resplendent white clothing, made of heavenly cloth.

As fast as it had descended upon them, the silvery cloud disappeared in the blue morning sky.

Young Avel, together with others who did not understand the power and glory of their Lord, trembled in fear.

"Do not be afraid, my beloved brothers and sisters!" exclaimed their Lord, extending His arms out. "Stand up so that I may see you and you may see me."

Everyone stood up, witnessing their resurrected Lord, clearly beholding the wounds above His palms. His clean and shaven face made Him look much younger and more radiant. Everyone noticed an aura around their resurrected Lord, which compelled them all to fall on their knees again.

"I am here, this Shabbat morning, to be with you one more time, my beloved friends. Soon I will go to My Father," He said, pointing to the sky. "Although I will be gone, my love for you and for all mankind yet-to-come will always be present within your hearts. My love for you will grow stronger as each one of you will teach others about love. Learn to love everyone, the beautiful and the ugly, for what appears to be ugly outside is beautiful inside. Love everyone, not matter what color is their skin, for deep inside we are all the same. We are all children of My Father. Love everyone, especially your enemies, for love conquers all. Love will conquer your enemies and they will become your brothers and sisters.

"In my name, with my love for all yet-to-come, and with your love that will keep growing within you go into all corners of this earth and tell everyone about my message of love. This will take time. It will take generations. It will take centuries; but I can guarantee you that this love that I speak of will conquer all empires!"

"Even the Romans?" asked young Avel.

"Yes, my beloved Avel, even the Romans!" answered the Lord. "But the secret to this conquest is love and time. If it would be instantly, it would be meaningless for it would not take any effort or suffering."

"Why suffering, Lord?" asked young Manasheh.

"Did I not suffer and die for all of you!?" exclaimed the Lord. "I could have had my angels crush the entire Roman Empire in an instant; but, that would have been as cruel as they have been. I will leave that for you: to conquer the Roman Empire and any other empire on earth. But it will be sinful to do it by force and with cruelty in my name. That would not last! You will conquer the Roman Empire and other empires with love and with time. Only through love and time will you succeed and understand my message.

"I must leave now for I must visit all the great men of this earth that I have met and learned from. I will see you one more time before I leave this earth. We will meet again in Hagalil, on the top of Har Tavor, on the fourth Shabbat from today. From there I will ascend to My Father. Cephas will be my first representative and his mission will be Rome itself. Joel and Daniel, two of My Father's messengers, will remain here on earth to guide you and to help anyone of you in difficult times. I will see you on Har Tavor where I will ascend to My Father."

Lord Ishia, the Only Son of the Almighty Yahweh, embraced each and every one before He left. No one recognized Judas for he looked so different without a beard; and, everyone welcomed back Yakov Bar-Yoseph, the Lord's half brother.

Ishia, Ghabriel, and Judas walked up the path, which led to the western plateau of the Ha-Yarden and disappeared into the horizon.

(April, 33 A.D.)

Most of the month of April was used for travels around the earth. Judas went with Ishia and Ghabriel to visit the great men and leaders of all the great civilizations on earth. They visited an ancient monastery up in the Himalayas, one on Kilimanjaro and another in the Andes. They visited holy men of Sindhu, of Chen, of the Maya, of the Chimu, and of the Sahar. With each meeting, Ghabriel would introduce Lord Ishia as the Son of God. In each ancient language, Ghabriel would explain Lord Ishia's mission on this earth: to suffer and die for humanity's sins; and, to be resurrected from death itself. Each and every leader or holy man had accepted the power and glory of Lord Ishia, which would later be incorporated into each culture's beliefs.

The last week was spent in Massilia, where Lord Ishia and Judas enjoyed their last days with their loved ones. It was a painful experience leaving Massilia and their loved ones. Miryam, the Lord's mother, went back to Hagalil with Lord Ishia. She would go with her son and live in Paradise as Ghabriel had promised.

Har Tavor
Saturday, April 25, 33 A.D.
(12:00 noon)

All of the apostles and disciples, men and women, old and young, had reached the summit of Har Tavor by Friday afternoon; and, they were waiting for their Lord, Ishia of Nazerat, the Krystos, to appear to them for the last time before going back to Paradise. All of the men and women looked up in the sky, waiting for Him to appear from the silvery cloud.

Lord Ishia and His mother, Miryam, had been walking up the trail, which led to the flat summit of Har Tavor. Finally, they reached the top. Ishia held His mother's hand, helping her up the often-steep trail. They saw the crowd looking up at the sky as they gently mingled into it.

Ishia stepped up on a large stone and began to speak, "My dearly beloved!"

The disciples were taken by surprise, never thinking that their Lord might have walked up the mountain before ascending into the heavens. They were equally surprised to see His wonderful mother.

"I am happy that you all came to see my departure to Paradise, to be with My Father. My mother, Miryam of Nazerat, will be coming with me for My Father longs to see her. I have chosen this wonderful spot to depart from this earth because it is sacred to me. I have climbed this small mountain many times, before I chose you. As a young man, I would often come here to pray and to meditate. Often, My Father's messengers met with me at this very spot. I have often sat on the stone that I now stand on. In the course of my life on this earth I have climbed this mountain more often than any other mountain that I have ascended on earth. For these reasons, Har Tavor will always have a special place in my heart. For these reasons, I have led you up this plateau several times since we have met. And, for these very reasons, it will be the last part of this planet that I walk on and touch before I depart.

"Seven weeks from now, on the fourteenth day of June, the day after the next seven Shabbats, it will be Pentekostes. On the third hour of that holy day, each and every one of you will receive a special power directly from My Father, through the Holy Spirit. You will know when the power is inside you for you will fear no evil and you will then be ready to be my witnesses anywhere on this earth. Some of you will remain in Yerushalayim; some of you will travel to Roma, to Athenai, and to every end of this earth.

"Now, it is time for my mother and I to depart. We will embrace all of you with our hearts for it is too painful to give you our last embrace. I leave you my love, which will never die, which will grow in each and every heart that is present. Love each other like true brothers and sisters; and, pass on my love to everyone you meet, friend or enemy, for with time it will conquer all."

As He had spoken that last sentence a wind stirred the trees and the dust on Har Tavor. The silvery cloud appeared from nowhere, hovering over them. It was so big that it blocked the sun, casting a dark shadow over the entire mountain and valleys below. The disciples were not afraid but felt its power, the Power of the Lord. All knelt on the rocky top of Har Tavor as they witnessed Lord Ishia, the Only Son of the Almighty Yahweh, and His mother, Miryam, ascending up into a column of light, disappearing into the vast silvery cloud.

Quicker than it had appeared, the silvery cloud climbed into the heavens, disappearing from their view.

Qumran, Mesad Hasidim

"Lord," spoke Judas, "I will miss your presence, and all of these wonderful people."

"I will always be in your heart and mind, my beloved friend, Judas," replied Ishia.

"We are approaching the monastery at Qumran," informed Ghabriel. "Joel and Daniel will accompany you to reprogram your time vehicle."

"What happens if it does not work!" exclaimed Judas.

"Do not worry, Judas!" answered Ghabriel. "Joel and Daniel can make anything work. Also, we will not leave until you have successfully gone back to the future."

"How is that possible?" asked Judas.

"You must trust in us. Have faith, Judas!" replied Ghabriel.

Suddenly, Judas understood. He had faith in them. These were the same people that had brought him back from the dead.

Judas embraced Ghabriel, Sha-el, Miryam, a few others present in the command chamber of the mother ship, *Paradise One*. Finally, he embraced Ishia Himself, gently kissing His cheeks, as it had been customary in Hagalil. Tears began to swell in Judas' eyes.

"Do not cry, Judas," whispered Ishia.

"When will I see you again, Lord?"

"On April twenty-fifth, two thousand thirty-three," replied Ishia, "Exactly two millennia from today."

"Why such a long time, Lord?"

"The earth is not the only planet that I must die for, Judas," whispered Ishia sadly.

Judas was silent, unable to speak, feeling such a strong pain within his brain. For the first time in his life, Judas had communicated with his mind, telling the Lord the pain he felt for His other future missions.

"Niihau," whispered Ishia.

"What does the word mean, Lord? What language does that word come from?"

"Hawaiian," replied Ishia.

"Niihau, Niihau!" repeated Judas. "What does it mean, Lord?"

"You will find out as soon as you go back to your future, my beloved friend. It will be wonderful for you."

"Niihau, Niihau!" repeated Judas as if it were a magic word. "I will miss You so much, My Lord. I will miss all of you!"

"Just remember, Judas," whispered Ishia, "For you it will be only ten years. You will always be in my heart, my friend. You have been a very important person in my earthly life. My mission would have been much more difficult without you and your knowledge. Farewell, my beloved friend, Judas!"

Those were Lord Ishia's last word as He broke the embrace. Judas, Joel, and Daniel were ready to be transported down into Qumran's Essene monastery. Ghabriel had given the GISA knapsack back to Judas. Judas wore it on his back, as did Joel and Daniel. Both wore an ultra modern pack on their back, which seemed to be made of the finest-yet-most-resistant material. Judas could only guess what advanced tools were inside those backpacks.

The three men descended through the beam of light, landing into the monastery's courtyard. Several monks, including the one that Judas had recommended to guard Judas-1 were hiding behind the trees and bushes of the courtyard, witnessing the angels descending from the heavenly beam of light. They knelt and bowed down in reverence. In perfect Aramaic, Joel told them to relax and that no harm would come to them.

Judas looked around for Judas-1. He found it at the same spot that it had landed on, except it was covered with off-white linen. The monk explained to them that they had covered it with the linen to protect it from dust. Judas, in appreciation for his care, took the flashlight from his knapsack and gave it to the monk. The monk switched it on and played with the beam of light as his comrades watched him in awe.

Judas removed the linen and gave it back to the monks, thanking them for it. Joel pressed the center of the frame of the glass bubble door, automatically opening it.

"How did you know?" asked Judas.

"I took an educated guess," responded Joel, smiling.

"Everything looks new!" exclaimed Judas. "How will you be able to reprogram it? It has been over three years since I left it."

Joel and Daniel studied the studded command board without touching it. Finally, Daniel announced, "It is ready, Judas. Simply, push the yellow topaz to activate it and the large diamond to return to the future."

"But you haven't reprogrammed it!" anxiously exclaimed Judas. "It has been a long time; and, Dr. Weinstein, my scientist friend, programmed it only for seven days! What happens if it won't work or if I go back to a different time?"

"Remember, Judas, that time is relative to many factors," reassured Joel. "We would not chance your life by our carelessness. We are positive that Judas-One is ready to go back to your future. You will be the last representative of Our Lord. It is all part of the plan."

"I am sorry for doubting you," answered Judas, "But I prefer to go back to Massilia than being disintegrated into neutrinos."

"That would go against Our Lord's plan," whispered Daniel. "Now, give me a hug, Judas. It is time to go."

"I will never forget you, Daniel!" exclaimed Judas, embracing him. "I will miss you, Joel," he continued as he embraced the other. "Will I ever see you again?"

"Sooner than you think," answered Joel. "You must get in now, Judas. We will remain here to make sure that everything will work perfectly. Farewell, my friend."

Judas sat on the leather seat as Joel buckled him into it. Judas took his miniature CD-player and set Billy Joel's CD to *Two Thousand Years* as Daniel closed the bubble door. Joel and Daniel backed away, making sure that all the monks were safely away from the time machine.

Judas pushed the yellow topaz and waved good-bye. Joel and Daniel waved back. He then pushed the huge diamond, which began a slow rotation of Judas-1. Billy Joel's voice resonated into his brain as the rotations picked up speed. Within moments Judas-1 had become a blur. As the machine reached the top velocity of its rotation it broke up into tiny particles and then into microscopic particles, totally disappearing into thin air.

September 15, 2023 A.D.
(3:30 p.m.)

The trillions of atomic particles, which made up Judas and Judas-1, began to reassemble. As the speed of its rotation slowed down, Judas-1 was once again clearly visible. Dr. Weinstein, Major Coolidge, Major Nichols, and Catherine stood up from behind the ruins of the ancient monastery as Judas-1 came to a stop. The bubble door opened and Judas stepped out of the time machine. No trees, bushes, or flowers were to be seen. Only burned ruins and charred desert soil.

Catherine ran to embrace her father as the others followed.

Each one welcomed Judas back with a warm embrace, happy that he was back alive and healthy-looking.

Dr. Weinstein noticed his nail wounds and asked him, "Were you the messiah, Judas?"

"No, my good friend," answered Judas, "I was Judas. I was crucified beside My Lord, Ishia of Nazerat."

"You were Judas, his betrayer!" exclaimed Dr. Weinstein.

"No, my friend, I was Judas, His best friend."

"I am so happy that you are back, daddy!" exclaimed Catherine.

"And, that you look so healthy!" continued Dr. Weinstein.

"I am cured, Jeff," said Judas. "Our Lord cured me."

"Our Lord!" exclaimed Dr. Weinstein, "Remember, Judas. I am Jewish."

"He is not only the Lord of this earth, Jeff; but, He is also the Lord of the Universe. I have so much to tell you…By the way, what does the word Niihau mean to you?"

"Nee-ee-haoo!" exclaimed Dr. Weinstein, thinking. "I am afraid I can't help you, Jude. It doesn't ring a bell."

"Niihau is a small Hawaiian island, belonging to Kauai, one hundred fifty-three miles west of Honolulu," answered Major Nichols.

"That's impressive, Major Nichols!" exclaimed Catherine.

"Hawaii!" whispered Judas. "How could He know?"

"Know what?" asked Dr. Weinstein.

"That they might be in Niihau."

"Who might be in Niihau?" asked Catherine.

"Judith and David!"

"Mom and Davy!" exclaimed Catherine.

"Yes, my love!" answered Judas. "But, how could He have known?"

"Through you," whispered Major Nichols.

"I never told Him about it?"

"Did He ever probe your mind?" asked Major Coolidge.

Judas stared at both majors, finally making the connection. His lips trembled as he asked them, "Who really are you?"

Major Nichols smiled. He whispered, "I'm Joel."

"I'm Daniel," continued Major Coolidge.

"Two thousand years!" whispered Judas. He looked up into the gray-covered sky and said, "My Lord, My God!"

"Will someone, please, explain to me what is going on!" shouted Dr. Weinstein.

"Let's first load Judas-One and get ready to go from this desolate place," answered Major Joel-Nichols, "And, I will explain everything during our flight back to Seneca Rocks."

Having loaded Judas-1 in the belly of the Stealth G-1, Judas sat with Dr. Weinstein and Catherine on the modified back seats while Joel and Daniel got ready to fly back. Slowly the Stealth G-1 lifted off straight up to two thousand feet, shrinking the charred Judean Desert beneath them. Then, faster than any bullet and as fast as any space vehicle ever invented by humans, the Stealth began to climb upward into the thermosphere piercing through the massive gray nuclear fallout that enshrouded the earth's atmosphere.

Major Nichols (Joel) explained their mission on earth to Dr. Weinstein and Catherine as Major Coolidge (Daniel) concentrated on piloting the Stealth. Dr. Weinstein and Catherine were both in awe and in shock after listening to Joel's narrative.

"Did you have any influence on my creation of the Judas-One?" asked Dr. Weinstein.

"No, Jeff. The invention of Judas-One is all yours;" answered Joel. "But, we were always around to see your progress."

"Where we predestined to annihilate ourselves?" asked Dr. Weinstein. "And where were you when we destroyed each other with a nuclear Armageddon?"

"Lord Yahweh, Our Father, gave humanity a genetic predilection into predestination," replied Joel. "You always had choices throughout the history of mankind. Unfortunately, leaders, scientists, educators, and parents chose the wrong way most of the time. They always had a choice; however, at times, the wrong choice may propel you into self-destruction whether you are an individual or a powerful country?"

"I understand that!" exclaimed Dr. Weinstein. "But why didn't you try to stop them from total destruction?"

"We did try!" replied Joel. "We tried so many times to influence key people to make the right choice. Sometimes we succeeded; but many times we failed. The final choice was theirs and that is why you have a free will: to chose between right and wrong."

"What was the main culprit of our wrong choices throughout history?" asked Catherine.

"I could answer that, my love," spoke Judas, who had been listening to Joel's explanations. "The main culprit throughout history was instantaneity. As we progressed into modern science we always took the fastest way. The faster the better—we thought! It was rare that we took the long way. Everything we did took less and less time, instant gratification in food, in science, in education, and in life!"

"Is that true?" asked Dr. Weinstein.

"Yes, for most of mankind," explained Joel. "But, there were always people like you, Jeff, who did things the right way, taking time, reviewing, retesting, making sure that you had not taken any shortcuts. Unfortunately, people like you and Judas were always rare."

"Was Einstein?"

"Yes, he was like you, always taking the long and difficult way," replied Joel. "And, for that very reason he was able to see what others had missed by taking shortcuts."

Everyone was silent for several minutes as Jeff, Catherine, and Judas ruminated over what Major Nichols (Joel) had told them, while the two Paradisians took care of flying.

"What will the immediate future bring us?" asked Dr. Weinstein. "Will we be able to invent a medicine to fight this horrible cancer that is quickly eliminating us? Who can help us?"

"The only man that can help whatever is left of mankind is sitting beside you, Jeff!" answered Joel without looking back.

"Judas?"

"Yes, Judas!" continued Joel. "Our Lord Himself has given him the power to cure, to lead, and to prepare the rest of mankind for His return."

"Judas," whispered Jeff, "Please, heal me."

"I can heal you only if you, without a doubt, want to be healed in the name of Our Lord Ishia, the Only Begotten Son of the Almighty Yahweh," responded Judas.

"I want so much to believe!"

"Wanting is the first step, my good friend; however, now you must truly believe with your heart, mind, and soul."

Dr. Weinstein closed his eyelids to concentrate and said, "I do believe!"

Judas touched Dr. Weinstein's forehead with his right hand, praying, "In the name of Our Lord, Ishia of Nazerat, the Mashiah, the Only Begotten Son of God, you are cured of this evil cancer."

"Thank you, Judas, my best friend."

"It will take a little time before your entire body will be cured. The battle of healing has already begun within you. Now, you must continue to believe and be positive."

"I will, I will!" exclaimed Dr. Weinstein, excited like a little child.

"Can you cure me, too, daddy?" whispered Catherine. "I do believe, daddy. My faith is strong."

"You are already healing, my love. You have been since you embraced me at Qumran." whispered back Judas, kissing her forehead.

"Prepare to descend, everyone," announced Joel. "We are approaching Seneca Rocks, West Virginia."

"Our home!" exclaimed Catherine.

As the Stealth broke through the clouds, they did not rejoin. Instead, a hole began to widen, helped by a strong wind. As the Stealth began its perpendicular descend the sun's rays formed a huge column of light, illuminating the valley below. It was still morning in the valley; but that morning was very special. For the first time, in the past two years and twenty-seven days, the morning sun was shining through the clouds. For the first time in what seemed an eternity, the valley was resplendent. People came out to witness the return of the sun and the Stealth G-1. Everyone, old and young, came out to welcome back their leader, Judas.

As the Stealth descended into the large field, hovering like a giant hummingbird, hundreds of people formed a huge circle around it. They were singing joyfully as the Stealth's landing gears touched the earth, setting into it.

The hatch opened and Major Nichols came out, allowing the other four to step out. When Judas was finally on the ground, a little girl, Jay Morrison's daughter, had broken away from the circle and headed towards Judas. She was holding something to her heart. She couldn't have been more than four years old. A sweet little soul thought Judas; however, he could clearly see the cancer eating her up. As she came closer, it was clear that she was holding a daffodil, a white daffodil with a yellow center.

"For you, Jude!" she exclaimed.

"Thank you, my sweet angel," whispered Judas as he picked her up to hug her. As he held her, he asked her, "How are you feeling, my little angel?"

"Not so good, Jude. Everything hurts!"

"Would you like to feel better and strong again?"

"Yes, I would very much."

"In the name of Our Lord, the Only Begotten Son of God…"

"Do you mean Jesus?" she asked.

"Yes, my angel, I do mean Jesus. Do you believe in Him?"

"Yes, I do. My mother reads to me about Jesus. He is the Son of God."

"In His Holy Name, you are cured, my child," Judas whispered into her ear as he kissed her.

"Look what I have for you!" she exclaimed.

"A daffodil…so late in the summer…where did you find it, my child?" asked Judas.

"By the river. There are more!" exclaimed the little one.

"Can you take me there, my angel?" asked Judas, putting her down.

Judas took the daffodil and smelled its sweetness. He held the daffodil to his nostrils and held Rose Morrison's little hand as she began to lead him towards the South Branch Potomac River, which flowed beside the valley of Seneca Rocks. Judas and little Rose reached the sandy bank of the river to the spot where several daffodils were growing. By now, everyone had followed them to see what seemed so important.

By the time everyone reached the bank of the river, Judas had gone into the water and had his hands outstretched towards the opening of the clouded sky. He seemed to be praying, totally impervious to the cold water and the current of the river. The sun, filtering through the large opening in the clouds created an aura around Judas. Also, the little community realized that their Judas looked extremely healthy and powerful. Not a forceful power but a loving power.

"My beloved brothers and sisters," cried Judas, "I have been away into the past to find if there was ever a Jesus Christ. To find if He truly was the Son of God or a simply a holy man…I can truly say that Jesus of Nazareth truly exists. He truly is the Son of Yahweh. He truly is Our Savior. I was there with Him for the last three years of His life on this earth. I chose to be crucified beside Him. I was also resurrected with Him."

Judas stretched out his arms to show the wounds above his palms, which had been inflicted by a Roman soldier. He began, "These wounds are my witnesses. But more than these wounds, His Love that I carry in my heart is the real witness. I give you all my love that I have been carrying for you within my heart. It is the very same love, which He gave me to give to you. Make it grow by sharing it with anyone you meet until everyone still living on this planet has received some of His love. That is my mission. If anyone would like to be baptized and cured from the awful sickness that plagues you, come forward with some faith in your heart. Come, do not be afraid."

The first one to step into the water was Dr. Weinstein. Judas took him by his hand and submerged him into the cool waters of the river, saying, "I baptize you, Jeffery Weinstein, in the Name of Ishia, the Mashìah, the Only Begotten Son of God. You have received His love and blessing. Go and share that love with as many brothers and sisters as possible."

One by one, each member of the Seneca Rocks community was baptized and cured by Judas. Every person, young and old, male and female, received the love of their Lord through Judas. For the first time in more than two years, faith, hope, and love glowed in every member of the little community.

Weeks passed and many strangers filtered into the valley to be cured by Judas, the Lord's messenger. People who looked no better than walking skeletons were cured and were looking healthier by each day. Word got out that a holy man who lived by Seneca Rocks could cure anyone. By the end of October, the valley was filled with people asking for food and for a miracle. The Seneca community grew larger, multiplying by the week. Its members had found a new life through Judas. They had become healthy and their love had grown bigger than Seneca Rocks. They had become more resourceful in finding food; and, some had begun to grow vegetables and other foods in homemade nurseries. And, they were eager to share that food and love with any stranger who walked into that valley.

Finally, one early morning at the end of October, Judas approached Joel and Daniel and asked them, "Is this a good day to, maybe, explore that small island in Hawaii?"

"You mean, Niihau, Judas?" answered Joel.

"Yes, Niihau," sighed Judas. "What chance is there that they might still be alive?"

"As good a chance as ours," answered Daniel. "Only Honolulu was directly hit. If they had gone to view Niihau by boat, they might have docked there after hearing the explosion. Niihau is a private island; but in a desperate situation a boat might be given permission to dock."

"When can we leave then?" asked Judas.

"Now, if you wish," responded Joel.

"First of all, we need to tell Catherine and Jeff," suggested Judas.

"Everyone is so busy that they won't miss you for a few hours, my beloved friend, Judas."

Vincent L. Di Paolo

Glossary

abba (Aramaic) - Father.

Abiatar (Aramaic name) - High priest of Israel and King David's friend.

Abshalom, Avshalom (Aramaic name) - var. of Absalom, King David's third son, killed by Joab.

ad (Latin, prep.) - to, toward, according to.

Ain Feshka (Aramaic name) - village on western shore of the Dead Sea, approx. 4 kilometers south of Qumran. *Ain* means spring; thus *Spring of Feshka*.

Alba Fossae (Latin name) - canyon on Mars. Literal translation is *Trench of Dawn*.

alii (Latin, adj., pl.) - others, some.

Amazonis Planitia (Latin name) - plain west of Olympus Mons on Mars. Literal translation is *Amazon Plain.*

Ammathus (Latin for Hammatha) - fishing village on western shore of the Sea of Galilee, immediately south of Tiberias.

Ammude Shelomo (Hebrew name) - redstone pillars by Har Timna (Mount Timna), approx. 27 kilometers north of Elat. Literal translation is *Solomon's Pillars*.

Andros (Greek name) - variation of Andrew.

Antipas (name) - Herod Antipas, ruler of Galilee, had John the Baptist beheaded and interrogated Jesus of Nazareth.

an (Latin, conj.) - or, perhaps.

apostolos (Greek, noun) - a disciple, one of the first 12 disciples of Jesus of Nazareth.

Arbela, Arbelah - town approx. 4 kilometers southwest of Magdala.

A'Ramathayim (Aramaic name), from the town of Arimathaea in northern Judaea.

Armageddon (Biblical name) - final battle at Magiddu (Megiddo). Final battle between the forces of good and evil.

'Arvot Yeriho (Hebrew name) - Plains of Jericho.

Athenai (Greek name) - Athens, capital of Greece.

audit (Latin, verb) - he/she listens.

autem (Latin, adv.) - however.

Avel (Aramaic name) - variation of Abel.

Bar-Abbas (Aramaic name) - Son of Abbas, Son of Father. A small revolutionary leader who was given freedom by the Jews over Jesus of Nazareth.

Bar-Abel, Bar-Avel (Aramaic name) - Son of Abel.

Bar-Alpheus (Aramaic name) - Son of Alpheus.

Bar-Amalech (Aramaic name) - Son of Amalek, descendants of Esau.

Bar-Jonah (Aramaic name) - Son of Jonah. Simon Bar-Jonas, one of the chosen twelve, Peter.

Bar-Oza (Aramaic name) - Son of Oza.

Bar-Ptolemais (Aramaic name) - Son of Ptolemy, or Bartholomew, one of the chosen twelve.

Bar-Thimeush (Aramaic name) - Son of Thimeush.

Bar-Yoseph (Aramaic name) - Son of Joseph.

Bar-Zebedeus (Aramaic name) - Son of Zebedee, two of the chosen twelve.

Bashan (Biblical name) - region east of Jordan River in ancient Palestine, famous for bulls.

Batanea (Biblical name) - region west of Golan.

Bat-Ybrahim (Aramaic Name) - daughter of Abraham.

Bayt-Lahm (Aramaic name) - Bethlehem, birthplace of Jesus and King David.

Be'er Sheva (Ancient Aramaic) - *The Well of the Oath*, named by Abraham, capital of Negev.

Bene Hezir (Aramaic name) - variation of *Bnei Hezir*, tombs of Hasmonaean family of priests in the Kidron Valley; believed by Christians to be St. James' tomb, Jesus' cousin or brother.

Bet-Ananiah (Aramaic name) - *House of Ananias*, Bethany, small village east of ancient Jerusalem, at the foot of Mount of Olives, home of Martha, Mary, and Lazarus.

Bet-ha'Arava (Aramaic name) - small village west of the Jordan River, midway between Jericho and Qumran.

Bethmaus (Aramaic name)- village approx. 4 kilometers west of Tiberias.

Beth-Saida (Aramaic name) - Bethsaida, a fishing village on the Sea of Galilee, northeast of Capernaum, home of Andrew, Peter, and Philip.

Beth-Shean, Beth-She'an (Aramaic name) - ancient name of Scythopolis, a town in Samaria, by the Harod Stream, west of the Jordan River.

Caesarea Palaestinae (Maritima) (Latin name) - Roman harbor in ancient Palestine on the shore of the Mediterranean Sea.

Caesarea Philippi (Latin name) - ancient city in northern Gaulanitis, built by Herod Philip, brother of Antipas.

camalots (noun, pl.) - modern day protective climbing devices that replace the old pitons.

canem (Latin, noun) - of the dog, or to the dog.

canis (Latin, noun) - the dog.

Capreae (Latin name) - Capri, a Roman island off the coast of Puteoli and Naples, famous for its natural beauty and used for vacationing by Rome's nobles and rich.

Cephas (Aramaic, noun) - rock or stone, Jesus changed Simon's name to *Cephas* (rock).

Chen, Ch'an (Ancient Chinese name) - ancient name of the Chinese culture.

Chimus (Ancient Andean name) - tribe of Amerindians that lived in the Andes before the Incas. They were later conquered by the Incas.

Chorazin (Aramaic name) - Galilean village four kilometers northwest of Capernaum, condemned by Jesus for their unrepentance.

Cleophas (Aramaic name) - a follower of Jesus.

commissa (Latin, ppp/adj.) - connecting, (*crux commissa*), connecting cross, connected to the main cross.

crux (Latin, noun) - cross, gallows, torment, most difficult section of a climb.

Cyrenaica (Roman name) - North-African Roman province, present Lybia.

Daberath (Ancient Aramaic name) - Deborah, a prophetess and judge of ancient Israel, considered to be a heroine.

de (Latin, pr. followed by an ablative) - about.

Decapolis (Latin name) - Roman Province between Peraea and Galilee.

decertarent (Latin, verb, pl. third person) - they have fought.

denarius, denarii (Latin, noun, sing & pl.) -Gold and silver Roman coin; one gold denarius (*denarius aureus*) equaled twenty-five silver denarii.

dicis (Latin, verb, sing. second person) - you say, do you say?, do you ask?

Didymus (Greek name) - literal meaning is *twin*.

Dium (Latin name) - a city in the northeastern part of the Roman province of Decapolis.

dixerunt (Latin, verb, pl. third person) - they have told.

ecce (Latin, adv.) - look! here is! there is! lo and behold!

ego (Latin, pron.) I. (**ego, mei**) - I, mine or of myself.

Efrayim, Ephrayim (Aramaic, Hebrew name) - man's name; a tribe of Israel directly descending from Ephrayim, son of Joseph; a village in Samaria; literal meaning is *very fruitful*.

Eleazar (Aramaic name) - Lazarus, brother of Mary and Martha, resurrected by Jesus; also son of Aaron.

Eli, Eli, lama sabachtani (Ancient Aramaic) - first verse of Psalm 22; literal meaning is My God, My God, why have you abandoned me.

Eli-jah, Eli-Yahw (Ancient Aramaic name) - Elijah; literal meaning is *My God is Yahweh.*

En Gedi (Aramaic name) - ancient town on the western shore of the Dead Sea; literal meaning is *Fountain of the Kid.*

eph-pheta (Aramaic phrase) - open yourselves up.

ergo (Latin, ad.) - then, so, therefore.

es (Latin, verb, sing. second person) - you are.

esset (Latin, verb, sing. second person) - you were.

est (Latin, verb, sing. third person) - he/she/it is.

et (Latin, conj.) - and.

etabuh (Aramaic word) - lote bush, used by Roman soldiers to make a thorny crown to mock Jesus.

ex (Latin, pr. followed by ablative) - out of, from.

fecisti (Latin, verb, sing. second person) - have you done?

flagrum, flagra (Latin noun, sing. and pl.) - Short whip with two tiny lead barbells attached to two leather strips.

Gadara (Aramaic name) - a town south of Emmatha, southeast of the Sea of Galilee, in northern Decapolis.

Gallia (Roman name) - Roman province of Gaul; modern day France.

Garaba (Aramaic name) - a town in Lower Galilee, five kilometers northeast of Cana.

Gat-shemanim (Aramaic name) - Garden of Gethsemane, by the Mount of Olives, where olives were pressed into oil.

Gaulanitis (Roman name) - Roman name for Golan, a province northeast of the Sea of Galilee, today's Golan-Heights.

Genne-Sareth (Aramaic name) - Gennesaret, a fishing town on the western shore of the Sea of Galilee, approximately eight kilometers southwest of Capernaum.

gens (Latin noun) - people.

Gergesa (Aramaic name) - a fishing town on the eastern shore of the Sea of Galilee, facing Magdala.

Gilead (Aramaic name) - name of land east of the Jordan River, called Galaaditis by the Romans.

Ginnat (Aramaic name) - variation of Ginae, a small Samaritan town, southwest of Scythopolis.

Givat Moreh (Aramaic name) variation of Giv'at Hamore, a large hill southeast of Mount Tabor.

Ghabriel (Aramaic name) variation of Gabriel, archangel of Lord Yahweh; literal meaning is *Power of God or God is strong*.

Gulgoleth (Aramaic name) - Golgotha, a small mound outside old Jerusalem, used by the Romans to crucify criminals and rebels. Literal meaning is *the Mound of Skulls*.

Gush Halav (Aramaic name) - variation of Gishala, a Phoenician town, midway between Tyre and Capernaum.

Hagalil (Aramaic name) - Galilee, a Hebrew state, a Roman province during Jesus' life.

Haggadah (Aramaic word) - the story of the Hebrew exodus from Egypt.

Hagolan (Aramaic name) - Golan, called Gaulanitis by the Romans.

Har 'Azmon, Har Hazmon (Aramaic name) - Mount Hazmon, near Cana.

Hare Ramim (Aramaic name) - Mount Ramim, overlooking the Valley of Hulah near Qedesh.

Har 'Eval (Aramaic name) - a large hill next to Mount Gerizim.

Har Gerizim (Aramaic name) - Mount Gerizim, east of the city of Samaria.

Har Ha-Zetim (Hebrew name) - Mount of Olives, east of old Jerusalem.

Har Tavor (Aramaic name) - Mount Tabor in Galilee; Jesus' favorite mountain.

Har Tir'an (Aramaic name) - Mount Tir'an, north of Nazareth.

Ha-Shiloah (Aramaic name) - Siloam, a pool in the southeast side of old Jerusalem.

Ha-Yarden (Aramaic name) - Jordan River, in ancient Palestine and modern day Israel and Jordan. It is considered a holy river by the Jews, Christians, and Moslems.

Hebrai (Aramaic name) - Hebrews.

Henoch (Aramaic name) - variation of Enoch.

Herodias (Hebrew name) - second wife of Herod Antipas while still married to his brother Philip, mother of Salome. Herodias asked for the Baptist's head.

Herodium (Latin name) - circular palace built by Herod the Great on top of a circular hill in the Wilderness of Judea, approximately eleven kilometers south of Jerusalem. One can still visit its ruins today.

Hervot Mezada (Hebrew name) - Massada. Literal translation is *Ruins of Massada*.

Hevron (Aramaic name) - Hebron, a town in Idumea, approximately thirty kilometers south of Jerusalem.

hic (Latin, pro., adv.) - this, here, at this point.

hinc (Latin, adv.) - from here, on this side, for this reason.

Hinnom (Aramaic name) - Valley of Hinnom, outside the walls of old Jerusalem, on its southwest side. Also means Gehenna (hell).

Hippus (Latin name) - town east of the Sea of Galilee, directly south of Gergesa and north of Gadara.

hoc (Latin, pro.) - it, this.

homo (Latin, noun) - man, human being.

hommus (Aramaic, noun) - variation of hummus, a dip made of blended chickpea, olive oil, and spices.

Horatii (Latin name, pl.) - The Horatius family, heroes and saviors of Rome, later given a noble status.

Horatius (Latin name, sing.) - Noble Roman family name. Publius Horatius Cocles (Roman hero).

hosh 'ah nna (Aramaic phrase) - hosanna; literal meaning is *save us now*.

hygieine techne (Greek phrase) - the art of bodily cleanliness.

Idumea (Aramaic name) - a state directly south of Judea.

immissa (Latin, ppp./adj.) - extended; the cross of Jesus was *immissa* (extended at the top).

Imwas (Aramaic name) - Emmaus, a town approximately thirty kilometers west of Jerusalem, where Jesus met two of his disciples who were escaping from Jerusalem.

Ishia (Aramaic name) - Jesus, Aramaic variation of Yeshua, syncopated variation of Yehoshua; literal meaning is *God is help*.

Ish-kerioth (Aramaic name) - Iscariot; family name of Judas; name of town in ancient Jordan; literal meaning is *from Kerioth, of Kerioth, coming from Kerioth*, possibly modern Arab town of El-Qereiyat.

Jairosh (Aramaic name) - Jairus.

Jannaeus (Maccabean name) - Alexander Jannaeus, Maccabean king (103-76 B.C.), succeeded his brother Judas Aristobulus as King of Israel.

Jebel Har Montar (Arabic/Aramaic name) - a mountain directly west of Qumran.

Jebel Tammun (Arabic name) - a mount north of the Tirza River in Samaria.

Jesus Justus (Latin name) - Jesus the Just, son of Jesus of Nazareth according to the Dead Sea Scrolls.

Judaei, Iudaei (Latin, noun, pl.) - Jews.

Judaeis, Iudaeis (Latin, noun) - to the Jews.

Judaeus (Latin, noun) - Jew.

Judaeorum (Latin, noun, pl.) - Of the Jews.

Keen'an, Kena'an (Aramaic name) - Canaan, ancient name of Palestine, land of the Canaanites.

Kfar-Nahum (Aramaic name) - Capernaum, a fishing town on the north shore of the Sea of Galilee. Literal translation is *Village of Nahum.*

Kaiaphas, Caiaphas (Aramaic name) - Yoseph Caiaphas was high priest of Jerusalem during Jesus' life. Caiaphas was the main force against Jesus, fearing the Nazarene's popularity.

Khirbat Mazin (Aramaic name) - ancient Essene village on the western shore of the Dead Sea, north of the Wadi Kidron; literal translation is *the Ruins of Mazin.*

Khirbat Mird (Aramaic name) - ancient Essene village, westerly equidistant from Mazin and Qumran. Literal meaning is *the Ruins of Mird.*

Khirbat Qumran, Khirbat Qumeran (Aramaic name) - most important Essene village on the northwest shore of the Dead sea; also called *Mesad Hasidim.* Literal translation is the *Ruins of Qumran.*

Krystos (Greek, noun) - the messiah, the anointed one.

Lacus Semechonitis (Latin name) - Lake Huleh, smaller lake north of the Lake of Galilee, along the Jordan River.

leptonis (Greco-Roman, noun, pl.) - Pontius Pilate's coins (sing.: *lepton*); literal translation is small coins.

libra, librae (Latin, noun, sing. & pl.) - pound, a weight used by Romans.

locus coeruleus, locus caeruleus (Latin phrase) - part of the brainstem in the human brain. Literal translation is *dark blue place.*

Machaerus (Latin/Aramaic name) - Herodian fortress in Perea, where John the Baptist was executed.

Magdala (Aramaic name) - a fishing town on the western shore of the Sea of Galilee; home of Mary Magdalene.

Mamshit (Arabic name) - restored ruins southwest of the Dead Sea, southeast of Be'er Sheva; in ancient Palestine it was called *Kurnub.*

Manasheh (Aramaic name) - a boy's name; Manasseh, Joseph's first son; tribe of Israel.

Mare Internum (Latin name) - Mediterranean Sea. Literal translation is *Interior Sea.*

Mar Saba (Latin/Arabic name) - an ancient monastery along the canyon of the Kidron River, southeast of Jerusalem.

mashiah (Aramaic, noun) - the messiah, the anointed one.

Massilia (Roman name) - Marseille, France; a Roman port on the northern shore of the Mediterranean Sea in southern Gaul, during the Roman Empire.

mater (Latin, noun) - mother.

me (Latin, pro.) - me.

mei (Latin, pro.) - My, mine (pl.).

meum (Latin, pro.) - My, mine.

Mesad Hasidim (Aramaic name) - fortress of the Essene; also known as Qumran, an Essene monastery.

Midbar Yehuda (Aramaic name) - Wilderness of Judea.

mikve (Hebrew, noun, pl.) - Pools.

ministri (Latin, noun, pl.) - Servants.

Miryam (Aramaic name) - Mary.

Mons Olivae (Latin name) - Mount of Olives.

Moishe (Aramaic name) - Moses.

mundum (Latin, noun) - to the world.

mundo (Latin, noun) - of the world.

(Nablus), Neapolis (Latin name) - Roman name for Shekhem, a town in Samaria.

Nahal 'Ammud (Hebrew name) - 'Ammud Stream in Galilee, empties into Sea of Galilee.

Nahal Hever (Hebrew name) - Hever Stream near Hebron, empties into the Dead Sea.

Nahal Mezar (Hebrew name) - Mezar Stream in Golan, near Gadara.

Nahal Tirza (Hebrew name) - Tirza Stream originating north of Shekhem, Samaria.

Nahal Yaboq Hebrew name) - Yaboq River in Jordan, a tributary of the Jordan River.

Nahal Yarmouk (Hebrew name) - Yarmouk River in Golan, a tributary of the Jordan River.

Nain, Naim (Aramaic name) - Nein, a village south of Mount Tabor in Galilee.

natus (Latin, verb) - to be born.

Nazerat (Aramaic name) - Nazareth, a town in Galilee where Jesus and his family lived.

Niihau (Hawaiian name) - a small island in Hawaii, west of Kauai.

Nikotheimos (Greek/Hebrew name) - Nicodemus, a member of the Sanhedrin and a follower of Jesus.

non (Latin, adv.) not.

nunc (Latin, adv.) - now, at present.

numquid (Latin, interr. particle) - emphatic form of num: do you? Does he?

Olympus Mons (Latin name) -Mount Olympus, largest and tallest mountain in Mars and in the entire Solar System.

omnis (Latin, adj.) - All, every, any.

pali (Latin, noun, pl. of *palus*) - Wooden posts.

Paradisians (name) - inhabitants of Paradise.

patibulum, patibula (Latin, noun, sing. & pl.) - Crossbeam (s) used to crucify offenders by the Romans.

Pehel (Aramaic name) - Pella, a city in Decapolis, east of the Jordan River.

Peraea (Latin/Aramaic) - region of ancient Palestine, west of the Jordan River and of the Dead Sea.

Pentekostes (Greek name) - seventh Sunday after Easter (Passover).

perhibeam (Latin, verb) - to assert, to call, to give.

Pesach (Aramaic name) - Feast of Passover, commemorating the exodus of the Hebrews from Egypt.

pollicis, pollices (Latin, noun, pl. of *pollex*) - Thumbs, inches.

pontifices (Latin, noun, pl. of *pontifex*) - High priests.

Pontius Pilatus (Latin name) - Pontius Pilate, Roman procurator of Judea during Jesus' last years of his life.

Praetorium (Latin, noun) - Pontius Pilate's house in Jerusalem.

Pharishaiya (Aramaic name) - Pharisees: an orthodox religious group who fervently opposed Jesus.

Ptolemais (Greek name) - Ptolemais, a port on the Mediterranean coast, south of Tyre; also called Acco.

Qana (Aramaic name) - Cana, a small town in Galilee north of Sepphoris and of Nazareth.

Qanaanites - people living in ancient Canaan.

Qedesh (Aramaic name) - Kedesh, a town in Syria.

Qidron (Aramaic name) - Kidron Valley, east of the walls of old Jerusalem; also, Wadi Kidron (Kidron Brook).

qodesh haqqodashim (Aramaic phrase) - Holy of Holies; Sanctum Sanctorum.

qui (Latin, interr. pro.) - Who, which, what?

quia (Latin, conj.) - Because, that.

quid (Latin, adv.) - Why?

rappel (English, from French, verb) - descend a mountain or wall with a rope; rope is doubled and passed through a device (*figure eight*) attached to a harness, or butt-rappel.

Rebekah (Aramaic name) - Rebecca, a girl's name.

regnum (Latin, noun) - kingdom.

rex (Latin, noun) - king.

Sanctus Christus (Latin name) - Holy Messiah.

San-hedrin (Aramaic name) - Sanhedrin was the highest ecclesiastical, legislative, and secular council of the Jews, headed by the high priest of Jerusalem, consisting of 71 members. Caiaphas was the head of the sanhedrin during Jesus last few years.

Sarephat (Aramaic name) - Sarepta, port on the Mediterranean Sea south of Sidon.

Scythopolis (Greek/Hebrew name) - city in Decapolis, west of the Jordan River.

sedili (Latin, noun) - seats, pegs used for supporting the bodies of crucified people.

Sedom, Shidom (Aramaic name) - Sodom, ancient city destroyed along with Gomorrah, at the southernmost section of the Dead Sea, at the foot of Har Sedom.

Sejanus, Lucius Aelius (Latin name) - commander of the praetorian guards of Emperor Tiberius. Sejanus was left in charge of Rome while Tiberius escaped the empire's problems. Tiberius ordered Sejanus' death upon learning of his conspiracy against him.

Sekhakha (Aramaic name) - Valley of Secacah in the Wilderness of Judea, directly southwest of Qumran.

Sennabris (Aramaic name) - fishing town in Galilee on the southern shore of the Sea of Galilee.

Sepphoris (Latin/Aramaic name) - Sippori or Safuriyah, a Lower Galilean town northwest of Nazareth.

Sha'ar Haarayot, Sha'ar Ha-Arayot (Aramaic/Hebrew name) - Lion's Gate or St. Stephen's Gate, on the northern section of the east wall of old Jerusalem.

Shabbat (Aramaic/Hebrew) -Sabbath, Saturday.

Shalem (Aramaic name) - Salem, ancient city in Canaan, sometimes associated with ancient Jerusalem.

Sharah (Aramaic name) - a variation of Sara or Sarah.

Shekhem (Aramaic name) - Shechem, a town in Samaria.

Shelomo (Aramaic name) - Solomon, son of King David, also a boy's name.

shekels (Aramaic/Hebrew) -A silver coin used by the Hebrews, originating from Babylon.

shibah, shivah (Aramaic/Hebrew) - a seven-day mourning period following a Jew's death. Literal meaning is *seven days*.

Shidon (Aramaic name) - Sidon, a city port on the Mediterranean Sea coast of Tyre, north of the city of Tyre.

Shimon (Aramaic/Hebrew name) - Simon, St. Peter's given name; a boy's name.

Shomeron (Aramaic/Hebrew) - Samaria, a province of Rome, between Judea and Galilee.

Shomeroni (Aramaic/Hebrew) - Samaritans, inhabitants of Samaria.

si (Latin, conj.) - if, if only.

silentium (Latin, noun) - silence.

Sindhu (Indus) - Hindu, from India.

sindon (Greek) - a fine linen used as a burial shroud.

stadium, stadia (Latin, noun, sing. & pl.) - A long racecourse for chariot racing; the length of the course (approx. 607 feet), which was used by the Greeks and Romans as measure for distance.

Succot, Sukkoth (Hebrew) - the Jewish Holy Feast of the Tabernacles was to reenact the forty years that the Hebrews spent in the desert living in huts after their exodus from Egypt.

sudarium (Latin, noun) - handkerchief or fine veil. Literal translation is *sweat handkerchief*.

summa cum laude (Latin phrase) - with the highest praise.

suppedaneum, suppedanea (Latin, noun, sing. & pl.) - Footrest, footrests; also, a piece of wood nailed to the palus of the cross to be used as a footrest for the crucified offender.

Sychara (Aramaic) - a village in Samaria, north of Mount Gerizim.

Tantalus Fossae (Latin name) - a canyon in Mars, south of the Alba Fossae and northeast of Olympus Mons.

Taricheae (Greek/Hebrew) - another name used for Magdala, a fishing town in Galilee on the west shore of the Sea of Galilee.

Tavor (Hebrew) - Tabor, a mountain in Lower Galilee, east of Nazareth.

Tayr (Aramaic) - a variation of Tyre, a city and port on the Mediterranean coast, south of Sidon.

te (Latin, pro.) - you; acc. & abl. of tu.

temetipso (Latin, pro.) - yourself, an emphatic form of *te*, acc. and abl. of *tu*.

testimonium (Latin, noun) - testimony, evidence, proof.

Thella (Greek) - a town on the southwest shore of Lake Huleh, a small lake north of the Sea of Galilee.

Theudas (Latinized Hebrew name) - a variation of Thaddeus, one of Jesus' disciples.

Tiberias (Latin name) - a town and harbor in Galilee on the western shore of the Sea of Galilee, south of Magdala, north of Ammathus.

Tiberius, Claudius Nero Caesar (Latin name) - Tiberius, Roman Emperor from 14-37 A.D., succeeded Augustus Caesar.

tibi (Latin, pro.) - to you; dat. of *tu*.

traderer (Latin, verb) - hand over, deliver, surrender, betray.

tradiderunt (Latin, verb) - they have betrayed.

Tsadduqim (Aramaic) - Sadducees, an orthodox religious group of Jews who fervently opposed the teachings of Jesus.

tu (Latin, pro.) - you; thou.

tuum (Latin, pro.) - your, yours, thy, thine, your own.

ut (Latin, adv.) - that, to, so that.

utique (Latin, adv.) - certainly.

VCDs - video compact disks, used only in this novel.

veni (Latin, verb) - I came.

veritas (Latin, noun) - truth, reality.

veritate (Latin, noun) - in the truth.

veritati (Latin, noun) - to the truth.

Verenike (Greek name) - stems from *berenikion*, a plant; Veronica (a girl's name); Veronica, a follower of Jesus who wiped his sweat and blood with a sudarium, thus imprinting his image on the linen.

Via Dolorosa (Latin name) - a narrow road in the Muslim Quarter of Old Jerusalem on which Jesus carried his cross to Golgotha. Literal meaning is *Street of Sorrows*.

vocem meam (Latin phrase) - to what I say; to what I speak.

wadi (Aramaic/Arabic) - a run; a stream.

Wadi Abu Gharaba (Arabic) - a stream in Jordan, originating from the mountains of 'Ammon and empties into the Jordan River facing Bet-ha'Arava.

Wadi Abu Sidra (Arabic) - a stream in Samaria, which empties into the Jordan River.

Wadi Mallaha, Nahal Mallaha (Arabic, Hebrew) - a stream north of Jericho, which empties into the Jordan River.

Wadi Qumran, Nahal Qumran (Arabic/Aramaic) - a stream in the Judean desert, which runs near the Qumran Ruins and empties into the Dead Sea.

Wadi Sekhakha, Nahal Sekhakha (Arabic/Hebrew) - a stream that empties into the Nahal Qumran.

Wadi Tavor, Nahal Tavor (Arabic/Hebrew) - a small stream by Mount Tabor in Galilee.

Wadi Yabis (Arabic) - a stream in Jordan that empties into the Jordan River.

Yakov (Aramaic/Hebrew name) - Jacob.

Yam Ha-Melah (Aramaic/Hebrew) - the Salty Sea; the Dead Sea.

Yam Kinneret (Aramaic/Hebrew) - the Sea of Chinnereth; the Sea of Galilee.

Yarden (Aramaic) - Jordan; the Land of Jordan.

Yehohanan (Aramaic) - John, a boy's name; John the Baptist; John, one of Jesus' apostles.

Yehuda (Aramaic) - Judah, a tribe of Israel and a state of modern Israel; Judaea, a Roman province.

Yehudith (Aramaic name) - Judith, a girl's name.

Yeriho (Aramaic) - Jericho, an ancient city in Judaea, northeast of Jerusalem.

Yerushalayim (Aramaic/Hebrew) - Jerusalem, the capital of Israel.

Yesha-Yahu (Aramaic) - Isaiah, a Hebrew prophet.

Yshak (Aramaic/Hebrew) - Isaac, son of Abraham and Sarah; also a boy's name.

Yibrahim (Aramaic/Hebrew/Arabic) - Abraham, the patriarch of Hebrews, Christians, and Muslims, who came from ancient Ur, Sumer, and moved into Canaan; also a boy's name.

Yisrael (Aramaic) - variation of Israel.

Yoakim (Aramaic) - Joachim, a boy's name.

Yoseph, Youseph, Yousef (Aramaic/Arabic) - Joseph, a boy's name.

Yoshiyah (Aramaic) - a boy's name.

Yousef-al-Gader (Arabic) - Joseph of Gadara.

Zebedeus (Aramaic/Latin) - Zebedee, the father of the apostles, James and John.

Zebulun (Aramaic) - variation of Zebulon or Zabulon, a boy's name.

Zechariah, Zekhariah (Aramaic) - a variation of Zachariah, Zacharias, or Zachary, a boy's name.

Vincent L. Di Paolo

Bibliography

Aharoni, Yohanan and Michael Avi-Yonah (1968). *The MacMillan Bible Atlas*. New York: The MacMillan Company.

Endo, Shusaku (1973). *A Life of Jesus*. New York: Paulist Press.

Grant, Michael (1977). *Jesus: an historian's review of the gospels*. New York: Charles Scribner's Sons.

Humber, Thomas (1978). **The Sacred Shroud**. New York: a Kangaroo Book.

Kidd, D.A. (1964). **Latin Gem Dictionary**. London, England: Collins.

Levi, Avraham and Ruth (1994-95). *Israel Bazak*. New York: Harper Collins, Publishers.

The New Testament of the Jerusalem Bible. Garden City, N.Y.: Doubleday & Co., Inc., 1969.

Pritchard, James B. (editor) (1996). *The Times Atlas of the Bible*. New York: Crescent Books, a division of Random House.

St. Joseph New Catholic Edition of the Holy Bible. New York: Catholic Book Publishing Co., 1961.

Stevenson, Kenneth E. and Gary R. Habermas (1982). *Verdict on the Shroud.* Wayne, PA: Banbury Books, a division of Dell.

Thiering, Barbara (1992). *Jesus and the Riddle of the Dead Sea Scrolls.* New York: Harper San Francisco.

Waters, Sr. Alyce L. and Kathleen A. Marsh (1990). *Journey to the Land of Jesus.* Lincolnwood, Illinois: Publications International Ltd.

Wilson, Ian (1996). *Jesus: the evidence.* New York: Harper San Francisco, Banbury.

About the Author

Vincent L. Di Paolo is a well-known archaeological artist, educator, and writer. He is a post-graduate from McGill University and presently teaches in Northern Virginia. He has done over fifty solo art shows and his artwork can be found in over thirty countries. He has traveled extensively, exploring and painting ancient ruins throughout the world. In the past twenty years Vincent has been researching *how the brain develops, how it learns, and how nutrition plays a major role in learning, memory, and longevity.* He has practiced martial arts since 1963 and he is a mountaineer and rock-climber. He is presently working on two books: *The Brain, Education, and your Child;* and Children of Yahweh. He is married with two children.